Everyone knows that when a Langtry falls in love it's forever . . .

"Aren't you going to invite me in?" Harrison Kane asked.

"You know you can walk into the house anytime you want." Michaela Langtry stepped back and let him pass.

He walked to the windows overlooking the Langtry fields. Michaela studied his tall, power-ful back and casual stance. He was always very relaxed, very poised. And she resented his knowl-edge of the failure that had caused her to return home.

He turned. "There's no need to be nervous. I won't bite." The words came purring 'round her, tightening her body.

"But I could," she countered.

Other Avon Romances by
Cait London

SLEEPLESS IN MONTANA
THREE KISSES

Cait London

It Happened at Midnight

AVON BOOKS
An Imprint of HarperCollins*Publishers*

AVON BOOKS
An Imprint of HarperCollins*Publishers*
10 East 53rd Street
New York, New York 10022-5299

First Avon Books paperback printing: November 2000

Avon Trademark Reg. U.S. Pat. Off. and in Other Countries, Marca Registrada, Hecho en U.S.A.
HarperCollins® is a trademark of HarperCollins Publishers Inc.

Printed in the U.S.A.

10 9 8 7 6 5 4 3 2 1

To those men who try to understand.
And, of course, to Lucia Macro,
a wonderful editor.

~ ~

Langtry Legend

It was said of the Langtry men that they were charming rogues, and of the women that they were as bold as their men, with hearts as soft and sweet as the summer mist over a mountain meadow. It was said that when the wild heart of a Langtry is captured, it will remain true forever.

prologue

Shiloh, Wyoming

Soft-ly, slow-ly . . . the mornin' will creep
Dream your sweet dreams and do not weep
Cornbread in the morn-in' it will keep
Drift soft-ly, slow-ly 'tis time to sleep. . . .

Soft-ly, slow-ly . . . 'tis time to sleep. . . . The intruder finished the old Langtry lullaby and knew there was little time left to finish her work. How she'd waited and planned for this night, and now, ruled by hatred, she would act.

The maid, deeply loyal to the Langtrys, had to die, of course, and now Maria Alvarez's body waited in the car. The Langtrys' two canine guardians slept peacefully—sedative tucked neatly in meat had been a meal they couldn't refuse.

A bitter hiss sailed through the night air, stirring the baby's nursery, and the intruder recognized it as her own. Hatred and darkness stormed over the intruder. Marriage hadn't brought happiness, nothing but raging arguments and bitterness. *Faith and Jacob Langtry had everything. They always had. There were two perfect children sleeping in another room. Roark and Michaela.*

The six-week-old baby, sleeping in her crib, was also perfect, a tiny image of Faith Langtry with her startling blue eyes. Gentle Faith Langtry wouldn't know how rage felt, how badly hands could tremble with the need to murder. The woman's lips tightened and her teeth grated. She knew well how many men desired the "artist-lady with the sky-blue eyes."

The woman smiled tightly, coldly. She held a secret that Jacob Langtry would die to protect; but this was better—taking a part of his wife's heart, this tiny baby. A powerful man descended from a Southern legacy and a Native American princess, Jacob Langtry was a tough westerner, capable of anything when it came to protecting his family. But tonight, dining and dancing and making love with his wife had left their brood with a babysitter—and she had been quickly disabled.

Soft-ly, slow-ly . . . the mornin' will creep. . . . In the nursery, the woman hummed the song she'd heard many times in the Langtry home. Generations earlier Zachariah Xenos Langtry, a displaced Southern veteran and western frontiersman had created the lullaby.

As a friend of the Langtrys, the intruder had had

her fill of their heritage and legends. *It was said of the Langtry men that they were charming rogues, and of the women that they were as bold as their men, with hearts as soft and sweet as the summer mist over a mountain meadow. It was said that when the wild heart of a Langtry is captured, it will remain true forever.*

The legendary Zachariah's journals were filled with the love he bore his half-blood Native American wife, Cleopatra. Unstained and honorable, respected in the community, the Langtry name tore at the intruder, whispers stoking her hatred—men did not love women and men were never honorable.

And Zachariah Langtry had been a deserter. He'd run from the war, a deserter and a coward.

She almost cackled, wild with joy and drugs, because after tonight, the Langtrys wouldn't be perfect any longer.

Moonlight slid through the window, striking a metallic disk on the table next to a rocking chair. A ripple of ecstasy shot through the woman as she reached for the large coin, tethered by a heavy chain.

She gripped the coin, and the metal seemed to burn her shaking hand. She hesitated, listening to the whispers in the autumn wind, the leaves slashing at the nursery window. *The perfect Langtrys were meant to be torn apart.*

With care, the woman took the baby and hurried into the Wyoming night.

one

Twenty-seven years later

"I've made mistakes, and I'm paying for them." A descendant of the legendary mountainman and westerner Zachariah Langtry, Michaela Langtry prowled her New York apartment. She could not blame anyone for her choices—the wrong man, the wrong values—decisions based more on career than the richness of life.

Her parents had found that depth, that richness, that meaning and truth. The only scar on their lives was the baby stolen from them.

Michaela studied the crowded New York traffic below, the rain-beaded tops of black umbrellas moving below on the sidewalk. At rush hour, the subways and commuter trains would be crowded. But then, she no longer had to worry about mass transit, or had the problem of waving down a cab, of pushing her own umbrella through a sea of others.

Stripped of the heavy cosmetics demanded by the television camera, her face was taut and brooding and yet masked the savage emotions tearing through her. They said her fighting temper came from her father's side, from her ancestor Zachariah's high-wide sense of honor and pride. They said when Zachariah's temper was raked, it was like looking into hell; a quick glance at the image reflected in her apartment window revealed that same savagery. Michaela wasn't startled by her deep emotions; she'd always known they were within her—and she had the strength to conceal them.

Now, facing her moment of truth—that she alone held her future—Michaela thought of the pine needles high on the Rocky Mountains, frozen by the clouds' icy crystals. The needles were thin and fragile, encased by ice—like her heart.

The window glass ran smooth and cold beneath her palm, just as her life had been, the texture of meaning and excitement gone. She had to find that meaning again. *She had to survive.*

Michaela clasped an old coin, claiming its warmth just as she needed to reclaim her life. She traced the L etched into the metal and held the coin tight against her chest. One of the Langtry's six original gold coins, it was her father's going-away gift. She'd been only twenty-two those nine years ago, her meteorologist degree tight and new in her hand.

Michaela had never believed in the legend of the

Langtry coins, how they protected the Langtry-wearer. When all six coins were united, the legend said the owner would become even more powerful. Lately, after a series of disillusioning experiences, she'd begun doubting the legendary love of Zachariah Langtry—the son of a displaced southern plantation owner—and his Native American Cleopatra.

It was said that when the wild heart of a Langtry is captured, it will remain true forever . . . Could love run so deeply that each would give up everything to have the other?

Against the windows filled with the gray March day, the former television meteorologist's tall, slender body was taut with frustration. With black shoulder-length hair swirling around her striking clean-cut face, Michaela was a fighter—a woman who dared resist sexual harassment—but the odds were against her. She was an outsider in an insider business, a labeled "troublemaker."

A wash of rain hit the woman's pale face mirrored in the windows, chilled by spring rain. Michaela studied her arching black brows, her shoulder-length hair pulled sleekly back from her forehead. "Photogenic" and "dynamic" were words they used to describe how the television camera caught her Langtry features and slid them across New York City. The startling effect of her brilliant blue eyes jarred her once more. They were her mother's eyes, framed by black, glossy lashes instead of light brown ones. Michaela's were slashing now, glittering with tears she would not shed. Her skin-tight black pants and a sports bra were damp from her aerobic workout. The design was expensive, just like the closet full of suits worn for the nightly camera.

Arms folded in front of her, nails digging into her flesh, Michaela listened to the television and to the woman who had easily replaced her at the television station. Tina Thomas was good, moving in front of the weather maps, her hands and body eloquent. She'd been well tutored on cosmetics and clothing and was just starting a career that Michaela had ended. But Tina relied strictly on computers, chatted about her dog, and forgot about reading clouds and winds and the moisture condensing on the outer surface of a glass—a telling sign of dew point.

Michaela wanted to feel the weather on her skin, to stand in it and be washed clean. She wanted to know the storms of her heart, to accept what she'd done and make a life from it.

She jerked the window open, allowing the rain to pound on her open palm. Her ancestor hadn't needed computers and reporting weather balloons; he'd foretold weather by the drift of it against his buckskins, his skin, the leaves turning on the trees, and by the look of the clouds in the sky. She missed the fierce elements, the wild Rocky Mountains, the sprawling Langtry ranch.

She'd come so far, moving, jostling for better positions, longing for her family. And for what? A high paying job with a high price tag.

She'd lived with a man for two years, believed he would support her in her battle against the man harassing her. And she'd been so wrong. Worried about his career as a newscaster, Dolph Morrow had run, not walked, away when she'd decided to fight James Charis's sexual harassment. A powerful man in the broadcasting community, James was capable of ruining lives and Dolph wanted his career more than Michaela; he did not support her fight against harrassment.

Truth: their surface-deep affair had been based more on careers and appearances than emotions. They had never once had a meaningful discussion about their emotions.

Michaela smiled tightly, confining the wild hysterical laughter bubbling inside her. She slashed away the hot wash of tears and resented the emotions that prowled through her, raking her confidence. Maybe it was her ancestors' blood stirring, the mix of French, English, and Native American tormenting each other. *Maybe this was the price she would have to pay for coming to life, the pain of reality?*

Did she love him? Not really. Bred to Langtry ideals, she'd tossed them and love away in her need to find a perfect mate.

Truth: she'd been comfortable with the non-relationship, the borders, keeping that fragile inner part of herself safe from harm. The two stress-filled months since James's harrassment of her had exposed her life and career. The daily trials of holding her own against his power sucked away the glitter and exposed the harsh bones of reality. She'd allowed her need for success to devour her.

The woman reflected in the glass flashed a brilliant smile that had won thousands of viewers. But inside herself, Michaela could not deny the cold anger and the emptiness.

Now she smoothed the gold coin in her hand. It ran warm beneath her fingertips, representing all the heritage she'd left behind, the need to test herself against the mountains, to stand in the swirling clean snow and know that her blood ran warm with life.

Truth: she missed Wyoming, the sense of needing the rough mountains, the jagged black rocks and acres of timber, firs and pines broken by stands of white-barked aspens. The wild freedom called to her, those midnight rides alone, pitting her against the wind rushing through her hair, the power of the horse beneath her. She could almost taste the fresh pine-scented air of the mountains, hear the rippling streams, feel the low, hovering clouds damp upon her skin.

Wind from the rugged mountains had always called to her, hissing through the black rock walls of Cutter Canyon as stirring secrets. In the wilderness beauty, she'd found peace and yet a restlessness tore at her. She remembered a passage from Zachariah's 1870 journals:

In these rugged mountains, I have found peace after the war within myself. A soft sweet haunting of truth would never let me rest until I met myself in those dark corners, the man that I was.

Did that same need run savagely within her, the need to hunt and to claim and breathe fresh air once more? To feel the weather on her skin, to know what the clouds would bring, ignoring the computers and the weather balloons? To feel the pine-scented wind flowing through her hair, to let her senses—she searched for a moment before coming to the right word. To let her senses *feel*. . . . More than anything, she needed to feel. Long ago, before the meanings became blurred, she'd known truth—

Truth: she couldn't run from herself. She had to return to Wyoming and find what she had lost.

Michaela frowned slightly. If she returned to Shiloh, even for a short time, she'd see Harrison again. On her last visit home, she'd been uneasy with Harrison Kane II. He'd returned to Shiloh three years before, setting up permanent residence for Kane Corporation and reclaiming his father's bank. Doing business with her family, Harrison was almost a member of the Langtry clan and his presence was certain to nettle her. Meeting infrequently through the years, she at first hadn't understood his dark contemplative looks, though the familiar shadows that circled him were the same as hers.

Her father trusted his advice, making the investments Harrison had suggested. Jacob Langtry was one of the members of Kane Corporation's board, but Harrison's interest in Langtry investments was very, very personal and intense. "The boy has talent. He can spot a good investment and rev it up to real money. But he's paid his dues. He's sacrificed to get where he is now, and it was no easy road. Nothing was handed to him," her father had said proudly, as if Harrison were *his* son.

Michaela's fingers bit into her upper arms. Her

instinctive dislike for computers and calculators and those who relied on them extended to Harrison Kane II.

Harrison's steel-gray eyes were too alert to her raw, exposed emotions. That familiar gesture, that one lean finger strolling down the broken line of his nose, could set her on edge. The gesture was too thoughtful, as if he knew secrets that nothing could tear from him, as if he would act on them when the moment was right.

He'd never told her what happened when he was fifteen, the night his nose was broken. On her way to the kitchen for a snack, fourteen-year-old Michaela had found him with her parents. Already tall, Harrison's usually neatly combed hair was rumpled. His clothing was torn, his face battered and his broken nose taped. His knuckles were scraped, the sight shocking Michaela—Harrison was always in control; he never brawled. *What could have driven him to fight?*

The expressions of her parents and Harrison's had caught and chilled her. Harrison, usually so shielded and in control, looked at Faith as though his soul had been shattered. Faith's tender, concerned expression was to be expected, but Jacob's was that of sheer rage. Michaela had never seen her father so angry, violence pouring from him, his fists held tightly. Her mother's hand upon Jacob's shoulder had seemed to be a tether, leashing him.

The room seemed to be filled with thunder and lightening, washing by confusing emotions from Harrison's unexplained pain to Faith's gentle, maternal sympathy. In a heartbeat, young Michaela had sorted through the dramatic scene and her instincts told her to rescue Harrison, to bring him back from whatever darkness was clawing at him. Despite the way his logic had always nettled her, Michaela knew he needed her strength now—whatever weight he bore was too much and for just a moment, until he reclaimed himself, Harrison needed a distraction.

Michaela knew that one soft question to him could destroy the fragile moment; that Harrison—unused to tenderness—could shred easily if it were offered. Her instincts told her that he was too close to a dark, deadly ravine and that she had to tear him away into life. She hadn't asked for explanations or permissions, she'd just acted, hustling Harrison off into the clear Wyoming night to ride horses. She'd challenged him at every turn, distracted him with fresh air and the beauty of the moonlit mountains, and slowly pushed him back from that uncertain, dangerous edge.

She had never known what happened to Harrison that night. He'd refused a doctor's help and his nose had never been straightened properly. Though they'd battled for years, she respected his right to whatever darkness haunted him. Jacob's lips were sealed, and Michaela knew better than to push her father.

Harrison had been sent back to military school, but he continued spending vacations at the Langtry ranch. Michaela desperately wanted to ask him about that night, but she knew that his shadows were better left alone.

Then when Harrison was eighteen, his father committed suicide, his embezzlement from the Kane First National Bank exposed. Harrison had discovered the body and the blood. A second time he came to the Langtry ranch, looking as if he'd been shredded.

Though his father was not a kind, loving man, Michaela had understood the loss of a parent; she hadn't understood Harrison's mood—self-disgust, fury, and shame. Once again her instincts told her taunt him, push him, pull him back from that dark torment.

Now, her hand against the cool glass of her New York apartment, Michaela saw herself at seventeen, furious with Harrison, battling to bring him back. She'd yelled at him. "I'm not having any of my friends say I couldn't manage a guy who might be thinking of stepping off some cliff and ending it all. You're not going to hurt my parents, Harrison. Or anyone else. You're going to pick yourself up and get back on life's horse and ride it. How embarrassing to think that you—a boy I cannot stand—might do something so dumb. Think of my reputation, will you?" she'd demanded hotly, pushing, saying anything to haul him back into life. "How dumb."

"I'm not dumb," Harrison had shot back, fury replacing that aching darkness.

"Bet you can't even saddle a horse right. Bet I have to help you—" young Michaela had taunted, and he'd taken the bait. "Bet you can't outride me," she'd said, and they'd raced into the moonlight, tearing across the fields and fighting against Harrison's darkness.

Was he worth it? Maybe. Maybe she was the only person who could have pushed him back that night.

As a banker in Shiloh, he'd dedicated himself to success and rebuilding the reputation his grandfather once held, benefitting the community. But Harrison possessed shields that were too cool and logical to suit Michaela's fierce emotions. *Some deep, instinctive part of her wanted to tear him apart, to pit herself against Harrison, to drag him into life.*

"So she's coming home in a month." Harrison Kane II replaced the telephone, Faith Langtry's cultured but excited tones still echoing in his ears. She wanted him to come see Michaela, because he was "family." He had grown up without the warmth of his own family, and had been taken into the Langtrys. Jacob and Faith treated him like their son. Roark had teased and tormented him like a brother.

He leaned back in the big leather chair in his office. After a long day and a board meeting, he was comfortable in his dress shirt rolled back at the sleeves, his opened vest, and his suit slacks. A quick glance at the window jarred him; he bore his father's dark brown waving hair and harsh features, a wide brow, lightly lined, soaring thick eyebrows, and silver, guarded eyes, shuttered with secrets. His body was more of a workman's than a paper-worker's, heavily made and thick with muscle. His father had been jealous of his size, and there had come a time when his father no longer chanced to punish Harrison physically—and then Harrison Sr. had gotten very nasty, tearing at his young son's confidence instead.

Harrison ran his finger down the broken line of his nose, an unconscious reference to the blow his father had served him when he was fifteen. *How could he repay the Langtrys for what his family had taken away?*

He'd carved out a life with Jacob and Faith Langtry's help and yet, there was that dark, brooding temperament he recognized as a gift from his father. A quick mind with numbers and just as frugal as the elder Kane, Harrison had founded Kane Corporation.

Older men with money had liked the "sharp newcomer," and listened to his investment theories, backing him. He wasn't wealthy, rather he was well connected with wealthy investors who trusted him. Once confident with their support, he moved to Shiloh and reclaimed his father's bank.

He placed his well-polished shoes on the sleek functional modern desk that had replaced his father's massive wooden one. Harrison had redone the bank's executive offices, ripping out his father's ornate furniture. He wished he could as easily tear away the legacy his father had left the Langtrys and himself.

As soon as he could, he'd donated Kane House to the Shiloh Historical Society. Upon his return to town three years ago, he'd built a home without the shadows of the past. A distance from town, his rock-and-wood home suited him. When he could, he'd enjoyed working with the contractor and Jacob and Roark. Without the opulent furnishings of Kane House, his new home provided a measure of peace—a commodity difficult for Harrison to find.

Outside his office, Shiloh had settled down into a small town's peaceful evening. Seeding fescue and alfalfa fields were top priority now with the cattle ranchers. Rural vegetable gardens were being planned, and life remained constant year to year. Drought and crop disease, cattle and market prices dominated the local cafe and the feed and grain store. Small farmers angling for more land and better equipment depended on Kane First National Bank. Young families needing additions to their homes and the elderly needing counseling on their retirement plans were a major portion of the bank's patrons.

Harrison breathed deeply, controlling the dark remembrance of his father's "deals," which had ruined too many people. Kane Sr. liked to play games with lives, and sexual payments were often part of his rules.

His son fought that look every day, of people wondering when he would change, taking his father's dark side. He wouldn't. He'd formed and managed a successful corporation and was dedicated to correcting his father's damage. Rural and steeped in ranching tradition, Shiloh would always be home. Harrison couldn't run away from the tragedy his family had caused the Langtrys, but he intended to help Faith Langtry with her dreams.

He reached to brush away a fleck of dust on his shoes. They were Italian and expensive and represented how far he had driven himself to reclaim Kane position and money. Then he'd skipped a few meals and worn shabby secondhand suits and taken part-time work doing anything that added a few more dollars to his investment portfolio. Initial success had ended his laborer's days in construction, and dressing well had paid off, getting him a better clientele. He found he liked hunting profit, for sport and pleasure, and doubted a woman would bring him as much satisfaction.

But then he had needed money to track a woman—his mother. Julia Kane didn't want to be found, leaving a path of destruction behind her.

A fragile woman, battling years of depression and abuse, Julia's high intelligence had thrived on deception. Skilled at paper trails, understanding people's vices, and obviously relishing her strength to deceive, she had layered the trail with pitfalls and diversions, each leading into oblivion and frustration. Using aliases, Julia could move into any lifestyle, blend with any community; she could always make money and hide it. A financial genius, Julia could forge signatures and documents to her satisfaction. If she needed to corrupt official data, to change her identity or to produce a death certificate, she would temporarily take a position as a file clerk. At Harrison's last count, there were twelve forged "Julia Kane" death certificates, all with unusual, dramatic causes of death.

Harrison had learned not to trust the obvious, and the trails were always twisted and deep, eventually ending almost at their starting point. *He couldn't serve the Langtrys the cruel hope that their daughter—his half-*

sister—lived. He couldn't bear to watch them tormented again, and it was best that he kept silent until—

Until what? Until the baby was found? Where? Julia had left too many trails. Dealing with his mother's almost criminal intelligence was like following the bouncing ball through quicksand loaded with land mines. Yet the people he'd interviewed said she appeared absolutely normal. Playing any role, Julia was first the mother of a baby, running from a potential child molester and abusive husband. She garnered sympathy and protection before she moved on. She always seemed to have money, the baby well-tended and happy. Suddenly, when the baby was almost two years old, reports revealed that Julia moved alone.

Harrison trusted nothing when it came to his mother.

He'd spent years and a fortune tracking her, with few pleasures for himself. Harrison ran his finger over his nose. It had been broken again by the ham-sized fist of a bare-knuckle fighter who didn't like "fancy college boys." Brundy really should have taken the cool warning; he didn't like the verbal price tag to escape from Harrison's fists. Harrison demanded that Brundy apologize, and the words came hard to the experienced brawler. "I apologize. You're okay, kid."

That back alley fight was a life-experience Harrison had enjoyed, despite the scraped knuckles and his broken nose.

But at the top of his enjoyable life's adventures was

Michaela Langtry. Each encounter with her was a revelation—how her mind would turn quickly, running on instinct rather than logic. His singular very private need, other than obvious financial stability and his goal of repaying the Langtrys, was to stir Michaela's passionate nature, the one she kept hidden. He could almost feel the burn of it lick at him, sizzle in the air between them. To a man raised in a sterile, cold home, Michaela's genuine, wide-open emotions were appreciated. Just a subtle brush, a look, or a word could nettle her. She didn't like being pushed or studied, and he'd found that he liked to do both.

A wash of snowflakes sailed past the darkened window, taking him back to when he was fifteen and to his father's drunken rages. He'd yelled, *That stolen baby was mine! Faith was too good for Jacob Langtry, an uncultured rough cowboy. I knew I had to make her mine, and so I did one night, forcing her. Women like force, remember that, boy. Jacob never knew who fathered that baby, or he would have come after me.*

Harrison inhaled sharply, the familiar pain clenching around his heart. He remembered little about his mother; she'd deserted them when he was five, but in his unleashed drunken rages, his father spared little affection for her. *Your mother couldn't have any more children, an infection of some sort after you were born. She took that Langtry baby. I damned her then, wanting that child to grow up and ruin them—my seed in the almighty Langtry family . . . the perfect revenge. I had it all planned and she ruined everything, running away with the baby. I never thought she'd go so far.*

His mind twisted by hatred and alcohol, Harrison Kane, Sr., feared death and losing his heir. His son, already scarred by life, would have walked away easily—if the Langtrys were hurt yet again. Faith's rape and gossip about the youngest Langtry's father weren't open for discussion.

Harrison's finger slid over his nose. He'd used the gesture many times to remind himself of what he had to do: help the Langtrys resolve their pain.

Back then, no one had suspected his mother. His father had supplied too many lies—that first month she was missing, she was merely "indisposed and needing rest." Her mental fragility was well known through the area, and no one had questioned her.

Then the suspect was Maria Alvarez, the missing Langtry housekeeper.

The oldest of the clan and taking her duties as big sister seriously, four-year-old Michaela had placed a fabled Langtry coin by the baby's crib to guard her that night—the coin was still missing.

But Julia Kane had left that night, taking the baby, her absence concealed by lies.

His search for his half-sister and his mother had lasted eighteen years; his demented mother had done her work well . . .

Harrison closed his eyes, grateful that his mother hadn't killed the younger Langtry children, sleeping in their beds.

Should he have told the Langtrys what he knew? He was fifteen by then, shamed and stunned by all his family had done to a family he treasured, worshiped.

He could then, and he couldn't now. Harrison carried that shame with him with every breath. He couldn't give them hope and then nothing; only hard evidence could bring peace to the Langtry family. A boy, uncertain of the shocking truths, had almost come apart that night, flying into pieces.

But Michaela wouldn't have that. That night, she'd pulled him back from the edge of nowhere, pushed him until he was drained, and then pasted him back together . . . Michaela had always fought for those she loved, and only fourteen then, she'd stepped into his bleeding young heart and told him of her dreams—and then he'd dreamed, too. His dream was to find the missing baby, his half-sister and Michaela's.

When he was eighteen, his hands bloody from the discovery of his father's suicide, Michaela had once more retrieved him from the edge of nowhere. Twice, she'd grasped, shoved, cajoled, and challenged him from that dangerous edge; she'd proven the Langtry legend, *the women were as bold as their men, with hearts as soft and sweet as the summer mist over a mountain meadow . . .*

While Michaela's family had given her heart and warmth; his family had none. Harrison stared at the man in the mirror. He was his father's image without the shadows of excess. He was very controlled, allowing little self indulgence, because there was always the edge, the fear that he could be like his father.

Michaela had moved away, but distance made little difference to a man who knew how to prowl through lives. Her lover of two years had deserted her, her career was gone. Harrison frowned, thinking of the narrow-faced, delicate build of Dolph Morrow. He didn't like to think of Michaela in Dolph's bed, all that steaming passionate nature given to— He pushed away that slight jealous burn and thought of the curved, sweet women he preferred.

Who was he kidding? Michaela's vivid image burned away other women. She'd always fascinated him, even when that saucy mouth was cutting at him. He smiled lightly; he'd known very early that Michaela's impatience wouldn't allow his slow but sure methods, his basic one-two-three logic. When they were younger, she'd move into a challenge while he was still debating; more times than not, he'd have to rescue her from disaster. Michaela moved on impulse and need and her instincts, while he'd long ago trimmed away anything but logic and essential purpose.

He ran his fingertip around the coffee mug that Faith had made especially for him. It was big and solid, like himself, a curved plug on the handle fitting his thumb. Michaela could always divert him from his thoughts and he didn't like that at all, not a man who built his life brick by brick and kept his mortar close at hand to mend problems. Quick tempered and passionate to his basic logic, Michaela had always stirred simmering emotions he'd rather not explore.

Michaela had come back to her family and four of the coins were reunited. Harrison intended to find the two missing coins.

A methodical, controlled man, he firmly placed his

thoughts of the missing coin back into a mental drawer. Harrison gripped the mug, curving his hand firmly around it. Michaela's return to Shiloh, even for a few days, meant they were certain to clash. Harrison resented the emotions she could ignite in him, testing his control. In his few relationships, he preferred less volatile women. Yet during her last few trips back to Shiloh, he'd enjoyed clashing verbal swords with her, watching those fabulous blue eyes narrow and burn at him.

He smiled grimly. They weren't children anymore and he wasn't backing off.

two

Wounded and the escapee of a Yankee prison, I'd gotten home, to Langtry Plantation. The mansion was sacked and charred, the Yankees coming to take what was left. At midnight, my father begged me to run, to take the last of the family gold. "The South will rise again with Langtry gold," he whispered as the fire burned and an ex-slave, Obediah, turned Langtry jewelry into coins.

Black as ebony and faithful to our family, Obediah's sweaty body had glistened. His feverish black eyes had closed, his lips muttering. He shook the chicken bones and tossed them onto the six still warm, gleaming gold coins, marked with a crude "L."

"He's calling his gods," my father whispered. "The coins are powerful protectors of Langtry blood *and united the owner will be as powerful as a god. Those without Langtry blood will be cursed for having them. Take them and go."*

And so it was that I came to this wild free country, the soaring mountains and the beauty with the six Langtry coins and Obediah's curse keeping me safe.

Zachariah Langtry's Journal

Four weeks later, Michaela stood next to the Langtry corral, savoring the moonlight—unwilling to go inside.

She caught the shadow surging out of the April night, the big man moving toward her. Roark Langtry's build was as lean as his father's, and Roark bore an edge of the untamed in his eyes, in the loose way he stood. Moonlight outlined his cutting cheekbones, slashing brows, and the hard set of his jaw, the wind whipping at his shaggy hair. For a time, Roark's wife, Angelica, had tamed that wild, searching hunger, but Roark now kept his secrets dark within him.

A month before, her brother had just "dropped" into New York for business, but Michaela had known that he was actually the Langtry family scout, checking up on her. As tall as her father and bearing that same long-legged angular power, Roark had squired her, pushing her, nettling her and getting her out into the favorite haunts of her former crowd. When a Langtry man dressed to kill, flashed that brilliant smile, women drooled. But Zachariah's fierce savagery, the need to avenge his sister amid the backbiting, career-climbing crowd, ran beneath Roark's smooth charm.

He'd come to New York to protect her, almost calling out the man who had harassed her. The ring of a western gunfight sounded through the cocktail party, and Michaela had been furious, tearing into Roark. "The rules are different here, little brother. I can protect myself."

"Some things are worth fighting for," he'd brooded darkly.

"And others aren't," she'd returned, aware that her life had to change.

Now her brother moved silently across the field, patting a horse's rump as he walked toward her. Roark would do anything to protect his family, yet he'd lost a wife he loved, blaming himself for her death. Angelica had been too finely made to bear their child, and within days, his son gave up the struggle to live. Roark bore his shadows every time he saw a pregnant woman. In his grief, he roamed when the darkness came upon him. She greeted her brother lightly, "Roark, you're night hunting again."

Stubble covered his jaw, his hair tousled from the wind. The moonlight caught the silvery gleam of his eyes, searching her face, seeking out the exhaustion and the haunting that would not release her. "So is my sister. Welcome back. But why are you out here? It's nearly midnight."

"I'm not ready to go to the house yet. I'm not ready to face Mom and Dad." She lifted her face to the night breeze, stirring softly, almost a caress in her hair, sweetly scented against her face.

"Every time I come home I have to deal with Mom's belief that Sable is alive. And my memories of that night . . . I placed a Langtry coin beside her crib that night to keep her safe. And I remember hearing that lullaby, '*Soft-ly, slow-ly . . .*' "

A frontiersman from the war-torn South, and having little to give, Zachariah had created the nursery lullaby for their children, to keep them safe in dreamland. Michaela had heard that song the night Sable was taken away; it was then that she knew "safe" couldn't be trusted.

She'd seen her parents in emotional shreds when their youngest baby was stolen by a trusted housekeeper and friend. Michaela had seen her mother valiantly try to hide a grief that would not heal, and for the first time, her powerful father had been helpless.

Jacob Langtry's fierce war to find Sable had shaken a nation, and yet the baby remained hidden— Faith believed her child was alive, and she looked for Sable in each young woman, always searching.

Michaela looked at Roark, his face shadowed by his western hat. He knew more than anyone how that night haunted her, that song clung to her. "Do you believe the curse—that anyone but a Langtry will be cursed if they have the coins, that all six are powerful?"

"I believe in truth and what is. Life comes and goes. We have to take it as it is and make the best of it."

Michaela smoothed the mare's mane and words from Zachariah's journal floated on the night air. *Feverish I was, but my father's terror was worse. I did as he bid, and ran from the war, carrying a bleeding heart and those coins. They would brand me as a coward, my honor gone. My wound opened, and in rage and pain, I fled with lightning crackling about me. I took with me my father's dreams as I was honor-bound to carry on in his stead. The Langtry stallion beneath me knew his deed and we ran on, the coward and the horse.*

Michaela nuzzled a mare, holding her close. There was nothing like riding a "Langtry" horse, of feeling the power and heritage in the muscles of the animal. The famous Langtry breed had descended from His Majesty, the thoroughbred stallion that had carried Zachariah and the six gold coins from the family plantation. His wife Cleopatra's mare had provided the endurance of mustang, quarterhorse, and Morgan to the heavier-built breed with shorter necks and larger heads. While the Langtry horses were sought across the world for their powerful endurance, the breed appealed for the mystique of Zachariah and Cleopatra's love, as if the new owners wanted a portion of that legendary romance.

But the Langtry family knew better than anyone that the fierce heart of a Langtry horse was truly powerful only in Wyoming, amid the sprawling fields fed by mountain streams, amid the clean air, spring bluebells, and winter snowfall. A keening hawk was said to raise their thoroughbred hot sporting blood, evidenced by the prancing and edginess before the hunt.

"Do you believe in a love so strong it could overcome anything? Such as Zachariah and Cleopatra's?"

"I believe in love so deep that it can tear a man's heart from him when he loses it."

That stark honesty, the brittle reminder that Roark had lost a part of himself with Angelica and their baby, was etched on his grim expression.

"I don't know that I believe in love. For myself. I'm going to be a grand old spinster."

Roark briskly rubbed her head, a brotherly gesture of affection. "That's because you haven't really loved. You're not willing to give up that last part of yourself to someone else, to trust them with your heart, your life and soul. You've got a wild, fierce heart, sister dear, but when you love, you'll know it. It won't be a sweet ride, because you like to control your life. You've been choosing men who let you do that. When a person loves, he gives away part of himself to someone else's keeping, and that's the joy of it."

Michaela gripped his hand, rough with calluses. "You think that's what I do? Choose a man I can control?"

Roark snorted in disgust. "Real sissies, sister dear. You're a hunter and you like challenges. You need a match, someone to stand up to you. Take Harrison, for example. You can't run over him and instead you run from him. You two have been battling for years. You stay here and the war is on—"

He studied the hat she had taken from his head and placed on her own, teasing him as she had when they were children. He grinned down at her. "Ready to go in now?"

"It's about time you came home where you belong," Jacob Langtry muttered gruffly, though just looking at his daughter made him feel warm and proud. At seven o'clock in the bright April morning, he was shocked by his daughter's exhausted appearance as she made her way into the ranch house's sunny kitchen.

At thirty-one, his daughter should be safe in her own home, snuggled with a good man and raising Jacob's grandchildren. With her life in pieces, Jacob wanted to offer his help and solve her problems for her. But then there was her pride—Langtry pride—and he recognized that well enough. She wouldn't want his interference.

Restless this morning, wanting to say the right things to his daughter, praying he wouldn't say too much, he'd finished milking Bess and riding Earl, his gelding, around the herd. He'd collected the eggs for Faith's light omelets, silly eastern-city fare. Though the ranch hands would have performed the chores, he loved seeing Faith's expression, the delight in her blue eyes as he gave the bucket of creamy milk and the basket of eggs to her. Still a city girl at heart, she'd delighted in making butter, a common, necessary chore in ranching country.

They'd made a good life together. She'd taken his heart and given him more than he'd expected of life. His wife's talents had softened the gleaming hardwood of the sprawling ranch house. Faith's woven rugs decorated the walls, her pottery, placed just right so as not to clutter a room, enhanced the spare decor.

Her paintings were large and bold and almost as striking as young Michaela's. At times, the shadows caught Faith and he was helpless, but held her close. Though Roark and Michaela flourished, Faith mourned a child she could not hold, or hear laugh, or watch grow into adulthood.

In the warm pink and brown tones of the Langtry's sprawling kitchen, sunlight passed through the skylight. Jacob marveled at the difference between his fair wife and their taller, raven-haired daughter. The grace of the two women he loved never failed to stun him, to tighten his throat with pride and love.

Dressed in a light pink sweater and tan flowing slacks, Faith was just as slender as when they'd met years ago, her blond hair, now streaked with gray, but still elegantly, neatly twisted upon her head. In her studio, amid her pottery and art and students, dressed in an old flannel shirt, she could be a tyrant, but her raging temper cooled just as quickly as her precious raku pottery.

His wife still fascinated him. Faith had that pink glowing look, blue eyes beaming at him, as if all her world was complete at this one moment. He looped an arm around her and brought her close, the woman he'd loved and cherished for thirty-three years, and studied their daughter.

In a red sweater high on her slender throat and long, slender jeans, warm white socks covering her feet, Michaela looked too thin, too haunted. Her dark, shoulder-length hair framed too-pale creamy skin. She needs the sun and the wind and plenty of fresh clean air, Jacob thought, aching for his daughter. Years ago, he could have brought her a new kitten from the barn, or given her a calf to show at the fair, and he would have made her world right. But now life had torn at her and she'd do her own mending, in her own time.

Circles haunted Michaela's blue eyes, startling against her black lashes and brows. Jacob mourned the tightness around her mouth, that too thin, tall body. Her face bore the mark of bad times, and Jacob knew there was no more difficult time than the one when you begin to sort through your life.

"I could use a hug," he stated roughly, the request still sitting unfamiliar upon his rough-hewn ways after all these years.

Michaela came to snuggle against him and Jacob wondered who needed who most. His heart filling, brimming, he held them close, his two women. Against him, Michaela's shoulders seemed too fragile, like that of a little bird who had fought too many storms. Jacob swallowed the rage that consumed him; he wanted to slowly squeeze the life out of the man who had sexually harassed Michaela, and the man who had run out on her. But that wouldn't do, because his daughter liked to rule her own life. "Sleep well, Michaela?"

"Just great, Dad. It's good to be home." She moved to pour coffee into the pottery mugs Faith had made, handing Jacob the one he preferred—big and sturdy, a tiny chip just there at the rim, Faith's first effort and a gift to him. This morning, he held it tight when Faith would have taken it away, replacing the battered mug with a new one. "You gave it to me. It's mine."

"Cowboy, you'll forget to guard it one day, and I'll have that poor old thing then. It's my first work, and not good at all," Faith teased him, and gave him a light kiss that still tasted of that first hunger, years ago.

"Leave me be, woman. It's mine," he repeated, faking a fierce scowl at her. He'd give his heart and soul to make her happy, to give her back the baby she'd lost long ago. When Roark came to in breakfast, he'd have all his children there—but one.

Jacob wanted his children safe and damned himself for not protecting the baby who had been torn from them.

He sat at the sturdy wooden table, smoothing the woven placemat which blended the dull pinks and browns of the kitchen. He caught Faith's hand as she placed his plate of pancakes on the placemat, his heart too full for words. Helpless amid his emotions, Jacob held her hand, lacing her small capable fingers with his workman's scarred ones. "Dammit," he said roughly, finally, humbled by his good fortune, the children and love Faith had given him.

Then Roark, tall and lean, almost a replica of a younger Jacob, carried the fresh air with him as he burst into the kitchen. "Hi, sis! I thought you'd be sleeping in. I was planning to dump a glass of water on you and watch the fireworks."

My son, Jacob thought proudly as Roark hurried to

wash up. With Faith's sky-blue eyes amid the raw-boned Langtry features, Roark had that hawkish, hunter look.

Michaela smiled then, that quick flirting of pleasure over her lips, and for a moment the shadows lightened. She poured more batter onto the griddle and scanned the ranch yard outside. "Where's Culley?"

Culley Blackwolf, a tall, lanky cowboy, had arrived in Shiloh ten years ago. Obviously of Native American descent and then somewhere around twenty-five, Culley had parked a battered pickup with Colorado license plates in front of the town cafe. Jacob had liked the western-bred look of Culley as he straddled the counter stool and quietly ate his meal, cleaning the gravy from the plate with the swipe of bread. The boy was hungry and worn, too thin beneath a shirt that was past saving. He had big scarred hands, the kind made from rope burns and barbed wire. A man who recognized hard times, Jacob had sat on the next stool. He signaled Megan to bring two pieces of her best berry pie—and one for the silent man beside him.

"I don't take handouts," Culley had said, shoving away the plate through his gaze lingered hungrily upon it.

"I need another good man at my ranch. My son and I ramrod it, but my top man is about to retire—his arthritis is getting to him. I'm just trying to sweeten the pot," Jacob had said, and eased the pie back again.

This time, Culley had taken the invitation. "I'll drop on by your spread."

He kept to himself, and other than those Colorado plates and the expert way he handled a horse and ranch life, the Langtrys knew little about Culley.

Jacob returned Faith's breakfast-table kiss, his hand caught when it wandered a bit too low. "Culley will be here soon enough. He always makes it in time for a family breakfast. He's got a few chores to do in the morning before he comes here for a workday. He's got a place out on the north forty," Jacob grumbled. "He and Roark built the house and dug the well. He's going to be an old lonely-wolf bachelor, set in his ways, and then no woman will have him."

"Now, Jacob," Faith soothed. "Culley always liked his privacy."

"Woman, it's you who does the worrying about this family, not me. I raise cattle and horses and crops." Because of Roark's tender loss, Jacob didn't say that he longed for grandchildren to sit upon his lap, to sneak to the ice cream parlor, and to rock to sleep at bedtime. But the way Roark was living, the Langtry name would stop with him.

Jacob's gaze shifted to Michaela. She was unpredictable as a filly—no telling what his daughter would do. Women were hard to understand.

Faith patted his head and rumpled his hair, gray now at the temples. "You know how that 'woman' talk gets to me, cowboy. So macho. Makes my heart just feel like a trapped butterfly."

His tirade blocked for a moment, Jacob's weathered face began to shift into a boyish grin. It widened when Faith dipped her head to quickly kiss him and sat upon his lap. He patted her bottom as she rose, hurrying to her pancakes, and for a moment Michaela held her breath, caught by her parents' obvious devotion and love.

Roark gave Michaela a knowing look. "Things are dull around here. No bagels on sidewalk tables and fancy coffee. No plays except the high school drama class and the Christmas pageant. I'll bet your rear end is too soft to sit a saddle now."

"Try me," she shot back, and the light banter eased the tightness in Jacob's heart.

"You'd better practice before you take me on." Roark eased into his chair at the long, sturdy table.

Hunched against the morning cold that had entered with him, Culley drew off his leather gloves and stripped off his coat. He hung them carefully on the hook beside Roark's and Jacob's. "Jacob . . . Roark . . . Faith. Hi, Michaela. Saw that flashy red four-wheeler of yours drive in at midnight."

Michaela glanced at a small battered economy car pulling beside her red S.U.V. Beside her, balancing a pitcher of orange juice, Faith spoke quietly. "That's May. Your father insisted that I have help with the house when I got so busy at the studio. It took a long time to get used to another . . . another woman in the house after Maria."

For a moment, the room was quiet, shadows of the

past haunting the Langtry family. Then Culley spoke, breaking the silence. "That little bull is doing fine, Jacob. The cuts from the barbed wire are healing."

"Good. Maybe he'll learn something for next time." Jacob turned to his daughter. "Ride with me? Your mare, Diamond, needs working."

"Not this morning, Dad," Michaela murmured quietly, the shadows humming around her.

A woman's time, Jacob thought, the mending of soft hearts and tender words that he couldn't always find. His daughter needed Faith's gentle care and his time would come soon enough. "Well, then. You need to see your mother's new studio. She's teaching most of the countryside and deserting me in my old age."

"You could come to my pottery classes too, dear," Faith returned with an easy smile.

"A man's hands don't belong in mud. I didn't give the studio to you to get sick watching that wheel go around, or mud splashing on my best boots." Proud of his wife, he tossed the familiar banter at her just to savor her reaction.

"He's too impatient, not centered enough, and he's a disaster in my studio. The clay goes spinning off the center more times than not. I want the studio to be on a self-supporting basis, not subsidized by my husband's gifts. I teach young children now and teenagers and senior citizens. I can't have them frightened away by his surly moods." Faith's words were softened by love. She fluttered her lashes at Jacob. "But he's all I've got to carry in clay for me, showing off all those big, strong muscles, those broad shoulders and that cowboy smile."

Jacob allowed his wife-fascinating grin to escape and didn't worry at all about the blush rising up his cheeks.

Later that day, Michaela wandered toward her mother's art center, a massive jutting building. Outside, Faith's use of sienna stucco and shrubbery blended the stark structure into the rugged mountains behind it. Inside two big gas kilns were in a separate room, gas pipes angling from the huge propane tanks a distance away. In a main room, shelves of unfinished pottery, some in the "leather-hard" stage, waiting to be trimmed, were the work of Faith's students. Glazed and fired, other work waited to be collected by the makers. Electric potter's wheels were placed in the big room, a sink stained with use, and nearby buckets for trimmed clay to be reused. An extruder machine, to press the bubbles from the new clay, was at the opposite end of the huge room, lined with southern windows and high skylights. Books of glaze recipes and building kilns and clay techniques filled a tall bookcase, and in the center of the room the skylight poured down on a long table for the students' use. A large outdoor patio served the painters in good weather.

Another large room had windows facing to the north, excellent painting light and devoted to those who would study painting and sketching. Faith's office was cluttered, numbers of the gas company, clay and glaze supply companies scrawled by the telephone, crusted with clay.

Outside were the raku kilns, placed close to beds of sand and hay, buckets waiting to be placed over the quickly cooling pottery. The hay would ignite and the chemical exchange of glazes, with heat meeting cold, would produce the shimmering, iridescent, and sometimes dull or cracked raku finish.

Michaela found Faith at her private studio, dressed in a shirt stained and laundered many times. She carefully trimmed the edges from a large bowl that had turned leather hard and glanced at her daughter. Faith smiled softly. "Your father is emotional. He's hiding out until he's pulled himself together. He'll rope a few cows, tighten a bit of fence wire, talk old times with the men working for us, and brood about his little girl growing up."

"Times change. I'm not a little girl anymore."

Faith's brilliant blue gaze was direct and clear, meeting Michaela's. She tossed a curl of discarded clay into a bucket to be reused. "No, you're not. You're having a bad patch and nothing more. But I'm glad you're home."

Michaela nodded and studied the rugged mountains studded with pines and fir and jutting rock ledges. *I knew I was home,* Zachariah had written. *All that had gone before was nothing but smoke on the wind. My heart is here, with my wife and family. She's a fine proud beauty, my wife. A little savage when angered, and always a lady. She believes in the power of the coins and the curse. Sometimes I feel as if her shaman blood told her the truth of Obediah's curse.*

Michaela badly needed to believe in herself, to find the reality she had lost. "I've got to find work."

"Mmm. You might ask Harrison if they need someone at his new television station."

"Harrison owns a television station?" Michaela repeated.

"With his investors. KANE isn't on line yet, but it will be. He's nearly rebuilt the inheritance his father's alcohol abuse exhausted. Harrison is very shrewd and he works hard. He's very caring. People trust him. He's absolutely solid. He's not at all like his father." Faith dropped another clay curl into her re-use bucket as though discarding a bad memory.

Michaela noticed that her mother's dislike of Harrison's father hadn't budged in all these years. Her mother always flinched when Harrison Kane, Sr., was mentioned; a placid, usually balanced woman, Faith Langtry kept her secrets, but her reaction was always there, palpable—she was repulsed by mention of Harrison's father.

Faith frowned slightly, her body clenched as if from a blow before she turned back to studying the large bowl. "His corporation owns several things around here, including the bank. And he's working to promote financial support to get attention to our art center. Selling a few pots now and then isn't cutting it. I told Jacob wanted to borrow money from the bank to get the studio more into a business. I had to battle that

Langtry temper and pride for a week later. We compromised on donations. They're tax deductible finally and not charity. I've always felt that art should support itself, and there's a lot of undiscovered talent here. You can paint any time you want, dear. You were good. Much better than me. I can teach basics, but flat surfaces aren't for me—my talent ran more to clay than to canvas."

Michaela scanned the large, vivid abstracts in her mother's private studio. She'd tossed away her feel for colors as she'd pursued her career, and now she felt nothing but empty.

Faith smiled and continued to trim the large bowl, the surface layered with finger groves. Her daughter must never guess her secret. With practice, she'd pushed away the memory of Kane Sr., his harsh, drunken taking of her. It was the only secret she'd kept from Jacob, because he would surely have killed Kane. She would have lost a husband then, and she preferred to protect her love and her two other children.

Despite the beautiful morning and her daughter's return, Faith tensed against the familiar pain of her lost daughter, Sable. From time to time, she studied Harrison and wondered if he knew. Would Sable look like Harrison now? Would her fair curls have turned to dark waving brown, glinting with red highlights. Would Sable be a feminine reflection of Harrison? Would her face have those same broad cheekbones, those wide-spaced eyes, and a nose more delicate than his blunt one, matching the wide span of his forehead?

Her missing daughter would always haunt her heart, and sometimes she thought Harrison understood, his gray gaze meeting hers. Visually, he reminded her of his father, and she'd caught herself shivering once or twice at the sight of him. But Harrison was big and solid and *without his father's cruelty*. With practice and strength, she inhaled and shoved away the aching loss of her stolen daughter and considered the bowl she was trimming. It was a good piece, she thought critically, in the basic style that matched other pieces. Her buyers loved to add to their Faith Langtry collections.

She smiled as Michaela frowned, chewing on the idea of Harrison's television station, and fed her daughter another tidbit. "We're rather proud of Harrison's efforts. He's put up a tiny radio station and the high school students interested in media are welcome to participate. It's just what we needed years ago, when you were a teenager and researching careers."

Michaela lifted a delicate black eyebrow. "Harrison still seems to be a part of the family."

"He needed a family back then, and I think of him as a son. He's always welcome in our home." Faith smiled and placed her trimmed bowl on a rack waiting to be fired into bisque. Her husband would bring up Harrison's suitability as a husband soon. Jacob's need to see his daughter safely wed and settled and bringing him grandchildren wasn't always subtle.

Harrison traced his broken nose. He hadn't expected the excitement in him, the need to see

Michaela, to ignite her. His experience with women was limited; fighting for financial safety had stripped away too much time and energy. *He wanted her.* At first, that fact had shocked him, then he realized he had always wanted Michaela. Admired her? Yes. Been irritated by her? Yes. But whatever roamed through him, stark and quivering and exciting, he knew that Michaela struck a primitive chord within him, something real and taut and alive that no one else could reach. He smiled tightly, anticipating their first meeting, and then, with the ease of practice, gave himself back to the numbers flashing on his computer screen.

Three days later, Michaela lay in her bedroom, the late April dawn skimming the shelves layered with dolls and the walls filled with riding trophies and pictures of her as a child and a teenager. Beneath her college cap and gown, a younger Michaela flashed a brilliant grin into the camera. Spacious and warmed by her mother's weaving, Michaela's bedroom was much the same as the rest of the sprawling house. A mix of cool tile and hardwood floors, the comfortable ranch house was a blend of Western life and Faith's cultured tastes.

Michaela's bedroom was part of the new addition, and the old nursery was just a few feet away. Though Faith had removed the crib, the rocking chair remained and the room seemed without purpose in a house carefully arranged and decorated. Michaela closed her eyes and heard the old song whisper through the dawn—*"Soft-ly, slow-ly. . . ."*

She'd placed the coin on the table to keep Sable safe, but it hadn't.

Her mother still paused at the room, her expression haunted. She'd turned once to Michaela, her eyes shining bright with tears. "I know she's alive. She'll come back to us."

Michaela's bedroom door opened wider and Jacob's tall, lean body filled it. As he had done in the nights before, he'd come to watch her sleep, to reassure himself that she was safe. He'd never forgiven himself for wanting his wife alone that night, twenty-seven years ago, and his midnight checks on Roark and Michaela had continued.

"I'm fine, Dad. I'm just tired. It takes a while to adjust."

At the sound of her voice, his body relaxed slightly. "I'm glad you're home. Go back to sleep, honey."

"Dad, Mom thinks Sable will come back."

Jacob inhaled slowly, and rubbed his chest where an ache for his wife and child never stilled. "I know. She'd be twenty-seven now."

"You never believed Maria took her, did you?"

"Not for one minute. I knew Maria's father, and I know her family. I'm sick about what this has done to them and that they had to move to find peace. But the facts say Maria was gone and the baby was gone. So was the coin you put by Sable's crib. I've had detectives on the case for years trying to find Maria, and they haven't found anything. You wear your coin. It will keep you safe. Faith doesn't need to worry about another lost child."

But Michaela knew that Jacob worried most of all, carrying his guilt into the midnight hours when he watched over his adult children. "I'll be fine, Dad," she repeated softly. "Do you think Obediah's curse is real? Do you think the coins bring bad luck to those who are not Langtry?"

"I'm goddamned praying so." Jacob's deep voice echoed with barely leashed violence. "What kind of a monster would take a six-week-old baby from her mother? They deserve any hell they get. Cleopatra was supposed to have used that curse to frighten men, and she managed to get all the coins united. Your mother needs closure to this—we all do. If those missing two coins turn up, we might have something to go on."

three

I never saw a woman more elegant, more queenly than the Indian woman who took my heart in the mountains. Daughter of a trader, she'd been picking berries and had come upon me, mauled by a grizzly. He lay in deathly repose nearby, my hunting knife still friendly in his throat. In truth, I wasn't that badly hurt and was searching for sinew and needle to sew my wounds. But my lady's hands upon me enticed and I fell beneath her spell immediately.

Zachariah Langtry's Journal

Michaela hesitated before answering the brisk knock at the door. Harrison Kane II was the last man she wanted to see while pasting herself back together.

Her mother would have invited him in of course, and his timing was impeccable, with Michaela alone and brooding and defenseless against his quiet logic.

She clicked off the soothing music from the sound system, used for the slow stretching exercises of her aerobic cool-down. Nothing about Harrison soothed her.

She frowned at Harrison's choice of vehicles, a high-powered gleaming black pickup without rural Wyoming's usual coating of mud and dirt. It resembled the man—expensive, made for impact and power, and unmovable in the Langtry's driveway. If she pretended not to be home and ignored his knock, Harrison wouldn't go away. He'd walk the distance to her mother's art center and Faith would bring him back to the house.

Harrison was always very careful to be polite and nonintrusive in her family and that trait irritated Michaela. She also resented Harrison's logic and his smooth manners. Most of all, she resented how he could stir her with one shadowed, dissecting look of those gray eyes. Since he was almost a member of the family, and likely to be invited to dinner, she might as well get the initial battle over with. She jerked open the door. "You took your time. Mother expected you *last* night for dinner."

She wasn't prepared for that smoothly combed dark brown hair, gleaming in the morning sun. She'd forgotten the impact of those fierce brows and lashes too long for a man, those deep-set gray eyes, the slash of his broad cheekbones. Not a pretty man, Harrison wasn't one to fade into a crowd with his broken nose and his hard set jaw. His hands were too big, square and powerful for a man who spent most of his time in an office.

"I called Faith. She understands." Harrison's gray eyes strolled down Michaela's black aerobic workout bra and tight yellow-striped pants. He picked up the end of the towel draped around her neck and patted the film of moisture on her forehead. Michaela jerked back, placing distance between her and Harrison's tall, well-clad body, and that soap and man scent. Her skin burned with the scrape of his hand across her cheek and she patted the towel there, trying to erase the sensation.

The tailored pinstriped gray suit was obviously expensive and not from rural Wyoming. He was usually meticulously dressed and pressed. She resented the warm, surging liquid tug on her senses the few times she'd seen him dressed for ranching in a cotton shirt and tight-fitting jeans. A muscle-packed six-foot-four man, he had shoulders that blocked daylight from her, and that humming, squeezing feeling had begun inside her. She disliked looking up those inches to his face, finding that shielded, watchful, close study of her.

Harrison's hard mouth curved slightly. "Are you going to invite me in?"

"So proper. You know you can walk into the house anytime you want." She stepped back and Harrison's clean soapy scent invaded her senses as he passed.

He walked to the windows overlooking the Langtry

fields and spreading up into the Rocky Mountains. Fog that could become drizzle layered the view, and Michaela pushed aside the need to analyze the layer of stratus clouds. She studied Harrison's tall, powerful back and his casual stance. He was always very relaxed, very poised and successful, and she resented his knowledge of her failure. "Okay, let's get it over with."

"No need to be nervous, Michaela. I won't bite." The words came purring 'round her, tightening her body and that curious sensation that Harrison could nibble quite effectively in appropriate places. Accustomed to men, working with them, appreciating them, Michaela was used to her father's and Roark's height and lean strength. Harrison's three-piece suit covered a hard-packed body, muscles shifting on his throat as he turned to study her fully, his shoulders needing no padding to block the rest of the room from her.

"I do."

"I know." Harrison turned slowly, the dim light catching on the harsh planes of his face. Michaela pushed aside the shiver that stirred within her because Harrison's blunt features resembled his father's more narrow ones. Michaela glanced away, remembering the time just before the suicide, when his father had caught her alone. She'd put the incident behind her, fearing that at seventeen, she had misinterpreted the raw look in his eyes.

"I'm sorry for what happened to you, Michaela," Harrison said smoothly. The low rasp of his voice seemed too intimate in the large comfortable room. The sound skittered across the gleaming varnished floor and her mother's woven rugs to quiver around Michaela.

She'd lost a man she thought she'd eventually marry, and a career that she'd staked her sweat and blood in obtaining. And Harrison in his safe nest was "sorry."

He was absolutely perfect for her dark mood, tempered steel to clash with hers. Theirs was a running history of clash and duel. She longed for that now, to test herself against Harrison, to jerk those finely leashed emotions and see that darkness in his eyes, proof that she had scored a dent in his shield. She needed that release more than the aerobic workout to slake the tension running through her body, her taut nerves and sleepless nights evidence of her reckoning. Harrison had always been good, dependable when she was in a mood, and she looked forward to tearing into him. She ripped away the rubberbands confining her twin braids and tossed them aside. "Are you sorry? How very polite and proper for you to extend your sympathies."

He lifted one eyebrow, studying her warily. "You're not going to call me 'nerd-boy' again, are you?"

"Of course not. I haven't done that since— But you were bookish and shy and—"

"And you held my hand the night I found my father's body. All night. You haven't called me 'nerd-boy' since that night."

Michaela ran her fingers through her hair and found them trembling as Harrison crossed the room. To keep from meeting that cool, studied gaze, she bent to stir the fire in the rock fireplace. "I've always felt that you resented that—me seeing into your pain, all the shields torn away. Anyone else would have done the same."

"No, not everyone," he murmured after a pause, and Michaela knew he was thinking of his father, a cruel man. Harrison smiled briefly, in that tight certain way that said he'd balanced the odds and was certain of the outcome. "Everything will turn out fine. You'll see."

He knew how to soothe, the words flowing easily from his lips, but now Michaela wasn't having any of it. Life hadn't turned out fine and she was battling nerves and shaken confidence, and a lost career that she'd slaved and sacrificed for. That cool controlled tone set her off. He'd always known what he wanted and how to get it. As though all her pain had waited for him, waited to strike him, she erupted, "Will it? What do you know about it?"

When he was too silent, she whipped back to him, her body taut and her fists tight. "You know everything, I suppose, and you've come here to gloat, haven't you? Well, go ahead, gloat."

"You're an intelligent woman. You could have a job anywhere. Why did you come back?"

There it was—that too-soft verbal jab. She was instantly furious with him for digging in too quickly, too intuitively. She wasn't ready to give him any part of her life; he'd dissect it too clinically. "That's absolutely none of your business."

"What's the matter? Didn't the fairy tales work for you, Princess?" The fingers that caught her chin were too hard for a man who sat behind a desk. His eyes were cold with anger that danced from his fingers to her skin, raising the hair on her nape. Few people challenged Michaela, opened their anger to her; she knew how to protect herself too well. But Harrison wasn't stepping back. "You're determined to wallow in this, aren't you? Let your bitterness wash over onto the people who love you?"

She jerked her face away from his touch. She felt too brittle, too exposed with him. She hadn't expected the sudden touch, the fierce slash of his eyes, that angry tense cord pulsing on his throat. Savagery wasn't an element she'd suspected ran within Harrison. "What do you know about it?" she shot at him.

"I know you've got your mother and father worried sick. It's time to grow up, Michaela. Think of someone other than yourself. If you can."

"Exactly what do you mean by that?"

"You're spoiled, Michaela. A golden girl who has had everything her way and now, suddenly can't cope with a picture that isn't perfect. You're afraid to fail, darling."

The "darling" hit her like a fist. Harrison knew how to pack his words, how to wield them, mocking her. "What gives you the right—?"

"They'll make it comfortable for you to wallow

here, to hole up and lick your wounds— Don't count on that from me. You fought and you lost. Pick yourself up and go on. Do not cause your family any more grief. Or you'll have me to deal with."

Harrison had taken her jabs through the years, and now he'd just threatened her. Her brewing temper wanted to fly at him, to throw something at a man who was too cool and untouchable, as if he'd already paid his dues to life and now nothing could hurt him. Michaela braced her hands on her waist. "What do you know about it? Were you there? Who told you what?"

Harrison took a deep breath and those cool gray eyes darkened and narrowed. "Before you go tearing strips off your family—because you feel betrayed— maybe you'd better know that I've followed your career. I've made it my business to understand what makes you so driven and so selfish that you can't see how badly you've hurt and worried your family. You deliberately picked a man who completed the picture you wanted, and now that picture is shredded and you're looking for someone to take out your bad temper. Well, come ahead, Michaela. Let's have it out. Your mother and Jacob and Roark don't understand your petty little dark streak, that perversity in you, but I do. And I won't have you hurting them."

Too stunned to move, Michaela stared up at him. The same cruel lines of his father were in Harrison's features now, menacing and dangerous. But she'd never been afraid of him, only surprised at the lengths to which he'd gone. "You . . . followed my career?"

He nodded slowly, watching her. "I found it interesting. Your climb up the ladder and your choice of bedmates suit the perfect picture."

"Leave my love life out of this. There's no way—"

"There's always a way, Michaela. I'm very good at details," Harrison murmured smoothly. "It's time to grow up," he repeated, and brushed a tendril back from her hot cheek. "Your frustration is showing, Princess. Use a big, hard pillow and a heating pad for those long, cold nights."

Harrison studied Michaela's battle for control and savored what would happen next; she never failed to excite him when she erupted, and she was brewing a good hot temper right now. He'd always been good at deflecting her moods and—

Her blue eyes tore at him; her head lifted and those fabulous cheekbones gleamed in the soft light. It was all there, the fighter, the woman, the hot, boiling emotions that rode right to the surface when scraped just right. His pulse stirred with the need to stroke that smooth, warm skin, to grip that sleek, gleaming hair in his fist, to hold her tight against him and to place his lips over hers and feed—

Harrison inhaled slowly, methodically. His relationships with women were based on physical need, on reminding himself that he was a man with a beating heart. He had selected his few companions carefully and left no doubt as to what he expected and what he would give. Those relationships ended years ago, because he realized they were pleasant, mechanical and empty, serving no more than the moment's need; Harrison wasn't a man to invest time and energy in events that did not give lasting rewards. He recognized the cool, analytical dissection of his emotions— perhaps he'd gotten that from his father. He saw Michaela as a good investment—she had been for years. There was a certain joy to sparring with her, to seeing those sky-blue eyes flash with anger. She'd always stirred life in him, even when he thought he had no emotions to touch.

To feel alive was very important to Harrison. His father's cold, ruthless training had almost stripped humanity from him.

The edge of nowhere, Harrison thought, remembering how she'd been that night when he was fifteen. Then when he was eighteen, when he was shamed and shaking from discovering his father's blood-splattered body, she'd been just as strong. She hadn't faltered the night of his father's suicide, staying with Harrison, holding his hand when he would have slipped away—run away into nowhere, losing himself for an eternity. She'd been his anchor; Michaela Langtry never worried about gossip as she fought to bring the boy he'd been back into the light.

Michaela had argued with him, had cajoled him, and finally, when she was frustrated, had thrown a pitchfork right at him. "You want to die? You would do that to my family? They love you, you idiot. You would tear my mother's heart from her, after what she's been through, and Dad aching for her? You think you're to blame for your father's sick mind.

Well, you aren't. But you are to blame for what you do, and no one else. If you want to kill yourself, go ahead. Here, let me help you—"

Harrison remembered the twang of the pitchfork, tines stuck in the barn board near him. "Your aim is off, Miss Langtry," he'd said finally, and Michaela had grinned.

"Harry," she'd said, teasing him with a name he hated, as she gripped his hand. "I liked you better when we were the same height. Eyeball to eyeball. Then you had to grow and it's a little hard to intimidate a guy taller than me."

He remembered the strength in those slender hands, the certainty of her voice. "Life is rough, and so is that gelding with your name on it. I'll bet you a dollar you can't outride me tonight."

They'd ridden across the Langtry fields, Michaela bent forward against the night wind, her hair flying around her face like a storm. She had been glorious, invincible and untouched, as she turned to him. "Ride, Harrison, and don't think about anything. Ride until you drop and I'll still be riding."

That night, just as she had done when he was fifteen, she'd burned the need out of him to run and a good portion of the shame he'd felt, too.

A fighter, she was down now, feeling defeated, and those fabulous eyes were glittering now with hatred and with fury. *Come on, Princess. Fight. Pick yourself up and fight.*

"I ought to cut you to shreds," Michaela said too quietly, fury quivering on her husky voice, the words evenly spaced for impact. "You've gone too far. You're not my brother and you're not a member of my family."

"Faith and Jacob have been kind," he murmured, just to set her off, and enjoy that quick toss of her head, the rippling of firelight dancing on her hair. He wanted to grip it in his fists, to bury his face in that silky mass, but he wouldn't.

Finding her damp with sweat and pulsing from her aerobic workout, the skin-tight black and yellow suit fitting her like a glove, clinging to those long legs and rounded curves of her breasts, Harrison had wanted to place his mouth on hers. He damned her for giving herself to another man, for waiting on him, coddling him, and worst of all, mourning him when he walked out.

Her anger pulsed through the room now, ricocheting off the natural stone fireplace, pounding at the smoothly varnished floors.

"I'm not spoiled," she said finally. "I've had to work for everything I got. I did not sleep my way to the top."

He met her furious stare evenly. "I never said you slept your way anywhere. But you're expecting everyone in your family to extend hugs and sympathy. It's time you figured out that the world does not revolve around you, Michaela."

Faith entered the living room, her cheeks pink from the cold. She gracefully unfurled the large shawl she'd woven and folded it. She was smaller and more softly made than her daughter. Faith's fair beauty was timeless. The visual impact of the two women, side by side, never failed to enchant Harrison. Faith's expression warmed when she saw him. "I just came in from the arts center. I thought I heard voices here— Hello, Harrison. I'm so glad you've come. We'll set another place for dinner. All my boys and Michaela will be sitting at our table again."

The delight in her mother's voice stilled Michaela's hand on the mug she'd just picked up. Every nerve in her body told her to throw it at Harrison, because only he would dare to cut away the softness and go right for the heart of her pain.

"Faith," Harrison murmured smoothly, and opened his arms for her quick hug.

His eyes closed then, the steely gray glitter gone, replaced by a softness only her mother could bring to Harrison.

Michaela sucked in air and replaced the mug on the fireplace hearth. She forced herself to breathe evenly and wondered at Harrison's obvious, unwavering affection for her mother. Harrison's father had always coveted Faith, quickly shielding his lust, but his emotions were deeper, more tender.

Michaela wanted to tear him away from her mother, because Harrison wasn't sweet. There was always that quiet, waiting study of her mother, as if he knew something the Langtry family had missed. Michaela ran her hand through her hair and found it trembling. *What was it? What ran between Faith and Harrison?*

"Harrison was just leaving," she said, anxious to

pry him away from her mother and the echo of his words from the room. *Did Harrison desire her mother?* Michaela considered his expression and found only tenderness.

"No, I wasn't leaving," he said easily, smiling warmly at Faith. With the ease of a man who had enjoyed the Langtry hospitality for years, Harrison asked, "What's for dinner?"

She laughed casually and reached to ruffle his hair, that smooth well-combed hair. "Pot roast. You'll have to peel the potatoes. Roark will be in later and my daughter will probably want to shower after her work-out. She's lovely, isn't she? She's got the Langtry bones, the proud way Jacob stands, that tilt of her head."

"She's got your beautiful blue eyes." Harrison bent to kiss Faith's cheek, the movement polished, re-served, classy and yet portrayed the respect he'd always had for her. He glanced at Michaela, who was studying them. He smiled briefly, as though moments ago he hadn't torn into her. Then his attention was back to Faith. "Peeling potatoes will cost a glass of Jacob's homemade wine. How's the art center going?"

Faith's blue eyes darkened. "We need more visibil-ity and more patrons. I can't allow Jacob to finance the art center. It's got to grow on its own. Vitality has to come from within and we've got to be self-support-ing."

"You'll get what you need," Harrison murmured, and Michaela gripped her arms around herself pro-tectively. Harrison was a man of few words, but each one seemed weighed and given as a vow.

What ran between Harrison and her mother? Correction. *What drove Harrison, an impassive, controlled man, to have such obvious affection for Faith?* She clearly regarded him as a son, but his careful attention to her was deeper.

Later, Michaela rode her mare, Diamond, across the field. The gamma grass glittered, jeweled with moonlit rain. Dressed in jeans, boots, and her father's worn denim and flannel coat, Michaela wore the black straight-brim hat as protection against the clinging cold fog that seemed to penetrate her soul. At ten o'clock that night, the Wyoming moon rose above the jagged snow-covered peaks of the Rocky Mountains.

Shiloh nestled in the small valley not far away, the lights of the small city presenting a twinkling, uniform pattern.

Night riding had always settled her, and after the family dinner with Harrison, Michaela needed soothing. One cool glance of those gray eyes and she'd wanted to bolt from the table. Or start yelling at Harrison that he had no right to enter her life.

Michaela sucked in the cold air, letting Diamond take her lead. Battling her frustration and nerves that only Harrison could lift to that edgy peak, it didn't matter where her mare took her. *Didn't the fairy tales work for you, Princess?* he'd asked. *It's time to grow up, Michaela. Think of someone other than yourself. . . . You're spoiled. . . . You're afraid to fail, darling. . . . I won't have you hurting them.*

Her fist tightened on the saddle horn. Harrison was

always right there, too up close and personal, nudging his logic into her emotions.

Maybe she had been wallowing in her damaged life, damn him.

Maybe she *was* afraid of failure marking her, damn him again.

"Harrison is right, damn him. The longer I put this off, the worse it will be." *She'd have to face them all, sooner or later, and she'd have to do it without her family.* Jacob and Roark would be too protective, her mother had enough heartbreak in her lifetime.

Michaela turned Diamond toward Shiloh. The town knew her. Shiloh was the best part of her past. They'd encouraged a younger Michaela, setting off into the world, so long ago. She might as well "lay it all out on the table," as the western saying went, letting them know she was back. After all, she was a Langtry and her family didn't hide from life. Forty-five minutes later, she rode down Main Street. With the ease of a western-bred rider, the reins held loosely in her hand, she let Diamond take her lead, stirring the fog layering the street. A hundred and fifty years ago, drovers and hunters had coursed through the swirling mists. The streetlights gleamed on the wet, smooth cobblestones of the street, music pouring from Donovan's Bar and Grill. On the other side of the street, Lomax Grocery's neon lights had been dimmed. Shiloh's Drug Store still wore the look of a 1880s cow town, a two-story building now with an apartment that overlooked the street. Faye's Beauty

Shop, Henry's Barber Shop, and the local teenage hangout, Morelli's, were all dark, windows gleaming and as empty as Michaela's heart. The trees were naked now, but in the summer, they'd shade the sidewalk spotted with planters from the garden club and benches for the spit-and-whittlers.

The church with its high white steeple, where her father had wanted to see her wed, soared into the night sky.

That street led to a country road, and a few miles from Shiloh, Harrison Kane II had built a new, sprawling ultramodern rock-and-wood house nestled among the mountain's pines. His parents' opulent family home at the very top of Nob Hill, overlooking Shiloh, had been donated to the local historical society.

Michaela closed her eyes, a cold shiver running through her as she remembered the lushly decorated home, as emotionally cold as expensive crystal. She didn't like remembering her earlier encounter with Harrison, how he had challenged her, those dark gray eyes like steel as he held her chin.

The waves of heat flowing from him, of startling, grim emotion, had startled her. She sensed the whipcord strength in his body, how he could hold a woman tight and hot against him if once he lost that control. Once that icy shield was torn away, Harrison's savagery would not be far behind. Who was he now? Why did he seem to see to much, understand too much? Why did he openly reveal his obvious affection for Faith when he kept others at a distance, even male members of the Langtry family?

Michaela didn't like the way her body responded to the heat of Harrison's, how her senses leaped when he was nearby. The phrase "too long without" crept into her mind.

She didn't want to think of Harrison's hard mouth, that taut, finely-honed body naked in bed with her, in her. She swallowed tightly, pushing away the unnerving memory of Harrison's taut body close to hers, the flash of steel in his eyes. She gave herself to the sense of homecoming, not wanting to be distracted by their instant clash.

The rumble of the station wagon pulling alongside Diamond, caused her to smile. C. C. Tomlin's broad, friendly face peered out of the driver's window. "Whatcha doin', sweet cheeks? Trolling for some good looking cowboy?" C. C. asked with a grin.

"You betcha," Michaela answered, returning the grin. "Tossed the last one back into the pond." A lifetime good friend, C. C. had married in high school and had set out immediately to produce a large, happy family. Her home was filled with friends and warmth and clutter.

The station wagon coughed and threatened to die, but C. C.'s warmth never faltered. "Had to go to my mother's house to borrow her sewing machine. Mine is broken and the patching basket is full. I'm going to call all the old gang and they'll want to see you. Boy, this is exciting. Michaela Langtry, out riding at night, just like the old days. Be back in a jiff with a carload. We'll cruise town just like when we were kids—"

C. C.'s cheerful, warm moods hadn't changed. Her

battered station wagon swept off in a cloud of exhaust and Michaela settled into the warm sense of coming home.

Houses lined the streets angling off the one in which drovers had herded their cattle to the railroad. The first houses in Shiloh lined one street, two-story white houses decorated with gingerbread trim. Marsha Jo Woolridge had graduated in the same high school class as Michaela. Now a colorful collection of plastic play equipment rambled across her front yard. Mrs. Edmonton, Michaela's first grade teacher, lived in the house with the beautiful summer rose gardens. On a dark side street, lined with newer cheaper houses, a white picket fence ran around the small pink house where Mrs. Emma Jones received her "visitors." Mrs. Jones, now a widow, had returned to Shiloh amid gossip that she'd sexually exhausted and finally killed her elderly husband. But now her visitors were usually older men wanting more of a listener than a sexual companion.

The "for sale" sign in front of the old Atkins place surprised her; then she remembered that the elderly couple now rested in Shiloh's cemetery. For years the elderly childless couple had lived simply, feeding and sheltering the small wild wandering band of burros deserted by the frontier miners. When Elijah Atkins passed away at ninety, his wife, Sara Belle, followed six months later.

Just up that quiet, well-groomed street was Nob Hill, ruled by society matron Mrs. Victoria D'Renaud.

In her sixties and originally from Boston, Victoria never failed to point out the difference between the nouveau riche and "descendants of royalty." She elegantly disdained the Langtry heritage as "crude, and breeding too-passionate children." Faith's elegant heritage equaled Victoria's well-bred background, which nettled the society matron even more.

On Nob Hill, flood lights hit Kane House. It stood like an eery, unshakable monument to Harrison's parents. The elegant parties Harrison's father had thrown in later years were hosted by Victoria. She'd preened then, with her social standing, and went into seclusion after his suicide and the embezzlement was revealed.

Michaela inhaled sharply, sucking in the cold mist and the bitterness that she'd have to tame before going on. She'd lost her dreams and she'd have to make the best of it. She hadn't asked for love from Dolph, but she'd expected his support. Did love really exist? *Zachariah and Cleopatra's love was legendary, his journal filled with the sacrifices he'd gladly made for her. Her trials were no less terrible than his, and she met them valiantly, for him.*

How could a man love a woman so much that he'd give up everything for her?

Michaela ran her hand over the Langtry medallion beneath her jacket. Cleopatra's struggle to return all but one of the coins had proven her strength, too. Then another coin had been lost the night Sable was taken.

Were the coins that powerful, to bring luck to the Langtrys? Michaela smiled grimly, wiping away the mist clinging to her cheek with the back of her glove. "I could use some of that luck," she murmured.

Smitty's Shoes was where her mother had taken her to buy her first pair of high-heeled shoes and her father had grumbled about his little girl growing up.

Over there were the city offices, and the road that led to the small local rodeo grounds. Michael nudged Diamond down the dirt road and stopped to view the arena where she'd raced around the barrels, taking first place in the girl's teenage division. She'd been a Shiloh Rodeo Queen, riding with flags into the arena, all fringes and long black hair flying in the sunlit afternoon.

She leaned down to unlock the gate, entering the arena. As Diamond moved slowly around the perimeter, Michaela thought of Zachariah, how he had left the war-torn South with plans to return, to wrest his homeland from the North. A southern gentleman used to running a plantation, he'd been little equipped for the raw West.

Michaela rubbed the coin warm upon her chest. There with the cold mist around her, the mare's easy gait circling the arena, Michaela wondered at how much she had lost, how much she'd given away. Why had she forgotten her family's heritage, the love of Zachariah for Cleopatra? Why had she settled for less than the charming rogue her father had been? Or Zachariah Langtry? His journal had expressed his feelings beautifully.

I never saw a woman so beautiful. Her hair gleamed coal black as a raven's wing, her eyes held mysteries a man could die for. Siren, I thought, watching the graceful movements of her body as she served the men in the fort. My Lady Siren. She was more lady than the high-blooded women of my upbringing, more compassionate, more delicate and honest. Clearly, I had lost my heart.

Circling the arena, Michaela thought of the lullaby that Zachariah had created for his first son. *Softly, slowly*, around and around . . . *mornin' will creep* . . . she sucked in the fog and the memories swirling around her, lifting her head to the mountains that beckoned.

She was a part of all this, bred of Langtry men who were rogues until their hearts were captured. Zachariah had made his home here, built his original cabin on that mound and kept his love safe. It was said that when Cleopatra died after a long full loving life, Zachariah's heart stopped beating at the same moment. *When the heart of a Langtry is captured, it will remain true forever.*

Michaela watched the other horses file into the arena, the riders familiar as they lined up in the mist to face her. "Dad . . . Mom. Roark."

"Your mother felt like a ride, too," her father said, his look that of a man enjoying the night, riding beside his family.

"I'm not so old that I have to stay by the home fire at night, cowboy," Faith returned easily.

Her mother rode straight and elegant beside her husband, a black straight-brimmed Spanish hat like Michaela's covering her fair hair. The long black duster covering her split riding skirt ran almost to her knee-high leather boots. Always elegant, Faith's pearl stud earrings gleamed in the dim light. Her chestnut mare matched her husband's powerful stallion. Jacob's features were honed and angular, shadowed by the brim of his western hat. His skin was dark against the pale wool lining of his shearling coat. He spoke to the large white, part-wolf dogs at his side. A younger version of Jacob, Roark sat easily on his gelding, sired by Jacob's "Apache Red." Unshaven and fiercely grim-looking, Roark's expression equaled his father's.

"You're not the only one who likes night riding, Mikey," Roark said, using a childhood nickname. "We thought you'd be riding this way and thought we'd join the party."

There in the swirling mist, with her family looking as if they'd always been waiting for her to return, Michaela released the tears she'd held for months, for years, filling and tearing at her heart. "It's good here," she said simply, her voice uneven and husky with emotion.

Jacob nodded curtly and as Michaela nudged Diamond to begin circling the arena once more, the Langtrys silently lined up to ride beside her. Each sat very straight, filled with a heritage and pride that nothing could tear apart.

As they circled the arena, tears burned Michaela's eyes. The sound of the hooves in the deadly, quiet night, the steam shooting from the horse's nostrils, and the mountains jutting into the night sky told Michaela she was really home. Why had they always called to her, especially in Cutter Canyon? Why had the wind sweeping through the pines always seemed to call her name?

Riding down Shiloh's Main Street now, her family beside her, the horses' hooves clipclopping on the cobblestones, Michaela glanced at the motorcycle gliding out from the mist. The single eye of the head beam cut through the fog and the finely tuned motorcycle pulled alongside Diamond. Moisture beaded the cropped red hair of Silky Morales, her black leather jacket and pants gleaming, her helmet tied to her seat. Michaela's childhood friend held the motorcycle at an even pace with Diamond's.

From behind, headlight beams shot through the riders and the horses. One glance at C. C.'s battered station wagon, and Michaela knew the car was packed with her friends. They'd left their children and husbands to ride with her, prowling behind the mounted Langtrys.

Illuminated by the streetlights slipping through the fog, Silky's upturned heart-shaped face revealed eyes too big, a mouth too lush, and a chin that said she'd met life and survived. "Life here isn't so bad," Silky said at the city limits. "See you."

The man standing behind Kane's First National Bank's darkened tinted windows watched the procession and smiled grimly. He tugged at the tie confining his throat, loosening it and then opening the buttons of his brown vest. Dynamic, filled with pride and heritage, the Langtrys were together again, and the town would start buzzing about Michaela's return.

If she stayed, if she took his challenge, Michaela would eventually have to meet him, to come to terms with him and what brewed between them. But then, Michaela Langtry was unpredictable and exciting, and yet soft and sweet. She might choose to leave Shiloh and then he'd find a reason to go after her.

He could wait. He'd waited for years.

four

At the fort, watching my lady Cleopatra serve in her father's tavern, it troubled me that her white father pushed her from the society of gentlewomen. I came back from trapping to find her fair neck within a hangman's noose. Only gold and marriage could save her, they said, for in protecting her honor she had killed a man.

It was no small thing to balance my father's dreams of the South rising again and my honor as a man against the life of the woman I suspected held my heart. I gave five coins freely, expecting to recover them when my lady was safely away.

I may have bought her life, but I had not won the fair maid's heart. I disdain to tell you of the fighting back then, when she ran from me and I caught her,

my captive bride. For she had to marry me and did so
before the hangman lifted his noose from her throat.
'Twas no ordinary woman I set about to win, but a
woman of fire, strong of heart. It was no easy task for
a man bred to my former life to let her set terms
between us.

Zachariah Langtry's Journal

"It's a job. I'll take it. You could have made this
easier on everyone if you had just called and offered
the position in the first place," Michaela stated
tightly and shoved her resume back into her briefcase. Harrison hadn't bothered to look at it.

Mid-May sunlight slid through the windows
behind Harrison, catching on his waving hair and
outlining shoulders too broad for a "paper-pusher."
In the shadow, his mouth curved briefly, then settled
into a hard line. She hadn't expected Harrison to be
wearing a night's stubble on his jaw, or that weary
expression.

"You're not a woman who likes things easy. And I
don't like being turned down."

"Why, Harrison. It's the only job in town that I
want. Why would I turn you down?" she asked too
sweetly.

Harrison leveled a cool look at her. "You might
have other, better opportunities elsewhere."

"I haven't looked. There's something I want here
and I've got to find it." There was no other job in
Shiloh suitable for her but the one at Harrison's as-

yet-unborn station. The salary was far below what she had been making, but then, the cost of living in a small town wasn't the same as in New York.

She needed the challenge now, needed to pour herself into the excitement of creating a worthwhile project, needed to work until she couldn't think of how much she'd tossed away, how much she'd forgotten. Whatever she'd lost, it was right here; she could feel it humming around her, waiting to be claimed. She could almost feel the air in Cutter Canyon, fresh and cold and whispering on her skin as though—

He'd outlined her basic duties briefly. "You can start today. We're set to go on air next month. Here's the contract."

Michaela studied the legal print, frowning in concentration. "It's for four years. Make that six months."

"Two years." Harrison had expected Michaela to set her own terms. He knew she didn't like to be confined, but she wasn't breezing into Shiloh and leaving that easily. Faith needed more of her than that.

Michaela shoved the contract back across the desk. "One."

He recognized that look, the bottom line from which she would not move. He found the legal clause, crossed out a word, and replaced it with "one year." "You'll have to initial that when you sign."

With a grim sigh, Michaela briskly signed her name and initialed the clause. "I'm not broke, you know. You didn't open my resume, but then you already know everything about me, don't you?"

"I've always been close to the Langtry family. You're a member of that family."

"It feels like an invasion of privacy more than an attachment to my family."

"Let's keep this on a business basis, shall we?" he asked tiredly, with just that lick of temper riding his dark tones.

"Yes, let's. I don't like being examined without my approval." Nettling Harrison's imperturbable exterior took the edge off her unsteady mood. She'd hated coming to Harrison, spreading her resume folder before him. His cluttered office in the new television station contrasted with his sleek modern office at the bank. Located a distance from Shiloh, the small, new station—topped by a soaring tower—smelled of fresh lumber and paint. Unpacked boxes stood in the entryway. The sound stage which Harrison had just shown Michaela was small and well arranged. She recognized that the two cameras and boom microphones were of the highest quality.

Several different-sized receiving disks were behind the station with another tower located higher on the mountains to direct the outgoing signals. A satellite far in space directed the signals to the contracted stations.

"The anchor desk and the weather set can be changed to suit you. Most of the work was done by contract—the video room, the studio, the news room, the production control room, and the rest were designed and built by top people. The cost of those two cameras in the studio was ungodly. Still, we're small and lean, and with the help of interns, we can—you're staring at me." He shrugged and the dark hair at the base of his throat gleamed in the bright morning light. His jaw dark with stubble, his eyes shadowed with fatigue, Harrison looked too powerful, too male, too dangerous. "I know I might look awful, but I run a corporation with other interests. I have investors depending on me. I worked all night on a project. Business emergencies happen from time to time."

"I understand." Michaela did not understand her need to smooth the deeply waving hair he'd just rumpled by running his hands through it, the gesture of a frustrated and tired man. She tensed, unprepared for her fingertips aching to touch that thick mane. She could almost feel the strands drag coolly against her skin, a clinging caress on her fingers.

"You'll be paid overtime to get this project off the ground. If you need an assistant, I'll consider it." Harrison rose from his cluttered desk, came around, and leaned against it, crossing his arms over his chest. "We're on a shoestring budget. Every dollar has to be approved by me, and we'll be sharing this office at times. You should have no trouble anchoring the news desk, but the local weather will have to wait—mainly because we cannot spare you. For now weather will be channeled in from affiliate stations. I want the full support of the community and it's your job to drum up interest and money. You know the community and the rural outlying families. Tailor our program line up to their needs, then consider those of other counties. Put together ideas, a bare bones start-ing calendar, and a list of anything you want. You'll get an expense account, of course. And I want high school and college students interested in media to be involved in a paid-to-learn program. You'll interview the applicants. Any questions?"

"We'll need a director, someone who writes news copy, and several production assistants for cameras, editing tapes, and lighting. I still think local weather is a must, but it can wait. But I'll need a computer to prepare the graphics and a remote control to use in front of the chromakey wall—the blue board they project the maps on." Michaela's excitement rushed on, ideas pumping through her.

Harrison carefully placed the pencil he was hold-ing on his desk. "Now listen. I'm not hiring you for the weather, Michaela. I need someone to bring in money—that is your priority. It's important to get this station up and running in a month. The equipment we have is topnotch. Now we need the staff to run it, and enough proof that we can manage the financial ads and profit."

"Ah, yes. You'll have to show your investors that you can manage this, won't you?"

"Lay off. There is a lot of risk here, and I don't want Shiloh and the surrounding area to lose."

"Harrison, is *your* job on the line with this project?" Michaela smiled; she couldn't resist nudging him just that bit.

"You could say that. Shiloh isn't exactly a prime choice for a television station. But it was my choice."

"You took a gamble? Good old safe Harrison?" He had always moved so carefully through life, meticulously planning the next step.

Harrison scowled at the workmen's coils of wire and new computer equipment rambling across the boxes. A man who liked everything in its place, he was clearly uncomfortable with clutter. "There comes a time. But I don't intend to let my investors down. Because of our transmitter's high elevation we've already gotten several radio broadcasting contracts— we'll work together on sales. I've just finished negotiating with national affiliates for their spots—news, weather, sports, some soap opera and game shows. Fill our weekends with paid slots. The budget is *not* wide open, Michaela. We've got one year to prove ourselves, or the station will be sold off in pieces." That cool gray gaze moved down her expensive gray suit, her cream business blouse to the loose-fitting slacks and practical black pumps. Harrison's gaze took in the Langtry medallion. "You might think about not wearing that so obviously. It's worth a great deal."

She resented that vibrating electric feeling, the hardening of her breasts as his gaze briefly considered that curve. "Does that mean you have approval over how I dress?"

"It's a caution. I'm certain you'll dress appropriately. One other thing—there are times when we'll have to work at my place. If you have any objections to that, I need to know now."

Michaela glanced to the big tinted windows, bald

and new and unwashed in the morning sunlight. Harrison's mountain home stood a distance from the station with its huge moon-shaped receiving disks and its tower. Designed to fit into the jutting rock and pines, his home was marked by sunlight dancing off the silver squares of his windows. "No problem," Michaela agreed.

"Good. Because I want you to have dinner with me tonight—to go over plans—and knowing you, you'll already have some more rough ideas by then. I understand that we won't be up to speed immediately, and that we'll have some empty hours to fill from midnight to six A.M. I prefer John Wayne westerns."

She smiled, remembering the efficiency and no-time-wasted attitude of a younger Harrison. He'd never played games, awkward and uncomfortable when he was younger, pushed too hard by his father to succeed. He'd made every moment count, putting his own needs aside.

"You might start thinking of how to frame Faith in a regular spot. I want to support her art center and she's going to do regular segments on fashioning and glazing pottery." Harrison studied Michaela quietly. "That's all. See you tonight. Talk with Silky on your way out and have her set you up with an expense account and overtime forms. She can introduce you to Dwight and Mooney. Mooney is from Texas and is our cameraman. Dwight—"

Harrison smiled tightly before returning to the clutter on his desk. "Dwight will be doing the local news, anchoring with you. Be prepared. See you tonight at eight."

Michaela rose and studied the man already deep in the forms before him. "One question, Harrison. Why? There is no profit in this for your corporation. Why do you want this television station? And here? There are any number of channels for rural viewers."

His smile was brief and icy. "I owe this community, Michaela. You should know that better than anyone. It's payback time."

For an instant, the image of Harrison shattered by his father's suicide enveloped her. Harrison's shaking hands had had blood on them. "You aren't responsible for your father's actions, Harrison."

The pencil in his hand snapped. "Eight o'clock tonight doesn't leave you much time to work up ideas, does it?"

His tone slapped her, because she'd cared deeply for that boy long ago, almost as much as she had her brother. "Let me get this straight, Harrison. Your station's first broadcast is set for a month from now. You really don't have a full crew, needing someone for sound and light, and you're stuck for ideas on how to raise interest locally. You're full up timewise, working for your corporation, and you need someone to take the pressure off you here, right?"

Harrison's gray eyes narrowed and a muscle in his jaw worked as though he didn't like admitting he needed anyone. "That's the situation."

"You're gambling on me, too. I've never done anything like this before. Why me, Harrison? Why not some ace fix-it manager?"

"You know the people here. I know your work ethics. You've got television experience and you've got a good mind. There's no reason you can't learn what you need to know. That's how it's done, really, isn't it? After the media and journalism classes, hands-on experience, learning from others?"

"Well, then . . ." Michaela didn't shield the purring pleasure in her tone. For the first time in months, energy and excitement surged through her. With a challenging new job ahead of her, ideas hitting her like lightning bolts, she couldn't let Harrison get the best of her.

He'd researched her private life, her career, and it was so like Harrison to think that he had everything in control, that he'd lined up life to suit him. There was just nothing like tossing him a bone he hadn't expected. Michaela flashed her best thousand-watt camera smile at him, feeling the charge of energy that only sparring with Harrison could give her. "You need me, don't you? My experience? You really don't have time to interview and secure someone else and I'm the only girl in town that suits the job, right? That's the bottom line, isn't it? You're in a spot and you need me?"

There was just nothing like pushing Harrison, watching that slow controlled burn. "You need me," she repeated, nudging him, watching his reaction.

"You could say that," he answered slowly in a soft low tone, and in the distance between them, the air quivered with emotions that Michaela did not understand. The intensity was enough to raise the hairs on her neck.

"Hey, Dwight, if you're wondering about the chilly breeze below your belt, your fly is open," Silky called to the man passing by the reception desk.

Unshaven, his hair rumpled, and wearing a New York Mets ball cap and a battered sports jacket with leather sleeves over his flannel pajamas, Dwight grunted. He lifted his coffee travel mug in greeting. "Where's the donuts?"

"This is our new mover and shaker, Dwight. Dwight Brown, meet Michaela Langtry. Michaela, you'll be sharing the anchor desk with him."

Dwight stopped his scuffling, sleepy walk and slowly took a sip of coffee. "Heard of her," he mumbled, before moving into the studio.

Silky grinned and punched her intercom button. "I'll ring Mooney up-front. He'll show you around. Dwight is a journalist. He used to work radio in L.A. He had a little problem with the local toughs when he questioned the leader's sexuality—over the air waves. Harrison got him out of that jam and a slander suit, and now he's lying low here. Dwight is okay, once you bust his ego down to size. He wants to write a blockbuster and Harrison offered him free rent on a house in town and a salary he wasn't going to get anywhere else. Dwight does have a little open zipper problem, at least he's not the sperm donor to underage girls, like my creep of an ex-husband."

"How is good old Fred?"

Silky's usually smooth expression changed to that of bitterness. "Living somewhere else and not meeting his child support payments. Krissy and I are better off without him. Harrison has been very generous with my single-mother status. The school bus will let Krissy off at the station, and there's a small play room for her with a cot. That will help cut down my babysitting expenses. During the summer, she'll stay part-time at Maxine's Child Center . . . oh, hi, Mooney. This is Michaela Langtry, she's our new mover and shaker for the station."

A big burley man dressed in a plaid flannel shirt and jeans that sagged low at the crotch stared at Michaela. She extended her hand. "Hello, Mooney. I'm certain we'll work fine together."

"You're beautiful," he said baldly, and continued to stare. "I'm in love."

"Don't trip over your tongue while you're showing her around, will you, Mooney?" Silky asked with a grin.

"You're not married, are you? Do I have a chance?" Mooney's big hand was more of a paw as he held Michaela's.

"Mooney is from Colorado. He's living with his sister, a widow who works at the dime store. He eats more than three men put together, so don't ever offer him your lunch. But he can do almost every job here, except anchor and write copy."

"I'm not married, Mooney and you can share my lunch anytime."

"I've just met the goddess of my heart . . . I'd be mighty pleased to work day and night with you, ma'am," Mooney crooned in his rough, growling tones. He opened the door to the studio and with an elegant bow invited Michaela to enter.

That evening Michaela pulled her four-wheeler into the driveway of Harrison's mountain home. Big and modern, the wood-and-rock exterior fitting into the pines, the house had big windows which gleamed in the light of her headlamps. A small herd of mule deer bolted from the natural meadow nearby. The dirt road to his home was surprisingly unmarked from the main road. In contrast, the driveway to the old Kane house in town was guarded by huge concrete lions.

Wild roses would bloom amid that bramble, and mixed with wild grasses; sunflowers would catch the summer breeze, waving gently. Higher on the mountain, columbine, Indian paintbrush, and primrose would color the savage black rocks, the muted blue of fir blending with the lofty pines.

Three rugged miles away, Cutter River tumbled through black rock canyon walls, and Zachariah Langtry was said to have transported his lush winter furs by canoe down the white water rapids and the sweeping, fast-moving stretches of smooth water. Spring snows had swollen the river now, making it too dangerous, but Michaela longed for the summer's cold water and calm, shady stretches in which to place her canoe paddle.

The primitive beauty of the mountains, stark

against the clear night sky, called to Michaela as she left her vehicle. Cold night air swept from the mountains, that strange beckoning to Cutter Canyon leaping into life. The moisture on her skin told her that mist hovered on the higher alpine meadows, the bear and the cougar hunting and hungry after a lean winter. *And she'd always known that something else waited for her there, something she feared and yet needed . . .*

In the field, Michaela noted the ghostly appearance of Harrison's gray gelding, sired by Apache Red, the Langtrys' stud. Not far away the small gypsy herd of burros grazed, probably missing the Atkins' care.

So much of her life was here, Michaela thought and the coin that rested beneath her palm seemed to warm with her heritage. Tucked into Zachariah's aged journal was a folded note from Cleopatra.

I can read now, my lord husband teaches me. I read his pretty words and take them deeply into my heart, for he is the light of my soul. But do not think that my love is an easy man to understand with his dark, swirling moods. At times our tempers lift like swords striking, sparks dancing on the steel. I knew from the moment I met my charming rogue that I would have to hold my own against his powers. He gave his family treasures to save me and I gave him little, save the claw necklace of the bear he had killed. Never was a man so magnificent and swaggering as he boasted to me of the kill. I suppose that beast lurks within most men, and only a softer touch can tame the wild heart of a man like this. He says I am bold, with a heart as

*soft and sweet as the summer mist over the mountain
meadow. He says I have captured his heart. So has he
mine. I have pledged to return the five coins to his
keeping, and I shall. . . .*

Michaela sucked in the fresh moist night air,
scented of pines. Cleopatra had managed to unite all
six coins, and now two were missing. Michaela
pressed her palm against the coin resting on her crimson ribbed sweater. The old nursery song that
Zachariah had created circled the night and a chill ran
over Michaela's flesh, despite her warm fleece jacket.
*Where were the missing two coins? Where was Sable? How
could Maria have taken the six-week-old baby and torn
apart the family who loved her and she loved in return?*

She closed her eyes, pushing away the haunting
mysteries and Faith's aching loss, too frequently
haunting her expression. Michaela braced herself to
encounter Harrison in his lair. She glanced at the
oversized television receiving disk, a distance away
from his house. Years ago, at the Langtrys, he'd
watched the game shows, testing himself as if he had
to succeed at everything, even that. Harrison Kane Sr.,
had made certain that his son performed well,
demanding too much of him.

Michaela gripped her briefcase. She'd shanghaied
her father's office, kissed away his grumbling, and
spent a grueling day at the computer. Her shoulders
ached and her head hurt. She was tired, but it was a
good feeling, proof that she could pull herself
together to focus and create. Her concept was intense

and basic, but good. She smiled briefly. The methodical layout of plans to develop interest in the television programs would require Harrison's approval. He was likely to protest the social events.

He stood at the open door, the light from the room behind him outlining his broad shoulders, those long wide-spread legs. Michaela inhaled abruptly, because whatever caused her senses to leap when Harrison was near was too primitive to examine. The physical attraction was there. But it couldn't happen. Not with Harrison.

Harrison set off-base emotions she didn't want to explore. He touched the need to tear away his control—and perhaps hers. She'd been controlled for so long, she'd forgotten the honesty of dealing with her family and with Harrison.

"Harrison," she murmured coolly, while passing into his house. She frowned slightly, too aware of his freshly showered soapy scent, of the darker masculine one beneath it. With his bare feet on the varnished boards of his entryway, Harrison's jeans rode low on his hips, with a flat stomach and a defined, muscled chest above it. The dark wedge of hair on his chest was still beaded with moisture, his hair bearing the even furrows of a comb. The damp strands curled slightly, the deep waves barely controlled by the comb, surprising her. The tanned flesh over those hard blunt wide cheekbones gleamed as though freshly shaven.

He studied her gleaming blood-red S.U.V. for a moment. "Now that's a statement."

"It isn't a statement of any kind. I saw it, I wanted to drive home from New York, and I bought it." She pushed back the thought of the payments looming ahead.

"You're not an impulse buyer. You're too controlled. You bought what suited your purposes."

"*I'm* controlled?" she returned, slightly on edge because Harrison knew her too well.

"Controlled. Meticulous. A brain that never stops working, stacking up the pros and cons. Creative."

"That's how you see me?" Michaela was stunned; that was how she saw Harrison.

"You're going to be perfect for the job. I think we'll make a good team on his project . . . you look tired." Harrison closed the door and eased her coat from her. Tossing it to a small chair, he held her face up for his study. "You have dark circles under your eyes. I don't want you killing yourself over this, Michaela. Your family would blame me. And it's certain to show up on camera."

"Thanks. It's always nice to know that I'm not looking tip-top. You look pretty tired yourself." She eased away from that hard warm touch. Those gray eyes slowly moved down her crimson sweater, the gold coin resting upon it, and then lower, to the jeans sheathing her legs. Michaela fought the instant heat and awareness zipping over her skin. She wondered why Harrison, too close, could affect her like that.

He eased the pencil from over her ear and handed it to her almost ceremoniously. "Right on time. I see you worked until the last minute. I'm afraid I'm running late, and yes, I'm tired. Make yourself comfortable, please, and remove your shoes at the door. I'm careful of my floor. I'll be right back."

After Harrison had gone into another room, Michaela shook her head. The mind-shaking view of the tiny water beads on his shoulders and centered low on his back had taken away her breath. Her body's barometer had just soared with the need to take him, to plunge her fingers into those dark gleaming restrained waves and curls and fist them. To twine her arms around him and press herself against those water droplets low on his spine. To take his mouth and feed upon it, to take his body and forget everything else but—

She gripped her briefcase and studied the large, bare room with its roughly hewn mantle and blazing rock fireplace. Though her family had visited Harrison's new home, she hadn't. The fire reflected a trail across the polished wide boards of the floor, the distinct square nails salvaged from the 1880s. Michaela bent to unlace her boots, placing them on the entryway's worn mat. The basically barren room was much like her parents', except that the walls were roughly covered with pale cream stucco.

The three huge modern canvases, mixed slashes of blue and brown and dark green, textured with freestyle palette knife were her teenage work. She heard her breath hiss in the silence, and then hurled through time when she was young and free and the world waited for her. There was a savagery in the paintings, bold and harshly layered, centered in the expanse of white canvas. She studied them closely, the girl who had painted them removed from the woman. Michaela traced her fingertip over a rippling cerulean blue slash, white representing the harsh white water rapids. That was Cutter River, the palette knife building jutting layers of gray and black and brown for the rocky canyon walls. She studied the next canvas, more green and blue, pines rising against the Wyoming sky. It was this that the young artist had loved best, the wilderness, the freedom. The third canvas was larger than the others, mere slashes of lime green meadows blended with yellow sweeps of sunflowers and cradled by forests of dark pine.

She hadn't expected the large framed collection of photographs she'd taken with her first camera. The Langtry horses, the herds of white-faced Herefords, a doe and fawn grazing in the field, a stand of milkweed, all white froth and seeds swaying in the wind. She'd given the pictures to Harrison when he'd gone to college that year after his father had died. He was only nineteen then, all angles and broad shoulders, and he'd seemed so alone. She'd wanted him to remember the good, clean, fresh land, and that he'd always have a home with the Langtrys. He'd been too thin then, still growing, too quiet and brooding. She'd given him what was in her heart, the pictures that had come less frequently to her mind as she'd enveloped herself in her career. *Who was she now? What had she lost? Why did the mountains call to her so strongly now, the winds in Cutter Canyon sweeping through her mind?*

At one end of the room, cornered neatly in the huge

windows overlooking Shiloh, was a long, rough pio-
neer table, covered with a protective glass top. Cluttered with papers and books and a computer, the
work area looked little like Harrison's sleek office at
the bank. A line of file cabinets were metal instead of a
style better suiting his home. Nearby a bookcase
loomed, stuffed to overflowing. On the floor near the
fireplace, a display case of coins caught the light,
gleaming and preserved beneath the glass. On the display case rested a jumbled assortment of coin and money collector—"numismatic"—magazines and books.
A quick study of the titles revealed that Harrison's
interest ran to Civil War monies.

In front of the fireplace was a large, comfortable
recliner, carelessly covered with an old, soft quilt.
Without a pillowcase, the pillow had been covered
with a towel, now still bearing the imprint of Harrison's head. Around the chair were an assortment of
magazines, mostly those of coin collectors, and a stack
of file folders. A nearby folding card table held more
pads and pens, a clutter of paper.

When Harrison reentered the living room,
Michaela turned to him. Used to Harrison in a dress
shirt, she hadn't expected the light Irish knit sweater
over his jeans, or his sock-covered feet. Clearly Harrison was at home as he bent to pet the large white cat
that came yawning, all sharp teeth and pink tongue,
and twining like a lover around his legs.

Home? For all the expensive gleaming floors, the
blazing fireplace, and the large room with the rough-
hewn beams crossing the ceiling, the house lacked

warmth. Nothing of the Kane family had been salvaged. By appearances, Harrison had cut himself clean of his family.

"Meet Mary Belle. She comes and goes, and tonight she's curious about you. Don't look so puzzled, Michaela. It's how I choose to live—without tangles and obligations, other than mopping up the mud from the entryway once in a while. We'll be working at the table there after dinner. You might as well make yourself comfortable while I see to whatever we're eating." Harrison frowned slightly and considered Michaela. "I'm not a cook. It's just pasta with a jar of sauce poured over it, a slab of lettuce I call a salad, and some bottled dressing."

"Fine with me. I'm not a cook either. I thought I gave those paintings to Sissy Elbert to remember me. I was too afraid Mother would show them, and now here they are."

Harrison lifted an eyebrow, his mouth softening. "Sissy had a yard sale. I needed something for my walls. Everything else was too small and cluttered."

"So much for keepsakes. *You* can't display them, of course."

"Yes, I can. They're mine."

"Take them off your walls," Michaela demanded, temper simmering now. She didn't want Harrison to have anything of hers, any part of her life, in his keeping. Because Harrison knew how to keep too well.

"Don't be childish," Harrison murmured coolly, and determined to argue, Michaela followed him into the spacious kitchen, filled with ultramodern stainless steel appliances. Small bags of plastic-wrapped snacks, nuts, and chips haphazardly filled a cardboard box, as if someone had shuffled through them.

The glass cupboards were empty and a mismatched clutter of cheap pots and pans were stacked near the metal monster of a gas stove. Paper cups and plates and an opened container of plastic dinnerware said Harrison wasn't wasting time on housework. "I think you're supposed to rinse that," she said, as Harrison dipped the rigatoni out of the boiling water.

"You want to do this?" he invited in a challenge.

"Nope. I always wondered what it would be like to have you slave for me," she returned.

His slow, indrawn breath said she'd scored a hit. She decided to take another opening shot. "Your home would make a really super place to hold our initial this-is-what's-up party. An informal little cocktail party—I'm great with hors d'oeuvres, especially stuffed mushrooms. What's *that*?"

She touched the brown hard surface baked into a square metal pan. "Making bricks?"

"Brownies. A mix. I didn't have eggs." Harrison turned slowly from pouring the heated spaghetti sauce over the pasta. He stared blankly at her. "What's this about a party? Here?"

Michaela allowed her smile to escape. "Don't look so shocked. Your home is perfect. People like to know more about you. We'll invite them to your open house and push the station at the same time, all very dressy, very classy. We'll entertain and charm Victoria and her cronies. Jon can play sedate music on his keyboard—"

"Jon." The single word ricocheted off the cabinets of the kitchen, skidded across the Italian tile floors to plop at Michaela's stocking feet. Harrison stared at her as if trying to understand her joke. "Jon," he repeated, and stabbed forks into the pasta. They stood upright, statements of his dislike for the idea as he picked up the two plates. "Bring that bottle of wine and those glasses. We'll have to eat in the living room. The idea of having any social event here is out of the question. I don't want people to see how I live."

"Oh, I see. It's fine for you to 'research' my life, to hang paintings that I'd rather forget on your walls. But let's not come too close to the great Harrison Kane, Jr. He doesn't like it."

"You know I dislike 'Jr.' " He tilted his head to one side, looking at her. "Are you going to ruin the dinner I cooked? Or are we going to be sensible about this? This is business."

"You're going to have to bend a bit, Harrison. People are interested in what you do when you're not at the bank, how you act socially, and the big one—do you have a sense of humor? We can use that curiosity to get support and interest. Think of how excited Victoria's clan will be to come to an all-out tuxedo bash. And Jon looks marvelous in his tuxedo," Michaela said smoothly, as she picked up the wine bottle and glasses and led the way into the living room. The mismatched glasses were cheap and unlike the glittering crystal of the Kane mansion.

Harrison's dark, brooding tone gave his opinion. "Everyone knows that Jon likes to wear panties. He had the bad taste to purchase them at Williard's Dry Goods store, size fourteen, I believe. They had to be ordered in with a special black lace garter belt."

"Everyone has his private vices. He had to order them somewhere. It doesn't matter what he wears under his tuxedo. And he's a marvelous musician."

Placing the wine and glasses on the floor in front of the fireplace, Michaela ignored Harrison's scowl as she spread the blanket near the fire. While he waited, a pasta-laden dish in each hand, she sat to pour the wine into the glasses. Harrison shoved one of the dishes at her and sat in the chair, still scowling at her as she handed him a glass of wine. "I have a sense of humor. I can laugh at a joke," he said finally, as if unable to bite back the retort longer.

"Mmm," she returned lightly, knowing that would nettle him more.

"Women." Harrison's rough, disgruntled tone reminded her of her father and brother when confronted with logic they could not understand. He placed the filled wine glass on the floor and jammed his fork into the pasta. Then he insert a tine into the pasta carefully and turned it, as if he were lining up his thoughts. "No. Not here."

"Fine, we'll have it at the studio and—"

Harrison stared blankly at her. "Do you know how much that equipment cost?"

Michaela met his dark look and smiled coolly. "Yes, and I know what curious fingers can do, all that prodding and turning knobs and flipping switches. Which is it? Here or there?"

"Hell," Harrison muttered darkly, before sticking the loaded fork into his mouth and chewing as if the pasta were leather. His narrowed consideration said he didn't appreciate the ledge she had placed him on. "I hate those things. But getting the station up and running has to be a priority. Where's your concept?"

She stood and opened her briefcase, taking the neat binder from it with its pages of ideas. She handed it to him, and when he reached to take it, Michaela held the binder tight against his tug. "You'll do it, then? Host a social presentation of the station? You'll charm, and wine and dine?"

Harrison's narrowed smile was more of a showing of his teeth than of agreement. "There will be conditions, of course."

"Certainly. Here they are— Harrison, take my paintings and burn them."

"No. I like to think of that wild, free, laughing girl who painted them. The girl with summer in her heart and sunshine in her smile. The girl who cried when she hurt, and loved so deep and fierce that nothing could hurt her."

"She's gone, Harrison. Dead."

"No, she's not. She's been hurt and she's tired, but she's still there."

five

My wife knows that my honor and pledge haunt me, that my home far away and duty call. Yet my true heart belongs here in the mountains, in this lush valley where we have built our log cabin. She can ride, my lady love, fast as the wind on the stud I rode from Langtry Plantation that night long ago, fleeing from the Yankee pirates.

I wonder if Obediah's curse rang true with those five coins given freely to save my love's life. What of their owners, do they fair well with Langtry gold?

My wife says she will have the coins returned. She is a fierce woman, with strong instincts in keeping with her shaman blood. Is it magic that places my heart in her small hands? Was she there before I

knew of her? Sometimes I think I have always loved
her—

Zachariah Langtry's Journal

Had he always loved her? Maybe. If a Kane knew how to
love. Harrison wanted to ignore the ringing telephone.
He wanted nothing to interfere with Michaela's obvious excitement and enthusiasm. Rising, binder in
hand, he slapped it against his thigh as he walked to
his work area. Michaela stared into the fire now, her
hands clasped around her bent knees. The firelight
danced on her silky black hair, her lashes sweeping
shadows over her cheeks. The line of her body, all soft
and flowing beneath her red sweater and jeans, caused
Harrison's breath to catch and his body to heat.

Except for the two nights she'd held him from that
edge, Harrison had never been as alone with her as he
was now. The graceful way she swept back her hair
entranced him, the way the firelight stroked her
throat as she studied her paintings. They were like she
used to be—wild, free, bold, earthy.

Michaela had always been a sensual woman, the
stroke of her elegant hand against a horse's flank, the
lifting of a wildflower bouquet to her face. She moved
with a woman's grace now, but the smooth stride was
the same, that stalking, feline flow of curves and inner
strength.

His senses still held the scent of her, the warmth of her
body as she passed by him. For just an instant when

she'd first arrived, she'd been sensually aware of him. She'd eased back slightly from him, too careful of coming close as she'd passed him in the doorway. The quickly shielded blue gaze had lingered on his chest and the impulse to tug her to him had run a hot stake through Harrison's lower belly. Aware that his body was hardening, reacting to her feminine scent, and shocked that he wasn't in better control, he'd quickly turned and left the room.

He wasn't prepared for her, for the jolt of dynamic life and femininity she brought with her, and wondered if he ever would be.

He listened to his Denver office manager list the weaknesses of the company Kane Corporation was considering buying. According to Sam Moreland, the small electric wiring contract company was prime for acquisition. Once finely tuned by a man now retired, the company's crews weren't working to full capacity. The balance sheets said that the company wouldn't last another year on its own. "Get me a report on the foreman, what contracts their crews have filled in the last year, and check out the profit and loss statement with our accounting people."

Completing his brief talk with Sam, Harrison tossed Michaela's plans onto the table serving as his desk. He stared out the huge windows overlooking Shiloh. He wasn't proud of his early career, tearing companies apart, dissecting the parts, and setting up the resale of them for a profit. Back then, sorting out his life, living on canned soup and day-old bread, his talent ran to black and white numbers, to graphs and logic, not emotions. The television venture was sheer economical whimsy, the need to build something good and clean and strong, free of his family's past.

"You're curious about my lack of furniture," he said, as Michaela turned to look at him, black hair gleaming as it crossed her pale cheek. He wanted to trace that strand, enjoy her warmth running beneath his fingertips. "You want to know where all the good stuff went, right? The crystal, the Monet paintings, the hand-carved pieces? After my father's death, his creditors wanted payment. I felt no regret in selling whatever we owned at a good price to pay back the money he'd embezzled. I wanted nothing from the house I grew up in. Nothing to remember. When I came back that first Christmas, when I was eighteen and he'd shot himself earlier that fall, I went to the house and stood there. The furnishings were opulent. Expensive collections almost stacked in every corner. I'd just come from your parent's house, filled with warmth and laughter. Jacob and Faith had always been good to me. In comparison, the Kane house had always been frigid. On his desk was a laundry basket filled with creditor warnings. His blood was still on several older envelopes. I needed college tuition, his will left everything to me. He'd used almost all the money my mother had laid aside for college. I managed to stall the creditors with Jacob's help until I was of age. At twenty-one, I sold everything. The mortgage company took my suggestion of a tax write-off, a donation of Kane House to the historical society. A mansion isn't easy to unload in Wyoming's rural real estate market."

"I get the feeling you've never told anyone other than my father that information."

Harrison sat down at his desk and flipped open Michaela's plans for the station. "There's no point in lying to you. I'm giving you fair warning that we need to be careful with the budget."

"Ad spots will bring in some."

"Not enough." His finger jabbed at a recommendation. "I know we're working with a skeleton crew right now. Here, this is the rough blocking of our schedule. The national affiliate slots are already taken. See what you can do with it."

He forced himself not to watch her as she walked toward him to take the clipboard with the rough schedule. He tensed as she walked away, slender hips gently swaying. Then, with the control that had allowed him to survive, Harrison forced his attention to her portfolio. Michaela's ideas were inventive and certain to arouse interest. "So you see us out there, promoting events such as the canoe race down Cutter River in July, when the water is less dangerous. I like that. Mmm. Local cooks preparing recipes in the studio. An interview with John Starbuck, an eighty-year-old musher. Features of wheelchair races, rapelling, country dancing . . . I like the student debate hour and the basic education programs. You'll have to contact a university to see about that, about the credits and classes."

She nodded and Harrison focused on the neat proposal in front of him. He glanced over the rest of the pages. "You actually think we can go on air in a month with all this?"

"You said you had a friend who was experienced at ramrodding jobs like this through. With his help, yes, I do." Sitting in front of the fireplace now, Michaela looked up from the clipboard she'd been studying. She yawned and stretched, rotating her head as though her muscles were cramped from working over the project. "We might have a little smoothing to do, but yes, I think so. One of my investors is experienced in this. I did what I could to cut down those empty hours you wanted filled with John Wayne."

"John Wayne is an American institution. Jacob and Roark will agree with me."

"Sure. I lost a lot of good television time every time one of his movies came on and you guys took over the set. Let me know if you have questions," Michaela murmured drowsily, and gracefully slid down to lie in front of the fire, drawing the edge of the quilt around her.

Harrison forced himself not to stare at the curves beneath the thick fabric. He wanted to place his palm just there, on the jut of her hip, on the softer curve of her bottom, on the long, smooth line of her thigh. He flipped another page, the words running without meaning before his eyes.

Roark stood, one boot resting on his corral, watching the mountains shrouded by night. The scent of smoke came from his small house, the mare nudging his back for attention. He rubbed her ears and then turned back to his thoughts. His sister was struggling with a sense of failure and fighting for her future. Langtry land was a good place to do just that. She was at Harrison's place now, probably slashing at his logic. They made a good pair, one creative, wide-open and dynamic, and the other certain to get what he wanted, a strategical player. From the look of Harrison when Michaela was near, he wanted her and the game was on.

Soft-ly, slow-ly. . . . Since that night, Michaela had difficulty feeling secure. At times she'd lift her head and stare at the mountains—toward Cutter Canyon— as if something drew her there. Roark remembered that she'd always been drawn there, even as a child and a teenager.

Roark inhaled the night air and with the experience of a hunter, listened to the slight crackling of dry grass, the deer moving in the shadows, coming down into the valley. He'd chosen to live in Zachariah's cabin, modernizing it. On Langtry land where he could be close to the mountains—the well-worn path leading into the forest offered him escape. The urge to free himself, to run away from everything on that path, called to him now.

From habit, he slid his finger through the gold wedding ring sharing the chain with the Langtry coin. He couldn't bear to part with his ring, taking small comfort in a time that would never come again. He rubbed the coin on his chest. His wife wouldn't wear it, saying it was meant for him alone. His heart tore again when he thought of her, dying in childbirth. At first he'd hated the baby, barely clinging to life, and the reason for his wife's death; then, just as he began to treasure the gift Angelica had left him, a tiny part of herself, his son had stopped breathing. . . . At thirty, Roark had had all he wanted of loving a woman.

The coin warmed in his hand, and he thought of Cleopatra and the notation in Zachariah's journal that she had written her own. Of the heritage they'd passed down, Cleopatra's ruby ring and her journal were missing.

The wind lifted Roark's hair, tugging at it, and he wondered why those two things, so intimately for women, would haunt him. A raven, always on the alert for something shiny, had plucked Cleopatra's ring from the cabin's open window. He'd flown toward the mountains' jutting black peaks. Zachariah and Cleopatra had hunted for it then, and she was to lose her journal on one trip. Kept in a rose-colored candy tin, it had slid from her backpack as she leaped across a creek, the water bearing it away. Zachariah had said she mourned the loss as if it were part of her soul, for they could not find it. Fascinated by handwriting, taught by her husband, she'd wanted to leave a part of herself for their children. She wanted them to understand how deeply she felt, how her heart had been captured by the rogue with the Southern drawl and pretty, charming ways.

Roark understood loss; he could not find his heart,

not the beating life in it. Cleopatra had treasured her wedding ring and her journal, and they were still up in the mountains, waiting— If she could unite the Langtry coins, Roark could do no less than to find her ring and the journal. They were meant for Langtry women, and he intended to reclaim them.

His instincts told him that he would find the missing treasures. Was it his Langtry blood that made him so certain he would find Cleopatra's beloved ring and journal? Was it because whatever called to Michaela from the mountains, called to him, too? Or was it because hope could live, if it weren't destroyed? As long as he searched for the ring and the journal, he had a purpose and a dream. Dreams weren't easy for him now.

He closed his eyes, trying to find his wife's image, his first love and his last. After five years, it was dimmed, but a sweet ache stayed with him. He didn't expect another love in his life—didn't want one—and had settled for the quest of finding Cleopatra's treasures.

Cleopatra needed closure, just as his mother did, aching for a child she had lost.

Roark smoothed the coin beneath his shirt, then turned to hold the mare close and tight. There would be no children for him, or another love. He couldn't bear to lose again and the "*Softly, slowly*" lullaby would never be sung to his children . . .

He swallowed the emotion tightening his throat, remembering Zachariah's words—*'Tis no simple thing for a man to hold his child in his arms and sing this simple lullaby to him. It goes beyond what words can express, the filling of my heart. . . .*

But Roark knew that his heart would never be filled, not again.

Harrison gave up trying to focus on the station's concept and crossed the room. He crouched slowly to study the sleeping woman in front of the fire. In all the years he'd known her, not once had he seen her asleep. Now, she seemed vulnerable as never before. The sweep of light across her cheeks, those beautiful high startling cheekbones, those glossy lashes, fascinated him.

Tenderness wasn't within his realm of experience, the soft, uneasy need to— His hand lifted away from her hair, that silky warmth gleaming in the firelight.

He envied the cat, curled close to Michaela's stomach. He wanted to touch those soft earlobes, run his thumb across that tiny indentation, free now of an earring. Her slow breathing fluttered the tendril near her lips. Such full lips, not tightened by anger or determination now, but parted and soft and—

He sucked in air and found it bearing her scent. He'd wanted women, especially when he was trying to escape the dark shadows of his father's legacy, wanting—no, *needing* some warmth, some kindness to help him manage. But the aching hole in his life never filled, even in the red haze in which he found release.

She sighed, and the parted warmth of her lips gleamed. He closed his eyes, almost sensing them against his, against his skin. She snuggled down into the quilt and stretched and sighed, and the urge to take her in his arms caused him to tremble. Easing away from her, fighting tender emotion he didn't want, Harrison settled into the chair. He poured another glass of wine, studying the rich, golden lights as he swirled the contents.

Harrison tipped up the glass and drank quickly, pouring another glass. He had no right to want Michaela, not after what his family had done to hers—the rape of Faith, the birth of a half-sister, and the theft of the baby.

With his father's death and embezzlement riding him, eighteen-year-old Harrison had been stripped of money. The first private investigator—hired to find the missing baby—cost a part of his tuition reservoirs. Inept, the investigator had bungled the trail. Lesson one for young Harrison was research more carefully the people he hired for services. Harrison had sometimes worked nights as a bookkeeper at an auto salvage yard to replace the money paid the so-called investigator. As a nineteen-year-old college sophomore, he was already taking on investment clients.

Haunted by his family's brutality to the Langtrys, Harrison began a very private account, one he tended with ultimate care. He began to research more carefully, to learn techniques of prowling through accounts and identities. He learned to appraise the remaining custom-ordered silver from Kane House, then sold it to finance his hunt. Cuff links, watches, tie clasps, anything that had been given to him was very carefully sold to the highest bidder. A priceless collection of his childhood toys was sold, piece by piece. They weren't well loved—they'd been showpieces of the Kanes, public evidence of how well they treated their lonely young son. He sold childhood collections of stamps and coins—anything to fatten the fund needed to find Sable.

He had to give Faith closure, to stop the nightmare begun by his father—and his mother. Julia Kane was a talented chameleon and her dark path twisted endlessly, just as her mind did. Had she ever loved her son? Had she hated him because his difficult birth nearly killed her and started the infection that left her barren?

Michaela stirred restlessly, her hands flung palm-upward by her face, much as a child would sleep. The silence echoed with the song she hummed unevenly, one Harrison recognized as Zachariah's offering to his son, a Langtry heritage.

"Soft-ly, slow-ly . . . the mornin' will creep . . ." As though her own voice had awakened her, Michaela sat upright, shivering.

The cat hissed and leaped from her as if sensing a beast stalking her. Harrison recognized Michaela's helpless, agonized expression. He'd felt like that since the day his father had told him those dirty truths. Her face was damp with perspiration, that fine skin too pale, tears gleaming on her lashes. Harrison knew little about comforting, but he ached to hold her. "Michaela—"

She placed her forehead on her knees, her arms

wrapping around them. The gulping breaths were too familiar to Harrison, the nightmares waging against reality, the strength and control necessary to send them back into the darkness. She straightened, her hand trembling as she reached to pour a glass of wine. She downed it quickly and poured another, drinking more slowly as she stared into the fire. "I haven't been able to sleep well lately. In New York, I was . . . so far away from all this. Then it's all here, as though everything waited for me, every memory. I should have gotten up that night. I should have gone into the nursery. I should have—"

"Be reasonable. You were four years old." Harrison controlled his rage, the harm that had been done that night by his mother. She could have killed them all, the entire family, and felt no remorse. His mother's hatred and frustration had eaten her fragile beauty and her mind. He remembered the power of those bony hands when her crazed moods took her, shaking him in her fury.

Michaela's haunted, shadowed gaze met his. "Something wasn't right about that night. I don't know what it was. I heard someone singing the lullaby but Maria didn't sound like that. And her hand was too cold as she came to brush back my hair from my face."

Harrison's blood rushed coldly through him. *His mother had considered killing Michaela and Roark.* "She could have been holding the baby's bottle, cold from the refrigerator before warming it."

Michaela placed aside the wine and scrubbed both

hands over her face as if to push away the nightmares. "I can't forget. Sometimes my mother—" Michaela broke off and frowned at him. "What is it with you and my mother? Why do you watch her like that, as if you know something we don't? Why does she look at you as if trying to see—something that isn't real? As if she's trying to see something in you?"

Harrison understood that close, intense study of Faith's and what she was seeking. She'd be wondering what her baby looked like, if his half-sister looked like him. If she were alive. "She's a fine woman. I admire her. That shouldn't be unusual. Not with Faith Langtry."

Michaela got to her feet, stalking the length of the room, and then back to him. "Don't try that Mr. Cool act with me, Harrison. If you've got ideas about my mother—"

He grabbed her hand and pulled her slowly, gently closer. "Watch what you're saying, little girl."

Her hands covered his, fingers digging in, her expression furious. "You'll have to get your kicks somewhere else."

"What makes you think I don't?" He admired that fire, those fearless warrior instincts slashing at him. Maybe he needed her reality, those raw, exposed emotions honesty to tear through him, to make him feel alive.

Harrison watched Michaela circle the thought, dissecting what she knew of him. There was never another woman like her, he thought, all hot blood once her temper was raked. The slam of desire caught him, twisted through him like white-hot electricity, skittering in the air between them. The flush on her cheeks rose as when she tried to ease away, Harrison held the chain firmly.

"Let's get this straight. I'm not interested in your affairs."

"That's good, because I don't want to hear you moaning about yours." So real, so passionate she burned him, Harrison thought, diving into the churning emotions between them.

Michaela's lips tightened with the taunt. "I never 'moan.' "

"Oh, don't you? Ever?" he taunted softly, and enjoyed that gentle, hissing gasp as the sensual double-meaning hit her.

He'd expected her to act, disliking his tether, the back of his hand just brushing her breasts. She shoved a hand through his hair, pulling it taut, her eyes blue fire. "Did you hire me for this job because you know my mother wants me to stay here? Because she's missing one of her children and she needs to have Roark and myself close? That she's afraid she'll lose us, too?"

The reminder that his parents had hurt the Langtrys forever poured icily over Harrison; he drew back from the sensual edge he'd never felt with any woman. He released the chain, freeing her, yet Michaela held his hair tightly. Her face was stark with fury, color riding her cheeks, blue eyes lasering at him. "I don't like you very much, you know."

"Did I ask you to like me?"

* * *

My wife says I must meet the past, so that the future is ours. She knows that in doing my father's bidding that night, the fever running through me, that I'd felt my honor was torn from me. The lack of honor is a sore burden for a man, and little to give his love. I am not a coward in my love's eyes, but a man with a heart and soul, honoring his father's wishes. I fear she is right, that I must meet what I was before I can be whole. Do I dare return to that home far away?

Zachariah Langtry's Journal

Michaela stormed into the Langtry home, despite the one o'clock quiet hour. Still angry with Harrison's dark mood, with whatever secret he held from her, she flung aside her coat and walked into the living room. She tossed her concept onto the couch and noticed Faith curled up by the fire, wearing a nightgown and covered with a knitted shawl. "Mom, you're up late."

"And Harrison has set you off again," Faith murmured knowingly.

Michaela kicked off her boots and sprawled upon the couch. "You've got it."

"Did he like your ideas?"

Michaela flipped through the concept binder, filled with exact notations in Harrison's bold scrawl. He'd added thoughts, queried on the budget of some projects, stated that he wanted more of a rural feel in others. "For the most part, and I'm going to do a good job."

Michaela shivered, pushing away the memory of Harrison's naked back, those enticing droplets gleaming upon it. She hadn't expected the unsteady mix of her emotions, sensuality and passionate anger.

Faith had turned back to studying the fire as though trying to see through the flames. The search for her daughter had scarred her, and now her thoughts slid into the past. While Jacob had pursued traditional missing persons methods, she had tried her own, by bringing in psychic Lelani Virginia. Lelani's perceptions had found other missing persons, alive and some who had been murdered. Lelani had held the baby's crib, her trembling shaking it.

Lelani had held Maria's turquoise bracelet found on the floor. "Her heart is good. She would never think of taking your child."

Then the woman's soft dark eyes had met Faith's. "The father of the child was not your husband. Does he know?"

For the first time, Faith had shared her dark secret, tears falling freely. "Jacob has never questioned me. He's accepted the baby as his own."

"An unusual man. He loves you deeply, just as his ancestor loved a woman forbidden to him. Your husband doesn't trust me, does he? You're going against his will?"

Faith had nodded, holding the seer's hand. "Find my baby," she'd whispered desperately. "I have to know." *Would she ever know?* Where was Sable? All proof pointed to Maria and yet Lelani had supported

Faith's belief that the housekeeper was loyal and loving.

Faith considered her daughter, who was also looking at the flames. "I'm glad you're staying. Maybe it's my time of life, my body and moods changing, but I'm needing to know that everyone is safe and well. . . . I fought with Jacob like you do with Harrison, you know. That cowboy was too confident in his ability to make women swoon. I had to knock him back a step or two, but I loved him from the first moment I saw him breaking those horses. . . . Harrison has too many scars from his childhood. He's tempered to be a hard man and he's struggled so to come back from shame and his father's—"

At the name, Faith's body chilled. For a time, she couldn't bear to look at Harrison because he so resembled his father. Although he was bigger, broader in the shoulders, Harrison's features were that of the man who had raped her. Then there was that fragile, quiet bookish boy with no one but the Langtrys for warmth.

Michaela glanced at her mother. "You're the one person he relates to warmly. Do you ever wonder why?"

"His parents were selfish and emotionally cold people. I imagine he's attracted to me as rather a pseudo-mother. I tried to give him the affection they didn't. So did Jacob. But when Harrison was fifteen, something happened—you remember that horrible night. He withdrew just that tiny bit from me, and I never understood why. It was as if he had—I don't know. He's hard to understand and with his background, he could be horrible. He's not. He's honorable and kind and he can't throw pots worth a darn, just like your father. I thought it would be good therapy for Harrison, and for my sake, he tried. The result was awful. But the point was that he did try to please me. He's facing so many shadows here in Shiloh. He could have gone anywhere and been successful, forgetting the past, but he chose to come back. Jacob said that's the mark of a good man, facing his troubled past. Harrison comes to help with calving, or to mend fences, and he seems to really enjoy running a tractor in the fields, cutting and bailing."

"I imagine every swath he makes is perfectly aligned to the previous."

"Yes, dear. And he's the best at chopping and dicing in the kitchen. He's very precise and detailed," Faith murmured with a tender smile.

"Okay, okay. He got to me." Michaela hadn't meant her bitterness to erupt, but her mother already knew that Harrison had the ability to nettle her.

"I'm certain that anything Harrison dedicates himself to doing, he will do quite thoroughly. By the way, I see that you've started wearing the Langtry coin. I know it's silly, but I'm glad. I've always felt the strength in those legends, that the coins kept the Langtry family safe. I tried to find the missing two coins, but failed. I felt—I sensed that my connection to them was too faint, that I wasn't powerful enough to have them draw me to them. I watched you for years, wondering if Cleopatra had—but oh, that's silly . . . to think that she'd give you an insight where I had none."

Faith turned to study the fire again. "My baby has to be alive. I'd know it if she were dead. I'd feel it. Those first years, I thought I heard her crying for me. Then I had to push away the sounds. I'd already seen how problems ruined Harrison's mother. Julia used to be a lovely person when she first married his father. She was always brilliant in business. That's her gift to Harrison, I think. Sweet, kind, and then she changed. I've always wondered what happened to her. Julia left town a month after Sable was taken. Harrison's father said she went to a European sanitorium to rest, but she never returned— My baby is alive. I know she is. I feel her heart beating in me, just like when I carried her in my body. It has not stopped in all these years."

"Mother—" Michaela went to Faith, kneeling to wrap her arms around her. Now, grieving for a baby she'd lost, Faith seemed too fragile, her years suddenly weighing her. She began to hum "Softly, Slowly" as she had long ago.

"I love you, Mom," Michaela murmured, trying to push away the memories that song evoked, of that cruel, heart-breaking night. "If you think she's alive, then—"

Faith held her daughter tight. Nothing could happen to her two remaining children, nor to Jacob. Everyone had to be safe and close. Was she demented, unwilling to take the reality that her child was probably—? Faith firmly pushed that notion away. "I *know* she's alive. I can't give up hope. Her name is Sable and she's alive, somewhere."

Then with the strength that had carried her through tragedy, Faith eased away from Michaela, smoothing that sleek black hair, so much like Jacob's. "I have something I want to give you. Jacob gave this to me not long after Sable was taken—"

From a velvet box, lush and red when opened, the bear claw necklace gleamed savagely in the firelight. Faith took the leather thong and carefully fitted it over Michaela's head. She studied the contrast of the gold coin and the black deadly claws. "It was as if Jacob wanted me to fight the darkness that grief can bring. That's what I want you to do—find who you are, what you need and toss all the rest away. Fight, Michaela. You remember your heritage and how much Zachariah loved Cleopatra and how they fought to stay together. You believe in love, honey. You believe in yourself."

"Oh, Mom—" Michaela placed her head in her mother's lap, the soothing familiar hands stroking her hair.

They sat like that for a long time, the fire crackling in the grate, and then Jacob, rumpled from sleep walked into the room. "Our baby is home," Faith said softly.

"About time." Jacob's deep voice was rough with emotion as he eased onto the chair opposite his wife and daughter. "You two make quite a picture. Michaela, you were good with a camera. They've got those fancy self-timers now and I'm expecting a family portrait."

"Jacob, she has a demanding job working for Harrison at his new television station. She hasn't time to pamper your whims."

"Harrison is a good man," Jacob said solemnly. "Don't take too much skin off his hide, will you, Michaela? I've always liked that boy."

"As long as he stays on his side of the fence, he's safe enough," Michaela said carefully, and tried to ignore her father's roaring guffaws.

six

I took my wife to Augusta and admired her courage and heart. I feared for her safety then, uncertain of our reception. The brand of a coward did not sit well with me, and more than once, she drew me back from anger. My dear departed parents had made the path easier, saying that I was near dead when they shipped me away on a death wagon, contaminated with a plague, my mind lost.

I'd hoped to find work, to make a life and regain Langtry Plantation, for it was a sore, sad sight at best. A coarse, hard-talking woman stood in my dear mother's dainty place, and I was hard put to ask favors of old friends. A new breed had taken the land, but I swallowed my pride and took work as a stable master. I knew and loved horses. I still do. 'Twas no

*easy thing to return with only one Langtry coin to
the land I'd promised to help rise again. My wife
accepted the hollow, stilted invitations of friends
because of my family's good reputation, and I loved
her more. She would not let me sell the last coin for
her ease, for the South had gone forever on the midnight wind . . .*

Zachariah Langtry's Journal

From his office, Aaron Gallagher viewed the pic-
turesque San Francisco setting, the townhouses situ-
ated close together, the colors pastel in the dying sun.
Like metal snails, the packed trolleys pulled up the
hills and then soared down.

Aaron listened to his accountant, ticking off potential tax write-offs. "It's the last week of May, Norman.
Give me a break."

"Here's a good one," Norman continued, pushing
his small, round glasses higher on his beaklike nose.
"A little struggling television station. Brand new. Goes
online in two weeks. We could contribute to their not-
for-profit broadcasting, fund an educational program
or two. Here, watch this film. One of the anchors did a
spot on the national affiliates promoting the new station. She's good—Michaela Langtry, I think. The station is largely based on internships for media students.
Owned by Kane Corporation, a good tight outfit, lean
with a top man. Unshakable reputation. Donating to
funding for education is always good for your image
and it's a good, hefty tax deduction. Yes, we've got to

get you out of the nightclub business and into something more respectable."

With a wave of his hand, Aaron dismissed Norman. The bookish accountant knew only the surface of what Aaron wanted him to know—just enough to keep the law from asking questions.

Ricco, a bodyguard, started the film. Upon Aaron's signal, another bodyguard—Ray—began making cappuccino. Aaron sat in his leather chair, prepared to be bored. Then suddenly he sat upright, freezing the film frame. Michaela Langtry was dynamic, sleek, professional, easily channeling the interview in the direction she wanted, highlighting the focus of the small community and rurally focused television station. "Classy," Aaron murmured approvingly, a man always alert to a quality he'd never had, always desiring it. Dirt-poor Oklahoma didn't offer much to a boy raised in a shanty.

As KANE's mover and shaker, Michaela promoted the features of the new and as yet, unborn television station. Articulate and poised, she was careful to detail the plans that had been in the making for some time, the efforts of which would soon be realized. Clearly out to draw attention to the first day the station "aired," and to list its potential. She knew how to fascinate and how to sell an unproven product. But Aaron was more interested in the woman than the potential tax deductions his account had suggested.

The dark red suit emphasized Michaela's silky black hair, her photogenic face and those fabulous sky-blue eyes. Aaron pushed away the lick of desire and focused on her necklace. Gleaming on her chest was the exact match to the coin Aaron had purchased earlier from a dealer needing fast cash. "Langtry," Aaron repeated slowly, the name catching and turning in his mind. The coin, the woman, and his institutionalized brother's ravings all were "Langtry."

Aaron leaned closer, framing the woman's starkly beautiful face, her vivid blue eyes seducing the camera. He wondered what it would be like to own a woman like that, then he zoomed down to the coin on her chest. "L" was etched deep in the gold. Aaron retrieved the coin he'd tossed in his desk, a whimsical purchase, "minted at midnight as the South was crumbling," the dealer had said.

Paul, Aaron's brother, had been committed years earlier to protect himself. Paul needed to be silenced; he was too open with what he knew, a danger to Aaron's less than legal activities. Paul's latest confines had echoed his ravings. The expensive personal attendant had offered to sedate Paul, but something in his mutterings now caught Aaron.

In a Seattle private sanatorium, Paul had met a woman who had raved about hating the Langtrys; he'd come to hate them, too. They'd treated her shabbily, but she'd had her revenge, taking the bastard baby her husband had spawned upon the Langtry woman.

"If Paul got the story straight, there were six coins," Aaron murmured, grasping his tightly. "I've got one and the Langtry woman is wearing one. That leaves four. What was that Paul said about power, Ray? That the owner of all six was powerful?"

Aaron could feel the power surging into him, rubbing his fingers over the Langtry coin. With power came the respect he wanted and craved.

"Uh. Paul has a problem, boss. He's not always on line, you know? But he did say something about a slave's curse and a man selling the coins to save his girl. The whole thing sounds nuts—stolen baby, six coins, legends."

But Aaron's attention was on the woman now, desiring her and the power that owning her and the coin could bring. "Let's visit Paul again, shall we?"

"Your daughter is expensive, Jacob. She's costing the corporation plenty over budget. She knows she's got the upper hand and she's using it. She's messed up my office at the station. 'Reorganized,' she said. In the time she's been on board, it's so organized I can't find anything. I don't like asking her for something that should be right where I put it last."

Harrison slid onto the cafe's chair and glowered at the cup of morning coffee the waitress had just placed in front of him. The scent of Megan's Cafe's plate-sized cinnamon rolls wafted over the room, filled with the rumbling voices of men; they met for comfort and conversation about crops and cattle. Roark and Culley shared looks that said they'd been where Harrison now trod.

"Women like to have things their way, especially when they're making nests," Jacob said. He remembered how he had raged at Faith in those early days, how she'd torn apart his lonely life and pasted it back with love.

Harrison grunted and tugged his tie loose, an unusual gesture for the usually precise chairman of the board of Kane Corporation.

"The point is," Roark noted, "is she doing the job you want?"

"Damn right, or I'd send her packing, contract or no contract. Dammit, I can't even use my own phone at the station. She's reorganized the switchboard with slots for recorded messages of weather and the time of local events. She's out at Faith's studio now, taping segments on the development of a pot. I've got one man drooling over her every whim and another— Dwight Brown—about to quit."

"Dwight who wears pajamas beneath his overcoat?" Culley asked. A westerner down to his boots, Culley had been amused by the newcomer to Shiloh.

"He's talented. He needed a job. I was lucky to get him. They were yelling at each other when I left. I had the odd feeling that both Michaela and Dwight enjoy tearing into each other. I can't see them sitting behind an anchor desk together, making friendly chitchat at the end of the program." Harrison ran his finger around the rim of his cup. A systematic man who liked quiet and order, he brooded, "I had ulcers once and I didn't like them."

"A good fight gets it all out in the open. I'd rather have that than a festering quiet war," Culley noted quietly.

"Michaela doesn't hold anything back. She's got this smirk and I— Never mind," Harrison brooded. *He went for that challenge every time, pushing her, and they would argue.*

Jacob studied Harrison's broken nose. He thought back to the time when the boy had been only fifteen. He'd stood there on the Langtry front steps, his skin bloodless, horror in his eyes as he'd stared at Faith. Harrison looked like he'd been run over by a Mack truck, his clothing torn, his eyes starting to blacken, one eye almost swollen shut, and blood still dripping from that broken nose.

He wouldn't agree to a doctor. Experienced with the results of brawls, Jacob had done his best with Harrison's nose, taping it securely. "I'm so sorry," the boy had repeated, his eyes never leaving Faith's.

He seemed to hang there, strung together with nerves, looking as if he'd crumble at any minute, his expression tormented.

"You've got nothing to be sorry for." She'd hugged him before, and Harrison had responded awkwardly. This time he shrank away, shivering and shaking his head.

"I've got business in town," Jacob had said back then, because he knew sure as hell that Harrison had taken a beating from his father. If Jacob had anything to do with it, the bastard would never touch Harrison again.

"No, you don't. You're staying right here." Faith had cleaned Harrison's bruised and scraped knuckles. Her look at Jacob said the boy had fought back. "Do you want to tell us what happened, Harrison?"

The boy had shaken his head, his eyes downcast. Then Michaela had come into the room, stiffened at the sight of Harrison, and had met her father's even, brooding look. She must have recognized the savagery in it, the need to avenge the boy, and the plea to help him. She caught her mother's worried expression, the tight grip on Jacob's tense forearm. Michaela had never been afraid of stepping into the fire and she did that night. "Harrison, I'm going riding. You'll need something warmer than that if you're going to ride across the field with me tonight. Can he borrow your jacket, Dad?"

Jacob stirred his coffee, letting the movement take him back to that night. Faith had reasoned with him that Harrison was no longer helpless. He wouldn't want a brawl—Jacob calling his father out. The boy had withdrawn from the Langtry family that night, holding something dark and hard inside him. He'd visited on the school vacations and later through the years. Whatever rode the boy had made him more of a man than his father could imagine—and the next day Kane Sr. looked worse than his son. It must have been hard for the boy to stand up to his father, but Harrison always did what needed doing. . . .

Harrison looked at the men around the cafe's wooden table. His words pulled Jacob from his reverie. "I'd already slotted national affiliates, and she's filling up the rest of the schedule. She's picking up advertising clients from farm machinery, to cars, to who knows what, and she's cutting down on John Wayne movies. I got every movie he ever made, and she's only slotting a few. For the most part, he's been replaced by a sitcom."

They stared him blankly. "Not John Wayne," Roark said finally.

"I'll have a talk with my girl. Maybe she doesn't understand the importance of a man's movie rights. We work a hard day. We've got a right to sports nights and righteous cowboy films."

"Monday night . . . Cooking with Leonora Brown . . . seven to eight. She's baking a Boston cream pie. The shoot is going to take place in her kitchen and we got ad money from a grocery store chain and from the hardware for their line of pots and pans. 'Women's Theatre Night' after that. You'll have to go to another station for what you want. We'll lose viewers we don't even have yet. We need viewers, so I'm counting on you to have your sets on our station. I'll say this for Michaela—she's pulling favors from some high-powered places. She knows how to network."

"Cowboy movies are an all-American man's God-given right," Jacob grumbled. "Talk sense to her, boys."

Harrison snorted in disgust this time, but Culley's dark eyes were gleaming with humor.

Roark was silent, studying Patsy Wright through the cafe window. Heavy with child and married to a long-time friend, she glowed just as his wife had done, carrying their baby.

He couldn't remember what a woman's body felt like against his, that sweet tender passion in the midnight hours. At thirty, he was certain that he'd never need a woman again, never hold one close and soft against him.

The weight of his father's hand on his shoulder brought Roark back to the present. Jacob's look said he understood how a man could love a woman so deeply, how badly he could want her child.

Michaela awoke with a start, Harrison's cat purring heavily against her face. His couch was new and sprawling and too delicious to resist as he shoved budgets at her from his work area. Her notebook slid to the floor as she moved, snuggling deeper in the blanket. Harrison's cat nuzzled her hand, begging for an ear rubbing.

"It's the first week of June, Michaela. Another week and we'll be ready to go on the air. Maybe." Harrison rose from his desk and stretched, his body outlined by the setting sun outside the windows.

She resented the sensual tug. Harrison had no right to have the body of a laborer, broad shoulders tapering down to narrow hips, his shirt stretched tautly against his chest as he rolled his shoulders. She closed her eyes, and when she opened them, Harrison was standing over her, watching her, his hands shoved in his back pockets.

Too rawly masculine and appealing, Harrison's

hard face was all shadows and planes, tinted by the firelight. His suit had been replaced by a T-shirt and jeans, his feet bare upon the wooden floor. Those cool gray deepset eyes flickered down the blanket covering her body and her senses leaped, heating.

The sensual snag danced in the air between them.

"You're exhausted," Harrison murmured, and the low drawl wrapped around her like electricity.

"No more than you," she returned, as she sat up and pushed her hands through her hair. Her fingers trembled, needing to fist and claim his hair. She wondered then how it would feel to feed upon him, to forget everything and lose herself in him.

But she wouldn't. Harrison wasn't a man to take anything lightly. He'd want more than she wanted to give—

He hadn't moved, considering her, and when she looked up at Harrison again, he breathed deeply. "Leave the interns alone, Princess. The boys are in love with you. A sensational scandal would ruin the station before it's even on the air."

She studied him, fighting the urge to— "You know, sometimes I just don't know which piece of you I'd like to take apart first."

"Come ahead anytime." The answer was too cool, nicking her temper.

"This isn't about the station, is it?"

"Is it?"

Anger surged out of her, unshielded, slapping at him. He was right—she was exhausted and he knew exactly how to push her. "I hate it when you hand questions back to me for answers."

"Do you?" His tone showed no change, no emotion. Those gray eyes flickered just once, as if he were enjoying their game of cat and mouse. In the past few months, she'd been through all the games she'd wanted to play with superior-looking men.

Michaela stood and fought for control. She hadn't realized how easily Dolph had followed her orders; Harrison was a different matter. *Was Roark's statement true? That she picked men she could control?* "The cocktail party here is scheduled one week after the station opens. You've got two weeks, mister, to get this house in shape."

He raised an eyebrow. "You like pushing people around, don't you? Me, specifically?"

"You wanted promotion for the station? I'm giving it to you. Oh, stop scowling. I'm not backing off."

He released the breath he'd been holding. "I don't like my home invaded."

"I'm here, aren't I?"

"Yes, you are," Harrison murmured after a moment, and then slowly lowered his lips to hers. The brief electrifying touch of his mouth stunned her.

When she could breathe again, she pressed back against the wall. "What was that?"

She hadn't expected Harrison's quick, boyish grin. "It shut you up, didn't it?"

Still smiling, watching her expression, Harrison ran his finger over her lips. "You're not going to fail, Princess. You never have. You've had hard times and you've met them."

"Do something with this house," she managed,

sucking air into her when she realized she had stopped breathing. Experience told her that when Harrison won the first round, it was always much safer to start another point of attack.

"Okay. I know just the decorator." Harrison stretched out a hand to steady the pottery lamp Micheala had just bumped, stepping away from him. "Your mother gave me this. I really should get a lamp-shade someday."

That Harrison would pay someone to furnish his lovely home incensed her. "A good decorator, I hope. Nothing showy or elaborate."

"Sheila Rainbird has always had good taste." Harrison walked outside, leaving Michaela to follow in her sock-clad feet. On the porch, he smoothed his nose and studied the television tower in the distance, his hands braced on his hips.

"Was she your lover?" Michaela's question shocked her. She couldn't imagine Harrison as a lover. Or could she? He'd choose meticulously— She swallowed, shaken by the churning storm within her.

Harrison turned slowly to her, his expression cool and hard, shoving her life back at her like a barb. "You've had lovers, haven't you?"

She fought the flush of heat rising up her cheeks, the curl of anger and frustration and something else in her stomach. "Yes, of course."

One lover, the wrong one. She didn't trust herself to choose another.

"Well," he murmured, turning to consider the station again. A muscle in his jaw contracted and released, his skin gleaming over it. "I suppose we're even, then, aren't we?"

She didn't want to think about the women he'd held in his arms, in his bed. That she should care infuriated her. "I will do your house, Harrison. Just the rooms that count. I want the right feel for that party. It's important to make a good showing for potential backers."

His hand found hers, his hard strong fingers twining with her slender ones. He brought her hand to his lips, kissing it. "I can always count on you, can't I, Michaela? You're very territorial, you know. Very possessive."

"Me?" His lips had burned her flesh and now his face was too close. She backed away and almost tripped over the step, but Harrison caught her. His big hands spread open beneath her arms; his thumbs gently stroked the sides of her breasts just once, before he released her.

She couldn't breathe, electricity skittering around her body, tightening her flesh as the long, liquid pulls began low in her stomach.

Aware that Harrison watched her carefully, Michaela shot out a hand to grip the rough wood exterior, her knees weakening at that dark heated look. "You're exhausted, darling. You'd better go home. Unless you want to sleep here."

She trembled then, aware that whatever churned between Harrison and herself wouldn't be satisfied easily.

* * *

"Stand by," the intern called as Michaela settled into the anchor desk beside Dwight. The first morning show introduced the viewing audience to the station, showing clips of the other staff. Harrison, dressed in a three-piece gray business suit, stood off set, his arms crossed in front of him.

"You're gorgeous," she said to Dwight, enjoying his quick freeze, that instant recoil of a man who had tried everything to dislodge her and couldn't.

"Witch-lady," he snarled back.

"I love you, too," she returned, then turned to the camera's "On Air" sign for a lead-in to the morning show. "This is Michaela Langtry with KANE Television. Welcome to our first show. We'll be here every morning at six with local and affiliate news. We ask your patience as we begin. This is my co-anchor, Dwight Brown. Dwight is new to our area, fresh from Los Angeles. What do you think about life in the country, Dwight?"

Dwight smiled at the second camera, focused on him. "Thank you, Michaela. I've always loved the country. You're from here, right?"

"Born and bred."

Dwight's tight smile said "bumpkin." "I'm looking forward to the interviews we've scheduled. The first is with Faith Langtry, the creator of the local arts center. Let's go now to her studio."

When the camera's green light snapped off, Michaela adjusted the tiny microphone in her ear and spoke to the director. "Try not to give me too much while I'm talking. I hear background chatter in the news room. Yes, Dwight is wearing pajama bottoms—"

She ignored Dwight's glare and watched the inserted film clip of her interview with Faith. Her mother was poised and elegant, explaining the process of centering the lump of clay onto the wheel. "Yes, I have three children—Michaela, Roark, and Sable. . . ."

When Faith mentioned Sable, her tone had changed from pride to longing, her smile less confident. A movement off stage drew Michaela's glance to Harrison. His hands tightened into fists, his mouth becoming a grim line.

When Faith's segment finished, Harrison walked from the set, his body rigid. Whatever rode him about Faith hadn't changed; for just a moment, he'd opened his expression and he'd been vulnerable. He'd seen Michaela watching him from her anchor desk and he'd closed down, shut her away.

She turned the pen she'd been holding, watching it gleam beneath the bright studio lights. *She'd tear whatever Harrison held for her mother away from him.*

Michaela forced her frown away. "Stand by!" the production technician called and Michaela straightened, smiling at the camera.

"All right. I want to know what's going on," Michaela said an hour later, her high-heeled shoe bumping Harrison's bottom as he crouched, unpacking new wine glasses. Dressed only in his jeans, his back bare and gleaming in the kitchen light, he'd taken her breath away. Muscles shifted beneath his darkly tanned back and a white scar tore across the padding of one shoulder. Her finger ached to trace it. Harrison was a man of interesting textures. She wanted to slide her hands over his back, feel the power in it.

He held a glass up to the light and the cut glass design sent a myriad of colors into the kitchen. "These cost a fortune."

"Take those out of the dishwasher. You'll shatter the crystal. It's Irish, you know, the best." It was always safer to tear into Harrison, tossing away the softer emotions. She plucked the glass he was holding from him and placed it on the counter. "I expected champagne in the office . . . a few hoo-rahs from the boss. We are a success, you know, and you ran out. I detest men who run out under pressure."

Harrison stood slowly; he wouldn't be compared to her ex-lover, that loss still burning at her. He ran his hand across his bare chest, soothing the ache that the sight of Michaela always brought. "I'm not running anywhere."

Her fist hit his shoulder hard enough to sting. "KANE is up on the air and you haven't said one word, one overjoyed compliment. Let's not get all emotional here."

He'd forgotten how dynamic she could be in front of the camera. How she could make it love her, how the sound could catch that soft purr, that exciting lilt to her voice.

The first live program had stunned him. She'd

pulled together a station schedule, pushed a rookie college media team into running smoothly, and now she was all nerves, jubilant, triumphant, and riding on success. She was also ready to tackle him for what she considered a lack of interest.

Michaela's cheeks were flushed, her eyes burning. She tossed her head, and her hair fanned out like smooth silk, waiting to be captured. His instincts told him to do just that, the impulse to stand, lock his hands in that fabulous hair, and take her glossy, hot mouth. The sight of Michaela's long legs caused him to want to run his hand up beneath her short skirt as he stripped away all pretenses that he wanted her and simply took—but he wouldn't. He planned a different game. He wouldn't let Michaela walk away easily; he intended to wait and make certain that she wouldn't forget him. He resented the power she had to distract him from very careful plans. "Don't you ever get tired of ramrodding everyone?"

"Not you. If you couldn't do it for me, you should have done it for the people who worked night and day. You could have spent time with the crew, especially with the college kids. It wasn't easy, you know. We've all been working overtime and some of them are commuting fifty miles and back a day . . . and carrying summer classes. Sometimes you can be absolutely dumb and bloodless." Michaela hitched her large leather bag over her shoulder and flounced down the hallway to his bathroom. On her way, she kicked a stack of unopened boxes—monogrammed towels for the guest bathroom, lampshades for Faith's lamps, and linen for a guestroom newly stocked with bedroom furniture—in case a guest had to lie down.

Harrison didn't want his bedroom invaded. He liked the mattress and box springs on the floor, the simplicity of the barren windows. There was nothing wrong with stacking his folded jeans and T-shirts on the floor, and lining up his shoes. The walk-in closet was fine for his suits, but a cardboard box was fine for his clean underwear and another for his neatly folded socks.

But at times, he liked to go into the bedroom Michaela had prepared for that potentially ill guest, lie on that new sprawling bed and think about holding her—

"I ought to let you fry," she furiously tossed back at him as she stopped to kick off her heels and throw them at him. "Why, my family thinks you—never mind. When this first frantic mess to get organized is all over, I've decided to strangle you slowly."

Harrison tilted his head to one side, enjoying the fast sway of her hips as she breezed into his bedroom. He listened to the mild shuffling of his cardboard boxes and shook his head, imagining her digging through them, ruining his neatly stacked, folded clothing.

She soared out of his bedroom, carrying his clothing and glaring at him. Michaela left nothing to doubt when she was angry, and he appreciated that wide-open emotion. He wasn't used to easy relationships, and Michaela had breezed through a lifetime of them.

She'd nudged and cajoled and somehow got the over-worked crew into enjoying the stress and challenge of "putting a cutting-edge station on the air." She had a soft, feminine way of getting her message across, or she could cut like cold steel. She'd run Dwight down when he was sulking and ask about the progress of his novel while she was sliding him tips on how to write his lead-ins.

Harrison gave her a moment, then braced himself for another cut and slash session that only Michaela could make seem enjoyable. He leaned against the bathroom door, watching her strip away the heavy makeup demanded by the camera. She wore his T-shirt, clean boxer shorts, and socks too large for her. A fresh flannel shirt had been tucked onto the towel rack, her suit and slip and hose tossed over the shower. His desire startled him, his body hardening, his blood rushing warmer as he noted the unbound softness of her breast, her bra hanging from the door-knob. It was lacy and softly shaped and— Past his early experimentations, he hadn't really cared about women's lingerie, but Michaela's preferences were another matter. Strange, he thought, that he'd never considered women's underwear, or the removal of it, the delicate lace easily torn, until Michaela had swept back into his life. Her scent, an erotic blend of woman, not exactly sweet, but very real and enticing, curled around him. "That's an interesting outfit. Make your-self at home, why don't you?"

"I've lived with a brother. You're contrary and dense as brick, but you still have the same closet pickings as Roark . . . only yours are too neat and difficult to sort through. I'm tired and disgusted with you, and I didn't have time to change before coming over here and letting you have a—" She looked at the long black velvet box he had just tossed in front of her. "What's this?"

"The special courier's truck broke down forty miles outside of town. I had to pick them up. When I got back, the party was nearly over. I saw no reason to do a job halfway. And there is nothing wrong with neatly organized clothes."

"What—?" Michaela's expression softened as she opened the box. "Commemorative gold pins, each embossed with the crews' name and the date. Keepsakes, Harrison. You actually thought of something sentimental."

Her delighted tone caused Harrison to feel as if his feet were inches above the floor, he wallowed in the feeling of being her semi-hero. He hadn't given many gifts in his lifetime and had been uncertain of her reaction. It was very important to please Michaela, when he hadn't invested in pleasing another woman. "Cost a fortune," he muttered, comfortable more with talk of money then emotions. "So will tomorrow's champagne and flowers and free dinners for a month at Megan's Cafe for the crew."

"Still—" Michaela grinned at him. She closed the box and lifted her hand to pat Harrison's cheek. "Nice boy."

"Don't." He caught her wrist, holding it. He'd seen her tempt her high school boyfriends with the same gesture, making them steam. "Don't think you can manage me like you have the others."

"Others? Just how many do you think—?" When Michaela's eyes darkened in anger, Harrison moved closer, backing her against the vanity. He held her nape, supporting her head with one hand as he took a tissue to gently ease away the glossy lipstick on her mouth. Her hand flung out, tipping her bag to the floor, but her other hand reached for his shoulder, digging in. As she breathed deeply, watching him, struggling with the currents flowing between them, the soft nudge of her breasts rose and fell against his chest.

"You're aroused," she whispered starkly as his hips pressed intimately against hers.

"Damn right. You're not wearing a bra. You smell like— How do you think I'd be?" He shouldn't have looked down at the hardened nubs against the T-shirt's light cloth. Very little kept him from tearing away the cloth and tasting the warm flesh beneath.

"Why, Harrison. Do you want me?" she asked softly, the purring taunt in her voice curling around him.

He recognized the challenge to bare himself to her, but he wouldn't give her that pleasure, not without an equal measure. She was playing now, the flirtation reminding him of how she had acted in high school and with the college boys she'd infrequently brought home. He wanted more than flirtation from her—a lot more. He smiled, watching those fabulous eyes widen as his fist caught her hair, stretching her throat back.

Arched against him, her hand flung out again, knocking the cosmetic cleanser bottles and cotton pads to the floor. Harrison ran his hands down her hips, around to her bottom, cupping her, then lifted her to sit on the vanity. He moved between her legs, felt that intimate warmth, that taut quiver running through her as he leaned closer. With one hand splayed on her thigh, he placed his other over her medallion, let the metal and the woman burn his flesh. "You're nervous of me, Michaela. I wonder why?"

"Let me go, Harrison." Her voice was husky, uneven, her fingers digging into his bare shoulders.

"When I'm ready." Would he ever be ready to release her? He smoothed her bare thigh, stroked the inner surface with his thumb and sucked in badly needed air. The impulse to kiss her there had startled him; that drumming sound was his heart, his body aching too hard and too soon.

She studied him slowly, taking in his bare chest. Her fingertips slid to circle his nipples and another painful jolt hurled through his body, throbbing low and hard. He could have answered the beckoning of those sultry blue eyes, the sensual way her lips parted, the rush of her breath across his face . . . he could have relieved them both. But he wanted more from her and himself; he wasn't hurrying with Michaela. "Looking for entertainment, Michaela?" he asked, more coolly than he felt.

It took a moment for the taunt to set in, but then Michaela was pushing away, furious with him. She grabbed the flannel shirt, jamming her arms into it. "If I wanted you, I could have you."

"Could you really?" he asked too softly and knew that he wouldn't be able to sleep at all that night.

"Really. Don't push me, Harrison. It isn't wise. Now are we going to unpack all those boxes or not?"

seven

My love almost terrified me as she held the remaining coin close to her breast, her eyes closed as if drawing something into her mind. She stood by Obediah's poor grave, the midnight wind lifting her raven black hair in a storm around her. She looked nothing like the woman dressed in blue silk who wore the bear claw necklace, my trophy, honoring me in her way at the ladies' tea. I should have told her, but I knew not that she had done so, until the whispers came my way, the ladies' quiet, deadly words that had slashed at her.

Zachariah Langtry's Journal

"Go away. The party is a success and you're not ruining my moment." Michaela stiffened, the hair on her nape lifting. She resented how Harrison, moving close to her, could send electricity darting through her senses. In a room full of people, the air heavy with talk and low music and clashing scents, her body—her senses—responded to one man.

Dressed in an expensive black suit, Harrison's body warmed her back, though he did not touch her. Her first sight of him, the wary grumbling male, obviously uncomfortable and dressed to kill, had knocked the breath from her. His dark brown hair gleamed in deep, neatly combed waves, his jaw taut and freshly shaved, those steely eyes narrowing on her, had almost caused her to grip the doorway for support. He smelled of soap and shaving lotion and man, a scent that would cause any woman to want to—

Harrison had such nice primitive edges, Michaela thought, all smoothly covered, and waiting to be raised. The challenge to tear him from his shields, to watch those gray eyes clash like steel when he was nicked, was too much to resist.

Michaela straightened her shoulders. She'd lived with a man and hadn't known him, hadn't felt that prick of awareness when he was near. Yet when Harrison came near she could feel his presence seep into her pores, warming her. That she wasn't immune to a former "nerd-boy," wasn't easy to swallow. Harrison had no right to look so delicious, the white dress shirt emphasizing his dark skin, those wide shoulders beneath that tailored suit and those long, powerful legs. From experience, she knew that he had few suits, all impeccably tailored, usually in three-piece grays or navy blues. She hadn't been prepared for Harrison's impact in dress black.

When he was near, her senses seemed to warm and simmer and liquify, the hair on her nape lifting, her skin tingling. She hadn't forgotten how he easily lifted her up to the bathroom vanity, his body hard. There was no mistaking the intimate, blunt nudge, his hand open and warm and hard on her thigh. No other man had touched her like that, as if he meant to keep and hold her and let nothing tear him away. That certain savageness, that elemental passion within Harrison had ignited her own deep needs, startling her. The need to grasp him, to fuse her mouth to his, had danced through her sleepless nights in the past week.

She smiled briefly at Victoria D'Renaud in all her pomp and glory, obviously thrilled to be socializing with the powerful, worldly and wealthy men in the Kane Corporation. Michaela understood business parties, how to work them, but she didn't understand Harrison. He wasn't a man to play games and yet—

His finger, cool from the wine glass, lightly traced the back of her neck. His low voice wrapped around her, placing the humming of the crowd's conversation at a distance. "Still mad at me?"

He blew the tendril that had slid from her sleek French roll and she shivered, easing away from him. Harrison took that bit of nervous reaction as proof that he was getting to her. She'd strike out at him next, putting him in his place. As expected, Michaela started defending her walls. "Did you really have to insist that everyone take off their shoes at the front door?"

"Roark, Jacob, Culley, and I worked too many hours on this floor not to respect it. Relax. The rest of the house may not be furnished, but that doesn't matter. Faith's weaving and pottery add a unique touch, and display her work. She'll get that backing for her arts center. The room is stuffed with money and they want to be patrons of the arts. Add a few jungle plants and the whole thing is pretty classy. Not bad at all, Michaela. You look good, by the way."

Better than good, Harrison thought. He'd had to shield his first response when she'd come early, hustling with Sissy and Jon to bring in the plastic trays of hors d'oeuvres, shoving her list of orders at him. The simple turquoise gown was an illusion of cloth and woman, swirling as she moved, the low V promising just a kiss of her breasts. The tiny straps were meant to be slid away from her shoulders, the striking savage bear claw necklace and the Langtry medallion contrasting with her chic appearance. "Come to show off, darling?" he'd asked, pushing away the craving to pick her up and run off into the night with her.

"The coin is for good luck. The bear claws are because I felt like wearing them. I think Zachariah and Cleopatra would have liked this, creating something to enrich lives here, to make my mother's art center more visible. I'm feeling on top of it tonight. I like success." She'd caught the ends of the tie he hadn't knotted, deftly fashioned it and straightened his collar, ending with a pat. "You're not going to ruin this for me, you know. You're going to smile and laugh and socialize. Not the baring of teeth you usually do, but try some real warmth. You can laugh, can't you?"

With her scent taunting him, Harrison had managed that smile. He enjoyed Michaela's reactions, watching her deal with the heat running between them. "It's always better to come at me swinging, isn't it? I wonder why."

Her answer cruised at him like a body-heat missile. "You've made me take off my heels. That ruins the hemline of this dress."

He studied the long, lean line of the simple designer gown, the dip and curve of it, the gentle caress on her hips before pooling almost to the floor. "You don't like looking up at me or standing too close, so close that I can almost feel the heat in you. Why?"

"Stop pushing me." She'd hurried away, her color rising, her hand sweeping upward. Her fingers smoothed that shining twist of hair he wanted to unfurl.

Now, standing beside Michaela, he studied the crowd. Faith and Jacob stood together, holding hands studying Michaela's paintings. Roark was easing away from a Seattle news hound who wanted to touch and explore the cowboy she'd just found. Michaela's choice of guests was meticulous, a blend of wealth and power, and she'd charmed them, moving through the groups, in perfect harmony with her role as hostess, seducing them into contributing for the public spots and expensive ads. Tax write-offs appealed, but so did the glamour Michaela brought with her. Affiliate station executives were interested enough by her invitations to leave the comfort of their homes and offices to travel to rural Wyoming.

Harrison leaned back into the shadows, studying the man who had just lifted his wine glass to Michaela in a toast. Aaron Gallagher was not like the others at the party, simply wanting to make a profit or use the money as a tax write-off. He wasn't like Victoria's group, drawn by social clout. Harrison recognized the dangerous look of a shark, the brutality and cunning buried beneath the custom tailored clothing. Gallagher wanted Michaela, his eyes following her as she worked the crowd, her sultry laughter flowing over the rumble of conversation.

Good old-fashioned lust was something Harrison recognized. He knew the impact of Michaela's body against his, that need to take, to possess, to make love to her until she couldn't think of leaving him.

But Gallagher—his bodyguards waiting outside in the long limousine—wanted more than sex. He was fascinated by the Langtry coin, his questions shielded but underlaid with purpose. What did he really want?

Harrison took a step forward as Gallagher smoothed the coin on Michaela's chest, talking intimately with her. As if sensing Harrison's primitive instincts to protect her, Gallagher's cold blue gaze swung to meet Harrison's and his veneer slid away. He was a fighter, sizing up another man, estimating his danger and power. Harrison lifted his glass in a toast, not bothering to spare a smile. Gallagher's mouth curved then, just that telling smirk that said he'd come for more than the party. His shielded gaze slid to Culley, standing at the door. Gallagher's look said he recognized Culley as a hard man to fight, and one he wanted to test.

Silent and uncomfortable in his worn cheap jacket and jeans, Culley had come for Michaela, for Faith and Jacob Langtry. His black eyes met Harrison's, and whatever clung to Culley, whatever dark secrets he held, surfaced for a heartbeat. Then he turned to meet Gallagher's steady appraisal and his expression shifted to hard and cold.

As if sensing he was under consideration, Culley's gaze cut back to Harrison. Harrison frowned slightly, rubbing his nose. He'd seen Culley looking at him like that before, as if trying to picture another image. Then Culley, a loner uncomfortable with a crowd, lifted his head and Michaela, sensitive to the moods in the room, caught his look.

Culley nodded and Michaela smiled warmly as if she understood that he'd come to show his support of her, but now he was finished with too many people, too many words and meanings he didn't like. Harrison noted that Culley's appreciative gaze swept down Michaela's clinging turquoise gown, but nothing sensual had passed between them. Harrison hadn't expected that jolt of jealousy until he realized that his muscles were tensed, his nerves edgy. He settled back into the shadows of the room and watched Michaela smile brilliantly at an investor, laughing at something he'd said.

Harrison preferred her wide-open emotions, not the glossy ones she served other men. Whatever ran between them was true and solid, a simmering fire. He nodded at the look she flashed him, that hot, steamy look as if she'd like to tear into him. She frowned slightly, indicating that he should circulate in the party. He smiled mildly back at her, refusing to be pushed more than he already had been.

Culley silently opened the door and made his escape into the night, and Jacob came to stand beside Harrison. "Gallagher is a hard man. He doesn't fit the rest."

"Most of my investors grew up with money, and some are self-made. But Gallagher has come up the hard way and it shows. Michaela's profile of him on the guest list said he's from San Francisco. He'd seen a promotional film clip and called Michaela. He wanted to invest in our fine arts project, to come here and see what we're doing." Harrison spoke too quietly, searching through his dark thoughts of Gallagher's real reasons for attending.

Jacob studied the younger man. With glancing interest, in the manner of a man who appreciated women, Harrison considered a buxom blonde, generous hips swaying through the room. Then he focused on Michaela, watching her, following her progress as she circulated with the guests. Jacob had tracked Faith like that. He found her now, dressed in a simple black dress and the strand of pearls he'd given her. Her blue eyes turned and locked with his and though their hunger didn't rage as feverishly as it had, it simmered between them.

He found his daughter in the crowd, wondering how he could have sired such beauty and intelligence—but then, he thought with a rueful smile, look at her mother. When Michaela turned, her gaze locking with Harrison's, the slow burn, the sizzling tension between his daughter and a man he respected, ricocheted across the room. Michaela looked quickly away, her hand trembling as it moved upward, smoothing the sleek coil of hair at her nape. Jacob smiled in the shadows. The boy had her thinking, wary of him, and when the two tangled— The match was a good one, but not an easy ride—just as Jacob's capture of his bride years ago. The Langtrys weren't exactly a gentle breed, but when love ran true, they knew and cherished it.

Gallagher also watched Michaela, and Jacob didn't like thinking of that man near his daughter, putting his hand on her bare shoulder. "His interests aren't in public television spots or in ads or in giving media students an opportunity to intern. I don't like him eyeing my daughter or my wife. He's got an odd feel to him, like a hunter tracking the prey, playing with it before the kill. He wants to know far too much about our family. And yours."

Roark flipped an olive high and then caught it in his teeth. "His men are packing Automatics."

Harrison smoothed his broken nose. Gallagher was

playing games, and he'd play rough. He'd focused on the Langtrys, especially Michaela. He'd be coming after her and whatever else he wanted.

Harrison wasn't letting that happen.

"Perfect," Aaron said to himself as his limousine glided over the rough road leading from Kane's ranch. "The woman needs taming, with just enough spirit to be interesting. She's wearing one of the coins and I'll bet the rest of the family has theirs. That woman, Silky, was easy, telling me what I wanted to know. She says Jacob and Roark both wear their coins—she's seen them. With my coin and the one from the crazy Mrs. Kane, add those to Michaela's and theirs and the whole ball game is mine. . . . Kane is suspicious, but I've dealt with men like him before. He'll take the money and— Ricco, why are you stopping?"

"Big horse, boss . . . standing in front of the car. The rider looks like a guy who means business."

Aaron stepped out of the limousine as Harrison was swinging down from his horse. "Nice party," Aaron said, and wondered if he'd misjudged the other player for the woman, the man who probably currently shared her bed. That would change.

In the moonlight, his white dress shirt turned back at the forearms, his tie dangling beside his unbuttoned collar, Harrison didn't look like the corporate banker. He looked tough, the planes of his face jutting and hard, the wind whipping at his hair. He had the narrowed look of a seasoned brawler, and for an instant, Aaron's street-tough blood heated, wanting to prove that he was still "top dog." But he could wait. He wanted to enjoy the game, see if the story Julia Kane had told was true—how she'd stolen a Langtry baby—Kane's half-sister.

"Let's get to the point," Harrison stated. "You're not here out of generosity."

Gallagher threw his cigar to the damp Wyoming earth and frowned when it landed in a pile of horse dung. He detested the country and the bumpkins trying to rule it. Harrison Kane was no easy match, though, and Aaron toyed with the idea of tangling with him. He really enjoyed beating that last hired sparring partner to a pulp. Kane could expect the same thing, if he didn't watch it. "My contribution is hefty."

"It will be mailed back to you."

Aaron stiffened; his days of being looked down on were over. "Take it easy, bub. You don't know what you're saying."

Harrison glanced at the two men moving toward him. "It's time you left."

Aaron wanted to beat him, a man with class and arrogance, to make him beg. "What will your girl-friend say about that? She was more than happy with my contribution to public funding."

Harrison's expression went flat, giving away nothing, his blood running cold and furious. Men like Gallagher would use a woman to get what they wanted, no holds barred. "She's a sensible woman."

"Is she as good in bed as she looks? Don't answer

that. I'll find out for myself. You know, Kane, I could ruin you. You've got a lot on the line with this project. It's better to play ball with me, if you know what I mean. Your family history isn't exactly sweet and it wouldn't be difficult to damage you with your fancy investors. Not difficult at all." Aaron slid into his car, closed the door, then rolled down the tinted window. "Call me anytime, Kane. No offense taken. You're like me. You want, you take. You didn't pull yourself out of the muck by playing nice. We understand each other."

When Gallagher's limousine glided off into the night, Harrison swung up on into the bare back of his gelding. "I knew a man like you once. I didn't like him. But I'm just enough like him to understand you—that you want more than a tax write-off."

Inside Harrison's house, Michaela was saying good-bye to the last of the guests. She kissed Silky and Jon, and Dwight winced when she hugged him. She beamed as Jon hugged Harrison, who managed a thin smile. She closed the door and turned to Harrison, her eyes alight. "We did it! We did it!"

Still thinking about Aaron Gallagher and what he really wanted, Harrison unbuttoned his shirt, letting it hang open. He rubbed his fingers across the hair on his chest. He'd had enough of smiling at people he didn't know, didn't want to know. He'd tolerated all the polite conversation he could take. He'd finished watching Michaela's curved body lean too close to too many men, of wondering if he would let Faith down—Michaela's light kiss tore him from brooding about Gallagher and the night. He frowned. "Hmm?"

Michaela grabbed his hands and danced around him. She paused to lift the bear claw necklace from her and drape over his head. "The party. We've got columnist interest, more ads, more investors. Our first event is a success!"

She danced around him again and the soft, pale flow of her breasts above the turquoise material stunned him. "You're not wearing a thing under that dress," he noted unsteadily.

"Not a thing. The fabric is lined, and underwear makes ridges."

"Michaela—" Harrison's arms closed around the woman who had just leaped upon him, hugging him. Then he stopped thinking about Gallagher and the station and the corporation. Michaela's expression had changed from jubilant to soft curiosity, her body warm and throbbing against his. She stroked his hair just once, her scent curling around him, taunting him. Her soft, slumberous gaze traced his face, settled upon his lips, and the world shook around them, spinning, heating.

Her breath came quickly, hurrying to caress his skin as his fingers opened to span her lower back, the womanly curves softening against him, her breasts pressed against his chest. With a groan, tossing away years of restraints, he simply dived into the taste and feel of Michaela, easing his fingers through her hair to release it, tossing away the confining pins. His hands framed her face, anchoring her for his mouth.

No man had demanded that she claim him, that she equal his desire. Until now, she realized distantly, she hadn't been held as if nothing could tear her away. Those hard lips didn't take as she wanted. They cruised and heated and nibbled; his breath mingled with hers, taking away a part of her she didn't understand.

She sucked in air, her head back, her body taut against his, hot and warm. She needed his mouth, needed his arms, her lower body already melting, his thighs thrusting against hers.

Michaela fought for more air, for sanity and found pleasure instead as Harrison held her face, her mouth aching for the full impact of his.

"Is this what you want?" he asked huskily, before sealing her parted mouth with his. She'd thought he'd be gentle and meticulous. Then his tongue came nudging entrance and he slanted her head, positioning her for a tighter fit as if nothing could tear him away from her. She shook, wanting more, wanting him full and hard within her, the thunder rolling in her blood, the lightning flashing behind her lids. He demanded and she gave; she asked and he breathed unevenly against her, his skin rough and flushed and sensitizing her own. Her body's needs ran on, tumbling, heating, aching until the taut cords hummed within her. "Harrison—"

His thumbs cruised her cheekbones and the kiss softened, seduced, his parted mouth roaming her chin, her nose, her lashes. "Do you want me, darling?" he asked against her mouth, swollen and sensitized now. "This would be so easy, wouldn't it? To bed good old Harrison while you're riding high on success. A little toss in the hay to relieve the pressure?"

Somewhere on that ledge of hunger, of wanting him desperately, to feel her body match his, Michaela paused. He held her face firmly now, watching her eyes as they drifted open. Through layers of sensual heat and confusion, she focused on those cool, steel gray eyes, that hard, rugged face. "What do you mean?"

"I mean," he paused to nibble gently at her lips, "that I don't intend to be used for occasional sex, for filling a need you may or may not have at the moment."

She stared at him blankly, marking the heat of his face, that angry slash of his eyes, the emotions riding him. "You're not unaffected."

"No, I'm not. But I'm wanting more, Michaela."

He held her when she would have shoved away. He wrapped her tight against him when she would have kicked him, held her hair to prevent her from biting him. Harrison was the one man who could both tempt and infuriate her. "I'm old-fashioned, sweetheart. We're going to play this my way."

She'd danced away from light flirtations; Dolph was her first and only lover, but she wouldn't let Harrison know that. She wouldn't let Harrison know how he had just paled her relationship with a man she'd intended to marry. Kissing Harrison was like stepping inside a hot tornado, having no control over the outcome. He'd want too much, demand too much. And he was too thorough, a strategic player. "I prefer to pick my lovers."

"You just did." Like a vow his stark words hit the empty room, cluttered with wine glasses and crumpled napkins and hors d'oeuvre platters.

Michaela inhaled sharply, catching that dark scent she knew as Harrison's alone. She glanced at the bear claw necklace resting on his chest; the image suited him now—raw, savage, wildly masculine, powerful, and man enough to fight to keep her. She wasn't prepared for his tender kiss, for the way his arms closed around her, fitting her to his body as if for a lifetime. "Take a memo," she whispered, as his hands caressed her back, flowing over her hips and cupping her bottom lightly. "I'm not that easy."

He grinned down at her, patting her backside as he eased away. "Tell me something new, darling."

Michaela couldn't have him taking her lightly. She rubbed away the too familiar touch of his hands.

"Don't shut me off," she said, as Harrison stood, the bear claw necklace looking deadly and fierce on his bare chest. He thumbed through papers on his desk. She swept toward him, and lifted Zachariah's trophy from him. She didn't want Harrison to have any part of her, of her life.

"Be logical," Harrison said too coolly, as if he'd never held her, never kissed her with that heat pouring from him, never captured her hard and tight against him. "You're exhausted and so am I. It's not the best time to wage an argument. I'll see you in the morning. We'll compare notes on potential backers and by the way, I'm returning Aaron Gallagher's contribution."

"*What?* I spent hours on the telephone, getting to his checkbook. *I cultivated that support money.*"

"Men like him always want something. You, for instance, and the coin you're wearing."

Michaela's fingers shook as she picked up a glass and poured wine into it. She remembered how Aaron had been interested in her Langtry coin, asking about the history. He'd wanted a memory of the night, he'd said, lightly probing as to the cost of the medallion she wore. She'd refused, of course and he'd laughed, saying he understood. "I'm certain he's only interested in the legends—in the history of our family."

Harrison lifted an eyebrow. "He wants you in his bed, Michaela. And he wants something else."

"I don't think so. He said he was looking for a good tax write-off. I believe him."

Harrison rubbed his hand across his bare chest again, and the liquid, sensual pull surged up to tighten Michaela's body. "Are you going to kiss me goodnight before you leave?" he asked quietly. "Or are you afraid?"

Harrison willed his heart to stop pounding so fast, his body to cool, to force that hot blood back into the logic he preferred. One taste of Michaela had set him off, the barriers down, and he wanted more than one feverish night from her. He wanted the woman inside—valiant, caring, tender, running true to herself, loving deeply, and fiercely dedicated to her family. He'd known her forever, and she wasn't certain of herself now, of who she was—of what he wanted. The soft warm feel of her body taunted his now, the ache painfully lodged low in his belly. Pulling himself back from the edge, pretending to give his attention to the papers stacked in his work area had cost him; his hand trembled, a visible sign that she'd aroused him.

He scrubbed his hands over his face. He was too tired to think clearly. Running on little sleep, working at the bank and the station and continuing to meet the demands of his corporation, had taken every drop of endurance, of energy. Tonight's party added to the weight. Once Michaela and the Langtry family discovered—if they ever did—that his father. . . . Meanwhile he had to face his own conscience and the knowledge that his mother and father had torn Michaela's family part.

"Goodnight, Harrison. Have fun cleaning up," she said coolly across the room, though fury burned in her low, husky tones.

But he was moving swiftly through the kitchen and out the back door. Michaela looked down at the bear claw necklace, resisting the need to follow him. Then the solid rhythmic whack of an ax biting into wood told her that Harrison fought his demons. She tossed the necklace aside and followed him into the night. He'd discarded his expensive shirt and tie and she held them close, protectively against her. "You're not him, Harrison. You didn't rob, cheat, or embezzle. You're not accountable for what your father did."

His body gleamed with sweat now, powerful muscles sliding, gleaming in the moonlight, the ax raising and falling faster. Wood chips flew into the air, just as his emotions were doing—had done when he was fifteen and when he was eighteen and had just discovered his father's suicide. Michaela wanted to keep him safe, just as she had then. She wanted to bring him back from the shadows, to distract him, to give him—

She moved quickly to the moonlit daisies, picking a bouquet. She held it out to him, but kept a respectable distance from the wooden chips flying through the air. "Harrison."

He suddenly hurled the ax into the old weather boards of a shed, the blade sticking deep. "I could be like him. Worse."

"No, you could never be like him. He liked to hurt, to twist people, to use them."

Harrison breathed roughly, dragging huge breaths that caused his sweat-beaded chest to rise and fall, his fists tight at his sides. The sight of him vulnerable, questioning, fighting a hell she did not understand, tore at her. "I could fail," he said unevenly. "This little television station went to market, this little—"

The bouquet of daisies hit him in the face. He didn't seem to see them for a moment, and to distract him, she took one and placed it over one ear, and then the other. "Hey. You've got me, remember. I'm not going to let you down."

"Daisies . . . a bouquet," he muttered, raising a hand to feel the one over his ear.

"Haven't you ever had a girl give you a bouquet, Harrison?"

She had his attention now, the distraction too complete, because now he was focused on her. "No. I never have."

She tried to shove away that burning intensity, that familiar shiver running over her body, every pore aware of him. "I'll bet you've given plenty of flowers."

He shook his head, then carefully took one daisy and eased it down between her breasts. He bent slowly to kiss her there, nuzzling the gentle rise of her breasts on each side. "No."

She couldn't breathe now, her heart racing out of control, her knees weakening. "You've had—"

"No." He straightened, studying her. "There wasn't time or money. I shared an apartment with a girl in college. We were both struggling, the arrangement was more of a convenience than an affair. I liked her. She could cook. She fell in love . . . not with me. End of story."

She'd thought that he'd had affairs, but she didn't want details. Thinking of Harrison making love to another woman nettled slightly. "You didn't have to tell me that."

He took the bouquet and tore away the long stalks, placing the flowers in her hair. He smoothed a tendril back from her cheek and framed her hot cheek with his hand. "I wanted you to know. I don't give myself easily. Neither do you. I can feel you burning, Michaela. I can feel you softening. You're very sensual, very feminine."

The intimate tenderness was so unlike the Harrison she knew. "Tell me why you look at my mother like you do. What happened between you?"

"Always seeking an opportunity to push, hmm, Michaela?" Harrison's fingers slid under the gown's strap on her shoulder, easing it slowly aside. He kissed the bare skin, flicking his tongue over it until she shivered. "I'd like to feel you against me. All that softness close and warm against me."

"No—"

He pushed aside the other strap until the gown barely clung to her body, sliding fractionally as she breathed deeply. The choice was hers; Harrison watched her closely and she knew that one word would stop him. He placed one hand over her breast, cupped and shaped it over the fabric. "What are you feeling now, Michaela? Why is your heart beating like a trapped rabbit's? Frightened of what might happen between us?"

"Harrison—" She dug her fingers into his wrists, needing his strength to support her.

His finger roamed across the fabric covering her breasts, then gently tapped the daisy slowly downward. She couldn't breathe as her gown slid to her waist, leaving her naked to those silvery eyes burning down her body. She shivered, uncertain of him, of herself, wanting him against her, within her, that hard body thrusting—

His fingertips smoothed her cheeks. "You're holding me very tightly, Michaela. Please be gentle."

"Oh, shut up and kiss me," she whispered finally, giving way to the need within her, and locked her arms around his shoulders. His chest burned her, pressed hard and warm against her, the wedge of hair erotically seductive against her breasts. She found his mouth, wound her fingers in his hair to tether him, and took the kiss she wanted.

His trembling hands opened on her body, caressed every line, shaped her waist and smoothed the material covering her hips. When she ached for more, moving restlessly against him, aware only of his breath upon her, his body taut against hers, Harrison shaped her breasts gently with one hand, the other riding low to press her hips against him.

His body shook, his breath rough against her cheek, his mouth slanting for a tighter fit. Then both hands slid beneath her, to lift and press her intimately against him. She held him tight, feeling as if the earth was spinning away and the only safety was in Harrison's arms.

But he wasn't safe. He wasn't safe at all. With a shudder, Michaela lifted her head to study him. She tugged back his hair. He'd look like that while making love, his blunt features taut, his eyes slitted, his jaw taut and his mouth swollen with her kisses. "I don't quite know how to get out of this, but—"

His face lowered to nuzzle her breasts, nudging aside the Langtry coin to find her flesh. The tender, intimate tone in his voice was that of pleasure and discovery. She was shaking now, caught on a ledge of unwanted need. "I can feel your blush . . . all over."

"I think you'd better put me down."

"When I'm ready. You feel good, very good," he murmured and grinned at her.

She hadn't expected that devastating, roguish grin, the magic catching her. "You can't stand here with me . . . ah, holding me up here all night. No, don't look."

He closed his eyes and his hands caressed her bottom. "Okay. I'll feel."

His fingers were sliding closer to her— "Let me down," she managed to whisper shakily.

Harrison's drawl was too sensual, packed with a lazy ease of a man wanting to make love slowly, thoroughly. "Let's talk about it. What are your terms? What have you got to offer?"

"Harrison!"

His low growl was impatient and frustrated, but he kept his eyes closed as he lowered her to the ground. She grabbed her gown, held it against her breasts as she quickly scooped up his shirt and buttoned it. Harrison opened his eyes just as her gown slithered to the earth. That hot, smoky lick of desire slammed into her as he breathed unevenly, staring at the pooled turquoise material. That slow ride of his gaze lifted, caressing her bare legs, pausing at her breasts, then slowly, darkly tasted her lips and electricity danced along her skin: the slow liquid heat tugged at her lower stomach, weakening her legs.

"I wouldn't hurt you," Harrison said finally, the rough edge of frustrated desire scraping at the soft night.

"I know. You wouldn't. I trust you in some ways."

She'd always trusted him to be gentle and kind, to hold that darkness within him and not release it to hurt others.

"In what way don't you trust me?" He whipped the words into the night air, cutting into the scents of the wild flowers and freshly chopped wood.

"I don't trust what is happened now, between us. Intimacy isn't easy for me. Or for you. I can't handle more complications. And you are definitely complicated. This is what you do, isn't it? Chop wood when you're in a mood, when whatever is riding you devours your control? The calluses on your hands say paper isn't all you handle."

"I haven't paid much attention to what a woman wants or feels before. It's very important that I understand what pleases you and what—damn it, Michaela. You're not the average woman. I never understood women anyway. You're fragile and sweet and yet tough. You're like a diamond with different facets shooting off into the sunlight at any moment. . . . I want to be under you, over you, in you. Is that so hard to understand?" He opened his hands, studied the broad expanse and power of them. "I wouldn't hurt you," he repeated. "I would try not to. I'd kill myself if I did," he said more firmly, as if questioning and fighting what ran within him.

Her body jerked, remembering the gentle caress of his open hands along her skin, the cherishing of them as he touched her, the reverence. She'd never been held or touched like that before and with just one step toward him, with just one kiss— Her nerves dancing, her senses simmering with the need to step back into Harrison's arms, Michaela knew that once that barrier had been breached, he'd want more—too much more. Harrison was very meticulous about keeping what he acquired. She kicked the gown with her bare foot. "That cost a fortune. I'd never worn it before. I was saving it for—never mind the reason. You can pay for the dry cleaning and repair, and don't have it done here in Shiloh. That's all I need—for the local dry cleaners to know—never mind. Okay, you can open your eyes now."

Michaela hurried to the house. At the back steps, she turned to him. "You're not to blame for anything, Harrison. You're not like him. You're not going to fail Kane Corporation or let your investors down."

His answer was grim and cold in the summer night. "You have no idea what a Kane can do."

"I know what you can do." Because she wanted to hold him—he looked so alone in the moonlight— Michaela feared that Harrison already held a part of her. She had never really opened the tender, soft part of her heart as she had with him, never really trusted anyone else.

That he did not return her trust, after all those years of sparring, of testing each other, hurt her. There had been a basic trust, and now Harrison wouldn't share the darkness that had begun that night—when he'd appeared at her house, his nose bloodied and broken.

She hurried into the house, racing from herself, from him. She grabbed the bear claw necklace, the primitive image of it around Harrison's throat jarring her for an instant. She hadn't suspected that dark power, the hunter in him, the elemental male seeking her. She hurried out the front door, leaping into her S.U.V. Her hand shook so badly she couldn't easily fit the key into the ignition. It wasn't until she got home and Jacob raised his eyebrows that she remembered she was wearing only Harrison's shirt and the Langtry medallion.

Culley jerked open his door, welcoming the stark simplicity of his small home. Forty acres bordering Langtry property wasn't much, but it was all his. He'd never had a home before this one, even as a kid. He tore off his jacket and unbuttoned his shirt, freeing himself from the unfamiliar tethers. Before he knew it, the whiskey bottle was in his trembling hand, snatched from the shelf where he'd placed it.

A bastard who didn't know his father's name, he'd taken his mother's—Blackwolf—and he'd known nothing but trouble until he'd come to Shiloh.

He recognized the look of Gallagher, that narrowed thoughtful hunter look, seeking out the victims. That look sized up the fighters, the competition, homing in on what he wanted—the weakness and the strengths of those protecting it.

Gallagher had that bull-of-the-woods look, a bully wanting to test himself, and he'd come calling for Culley—it took a barroom brawler to recognize one.

Not that Culley worried about his hide; he worried

about the Langtrys, because a man like Gallagher couldn't leave good people alone.

Culley looked at the amber liquid, the whiskey calling to him, and placed it firmly back on the shelf, unopened. Jacob Langtry had seen him through a few rough nights, and Culley wasn't repaying that good man and his family by drinking his way back to hell.

He looked around at the small house Roark had helped him build. Meticulously clean, barren except for his few essentials, it was his. Roark's cabin across the way had been Zachariah's first home. Roark kept his wedding band on the same chain as the Langtry coin, and his home was still a shrine to his wife.

Culley breathed slowly, wondering what it would be like to hold a woman and love her, wide-open, and know that she loved him back. Unless he missed his guess, Harrison was going to know that feeling, because Michaela Langtry was a firebrand when she was stirred up.

He stretched his taut muscles, unused to the confinement of chitchat and too much talk. He'd dreamed about Michaela for a while, but he knew she wasn't for him.

He rubbed his hand across his heart when the pain lay deep and strong. He knew what he was and it wasn't much past being a good ranchhand. But he wasn't drinking anymore. He wasn't finding himself in a back alley brawl and he wasn't going back to where he'd been—a man for hire, no home, no life.

The Langtrys had given him a good look at what a home and a family should be.

They were going to need him when Gallagher came calling . . . and Culley would be there for them.

Soft-ly, slow-ly . . . the mornin' will creep. . . . The woman wrapped her bony fingers around her arms and stalked the institution's cell as she hummed the Langtry lullaby. Julia Kane liked the Gallagher boy who shared her crafts time. Paul's brother, Aaron, had wanted to talk with her. Aaron had something in him that was dark and hurtful and she didn't trust him; he reminded her of another man she'd hated. *Who was it?*

Somehow Aaron had gotten the coin they had taken away from her and he'd brought it to her, for her to remember. She'd wanted him to have it, because it was bad and he was bad. It hurt her hand, burned her flesh, though there was no mark. She heard voices rush through her head like a cold wind. Aaron had seen that she was moved to a more comfortable room. He promised to check on her investments—to keep her bills paid, to see to the executor watching her accounts.

She knew her mind danced between reality and darkness. In her lucid moments—which were becoming less frequent—she feared the other, of what she was. Who was she now? Mary Talbert? Leonora Black? Was she a bookkeeper, a courthouse file clerk, a banker's assistant?

She rubbed her temples, the roles and names she'd

used swirling inside her brain, hurting her. Then one name snagged and she slid into being Julia Kane. Julia Kane had known that her mind was slipping; she'd committed herself, but only after acquiring a lawyer she could manage. She'd chosen the sanatorium well, the administrator agreeing to keep her records under yet another identity very private—for a fee. There were always fees, and she had paid them. She served her keepers' pocketbooks as long as they cared and protected her. Tit for tat. What was the name she'd used on the sanatorium records? Julia Monroe?

Julia shook her head. It didn't matter. The nurses and doctors called her the name she wished: "Julia Kane." She was brilliant in her lucid moments, protecting herself against the weaknesses when it came. But the weakness, the sucking dark well was visiting her more frequently. In and out, in and out. Now she was Julia Kane—

Julia Kane had once had money, and the incredible talent for investing. A long time ago, she'd had jewels and cash and she'd begun a new life with them. Julia had learned how to create new identities and how to leave them—there were convenient manuals everywhere. Her mind whipped through the columns of figures, the paperwork her power-of-attorney lawyer showed her. He might have signed the investment papers, but he didn't doubt her choices. She was worth a small fortune now, her care insured. Her attorney was making money every time she picked a stock or sold her investments; he was filling his pockets and would take good care of her. She wouldn't miss the gold coin she'd kept as a souvenir.

The baby had been too much trouble though and— Julia frowned, trying to push through the cobwebs of time. *Where was the baby?*

No matter, Julia thought, the Langtry baby didn't matter; the coin had hurt her, and she was glad to be rid of it.

Paul Gallagher reminded her of a small boy, the memory hazy. Though the room was not cold, she shivered. The small boy haunted her, reminded her of a man she didn't like, a cruel man. She cackled then, glad she'd hurt the man, taking away the baby he'd prized, his unlawful seed with Faith Langtry.

eight

Fog layered the dueling oaks at midnight, torches lighting the distance between the man who had laughed at my wife's honor and myself. With a blast of sulfur and thunder, he lost his life, the lawman who thought himself above harm.

'Twas no faint-hearted lady who covered my back, who rode behind me that night, making for the mountains, safety and life. The law would not set gently on my side, not with his ruffian friends calling me out, wanting to blacksnake my hide. She shared that pitiful journey back to our wilderness home, complaining not at all.

She has locked her mind upon uniting the coins and I believe she honors me by carrying my child.

Zachariah Langtry's Journal

Too restless to sleep, too furious with herself for not understanding her emotions concerning Harrison, Michaela swung down from Diamond's saddle at three o'clock in the morning. The former Atkins property was small, perfect, and she'd spent the last of her money on a down payment. In a five-acre field, the burros were grazing, descended from those abandoned by miners long ago. A small fruit orchard badly needed tending, and the shamble of herbs and roses around the house led into a garden that hadn't been tilled or planted, the picket fence leaning and weathered.

Michaela rubbed her hands across her face, then slid the key into the old brass lock. She'd always loved the tiny house, and she needed privacy. Her mother was uneasy and worried about her, and her father's sleep disturbed by Michaela's restless midnights. She'd lived alone too long, because those two years with Dolph hadn't been a sharing—they had been more like reflections of what suited them for a career partner. She'd protected her safety by subconsciously choosing a man who did not stir her emotionally—and very little physically when compared to Harrison.

Tonight, Harrison had just thrown her an unexpected curve. *She hadn't expected that heat, the wild churning of her body, that softening and melting hunger—he'd held her tight, when she would have moved away, setting his own terms for that mind-blowing, intimate kiss.*

She hadn't expected the rough, stark demand, a

man who knew what he wanted, his body hardening intimately against her. For just that moment, Harrison's cool shields were torn away, and she'd tasted a wild erotic heat that had frightened her.

Under the bald lightbulbs, the linoleum flooring was worn and discolored. The kitchen cupboards needing replacement, the sink chipped, the old gas stove—Michaela considered it carefully. It was a beautiful chrome and enamel gas stove, dusty and badly needing cleaning, but huge and dependable and complete with ovens and warming shelves. It was solid and meant to last, just as everything was in Shiloh. "I think I love you," Michaela whispered and with a grin, mocked her lack of cooking experience.

The wallpaper on the two bedrooms was faded and peeling, one room small and perfect for an office, overlooking the pasture where the burros now grazed. Michaela inhaled sharply, a framed newspaper picture, faded with time hung on the wall. It left a light square when she lifted it away from the wall. Elijah Akins, a collector of mountainman memorabilia, had adored Zachariah. The picture, taken from the newspaper's archives, had been cut from the centennial issue. It showed Shiloh's Founding Families Celebration and featured Zachariah, dressed in full leather fringes, wearing an elegant pristine dress shirt, and knee-high calvary boots polished until they gleamed. The bear claw necklace and a Langtry coin gleamed on his chest, tucked into the wide leather belt at his waist were crossed dueling pistols. His "long rifle" was held at one side, and his other arm circled Cleopatra's shoulders. She was dressed in the blue silk gown Zachariah had described, and another Langtry coin gleamed on her lace bodice.

Holding the framed picture, Michaela walked to the back porch and sat on the steps. What was it about Cleopatra that had always—? The moon was still bright and she recognized her brother's large shadow gliding by in the night. "Roark what are you doing here? Come sit by me."

"I saw lights. I like this place . . . it's got a warm, homey feel to it. You made a good choice."

"My work hours are too unscheduled now. I need this—privacy, rebuilding. It feels like love passed through it, grew, and remained, hoping for another chance to bloom." Michaela ached for her brother, always restless, prowling the night. She handed him the picture frame with the faded photograph. "Why do you go to the mountains, Roark? What makes us so restless?"

"My wife and child lie up there."

She leaned her head against his shoulder, a younger brother that had grown into a tall, strong man, circled with shadows. "And something else?"

He studied the picture. "Cleopatra fought to bring back the coins to the family. And she did. She lost her ruby wedding ring—Zachariah's mother's ring—a poaching raven stole it and flew toward the mountains. She strapped on her revolver and went after it, nearly driving Zachariah mad with worry. He tells about it in his journal, how they battled. Her journal is up there too, hidden somewhere. I think it would give her ease to know that you and Mom have a part of her, know her thoughts, and that the ring was returned to the family."

"Roark, there's no way you can find either one. You're a romantic." Michaela kissed his cheek.

"Tell me you're not," he returned, nudging her with his shoulder. "I'm a Langtry, and if Cleopatra can reclaim Langtry goods, then I can, too. You look like Cleopatra in a way, when you're not taut and angry with yourself, feeling like you've failed. But you've got a bit of old Zachariah's temper when you're stirred up . . . and Harrison is doing plenty of that, isn't he? He's got you on the run and you don't like someone else making rules for you."

"Harrison Kane is bull-headed, arrogant, swaggering, and—" Harrison was no easy man. He'd set terms between them, just as Roark had said. Harrison moved into emotions she hadn't wanted to explore, that she feared. She wasn't certain of herself on those levels, the dark simmering ones that said he could take her heart. Michaela resented the memory of his kiss, that stark hunger, the fiery shaft of heat he could draw from her. His hands had opened on her possessively, splaying across her back and lower, pressing her intimately against him. She resented the knowledge that she hadn't really been held and desired, that all that had happened before was mechanical and cold, a dim simulation of the sensuality Harrison had drawn from her.

But she resented the tenderness most of all, the

fragile feminine feeling of being cherished by a man who could make her feel so much that he tore her from her safe, protected emotions.

"Whew! The image has changed. You used to call him 'nerd-boy.' From your reaction every time he came close tonight, I'd say our boy has you on the run. He's meticulous when he wants something. From the way he looks at you, I'd say it's only a matter of time before—"

"He hasn't got me running, and he's not our 'boy.' I grew up with him. I know him and I'm not about to enter a relationship with him. I will not come close to a man like him—do you know that he folds his socks, not balls them?"

"Now *that's* a reason to shoot a man." Roark's grin flashed in the darkness. "Sometimes we don't have a choice, sister dear."

"I do and so do you." Michaela inhaled the damp smell of fertile earth waiting to be planted. "I think we lost a feeling of safety the night Sable was taken. I did, anyway. Trust comes hard for me. A piece of Mom and Dad is missing, and I don't think we've ever completely healed. We're all hunting something, and there is something haunting me, as if I try hard enough I'll understand, I'll find the answers. It seems to me that if Cleopatra was strong enough to return the coins, then we should be able to resolve that night. I can't bear to listen to that old song—"

"It's time to stop blaming yourself for that night, for not getting up. You could have been taken, too . . . or worse."

"Not Maria. She loved us. I remember."

Roark was silent, watching the burros in the field. "Let it go, Michaela."

"I can't. It's like we were all torn apart that night. Mom, Dad, you, me."

Some things never change, Michaela thought the next day, as Jon placed cucumber slices over her lids to cool and refresh. Her eyes were tired from working at the computer all day. Roland's Funeral Home was quiet, Jon's parents relaxing in Tahoe at a funeral directors convention. As teens, they'd all gathered there when his parents were away. The music playing now wasn't for grieving, and Benny Goodman's dance band clarinet trilled through the somber room, alternating with a mix of Louis Prima and Sachmo Armstrong.

Michaela opened her lips to accept the straw Jon had placed against them. She sipped the Mai Tai. "I love you," she murmured as Jon tested her hardening facial mask.

"You needed this. You're wound too tight. Working like a dog," Jon said darkly.

"I think Michaela could use a little mattress dancing. I know I could," Silky stated. "I've tried to rattle Culley's cage a few times, but he passed. Didn't make a dent, even with my best red leather pants. Harrison's buns are so cute, when he bends over, I get all quivery. Don't they just do something to you, Michaela?" she teased. "Too bad all that beef is run by a cold calulator for a brain—"

"Shut up and drink your Mai Tai."

"Service over here, Jon," Marsha Jo—another friend of Michaela's—called. "This is the first time we've done this in years. It's my only night away from the kids and you're falling down on the job."

"Grump." Jon's good nature came from years of tending the women. "We haven't done this since Michaela was home from college. I'm a little out of practice. . . ."

Michaela let herself float in the familiar babble and thought of when she'd come from the news room, munching on a breakfast donut, reading her copy before air time. Harrison had been talking to a production tech, noting the cuts to pre-recorded film. He'd turned, that smoky heated gaze raking down her maroon suit, sliding almost like a caress down her legs to her high heels. A hot jolt danced across Michaela's skin and lodged deep within her, she recognized the sensation—the urge to push her fingers through that neat hair and claim that hard mouth causing her to tremble. Harrison stood too still, the air beating, tangibly warm and simmering between them. He'd caught her chin then, careful of her makeup, to brush his thumb at the corner of her lips—"Crumb," he'd explained, those cool gray eyes locking with hers. "Aren't you sleeping at night? Missing me?"

"If I wanted you, I'd have you," she'd returned breathlessly. "You're not on my menu."

"You're on mine," he'd murmured softly before turning away.

Furious with him, with her own need to kiss his

lips again, Michaela had punched his shoulder. He'd turned to her slowly, as if setting his own time, his own terms. "No, it's not sexual harassment. I know it, and so do you," he'd said, cutting her off, taking the wind out of her charge. "If you weren't so edgy around me, we'd be getting to know each other better. What is it, I wonder, that makes you so nervous around me?"

That hot smoky gaze had ripped down her body again, tearing at her control, her body already answering, melting to the heat of his. She'd dropped the donut and the napkin, her fingers trembling. Harrison had cursed, stooping to collect and toss them into the trash. "Go ahead. Run away, little girl."

Roark was dead wrong—she wasn't on the run from Harrison. Then she shivered and knew that Harrison was not a man to play games.

July settled over the alfalfa fields, the cattle grazed in the pastures, the vegetable gardens thrived. KANE was running semi-smoothly, thanks to a friend of Michaela's who'd stepped in to help. Josy Daniels, a petite blond who had lost her battle against the age and wrinkle stigmas of her longtime network, was happy to take the reins of the harness. Josy's capable presence allowed Michaela more time to renovate the basic needs of her new home.

At six o'clock in the morning, Michaela looked at the mountains in the distance; she listened to the new washer and dryer humming and leaned her palms against the sink. She'd scraped together a bit of peace by buying the house, working with her hands, scrubbing away dirt, and tearing out weeds when her moods drove her. She'd given away too much to her career and to the people who controlled her life. Reclaiming herself wasn't easy. Neither was the haunting sense that something waited for her amid the delicate Queen Anne's lace, the sunflowers and daisies, in the wild bramble of roses, the cottonwoods, firs and blue spruce forests, something called to her. There, she'd find badly needed answers to questions.

Michaela frowned at the bumble bee nagging the screen for entrance to the house. Harrison and she worked well together, each precise and controlled—until that heat flashed, that moment stood still and sparks caught between them. Wary of him, she rarely came close, but when she did, his unique scent plagued her for hours.

Michaela reached for the ringing wall telephone and Josy's husky tones purred over the line. "Big boss took off last night for a little rest in the mountains. Your brother delivered him up somewhere on Cutter Canyon. They were pulling a horse trailer, so that meant they'll be riding when the roads end. They must be going up that old canyon road. The state doesn't maintain it anymore because of the rockslide and snow avalanches. Harrison is camping and rafting down river, checking out the safety of your river kayaking and canoeing promo idea. You've got the next week off, too. He said you're looking tired. Boy, there is just nothing like having a man tell you you're aging and haggard, is there?"

"*He's what*? He's checking out my idea without me? I've worked on that idea for a solid two weeks. There are no white water rapids like those of Cutter Canyon, no smooth stretches of water, so clear you can—"

"Seems so. Hey, LeRoy and I could come over tonight and help you paint that picket fence if you want. Rather, LeRoy wants to do it. I'd like to sit on the front porch with you and enjoy the summer."

Michaela forced her tight fingers to ease around the telephone. "I won't be home, but I know LeRoy loves to putter, so stop by if you want. The key is under the front mat."

"Hot date?"

"You could say that. I'm going to go kill Harrison. That special was my idea. I wanted to plan the camera shots, the interview sites, the—talk with you later, Josy. I've got to go."

Harrison shaded his eyes against the bright early afternoon sun as he watched Michaela scramble down the rocky incline from the old state road to his campsite along Cutter River. Dressed in a bright yellow T-shirt, jeans, and hiking boots, she could take away a man's breath . . . and his heart. Sweating, panting, furiously eyeing him, already shouting threats at him, balancing a backpack, a sleeping bag, and a camera bag, there was no other woman like Michaela. He could have asked her to marry him then, to have his children.

Harrison blinked once, stunned that the gentler

thoughts roamed his heart while desire rode his body. He hadn't thought about children of his own, wasn't certain he was capable of loving, of cherishing.

He wasn't certain of himself with her, that he wouldn't hurt her. . . .

He desired the woman he could hurt most and guilt wasn't an easy shroud upon him. He'd kept secrets too long, hoarded them, trying to find the answers when there were none. His father had raped her mother; his mother had stolen the child resulting from that rape. He should have left, withdrawn all contact from the Langtrys. . . . But he couldn't. His investigations had hit a dead end years ago, but he was still trying. If one thread unraveled and the secret he'd carried with him since he was fifteen burst into light, the Langtrys would hate him.

The investigator's letter he had just received before leaving was probably just another wrong lead. Julia wouldn't be so obvious as to label a grave with the name "Sable Kane Langtry." Or would she? He'd learned enough about her to know that nothing was as Julia wanted it to appear. Just as he had the other trails, Harrison would visit the site and dig out the details, wary of their truth. But not now, not with Michaela Langtry in his immediate sights.

Truth: the need coursing heavily through him was old-fashioned and primitive, the need of a man to claim his woman. To make Michaela his. To hold her so tight, and bury himself so deep in her that they would be joined forever and nothing could come between them. He'd fight to win her, to keep her, to give her what she needed, and he wouldn't hurt her. The emotional gamble—balancing the dark secret he held and his instincts to cherish and love Michaela— was worth the torment.

Okay, he admitted. He needed a little encouragement from her. He wasn't that certain of Michaela, or her response to him. He'd wanted her to come after him, to need him, to ease the bruising of his ego. Other women—those few in his past—hadn't really mattered; he hadn't cared if they sought him, but it was important that Michaela come for him. He wanted time alone with her—he wanted her, bottom line.

"Harrison, I'm going to kill you. What gives you the right to take away a project I've been working on?" She steamed across the sand bar to him as he sat, tossing rocks in the gently churning water. She dropped her camera bag onto the sand and swung her backpack at him. Blocked by his arm, the pack fell at her feet. Off balance, she tripped, floundered, and fell onto her bottom in the creek.

He wanted to fall upon her, laugh and hold her and kiss her until they were both breathless and hungry and— But then he didn't know how to play those games, did he? Instead he reached out his hand, snagged her wrist and hefted her over his shoulder the few steps to the sandbar.

Michaela blinked at him. "You just manhandled me, Harrison. Picked me up and—what are you doing?" she asked as he dragged the small inflated raft close to the water and began loading his backpack and bedroll.

"Leaving. You can either climb back up that hill to Roark—he's waiting there to see what you do—or you can come with me. Which is it?" He wanted to be alone with her; she'd been dancing away from him since the party, since he'd seen her in the moonlight, kissed her breasts, longing to be inside her. . . .

The daisies had glowed in that silky black hair, the gentle night wind had webbed it across her cheek. His need of her was more than sensual, the stroke of his finger against her kiss, that sweet valley between her breasts, the soft flow of woman warm and melting within his arms. Michaela filled a part of him that had been empty forever; she was unafraid to meet him on a plane where no one else had dared.

At any moment, any part of the past could shatter her trust in him. Did he deserve that trust, and the Langtrys'? Maybe not, but his instincts told him that he could no more resist his desire for Michaela than he could stop breathing.

"It's a full two-day trip down the canyon. It's afternoon now and— That's overnight—two nights now, Harrison."

He treasured that wide clear blue gaze, the tilt of her head, the sunlight gleaming on her hair. Yet he wanted to be deep in her, consumed by her. Was that how his father had felt? That primitive, fierce need to take— Harrison breathed in sharply. He wasn't certain of his emotions, of how they could tangle and threaten his restraint when making love to Michaela—if she let him. With Michaela, the only thing that he knew for certain is that he wanted time alone with her, and he desired her. His emotions with Michaela were always too ready, and not exactly logical. He wasn't an instinctive man—yet with her . . . "True. People would talk. It's your choice."

Michaela breathed deeply, scanning the golden reflection of the sun on the swirling river. She turned her face to the wind that rushed through the willows, making them sway and sweeping her hair away from her face. "I missed this."

Harrison hadn't realized how uncertain he was of her until she waved to Roark, and his body relaxed.

They spoke little as the raft drifted on the gentle water, Michaela leaning back, almost dreamily, her fingers dragging in the clean water. Deer stopped drinking from the river, lifting their heads to watch the raft pass by. An occasional fish leaped in the river, feeding on the fat July insects, schools of tiny fish darting around the dark rocks. A hawk soared into the sky, a beaver lumbered near the tree he'd been gnawing. "This is good," Michaela said, her voice drowsy and soft. "Roark and Dad are placing bets on which one of us comes out alive. We don't exactly get along."

"We work together at the station. I let you bully me into that damned party. We haven't killed each other yet."

She laughed at that, the sound wild and free and happy. She reached to playfully ruffle his hair and Harrison dodged the touch. He wasn't certain about her mood, how to—

"Harrison, it's really a shame you weren't allowed to play, to be a child," she murmured, reaching more slowly now to smooth his hair. "You never came to the school dances, you never played football or baseball, or the other sports. They took too much away from you. It wasn't right."

"Would you have danced with me?"

She grinned and punched him lightly in the shoulder with the ease of a woman used to dealing with a brother. "Not me, nerd-boy."

His own smile surprised him, mocking her. "Liar. You would have dragged me out on the floor and taught me the latest steps and embarrassed me."

She laughed then, the sound ringing clear and free and rich in the afternoon light, the shadows of the pines and trembling aspens sliding across the smoothly flowing river. "Oh, yeah. I would have."

Howling through the black canyon rocks, sweeping down the deep gorge and whistling through the pine boughs, a sudden sweep of canyon wind lifted her hair. Michaela closed her eyes as though giving herself to the sound. "I've missed that. The sound of secrets. I've always felt that they were meant for me."

Roark swept his metal detector over the spot where he'd seen the big raven land, cawing at him, the human intruder. Attracted to pretty baubles, ravens were known to carry them miles away. The ring could be anywhere . . . Maybe Michaela was right, maybe he was a romantic, seeking Cleopatra's ring and her journal. But the hope and dream drove him, lured him like a siren to the mountains. Everything inside him told him that the ring and the journal were meant to be returned to Cleopatra's descendants. He lifted his face to the gentle mountain wind and the dappled sunlight passing through the trees and knew with certainty Cleopatra's treasures waited to be found.

His sister's temper had burned him on the way up the mountain. Strangling Harrison was at the top of her list. Or drowning him. Michaela's fierce, dark mood had stormed through the cab of his pickup. She saddled her horse expertly, not waiting for Roark as she set off those few miles to Cutter Canyon road to find Harrison.

From the look of Harrison earlier, that was just what he wanted.

Roark smiled at the chipmunk racing up a lodgepole pine. Michaela had always pushed Harrison, slashing at him, while she covered her emotions from other people. Roark doubted that the man who she'd trusted and who had deserted her had ever seen the real Michaela. Now Harrison had picked his time to claim her; he'd made her chose to come to him. Harrison was methodical, logical and he wanted Michaela. Roark wondered if Michaela knew how she watched Harrison, how she moved when he was near, as though every molecule of her body responded to him. They'd be battling now—sorting out the difference between longtime friends and the simmering heat between them. They were good for each other, Michaela wide-open, fiery, pushy when it came to Harrison. And Harrison moved steadily onward, circling her, maneuvering her. But there was no doubt that Harrison's emotions ran deep with Michaela, for there was a surprising tenderness within him as he watched her—as if he knew she would never fail those she loved, that her strength and beauty came from her heart and soul.

It was said that when the wild heart of a Langtry is captured, it will remain true forever . . . Roark's love had been gentler that what flew between Michaela and Harrison. Angelica wasn't that fiercely passionate, nor that difficult to understand and court. They'd simply come together as high school sweethearts, marrying later and sliding into a good life.

Roark frowned slightly. Whatever prowled dark and stormy within Harrison, the Langtry family was a part of it.

A big black bear, lumbering through the brush in search of summer berries, sniffed at the air, catching the human's scent. Roark stood still, eyes lowered, not challenging the bear's territory. A bigger bear than this had met Zachariah's blade, but Roark was not eager to be mauled now. The revolver strapped low on his thigh would be little resistance. The raven flew up high, perching on a limb, watching the man and the bear. The bird's beady eyes fastened to the gold coin and the ring on Roark's chest. "You can't have it," he said softly. "You made her cry. One of the few times in her life."

High on the black rock peaks, a wolf's lonely eery call began, and Roark understood. The wilderness called to him, sank inside him. He knew how the old hunter had felt in another century, his time passed, as he settled down to die in the cabin nearby. He'd wanted the wild for comfort, the deer and the bear, the sweet scent of earth and wild flowers.

Perhaps he was like Zachariah, as Michaela had noted. Roark readily admitted that fighting savagery within him, especially when he'd seen Gallagher circling his sister. Expensive clothes didn't hide the animal that Gallagher was with his too-ready smile, his capped teeth, his spa tan and those greedy, cold eyes. There was nothing inside but the need to tear and hurt.

The bear lumbered away and Roark's thoughts turned to the bird, waiting high on that bobbing limb.

The sun shafted through the shadows, blinding him and warming the gold coin. Was it so strange to want to reclaim something well loved, lost and mourned by one very unique woman? To want to give it to the Langtry women?

Roark rubbed the coin again, watched the bird's head angle, peering at it. He had nothing to give a woman now, his heart was gone. But if Cleopatra could pit herself against a countryside, returning the coins to Langtry keeping, he could do no less.

Firelight spread across Harrison's detailed maps, pinpointing the camera shots Michaela had noted to him. She studied each page, made notations and then munched on "trail mix"—a combination of raisins, nuts, and dried fruit. Somehow, it was the perfect dessert after the tuna and noodle skillet meal Harrison had prepared. He seemed adept at dumping dried prepared packaged and canned food together, stirring until finished. He was a man who didn't like cooking, but who had tended to his own basic needs. All in all, Michaela thought, she'd needed a trip like this, away from the frantic push-push of the last few months, of pasting her life back together. The small river splashed gently against the rocks, a night owl called to the moon, and the scent of clean air and campfire smoke intoxicating.

Michaela laid the notebook aside and stretched on her sleeping bag. She watched Harrison carefully remove his watch and place it in a zipper compartment of his backpack. He was like that, taking very good care of what belonged to him. "I like you waiting on me. I deserve it after climbing up that rock to lay out these camera angles. You only took notes and drew maps—though they are above average quality. I think we can camp on that first sand bar to start. What do you think is best? Canoeing or kayaking? Of course, any novices to kayaking are going to use rafts, we can't endanger their lives. There is enough depth to the water to swim and test skills. Helmets and life jackets—all marked with KANE logos . . . Harrison?"

"Mmm?" He lay on his bedroll, turned to the fire, watching the flames. The firelight cut across his features, hardening them, the dark growth of a day's beard making him look very dangerous. The black T-shirt and worn jeans added to the masculine picture. She'd known him forever, and yet this man, locked in his thoughts, intrigued her more than any man she'd known.

He desired her; that was easily read in those long slow, simmering looks. Yet Harrison would wait for her to choose. And then there would be no going back. No forgetting what had passed between them, there with their bodies locked, riding the fever between them, skin against skin, mouths hungry for a taste, a sound, a breath.

That long finger reached to stroke his nose, as if he were remembering— She knew the gesture well, for it was then that Harrison seemed to draw into himself, to raise his shields. She had to draw him back from that dark ledge consuming him, from the past, or whatever ruled him now. "Harrison, you're going to tell me about that night, when you were fifteen and you fought with your father."

"You've given me orders all afternoon. I'd like a little peace and quiet." He turned on his side away from the fire, his broad back an efficient notice that he was sealing her off for the night.

"You sound like Dad and Roark. Tell me." She nudged him with her foot and he grunted. The sound said he'd acknowledged her just to keep her quiet. He'd passed her off on his way to sleep—that wouldn't do.

She nudged him again and Harrison slowly turned over. The desire etched on his face caused her to shiver, to heat. With one touch, she could ignite them both.

Then Harrison turned slowly again, his back to her. She'd have to come to him, to let him know that she wanted him—and those were his terms for the night.

nine

We came home to the mountains and new lives. I realized that in the mountains and streams I would find
peace. And with my wife, the other half of my heart
and soul, I would find joy.

Cleopatra is not so easily pacified, for she is hunting now for the lost coins, determined to return them
to Langtry keeping. Perhaps a woman with child is
allowed such fantasies. She is no easy woman, my
love, and once set upon a course, not even the devil
can detain her.

I think I do enjoy the battle, though each time I
disdain Obediah's curse and in jest, remind her that
she is only a woman. But it was no ordinary woman
to take the hardships of our journey without com-

plaint. She is no faint heart, but sturdy of soul and most loving.

Zachariah Langtry's Journal

"Michaela . . ." Before dawn, when the mountains were starting to come to life, Harrison's body was ice cold, though he lay in his sleeping bag. Through the dim shadows, he saw the bears. Standing on her back feet, the female bear swiped at the food bag, hung high in a tree. A claw snagged the canvas, bending the branch supporting it, and her jaws tore the bag free. Food for the camping trip spilled onto the ground.

Fear tore through him for the woman sleeping soundly, as the black bears milled through the camp. At six feet and three hundred pounds and intent upon tearing open the plastic bag of trail mix, the mother black bear wouldn't want humans around her two cubs. She'd kill to protect them. One move from Michaela and— "Michaela," Harrison whispered again and breathed quietly, praying that she would hear him.

One of the cubs had found the raft, playing with it. He suddenly danced back from it with a loud "Wah!" A hissing sound cutting through the chirping of birds and the rustling of wildlife in the brush told Harrison that escape by river wasn't possible. Michaela's eyes were wide open now and frightened. With a nod that said she understood the danger, she began to slowly unzip her sleeping bag. Harrison was already free, ready to leap to his feet. He carefully eased jerky strips from his backpack, opened the package and when the mother bear wasn't looking, tossed the strips a distance away from Michaela. The mother and cubs quickly found the strips. With a glance, he signaled Michaela to move toward him.

Harrison held his breath, inching his fingers toward his boots and backpack and standing slowly, watching Michaela ease to her feet. She was fully dressed in a white T-shirt and sweat pants, her boots already in her hands. "Good girl," Harrison murmured silently, nodding to her. She looked back at her sleeping bag, camera and backpack and he shook his head. When she was close, Harrison took her hand, carrying his backpack in the other.

He paused, frowned, and eased the backpack over her shoulders. She scowled at him; he'd given the only protection from the bear's powerful jaws to her. When Michaela would have run, Harrison held her back; the bear was certain to pursue, if they fled too quickly.

They eased slowly through the brush, frightening a deer that leaped in the direction of camp. The mother bear lifted her head, sniffing at the air, and with care, Harrison pulled the tabs of a small tuna can tucked in his backpack. He hurled the can into the camp and the bear was soon distracted by the fish.

They didn't speak, making their way through the pine trees away from camp, Harrison following Michaela. They paused on a jutting rock ledge just as dawn lifted over the ragged mountains, shafting down into the camp. "Damn it," Harrison muttered as

Michaela sat to draw on her boots. "They've shredded the raft and our sleeping bags. Even if we could wait them out—"

He pointed to another bear lumbering into camp, a big male. The mother bear, smaller and fiercely protective of her cubs, charged at him. The big male moved a distance away, wading into the water and scanned it.

"You're buck naked, you know," Michaela stated in a voice that said laughter wasn't far away. "Standing there without a stitch on. Aren't you cold?"

"We picked a bear hotel to camp. You know that, don't you?" Harrison demanded, disgusted that he'd left her so unprotected, that he hadn't kept the fire burning bright through the night. The big bear neatly scooped a native cutthroat trout from the water. With it flopping in his teeth, he lumbered to a flat rock to enjoy his meal. "Look at that. That's a pool where they fish. Well, mark that campsite off our potential list. Damn it, there goes your camera, right into the water!" He began to pace across the large boulder. "Hell, here we are and without a raft, we can't go down that canyon, the walls are too steep."

"So we'll go up. To the old state road."

"You're grinning and you're enjoying this, aren't you?" Harrison asked darkly, placing his hands on his hips. She was his to protect and he'd failed and— "This is serious, Michaela."

Sprawled on the rock, her arms behind her head, Michaela grinned up at him. "I've never really seen you rant and rave before. It's every interesting. You're making me hot, you know. All that muscle and man stalking back and forth on this rock, raging at the world . . ."

He stared at her blankly. " 'Hot?' "

"You've got a really nice bod, Harrison. Really nice backside." She dug into his backpack and tossed a pair of boxer shorts at him. "Ah, an old-fashioned man. I figured. No itsy-bitsies for you . . ."

"I like my space." Harrison wasn't certain if he liked sharing his intimate preferences with a woman who was in an undetermined mood. She'd trusted him enough to come with him, and he hadn't taken care of her. "The situation is critical, Michaela. We're without camping gear, proper food, and we've lost time . . . To say nothing of your camera and notes. We're not on a picnic here, you know."

"Neither of us is hurt. We could have been mauled by Mama Bear." She rummaged through the contents of the backpack. "I knew it. Good old Harrison packs well. Sewing thread, fishing hooks and twine, flashlight and extra batteries, note pads and pens, salt and pepper. Men's hand cream. Toothpaste. Everything is in here that we need."

She tossed a new box of condoms to him and studied him intently as she used his comb to tend her hair. "Yep. Always prepared, good old Harrison."

He inhaled slowly and slid the box into his backpack. This was the part where she would define exactly why she didn't want him for a lover. But there was that clear sky-blue searching look, gauging him, seeking out his intentions for the trip, and he fought the flush rising up his cheeks. There was nothing like a man's plans for romance baldly exposed before their time. Trust Michaela to ruin any mystique he might have planned. "I packed that bag very carefully. It *was* neat and arranged. And a man's underwear is private."

He jammed his legs into the boxer shorts; they were a dark muted pattern, like his life. "You're taking this well. It's at least a three-day hike up to the road and then some down it. Your father and brother will have my hide tacked out to dry."

"True. I like playing the innocent and watching you squirm. Or if you're real nice, I just may protect you. Remember how I had to lasso Roark that time to protect you? So is this our first date, or what?" She shook free his flannel shirt against the cold and eased her arms into it.

"I'll get back with you about that," he stated darkly and dug a candy bar from his backpack, opening it for her. She took the bar, broke it, and handed one half back to him and the Langtry coin caught the rising sun, gleaming. Dressed in a T-shirt, sweat pants, and his flannel shirt against the cold, Michaela was the most enticing woman he'd ever seen. "Would you like to date me? Dinner, dancing, movies?" he asked after a moment, curious now as she munched on the candy and sprawled back on the rock as if she didn't care about their predicament.

His mind began to plow through schedules, through what might please her—little gifts, jewelry and flowers. He'd have to take dance lessons or she'd know that he'd never taken time to learn. He needed to know what made her happy more than anything else. Michaela looked happy enough now, at ease with herself for the first time since she'd arrived. Harrison sat beside her, watching the big male bear efficiently snag a fish, dancing it from paw to paw before sinking his teeth into it. "Why were you saving the dress? The one I had to ship out of town for repair and dry cleaning."

For an instant, Michaela's mouth tightened as if tasting a bitter memory. "Gown, Harrison. A French designer gown. I was saving it for an engagement party. I was going to throw it away, but—"

Harrison bent to brush a kiss across her lips. "I'm glad you didn't. I've got a hunch that's always going to be my favorite dress."

Michaela returned the favor, a gentle press of her mouth against his. "Don't blame yourself for this, Harrison. I don't. We've got our boots, a candy bar—I didn't know you liked nuts and caramel—hmm, I would have thought you'd be an energy bar sort of guy, like granola."

"A good brownie with nuts and a cup of coffee would hit the spot right now," he muttered and resented the confession, the weakness.

"A piece of berry pie from Megan's Cafe? Or chocolate cream? Or—"

He scowled at her. Michaela was the only person to ever tease him, to step beyond his shields and torment him to her delight. He'd have to learn how to keep control, but right now she knew she had gotten to him. He smiled briefly; at least she'd noticed what he preferred during their business breaks at the cafe.

She began to laugh outright, holding her sides and doubling up on the rock slab, tears coming to her eyes. "You were so funny, hopping a bit when your foot hit a rock, all nude and big and hopping mad."

"I'm glad you enjoyed it," Harrison said tightly.

Michaela wiped the tears away, grinning happily up at him. "At one point, you picked up a club and actually paused. I thought you'd be like Zachariah and go back for the kill, taking the claws."

"I should go down there and do just that." Harrison continued to frown at the bears prowling through the ruined camp. He'd felt like that and would have fought the bears to save Michaela. The sleeping bags he'd hoped to zip together were shredded and useless. "We've got a long way to go. We'll be lucky if a cougar doesn't have us for dinner. That's a rough, rocky climb up to the state road from here. . . ."

But Michaela had stopped laughing, her arms folded around her bent knees as she stared at the rugged mountain forests, the jutting black rocks. "We'll make it. I'm not worried. . . . I gave away too much of myself, Harrison. This is what feels right— the sunshine and fresh air . . . freedom. I thought I could make things work with Dolph, but it wasn't there. Nothing to build on, all surface, for-show emotions, going through the mechanics."

"Leave it," Harrison ordered. He didn't want to think about Michaela with another man, no matter how empty the relationship. Territorial? Possessive?

New, but true emotions for him and only concerning Michaela. He tugged on socks, laced up his boots and stood, glaring at the bears. "Come on. We're not going to be able to retrieve anything from that mess. Your panties are stuck on that bear's muzzle."

"Briefs, Harrison. We call them 'briefs' now."

"Well, hell." He had plans for Michaela's underwear, like drawing them off and—

But Michaela was rummaging through his backpack, drawing out another pair of undershorts. "I'm going to save my sweat pants until we get close to home. Okay, I know you're always prepared. All I need is—" She pulled out his jeans belt. "Ah! This! Turn around, Harrison."

He eyed her, wondering if she would undress in front of him, and there was nothing like testing Michaela, seeing how far he could push her. He crossed his arms over his chest and looked at her. "I'm not feeling like much of a gentleman. I really enjoy my morning coffee and since I can't have that pleasure, I'm not turning around."

"Fine."

Later, while one of his hands was on Michaela's bottom, pushing her upward on the sheer rock face, he wished he hadn't watched her peel off her sweat pants. His undershorts, tightened by his belt with an extra notch for her smaller waist, were entirely too seductive. It was then that he realized Michaela had left camp without her bra and those beautiful, responsive, desirable female curves were within easy caress. A man who had dedicated himself to achieving in business, Harrison realized he was not far from drooling. His lower body ached with desire, and he wasn't exactly certain of maintaining his control—not when his fingers were inches from that heat . . .

Harrison wiped the sweat from his forehead and realized his hand trembled. It smelled like the lemonly sun screen he'd used on her face, arms and legs against the stark mountain sun. Distracted as they paused on another ledge, Harrison caught her wrist and tugged her toward him. The movement was natural, instinctive, playful, surprising him. He tensed then, uncertain of her, of how she would react. She smiled, her face gleaming with the sun screen, and her arms circled his neck. Encouraged he nuzzled her cheek and when she giggled, twisting against him, he couldn't help laughing.

He liked tugging her to him. He enjoyed the gentle play, loved her laughter and the feeling as if nothing could touch them, tear them apart. Boy-girl play, he thought, dizzy with happiness—his first. Flirtation, tenderness, and Michaela in his arms, squealing as he nuzzled his overnight stubble against her throat, gasping for breath and hugging him tightly. It seemed almost as if nothing had happened all those years ago, the mountain sun burning away the past.

On a course set for the old state mountain road, they crossed a rock avalanche and a small stream with water that needed no filtering, fresh and tumbling and sweet. Michaela lay on her stomach and Harrison couldn't resist reaching to place his arm around her as she drank. There, lying side by side near the stream, she leaned to kiss him lightly before easing away and standing. The kiss lasted only a heartbeat, but it spoke of affection and trust and tightened Harrison's throat. He stood, rocked by his tender emotions, watching her leap over the stream. Affection, he repeated to himself, when had he every known affection? On the other side, she pushed back her hair. "You look stunned, Harrison. Why?"

"I'm having a good day, that's all," he managed to say when he could speak.

At sunset, Jacob Langtry leaned against the corral fence and stared at the rugged mountains hiding Cutter Canyon. His daughter was up there somewhere, with Harrison, a good strong man. Years ago, Jacob had done the same with Faith, picked his moment, testing to see if she would accept what he offered. His wife came to stand beside him now, slipping easily into his circling arm and the sweet homecoming always surprised him. She touched his weathered cheek and smiled softly. "That wouldn't be a tear, would it, cowboy?"

"They'll kill each other up there. One of them will come down in pieces."

"Or both. Michaela is a strong woman. She's not going to let Harrison run off with her, set his terms, like you tried to do with me."

"I couldn't get you alone, woman. What else was I supposed to do? I wanted all of your attention without all those yahoos fawning over you," Jacob exclaimed roughly. "It's too soon, Faith. My little girl just came back. She's moved out and she'll be leaving us soon."

"Mmm, we'll see. Harrison isn't a man to let much escape him, and think of all those beautiful grandchildren. I wonder . . . I wonder if Sable has children now."

"Honey-girl," Jacob whispered achingly, drawing her close to him. He'd tear his heart out, if it meant giving Faith the child she would never forget.

Michaela smoothed the large coin and stared at the campfire as the night settled around them. She wore her sweat pants and Harrison's flannel shirt against the night's chill. He sat beside her, clean shaven and hair brushed, the firelight gleaming on his bare, powerful shoulders. Coyotes howled in the distance, a lonely forsaken sound. Odd, Michaela thought, but she didn't feel lonely. She only felt the call of wild beauty, the feeling of coming home and uniting with herself. With a sigh, Michaela gave in to the unfamiliar impulse to rest close to him, to lean her head on his shoulder. His arm went around her and the night smoke curled into the sky. He gathered her closer, tucking her warm and safe against him as they watched the fire.

"You could be in your New York apartment now, throwing a cocktail party with what's his name. Maybe he'll come here, fall in love with country life and become a rancher."

She lightly elbowed Harrison's side. "I'm enjoying this. Don't ruin it."

"Someone should have taken good old Mr. Sexual Harassment and plowed him."

Michaela shook her head. "He wasn't worth it. And now you're talking like Roark and my father."

"There you were, a defenseless woman."

"Stop grumbling. And I'm not defenseless. I can manage you quite nicely, can't I? Especially when you're in one of those 'cut-expenses moods.'" She reached for a small box of raisins and put a few into his mouth. "Good old Harrison. Provider of cracker snacks and packaged dried onion soup and peel-tab tuna cans. It's a good thing you like snacks." They'd kept the cans for cups and to mix the soup with water, eating it cold.

"I got used to carrying snacks when I was working several jobs and hadn't enough time to pack lunches or cook, or eat right. I'm really sorry about this, Michaela."

"I'm not. It's been a long time since I've been mountain berry picking, and they are the sweetest anywhere. I've been wanting to come up here on the mountain and Cutter Canyon has always been very special to me. Zachariah used to bring his furs down the river, you know, and he met Cleopatra here. But there has always been something calling me here. I've always felt—don't you laugh at me, Harrison."

But he nuzzled her hair and smoothed her waist. "Mmm. There's nothing like a woman who smells like men's soap. Go ahead, tell me. I want to know."

Michaela picked through her thoughts, deep and secret within her for years. She gripped the Langtry coin in her fist. "I've always felt that Cleopatra wanted to tell me something. I look at her picture and I just feel this strange tug, as if she's restless, and needing me to do whatever she can't. Maybe she wants me to do as Roark is, hunting for her wedding ring and her journal. They were both so important to her."

"I'm listening."

Michaela turned to Harrison and realized that she trusted him. She'd given her body, but not her trust to another man. "Harrison, I really believe in that curse. So did Cleopatra. I can almost feel her willing me to return all the coins to the family, just as she did. She believed in Obediah's voodoo curse, that anyone other than a Langtry would be doomed if they possessed the coins. I'm certain she used that to frighten some of the bargains she made, obtaining all six coins. Two are missing. One stolen years ago from Grandma's kitchen table, and one stolen with Sable—I hope whoever has them is experiencing Obediah's curse. *I've got to find those coins.*"

Harrison stared into the fire, and the darkness that seemed to always hover around him when she spoke of the coins, returned. "I've tried for years. I wanted to give something back for all the good your family has done for me."

"I thought so, from the magazines and books at your house. Do you think Cleopatra is trying to tell me something?" The canyon wind howled eerily in the night, as if whispering secrets that began long ago. "I feel her so strongly now, up here on the mountain."

"I think you should listen to your instincts and your heart. They've always been good."

"Why do you always slip behind those pat sayings, slide away from me when the coins are mentioned?"

Harrison slanted her a cool glance that said to back off. That was a mistake. Michaela leaned closer to tease him. She looked up at him and fluttered her lashes. "Oh, Harrison," she sing-songed.

"I'm glad you're having a good time with all this. It's going to be a long, cold night without our sleeping bags." He glanced at the soft mat of mountain grass she'd collected to buffer the cold rocky ground. The underwear, jeans and shirts from Harrison's backpack would serve as covering. He looked wary and delicious. "I don't know how we're going to sleep on that—"

He blinked and jerked back from Michaela's quick kiss. "Now, what the hell did you have to do that for?"

"I wanted to see what you'd do. You're on edge, Harrison. Why? Can't you take a woman who uses a man's soap?"

"Oh, I could take her all right and your scent isn't that of soap, but of all-woman." Harrison's hand slid behind her head, lifting her face for his mouth. "Are you asking?"

"No." She wanted him to take her, to feed upon her just as she wanted to give herself to him. Not because they were cold and of the necessity, or by accident as they brushed each other in the night—a man and a woman alone—but because they both desired what would happen, had known what would happen with each kiss, each touch.

The need to be claimed was old and instinctive as time, the need to be desired and wanted, and the need to take one special man into her, to hold him close and tight and protect him and warm him and make him want more— She rose to her feet and Harrison stood beside her, the firelight flickering over his powerful body. Desire for her was there in his stance, lodged immediate and hard and visibly shaped within his jeans. There was that arrogant tilt to his head, that honed intense expression that said he wanted to hold her without the barrier of clothing, to love her.

Had she really been desired so intensely before?

James Charis's lust-sharpened features flashed in front of her for just a moment. His idea of seducing a woman into lovemaking was pushing her against the wall, biting her lip and grinding his pelvis into hers. He took her resistance as a come-on, tearing at her clothes and making certain that she knew her sexual favors would be well rewarded according to her "performance."

Michaela shivered slightly, pushing James's fleeting image away. She was about to enter a relationship with Harrison, whose very concern for her was a seduction.

Truth: nothing compared to Harrison's expression now, that wary, hard look, as if he were gaging how to first touch her, how to frighten her, how to love her—

"Then I'll ask. Will you let me have you?" His deep

uneven tone told her that Harrison could answer her primitive instincts, the needs she had not exposed to another man. There was tenderness there, too, blended by years of sparring and trusting.

For her answer, Michaela eased away his flannel shirt. Silvery in the night, his eyes followed her hands as she bent to unlace her boots. She stripped away her T-shirt and tugged away her sweat pants. In the firelight, the huge Langtry coin gleamed and she gripped it in her fist, fearing that she would give more than her body away this night.

In his turn, Harrison unsnapped his jeans and when her hand flattened on his chest, prowling lower, he tore away his jeans quickly. There was just that hesitation as she watched him, that bit of uncertainty that she knew sprung from his fear of hurting her. "I want honesty," she whispered, skimming his tense shoulders with her palms. The ripple that shot through his big body told her that he badly wanted her, but wanted to take her gently. "Love me how you feel. No pretenses. No restraints. Tonight, here on this mountain, I need truth."

For a moment, he breathed heavily, watching her, and then suddenly, he pulled her into his arms, flesh against hot flesh, thrust against softness, his desire already rushing, nudging for entrance into her. His mouth slanted over Michaela's and she held him tight as he lifted her, carrying her to the pallet they had made, upon which they would make love.

He bore her down, his mouth feverish, matching

her own, his breath rushing against her hot cheek, his body covering hers. "Is this what you want?" he asked roughly, pulling her hair back from her face, framing it with his hands.

"Yes. I want you. Now."

There was that brief smile, too fierce to be tender as their hearts pounded against each other, his hips lying within the cradle of her legs. He was shaking now, trying to leash himself as he reached for protection, fumbled, and found it. She smoothed his hair gently, for Harrison, a controlled man, was about to lose control. She wouldn't have less.

His head turned; his breath held as he looked down their entwined bodies, then to her breasts and lower where they would join.

She knew she would never forget his expression this first time—fierce and primitive and yet in awe. His hand opened on her breast, and he studied the dark contrast of his skin against hers. Then his touch slid lower, spanning her stomach, cupping her intimately, delving gently until she cried out, needing him, her legs moving restlessly, her hips rising—

"Michaela . . . Michaela . . . " he repeated against her throat, his body shaking within the caress of hers.

The flood of liquid warmth surged through her, muscles tugging within her body. The primitive need to lock herself with Harrison, to bond with him, shocked her.

She hadn't expected the gliding, smooth push to begin to stretch and fill her, leaving her grasping and shaking and rocketing too soon. She fought for more, digging into emotions that she hadn't experienced before, reserves torn away. Beneath her palms, Harrison's muscles bunched and his body trembled, yet he held away just that bit from completion, from the center of her pounding desire. Just there, at the peak of taking and giving and the wildfire heat where nothing else mattered, Harrison pushed her higher, took more, demanded when she would have—

When his lips tugged at her breasts, suckling them, his hands shaping the softness, he surged within her again, stretching and filling until he rested so deeply within her. He caught her hands then, lacing his fingers with hers, watching her as their heartbeats racked their bodies, deeply joined. They rocked slowly then, man and woman, a testing before the blinding, rushing summit.

Thundering through the night, unbidden and hot, their hunger needed feeding. The tempest raged, and they whirled out into the fierce storm. She held Harrison tight, gasping, fighting against the pounding within her, the riveting urgency that sought and held and asked for more.

She cried out, startled by the beauty, by the feeling of completion.

His heart beat savagely as Harrison sucked in air against her hot face, slowly lowering himself to her. She shivered then, as Harrison's hand swept down her, the gesture of a man who had possessed and enjoyed a woman. He settled heavily against her, warm and safe and relaxed. She kissed his shoulder and bit it gently and caressed his back. "I've never known you to be so relaxed."

But Harrison had begun nibbling on her breasts, tasting and suckling and quite efficiently stopping any more discussion.

Michaela slept soundly, drowsily awakening to a sensual dream that was the reality of Harrison turning her on her back and kissing her just as he was easing her sweatpants away. She opened herself to the dawn and the man in her arms, filling her, stoking the trembling, tugging warmth that burst quickly, deeply, and very efficiently.

After they bathed in the creek, he tightened his belt around her undershorts and drew on one of his clean T-shirts for her. He smoothed her breasts, escalating heavy ache within them instantly, and considering the darkened, peaked nipples against the cloth. He could unnerve her so easily, each touch and look so intent, as if he were memorizing her, cherishing her. "Harrison?"

He met her look. "I tried not to hurt you, Michaela. But you were so—"

"It's been a long time. And not like that." She shivered, remembering how she had demanded and he'd fed and then how he had entered her so quickly this morning, her passion out of control before she could— She looked away, uncertain of him, her body aching slightly, reacting, quivering near his. She'd opened to him and given him everything, unafraid of the consequences, unafraid to trust him. "Never like that."

Was it too soon to feel so much? She'd trusted one man and lost part of herself. Was she ready to really trust again? To trust Harrison on a different level than their past relationship?

Was Roark correct? Probably. She'd once chosen a man who was little danger to her inner heart, but Harrison would want everything. He was always very thorough.

ten

I have nothing to give my wife, but the ruby ring that came from my little finger, my dear mother's ring. For our child, I give this simple lullaby from my heart.

> *Soft-ly, slow-ly . . . the mornin' will creep*
> *Dream your sweet dreams and do not weep*
> *Cornbread in the mornin' it will keep*
> *Drift soft-ly, slow-ly, 'tis time to sleep*

Zachariah Langtry's Journal

"Give a man a compass and a map and he knows all there is to know. Well, you're wrong, Mr. Kane. I've camped here enough to know my locations," Michaela muttered the next afternoon. She pointed toward a stand of lodgepole pines. "If we head up that ridge and down that little valley, that will put us up close to the service road that leads into the old state highway."

"There's not a service road marked on the map, Michaela. If we go to that big rock ledge, and then go straight up, we'll be in a direct line with the state road." Harrison jammed his compass back into his backpack and scowled when he tore the map, flipping it back into its folds. "Don't forget I've camped here, too. Your father brought me up here with Roark, fishing for cutthroat. Did I get to do that on this trip? Hell, no! If we would have taken that other cutoff, I could have put my line into that water and pulled out the biggest—"

Harrison clamped his lips closed, unnerved that he'd wanted to show off for Michaela. The age-old instinct, male providing food for his mate, proving his worth, was unfamiliar and frustrating.

Michaela leaned close to his face, frowning at him, her hands on her hips. "You're yelling, Harrison. It's not my fault those bears came into camp."

"Hell, yes, it is. You smell like honey and flowers . . . and I never yell." He resented the biting defensive edge to his tone.

"Give me that." She jerked the backpack and he tugged it back. "Sometimes, Harrison, you can be so—nice. Give me that pack. I need the fingernail clippers. I've broken a nail climbing up that last rock ledge. *Which we didn't need to climb up if you would have just crossed the creek like I said.*"

"You've messed up my backpack. Things are out of order." He was feeling delicate. He knew why—he wanted to cuddle and whisper sweet nothings. Their morning trek had been spiked with several yelling matches—the arguments arising from his logical assertion of using the map and compass versus her illogical instincts. Along the way, they reopened old battles, all free and open and leaving nothing unsaid. Harrison was always controlled and picking his words, but Michaela's fiery attacks left him no option but to defend himself. The strange part was that after a lifetime of quiet deadly barbs from his father and years of control, a wide open mountain-yelling match with Michaela seemed just perfect.

Now that was illogical. He'd have to think about that.

Michaela had a lot to say about men who thought they knew directions and safety. "It's only common sense, Harrison. Cutter Falls is down there, the service road is up there. Gee whiz, what is so hard about fig-uring a straight line between the two?"

Michaela smiled too sweetly as she foraged in the backpack, tossing his map and compass to the ground. She dug out his clippers and whipped out the tiny file, using it briskly on her fingers. "Just what is the 'order' of things, Harrison? That everything has to be your way? That we have to—"

He scooped up the compass with the map, replac-ing them into the backpack. He almost winced when the map, stuffed down carelessly, tore again. "I'm responsible for you."

"I'm responsible for myself. I make my own decisions—like last night. And then making love to you again this morning."

That attack hovered on the fresh afternoon air. Birds chirped gaily, and the slight breeze flipped the trembling aspen leaves as Michaela's words echoed silently around him. Harrison rubbed the rough stubble on his jaw. There was no dreaming about the way Michaela had come to him in her sleep. "Twice, huh?"

"Leave it to you to drag out that calculator for a brain." Michaela tossed the clippers to him and pushed her hair back from her face. "We could have crossed that creek back there simply by leaping across from rock to rock. But oh, no. We had to go around the falls and climb all the way back."

She tromped across the clearing and tore a columbine bloom from its stalk, adding a flaming red Indian paintbrush and several daisies to her bouquet. "Here. Get sweet," she ordered, thrusting them out to him.

He took the flowers, contemplating the woman glaring at him. Some secrets were better cherished and left silent—Michaela had made love with him three times, not two. She'd turned to him in the night, holding him as he stared at the stars and wished he could give her peace, erase everything that his family had done, give her the coins she wanted and the sister that was of his blood, too. He'd been damning himself for not making their first time on a proper bed, with a proper bathroom and wine and flowers and more than the savage need to seduce her.

She'd turned to him then, in the night and in his dark thoughts, and held him, nuzzled his throat and kissed him softly. Her coming to him was so soft and natural and sweet, that he'd held very still, shaken by the tenderness and awe within him. She sighed his name sleepily, arching gracefully as his caress slid over her, in her. Leashing himself, Harrison shook as she reached lower, touching him, bringing him into her keeping.

"Harrison—" she'd sighed again, as she drew him over her.

"Harrison," Michaela said now, still glaring at him as he picked a leaf from her hair. "Don't you ever do anything instinctively?"

"Sometimes. Once or twice or three times," he admitted, still in awe that she'd needed him in a way so natural that he wondered if he were dreaming.

"Well, my instincts tell me we should forget the map and compass and work up to that ridge, find the service road that must be overgrown by now and take it to the old main road."

"You're wrong, Michaela. We'll lose time, probably get lost, but what the hey, let's do it your way," he said cheerfully and tucked the wild flowers into the leather belt she wore.

"We're not going to get lost. See that peak up there, where the sun is hitting that flat rock face and those ravens are feeding? Zachariah's journals often mentioned that peak and Dad said the old service road was directly opposite that flat rock." He swept away the gleaming strand of hair on her damp cheek and she tilted her head, studying him. "You gave in too easy. I don't know that I trust you when you're like this—you're glowing, Harrison. Grinning and glowing."

"You trusted me last night."

She closed her eyes, holding still, her face turned up to him as he applied sunscreen mixed with insect repellent to her face. The elegant bone structure—high cheekbones, that jaw—would keep her youthful-looking when she was elderly. He hoped that he would be a part of her life then.

"Yes, I did trust you—on a certain level—not when you're teasing or looking at me as you do now, as if you know everything about me. And if you think that's easy, think again. I made love to a man who won't let me help with whatever is tormenting him ... I've told you everything, even how I feel about Cleopatra trying to tell me something. You think I don't know you? That I don't know something has been eating at you for years?"

"It's nothing ... I wish I could give you those coins, give you what you need," he said, meaning it as he capped the tube of cream. He realized how Zachariah must have felt, having nothing to give his wife, no family treasures, nothing of himself but a ring stolen by a raven.

"It seems that peace isn't going to come easily to either one of us. But as for my needs—oh, I think you gave me what I needed quite well." Michaela took the cream and began working it into his face. He stood very still, entranced by her concentration, her fingers moving over his skin—he felt as if he were being petted as she said, "You're just emotional and you don't quite know how to handle the situation. We've been friends—sort of—for years, and now we're lovers. You're feeling insecure. You're threatened because you didn't follow a lover's protocol, whatever you suspect that is, of the morning after. . . . You're a very scheduled, predictable man, part of the reason I like you—good reliable old Harrison. In your step-by-step logic, you should be—say, cooking breakfast, bringing it to me with a nice little gift tucked near the rosebud vase?"

"Something like that." How like Michaela, to lay open his plans. When they returned to Shiloh, he intended to make her quite comfortable in his bed, in his life. He tugged at the belt circling her waist. "Someday, I'm going to do something you don't expect. I know of one gift that I'd really, really like now."

"Again?" Harrison tugged her to him, tasted the laughter on her lips and forgot everything, but the woman flying through hungry passion with him—

Later, as Michaela forged up a wooded stretch, Harrison tilted his head to study that fast sway of her hips. His borrowed undershorts fluttered, exposing a tantalizing curve of her buttock. Her long legs gleamed with sunscreen ointment, slender muscles bunching slightly in her thighs as she hiked up to a massive rock and placed her hands on her hips, scanning the rugged distance they had just climbed, shading her eyes with her hand. She looked little like KANE's dynamic anchor, the canyon winds tossing her hair, her T-shirt damp with sweat, clinging to her. "When this is over, I'm coming back. I may build a cabin up here. I've always felt—a part of this, at home. I needed this trip more than I knew. I feel very strong here."

Harrison smiled briefly; he was intimately aware of Michaela's strength, of her hungers. He rubbed the stubble he intended to shave before they made love again. He'd left marks on her this morning and again this afternoon.

He should have told her what he knew, given her a choice to make love with a man who had kept too many secrets too long. He'd forgotten with her breathing running close and fast upon his skin, his hands and arms filled with her, that savage heat surprising him, that he was a Kane, son of his cruel father.

He'd forgotten everything, but Michaela and how she opened to him, leaving nothing in the shadows, taking him beyond reasoning, beyond those layers of empty relief he'd had with a few other women.

She'd been too tight, too warm and damp and welcoming, objecting when he would have drawn away, would have gone slower. Giving herself to him was no easy matter, to make the decision to trust him, to let him have her. Yet she held nothing back, gripping his hair, burning with him—

Harrison rubbed the broken line of his nose. He could hurt her. Ugly truths could emerge at any twist and she'd hate him. Had he cared as she melted in his arms, flew with him into the heat? Selfish bastard, he mocked himself, and knew that he had to tell her—

His T-shirt knotted beneath her breasts, wearing a man's jeans belt and dark plaid undershorts, Michaela frowned slightly, studying the jutting rock ledges, studded with brush and pine. She pointed to a small herd of deer lying in a lush meadow, surrounded by alpine daisies. A big buck drank warily from the icy blue snow lake, his head lifting to the hawk soaring overhead. But Harrison was feeling the tight squeeze of desire, that burning taut, primitive memory of how she had held him close, her fingers digging into his shoulders, her breasts pushing against him as she fought the flashpoint of their desire.

She caught his look and flushed, looking away at a chipmunk racing up the rough, red bark of a pine. He waited as she decided to come to him, eased his backpack away, his body tightening with the almost liquid movement of her hips, the gentle sway of her breasts. He could already feel her body against his, flowing around him, and enveloping, her fingers digging in slightly, the surge of her hips, and the incredible heat—

There, moving through the dappled shadows of the pines, the dried needles crackling as she walked, Michaela's expression was that of a predator, a sensual woman prowling to take what she wanted. She unknotted the T-shirt and let him draw it away, her hands smoothing his chest, his waist, fingers sliding beneath the waistband of his jeans. Harrison quickly unbelted hers, and she stepped free of them, her sultry gaze never leaving his, darkening with desire.

She shivered when he bent to kiss her, arched taut and strong within the frame of his embrace. He caught her sigh in his mouth, gave it back to her, slanting his open mouth over hers, taking when she would tease, gathering her closer as if she were his heart, his soul, already a part of him. She tasted of dreams and woman and things he'd forgotten. Of homecoming and tenderness and whispers long into the night.

Harrison held her as he eased down onto their tumbled clothing, drawing her over him. There was no going back, no forgiveness for a man who had kept his secrets too long, he thought hazily as she eased upon him, rocking gently, holding him tight and close.

They fit so perfectly—the soft drag of her breasts across his chest, the meeting of their stomachs, her hip bones jutting slightly against him, those soft thighs pushing against his. He closed his eyes, feeling the heat rise too sharply to be controlled, and opened them to Michaela's dark blue ones, so close he could see himself in the black centers. She cried out, pressing down on him, her body taut and melded to his, arching to her desire, her arms braced beside his head.

He found her throat, nibbling on that warm scented flesh, dragging across it to find her breasts, nuzzling them as she cried out, passion rippling her.

Then when he could wait no longer, Harrison caught her close and they soared into the heat, the raging storm where nothing else mattered.

At dusk, the night settling cool and sweet in the mountains, they circled an old rock slide and argued about the best way to the top. Michaela was certain that at the top they would reach the old service road. Watching the humans, a small herd of mountain sheep studded the black rocks on the opposite side of the canyon.

A sudden gust of canyon wind swept against Michaela, sailing through her hair. It whispered against her skin, chilling it, and the leaves of the trembling aspens fluttered, a gentle comforting rustle. She stood very still, listening to the earth's sounds, the eery whining coming from Cutter Canyon, the too quiet lodgepole pines, the mountain sheep poised in the dimming shadows. "Harrison? Do you feel that? How quiet it is, as if something is waiting? Someone?"

She gripped the Langtry coin and turned to him, standing below her. The soft wind played in his unruly hair as he frowned slightly. He wasn't the well-groomed Harrison she'd known, but a gentle man, careful with her. A man who would last, his shadows slightly lessened now. He'd always been there, she realized, strong and waiting for her. But he didn't understand what called to her, what she could not define. Harrison understood logic and facts and—

"Yes, I do," he murmured, watching her.

"I've felt it before, when my family came up here and camped. It's too quiet now—"

Then a shaft of the dying sun cut through the craggy mountain peaks and shadows and high on the old avalanche, a big raven prowled on a rock. It plunged at a rabbit, frightened from safety; the rabbit bounded from rock to rock, the raven tormenting it. A tiny rock slide began, growled and died. Harrison gripped Michaela's hand. "Don't move. This avalanche is old and settled, but—"

One rock shifted precariously and tumbled away, settling into the wedge of a huge boulder. Metal gleamed dully from where the rock had been dislodged. Michaela's hand darted to lock onto Harrison's—every instinct, every sense in her chilled, telling her that—

"An old beer can," Harrison offered. "And some red cloth."

"No." Michaela began climbing, fiercely pitting herself against the dying light, her hands torn by rocks and brush. She reached the small rock ledge before Harrison and couldn't move, pinned by the sight of the big turquoise and silver ring.

And the skeleton hand bearing it.

"Michaela?" Harrison's tone was urgent as he stood by her. He glanced at her face, at the hands covering her silent scream, and then down to the ring. Entombed by the rock that had just been dislodged, the red cotton cloth, tattered and dirty, fluttered. The movement brushed the ring, polishing the silver gently.

"It's Maria's," Michaela whispered unevenly. "She didn't leave. She's here. Oh, what if Sable is under those rocks with her?"

She bent to lift a small rock covering the skeletal arm and Harrison gripped her upper arm. "Don't. It's too dark. One wrong move and this old avalanche could shift. And then we'll never know. We'll do what we can first thing in the morning—"

Michaela turned to press close against him. "She didn't leave after all, Harrison. I remember that dress, red cotton with white dots. She let me make a flag from it for Roark's play fort," she repeated shakily. "Sable could be with her. We'd know then."

Aaron Gallagher looked at the hair tangled in his comb and frowned at his morning mirror, the Langtry gold coin gleaming on his bare chest. He was losing his hair, and the woman lying in his bed wasn't Michaela Langtry. He would have had no trouble with impotence with Michaela, enough woman to make him hard. Beneath the gloss, Michaela was a smart, strong, savage woman, just the mate he needed. She moved like a cat, sensual, feminine, but always prowling, thinking, arranging life her way. She'd make a good alliance.

Julia Kane was both crazy and smart, ruling her power-of-attorney lawyer, making him rich. One look at a financial sheet, and the woman knew if the investment was good, the stock ripe.

Before she sailed off into worlds she alone traveled, Julia Kane spoke of a son she'd once loved and a husband she hated.

She spoke of a slave-curse on the Langtry coins and how she'd been plagued with whispers ever since she'd taken the baby and the coin.

Aaron smiled coldly at his reflection. It was likely that the Langtrys had the rest of the coins and soon he would have all six and the power of a king. Harrison Kane needed to be taught a lesson—that no one messed with Aaron Gallagher.

Harrison wanted Michaela Langtry, but once the secrets were out, the Langtrys wouldn't have anything to do with him.

Aaron's smile died as he watched a hair fall from his head and slide into the basin to join several others. With all the Langtry coins, and Michaela Langtry, he wouldn't be impotent, or balding. He closed his eyes and tried to see her, dynamic, beautiful, sensual.

Instead he saw another woman, her skin dark with Native American blood, her hair black as Michaela's, but neatly tethered in two long braids. Set in a narrow, sharp face, the woman's black eyes burned at him, devouring him. He felt her power suck away the air in his lungs—

When Aaron opened his eyes, he met the stark reflection of his terror, the sweat on his face, the silent scream.

He gripped the counter, clawing at it and pushed away the lingering image from his mind. There was nothing in the mirror, but steam, he told himself. He'd never been afraid to take what he wanted. The image of Cleopatra Langtry's face was only because he remembered her picture from his research of the family and the coins. Nothing more, he reassured himself.

eleven

Nightmares filled with war cannons blasting and men dying haunt me. I saw the evil in men, and in myself. But a devilish secret kept too long will eat at the soul, and I have my dark storms, as does my wife. I see her now, staring at the campfire, our child at her breast. What does she see in the flames at the midnight hour? The lost coins haunt her, for she has promised to bring them back to the Langtry family.

Zachariah Langtry's Journal

"Soft-ly, slow-ly . . . the mornin' will creep . . ." At midnight, Michaela sat with her knees bent, arms around them, as she watched the campfire dwindle. She rocked, holding the Langtry coin in her fist and humming the song that had plagued her since that night. At dawn, they would be trying to reveal the skeleton, lifting away the rocks to find Sable's tiny body.

Then it would all be ended. Faith would have the closure she badly needed, not a happy ending, but an end to an open wound.

The stripped branch spit across the fire was black and empty now ... as empty as all those years of searching. The rabbit Harrison had killed and roasted had been carefully wrapped and packed away for morning.

Moving to Harrison's direction, her mind torn by the past, but the ring clutched in her fist, Michaela had climbed up the rocks to the old service road. He'd placed her in the middle of the pavement, weeds growing up through the cracks, and had dressed her warmly. He'd talked to her then, the words didn't matter, she was beyond that. It was the constant reassurance that she locked onto, rocking her body against the blow she had just taken—that Maria had been lying under the rocks all that time, that Sable's tiny body could be with her.

Michaela had started humming *"Soft-ly, slow-ly,"* turning within herself, remembering that night. She barely noticed the fire that Harrison had efficiently built. He'd said something then, crouched beside her, and he'd smoothed her nape, her shoulders, her back. Then she was alone, briefly, with the haunting memories.

Somehow, he'd managed to kill and and dress a

rabbit, washing it in the tumbling tiny stream. He'd talked calmly to Michaela as the rabbit cooked on the spit, and had washed her face and hands, as if she were a child. He'd unlaced her boots, and stripped her dirty and torn clothing away, dressing her in his jeans and T-shirt and socks. Then he'd held her on his lap, rocking her, talking to her until the rabbit was cooked.

"You've got to eat," he said quietly, firmly. It was tough mountain rabbit and he'd cut it into tiny pieces for Michaela. He'd fed her, urged her to eat, talked about the new camera she'd get, about how he'd always wanted to cook and garden and never had time. While the lullaby circled her, she'd stared out into the night. Maria rested and perhaps Sable . . . and Harrison had talked, cajoled, and urged her to chew, to swallow, to drink.

Then he'd held and rocked her, keeping her warm and safe while she struggled with the past and the morning that would come.

"Maybe we shouldn't disturb her, or any evidence found with her remains. Maybe we should notify the authorities and wait," he'd suggested quietly, thoughtfully.

"I just can't," she'd returned fiercely. "I've got to know. *Now.* It's been too long. You'll help me, won't you, Harrison?" she'd demanded, desperately fearing he'd refuse her. When he'd hesitated, she'd asked again, "Harrison?"

"We'll do what you want . . . now come here, dear heart," he'd said, easing her onto the pavement, still warm from the sun, curling his big warm body around hers. Somehow, tucked against Harrison, her body and mind drained, she'd fallen asleep to the caress of his hand on her hair. She'd awakened to his restless movements, his body straining against invisible tethers, his soft, undefinable cries protesting—

He'd been stunned, his face paling, she remembered now. It seemed as if he were still staked to that rock, staring at the skeletal hand and the turquoise ring, frozen by the sight. Michaela knew that the ring she'd clutched had been safety tucked away. Harrison was like that, ever careful, taking care of details. The firelight rippled across his harsh face, his frown, his lips moving without sound.

Then the words came in soft jumbled mix of song and words. . . . "That lullaby . . . It's too terrible . . . how could he have? She wasn't there . . . couldn't find . . . Faith, I'm so sorry. . . . She took your baby . . . Damn it!"

The jumbled words cruised frantically into the lullaby that had haunted Michaela's life, *"Soft-ly, slow-ly."*

"He raped her . . . he raped your mother. Damn him! Damn her!"

Michaela froze, watching Harrison turn and twist on the mountain pavement, fighting his past. Tears streamed down his cheeks, his hand slashing at his face as if to wipe away his nightmare. "Harrison?" she asked, fearing what tormented him now, what it could unlock.

"My God!" He sat upright, still caught by his nightmare, his expression of horror and revulsion. "He raped Faith Langtry! *She* took the baby!"

Michaela tried to understand, tried to push back her fear, but her senses told her that whatever Harrison knew, was so evil and dark that it tormented him. *His father had raped her mother? No—* "Harrison! Harrison! Wake up!"

She crouched beside him, trying to shake him awake, and he flung out an arm, sending her sprawling to the pavement beside him. She wasn't hurt, but terrified by the horrifying facts Harrison had just hurled into the midnight air. He rubbed his hands roughly over his face, his big body shaking. Then he leaped to his feet, still caught by his nightmares, braced as if prepared to take a blow, trying to orient himself with his surroundings.

Breathing heavily, as if he'd just raced down a twisting, dangerous, rocky path, Harrison rubbed his face again as if to remove the dregs of his nightmare, crossing over into reality. Agony was etched in his face, the lines deep, his jaw moving rhythmically beneath the stubble. Every muscle of his powerful body was locked in horror, standing out in relief. His hair stood out in peaks by the fingers he had just thrust shakily through it. As if drawing back his senses into him, reclaiming them at her soft whimper, he slowly turned to watch her rise to her feet. "Nightmares, Michaela . . . sorry," he stated unevenly, wiping away the sheen of sweat on his face with a rough hand.

"More than nightmares, Harrison." Her throat was constricted tight and dry, fear clutching her stomach, her blood chilling. One fist clenched at her side, and the other over her pounding heart, Michaela couldn't stop shaking. "You just said that your father raped my mother."

He released his breath as if a fist had slammed into his chest, he looked up at the moon as if gathering his next words close and well chosen within him. He rubbed his hands roughly over his face again. He breathed deeply, his bare chest rising and falling quickly. He swallowed and his fists curled so tightly that his knuckles pushed palely against his skin. "Maybe it is time . . . past time. Twenty-eight years ago, during that blizzard when your father and the other ranchers were out fighting for their ranches, stacking up dead and frozen cattle like cordwood . . . trying to salvage what they could, helping each other, my father saw his opportunity. He took her. Nine months later, Sable arrived."

"No one ever—" She couldn't move, staked by the ugly story, too ugly to be true.

"You're shaking. Let me—" He moved toward her, briskly picking up a flannel shirt from the backpack.

"Don't touch me!"

Harrison stood very still, his expression that of regret. He dropped the shirt to the pavement, unlike the Harrison who always neatly packed away, who stored his belongings very carefully. "Of course. I understand."

"Tell me what you know."

"The dirty truth that I've kept for all these years? That Sable was my half-sister? That when she was born, she had the same cap of red curls that all Kane children have at first? That her face was a little broader, that her eyes were blue as Faith's and yours and Roark's, but that her hair wasn't black and glossy as yours?"

"That can't be true. My father would have killed him."

Harrison studied his trembling fingers, opening them as he was revealing the foundations for his nightmares. "Yes, he would have. That's why I don't think she ever told him. I think that Jacob might have noted something had changed when he got back two weeks later. But Jacob isn't a man to doubt his wife, or his wife's fidelity. Your mother never encouraged my father—he was just like that, he enjoyed taking women. She wouldn't oblige and then—that's what happened . . . I think that your mother was protecting your father by not telling him. She knew what he'd do."

There were times, Harrison well knew, that a man needed a good stiff drink . . . and now was one of them. Michaela stood rooted in the firelight, her body trembling and taut, her fists at her side, her feet braced apart. Her face was pale in the moonlight, her eyes were wide, reacting to the painful blow he had just served her. *"How do you know all this?"*

It is time, he thought wearily. She deserved to know everything. She'd hate him then, but he had to tell her. The dark secret had been kept too long, festering, hurting everyone, never giving Faith peace. Had he betrayed the Langtrys by keeping silent? He'd wanted to protect them and now nothing but the truth would do. He touched his nose. "Remember that night when I came to your house, my nose broken? My father was kind enough to tell me about his conquests during his drunken rage. I think Faith may have suspected something when she saw me. But your mother is quite the woman."

Shaking, sinking to the pavement as if the invisible strings holding her upright had been cut, Michaela put her face in her hands and began rocking her body. Harrison rubbed his chest, where his heart lie in shreds. "It's best all this is said now. It's waited too long. I doubt that we'll find Sable's body with Maria's . . . You remember the rumor about how my mother was going to rest at a spa and she never came back? Everyone believed she finally left my father, I was five when she left. She'd planned carefully, taking jewels and small items she could sell. Julia Kane could look at a stock market report and pick a winner with her eyes closed. She could divert funds and manage bookkeeping records, and she basically turned everything my father had, and those funds from her inheritance into cash. When she left, she'd stripped away money from accounts in the bank, eventually ruining my father as he had ruined her. Oh, yes. My wonderful parents were a perfect pair."

Michaela stared at him blankly, then back into the

firelight. Harrison had lost her. Lost whatever he'd had with the Langtry family and it was his fault. "I was fifteen when I learned all this. Fifteen and an old man already. That was the last time he touched me. That was ten years after Sable was stolen, Michaela. Ten long years. I tried to find her, but my mother was very cunning. It's taken—"

"What does your mother have to do with Sable?" Michaela was on her feet, thrusting her hands against his chest, furious with him. "You've kept all this for all this time. My father searched until there was nothing left to know, to do—"

She shoved Harrison again, and turned from him as if she couldn't bear to look at him for another heartbeat. Pain slid through him. His hand, reached out to touch her, dropped without her warmth. It was better now to make a clean cut—"You asked what my mother has to do with Sable. I believe my mother took Sable that night. I believe she killed Maria and that she wanted to ruin my father's crowing about how he was 'passing off a Kane bastard in the almighty Jacob Langtry's brood.' "

Michaela's slender back stiffened beneath the layers of his flannel shirts. Her hair swung around her face, fanning out as she turned to him, eyes flashing. "You knew this all this time. *She* would have known the family nursery song. *She* would have known about Zachariah's coins. Harrison, your mother was my mother's best friend. None of this makes sense. It's all so—"

"Gruesome? Terrifying? Ugly? Twisted? Yes, hurting people seems to be a family trait. I'm sorry, Michaela." This time, it was Harrison who sank to the pavement, bowing his head in his hands. He'd held the secret too long and now it was gone, hurting those he'd tried to protect. Was his blood still warm? How could it be? Did his heart still beat? Or was that a hard cold rock in his chest? Nothing he could say would help, wash away the truth. "I'm sorry."

Michaela wiped her shaking palm across the tears dripping from her cheeks. She forced herself to swallow, to try to understand. In only a few hours, the twisted past had been torn away and yet none of it made sense. She glanced at the moon, at the jutting black mountaintops, and the man she'd known all of her life, trusting him. "But why? What would possess her to take a baby from its crib?"

Harrison tossed a stick into the flames, watching it catch fire as though he was seeing the past. "He tormented her. That was his specialty—tormenting. She couldn't have any more children, and Faith already had two before Sable. Then she had a 'Kane bastard,' as my father said that night. He never said it again. Not to me. The odd thing is, that though I was only five, and the memories are dim—I think Julia loved me as much as she could."

Michaela sat down, her mind churning, tears dripping freely from her cheeks. "Do you think she could have killed Sable? A helpless baby? Do you think Sable could be lying there with Maria? Or—"

Harrison shook his head. "I don't know . . . I don't know."

When he turned to her, the firelight tore across his craggy, tormented expression. "That is the link between Faith and myself. I think when she looks at me, she wonders what Sable would have looked like as a twenty-seven-year-old woman."

Michaela eased to her feet, pacing restlessly on the strip of cracked pavement. Her sister—half-sister—could be dead . . . or alive. She looked at the man staring into the fire, his face rigid. The past, torn from him, lived in dark memories that she could not even imagine. She remembered him as a fifteen-year-old boy, his eyes begging Faith, blood dripping from his nose, spotting his clothing. He'd been shamed then, unable to speak, to reveal what he'd learned. "You didn't know what to do then, did you? When your nose was broken?"

"At first, I thought it was more of his drunken ravings. I didn't trust him. He liked to taunt. But I finally found my old baby pictures—he'd hidden them—and it was only after he died and I was going through his things . . . I was eighteen then, when I found them. Sable had those Kane features, that cap of red curls. I tried, Michaela. I really tried. I was a boy, and I bungled the trail. Mucked it up with a private investigator who was only out to make money." He crossed his arms over his bent knees and she knew that neither one of them could go further in the terrible twisted secret.

"Harrison." Michaela ached for him, for a boy who had been tormented, for the man who had tried to repay Faith and Shiloh for crimes he didn't commit. She walked to him, and placed her hand on his shoulder. "Don't."

His arm swept around her legs, holding her as if she were his anchor. But he didn't stop staring into the fire, as if the ugly past were locked inside him forever, branded into his soul.

Sable Kane Langtry. Harrison closed his eyes, sickened by the past. The investigator's letter listed the monument's correct birth date for Sable. The date of death matched the last age Harrison had been able to pinpoint. He should have taken time to investigate before whisking Michaela off alone. . . . He should have—

What if the baby's remains were with Maria? Was the grave real? Why, after years of searching desperately, did information about that tiny grave suddenly surface? Was Sable beneath those rocks with Maria?

Before dawn, Michaela awoke from a restless sleep; she listened to the solid clunk and rattle of rocks being tossed aside. She leaped to her feet and ran to the edge of the road, peering down into the pre-dawn shadows. Harrison was already at work, his body gleaming with sweat, his muscles bunching as he tried to lift a large boulder away.

Gripping brush and easing herself down to him,

Michaela noted the blood on his hands, on his jeans where he had wiped them. "Harrison!"

"It's too much," he gasped, straining for breath. "The rocks are too big. We've got to go for help."

The scraps of red cloth fluttered gently, escaping the tomb where they had been kept safe. "We can't leave her here, Harrison."

"She's been there for a long time. The sooner we get help, the proper equipment, the sooner we'll know—"

"Harrison, your hands. They're bleeding."

"They don't matter." He stared at them as though seeing his father's blood all those years ago.

Michaela tended them carefully with the antiseptic from his backpack, tearing apart a T-shirt to wrap around them. The blood seeped through, staining the cloth. Within two hours of the trek down the mountain, using the old state road, they met a day hiker. Within another hour, the day hiker had led them back to his car and phone. Harrison had insisted on making several calls in private. By noon, Faith, Jacob, Roark and Culley appeared on horses.

"It will take until almost dark to get the right equipment up here," Roark said. "The sheriff is bringing a forensic team and said not to touch anything."

Culley began silently, efficiently, setting up camp, and Faith couldn't move, her body shaking, her face pale, her lips tremulous and tears not far away. Jacob was never far away, his arm encircling his wife.

"You'd both better eat something," Roark said to

Michaela and Harrison. "And clean up. Harrison looks like he's been through a war, and you don't look much better, Michaela. Culley is heating water. Use it. You can't do any more now."

Roark took Harrison's hand and unwrapped the cloth. "You've butchered your hands. They need to have the gravel and dirt cleaned out, and re-dressed."

"I'm fine."

But Michaela knew he wasn't. Harrison looked as if he'd been shattered, his big body seeming to hang suspended as it had that night when he was fifteen. He'd been her antagonist, he'd been her lover and friend, and now he looked so empty, so haunted. "I'll take care of him."

Roark studied her and between brother and sister, the look coursed with meanings. *You claim him, then? Is that the way of it?*

"I've made mistakes before. This isn't one of them." Michaela met her brother's look steadily. *I don't know what's going to happen from now on, but for now, he's mine.*

As she worked over his hands Harrison watched her. "They won't find the baby there, Michaela."

His tone was deadly quiet. "How do you know?" she asked, her nerves dancing icily, fear skittering up her spine.

"Because I think she's buried in a tiny grave near the Oregon coast. The stone reads 'Sable Kane Langtry.' Those calls I made from the hiker's car phone? I called an investigator who had just sent me a letter about a child's grave. I hadn't had time to

research myself after receiving the letter—I was in too
much of a hurry to get you— The trails had been dead
for a long time, and suddenly he was sent a postcard
with information leading to the grave site. Julia must
have known he was hunting for her, because she
signed the postcard—it was one of her games, sending little tips. But it's been too long since she's done
that. This time, I think it may be real."

The morning news camera panned the avalanche
that Harrison and Michaela had climbed the previous
evening. Then the camera shot swung to Michaela,
the wind tugging at her hair, her face pale and
strained. Her voice was controlled, professional, and
only a man who had made love with her knew how
deep her emotions ran.

"This is Michaela Langtry with KANE Television.
We're coming live from Cutter Ridge, where a body
was discovered last night by hikers. A team of forensics experts are now examining the body, suspected to
be that of Maria Alvarez. Ms. Alvarez has been missing for twenty-seven years and was well respected in
the small community of Shiloh, Wyoming. Update at
noon on KANE."

Harrison leaned back into the shadows of his
house. Last night, the Langtry family was too stunned
to come after him. *He deserved what he got. That was the
end of the Langtry family's friendship.*

He tapped the thick files, representing his years of
work to find Sable, and knew that Jacob Langtry

would come hunting. Harrison ran his finger down his nose. He'd wanted another anchor on the story, but Michaela hadn't listened. She'd washed her face in creek water, used her mother's cosmetic bag, and borrowed one of the male forensic team's white shirt and jacket. The camera panned the Langtry family, Jacob's arm around Faith. Roark's hand rested on his mother's shoulder. Culley glanced at the camera and scowled, turning away.

Harrison had kept away from the Langtry family, trying not to remind them of more pain. He'd showered, shaved, dressed, and driven to the bank, burying himself in mechanics as he'd always done. The town buzzed with the discovery of Maria's body, but after answering the sheriff's questions, Harrison had kept in his office. His hand had reached for the telephone too many times, then had drawn back. Words were useless now, Faith Langtry was stunned, pale and shaking. Jacob and Roark would come after Harrison and he didn't blame them.

Michaela. . . . He ached to hold her close, to protect her. But then he'd hurt her most of all, hadn't he?

He rewound the film clip he'd just taped, playing it again. He frowned slightly and replayed it once more. Just there, when Michaela's crisp professional tone hesitated just that fraction of a heartbeat, the tiny flinch was almost imperceptible. "Update at noon on K . . . ANE."

Harrison realized then that his fist had hit the desk's papers, the note to Kane Corporation attorneys to facilitate the release of Michaela from her contract—if she asked. The other letter, torn open impatiently and tossed aside, was a too-friendly offer from Aaron Gallagher to meet and discuss the potential sale of KANE.

The blood from Harrison's injured hand spotted the papers, a reminder of another desk and his father's blood. . . .

twelve

*Cleopatra rode without my leave. She tore the heart
from me, racing my stud across the meadow. Her hair
flew wild and free behind her, a black silk river in the
wind. She won the race, bent to sweep the prize, a
Langtry coin, into her hand, and with a cheeky look
tossed it to me. 'Twas no easy time between us then,
me fearing for her life, and her set upon the coins. I do
not understand the female mind. Yet I know she needs
me in the softest of ways.*

Zachariah Langtry's Journal

At midnight, a movement outside her front window caught Michaela's attention. She recognized
Harrison's big, pale gelding. There was no mistaking

the tall, powerful man in the saddle. Harrison swung down, took the briefcase from his saddle horn, and started toward the gate in her picket fence.

"So you're here, now, are you, Mr. Harrison Kane the second? Where were you earlier?" Too furious with Harrison to wait, she hurried into the bathroom, picking up a small bucket along the way. She dumped out the apples for the burros, scooped up the warm scented bath water and hurried back through her house. She found Harrison on her stone walkway, just by the lavender bed.

The jasmine scented bath water, complete with bubbles and skin softening oils, hit his face. While the bubbles shimmered on his hair, sliding down his face, Harrison blinked at her. Water dripped down his hair, tiny rivulets snaking down his unshaven face, drops lingering on his nose and on his chin. From the force of the water, his usually neatly combed hair waved at odd angles across his broad forehead. His white T-shirt clung damply to his chest, his worn jeans were wet, and his boots stood in a pool of Michaela's bath water. Some of the water had splashed onto Michaela's T-shirt, unwashed from their camping trip and still carrying his scent. "Now look what you've done," she said between her teeth. "This has been one of the roughest days of my life and now I'm going to have to run more bath water. That brand of bubble bath cost a fortune."

She knew she wasn't logical, that emotions ruled her, but Harrison deserved all her emotions. He was guilty of being the only man she'd ever wanted. And he hadn't been with her—not when she needed him. She'd wanted him to hold her safe and warm, she'd needed him fiercely, needed that sensible logic when her world was spinning out of control. For the first time in her life, she needed Harrison's sturdy logic and—she'd needed him to hold her. . . .

After the first shock, he looked out into the heat of the summer night, the burros grazing near her house. "Okay. I deserve that."

Harrison's face was lined, shadowed, his blunt cheekbones thrusting at his skin, his mouth drawn into a tight line. "I thought you'd want this—"

Too charged with emotion, too exhausted to control them, too furious with Harrison, Michaela hit his chest with her fists. "I could kill you. *Where were you today when I needed you?*"

A drop of water clung to the end of his nose and Harrison blew it away. "I thought you might want these—"

He blinked and frowned and shook his head; water spun off his hair, hurling silver beads into the night. He rubbed his bandaged hand across his eyes as if trying to tear himself from one world into the next. "Huh? Where was I when you needed me? *You* needed *me*?"

"Swaggering, overbearing idiot. Get off my property—" Fearing she would say more, Michaela turned and hurried into her house, slamming the door behind her. Because that wasn't enough and Harrison stood in the moonlight as if he were bolted to the earth, she opened the door and hurried out again.

This time both of her hands hit him flat on the chest. "You've got the best feminine side of any man I know, Harrison. *I needed you and you weren't there!*"

"Uh, 'feminine side.' Thanks," he mumbled, as she hurried back to the house.

Inside, Michaela ran her shaking hands over her face. She was acting childish, out of control, vindictive to a man who was obviously shattered by guilt, by his parents' cruelty. But as a woman—she wanted to cry in his arms, to hold him.

Harrison's firm knock on her door said he wasn't going anywhere. He opened the door and caught the shoe she threw at him. "Michaela?"

"Why weren't you with me?"

Harrison tossed the briefcase to her couch, which was littered with the clothing she'd been washing and folding. He picked up a rose-colored towel and wiped his face. The towel came away lightly spotted with blood when Harrison impatiently ripped away the loosened bandages. She closed her eyes, seeing his hands torn and bleeding from digging at Maria's rock tomb. "I needed to see about your hands. Don't you understand?"

Harrison shook his head, his big body braced as if to take a blow. "No, I don't. I thought it better to stay away from you, from your family. I want you to know that you can be released from your contract anytime you want—"

"Just like that? Are you afraid of having a relationship with me? Didn't you feel anything up there on the moun-

tain when we made love?" The nagging thought, pushed
into the tension between them, had been there
throughout the horrible day.

"You know I did." The answer came back like a
vow he would keep until he died, defend against all
others.

"I've never needed anyone like I needed you today,
Harrison. It wasn't a pleasant discovery, on top of
everything else. I've just had one man run in the face
of turmoil—I thought I could depend on him, too.
Well, I couldn't. You just could damage my confidence as a woman. I'm going to take my bath now, a
good long soak, and I'm not going to think about you
anymore." She ignored the tear dripping from her
chin. Of course she was going to think about him—
especially when he stood as if rooted to the spot, staring at her, looking haunted and torn as if he'd been
dragged through hell and back. That he didn't understand her need of him hurt.

She hurried to her bathroom, closing the door and
tearing off his T-shirt, discarding it onto the floor. She
eased into the bubble bath, added more water, and
settled down to cry.

When she opened her eyes, Harrison was sitting on
the closed toilet lid, his damaged hands hanging
between his knees. He'd taken off his damp shirt and
it lay, carefully folded, on her vanity. He was watching in that shielded, careful, logical way, dissecting
her emotions. "My hands aren't so bad, Michaela. You
already tended them at . . . at the site. There is no
need for you to—"

"My needs are my own. Go away." She slid deeper into the fragrant water, and Harrison noted the discarded T-shirt, picking it up.

"This is mine. Why were you wearing it?"

"It was there. It was a part of you. Since I didn't have the real thing, putting on the T-shirt seemed logical." *Logical?* She wasn't now. She was on edge, and too exhausted to deal with her torn nerves and emotions. She twisted open a tube of apricot exfoliant, squirted too much on her toes, and began scrubbing. She wished she could scrub away the whole nightmare—

He was silent for a long time, watching her work at her toes and heels. "What's that stuff? It looks grainy."

"Something to scrub away the dead skin. I—" She clenched her lids shut, seeing the skeleton again, the tattered red shroud of Maria's dress.

That long hard finger ran down Harrison's nose, which meant he was doing some heavy thinking. "Let me get this straight—you needed me? You wanted me?"

"You're supposed to be dependable and logical and *there*, just there . . . like you've always been. That's always been your job. I'm alone here, Harrison, and I needed you with me. Do you think it's easy for me to admit that? Mom and Dad left immediately, flying to Oregon and Roark with them. Mom wanted to see Sable's grave, just to see it, as soon as she could—in the morning, she will . . . the sheriff said—unofficially—that it was likely that Maria's body was dragged a distance down the embankment and then the old rocks stacked beside the road were pushed to cause the avalanche. Culley is staying at the house because there was a break-in around nine—nothing was taken. We decided not to report it—"

"That house is wired for alarms. I helped install the new ones. After the—after that night, Faith has always wanted alarms, and the dogs outside. Why didn't the alarms sound, or the dogs raise a ruckus?"

Michaela shrugged and tried to grasp control of her shaken emotions, tried to relax, to center, to calm enough to deal with the man she wanted to hold her. "Culley said it was 'real pros, looking for something special.' He thought that high-sonic equipment had hurt the dogs' ears because he could hear them howl and yelp before he went into the house. They were in obvious pain, rubbing their ears and rolling on the ground. We thought it best to let Mom and Dad deal with what they have now and tell them when they get back. He'll stay there, cleaning up, so Mom won't see—"

"*Why didn't you call me?*" Harrison's deep tone echoed in the feminine bathroom, filled with delicate ferns and rosebud wallpaper. Harrison's rough appearance, the size of his shoulders seemed to fill the tiny room. His long jeaned legs stretched out, his western boots careful not to touch the cream cotton rug on the pale linoleum.

"Because I thought you would already be beside me, if you cared." That truth hurt and Michaela closed her eyes against the man who could hold himself away from her, with whom she had known so much, in the past and as a lover. Too tired to deal with more, Michaela leaned back to close her eyes.

"I thought women washed their hair when they bathed."

Harrison's wary tone said he didn't know how to deal with her tonight. Well, neither did she. She felt as if she would fly apart at any minute, maybe she already had. "I may stay in here all night. You'd better go, and I didn't have more than a chance for a quick shower today, and the shampoo wasn't my brand. You see the claw feet on this old tub. It's a special, elegant tub and I got it just for nights like this, to get away from everything. I was going to shampoo my hair in the kitchen sink later and relax with a cup of tea. Tomorrow is going to be another—"

Harrison sniffed lightly. "What's that other smell? Not the laundry one, or the—"

"The jasmine one you're wearing? It's brownies. I've been doing laundry, cursing you, and baking brownies since ten. It all seemed logical somehow. I needed logic and I didn't have you." Beginning to feel the affects of the luxurious bath, Michaela almost smiled, seeing herself plummeting down the old pathway, wearing Harrison's still dirty T-shirt as her only clothing and sloshing him with the bucket of bath water. Odd, that talking with Harrison while he sat on the closed toilet lid, trying to understand her, should calm her. But then, Harrison had always made her feel safe, even when they were battling. She needed him now more than her pride. She forced one eyelid to open and found his puzzled expression. "I changed my mind. You're staying the night, you know. You can take care of your horse and put him in the little lean-to behind the house—from the look of the clouds tonight, we're in for a summer storm. But you run off and I'll hunt you down like a dog."

"Sounds good to me," he said with humor in his tone.

An hour later, Michaela slowly surfaced from sleep; she listened to Harrison breathing steadily, deeply beside her, still dressed in his jeans. He smelled of brownies, her jasmine scented bath water, and safety in a world torn apart.

As though sensing her awakening, Harrison slid his arm around her and drew her close. His kiss was a reassuring light brush across her lips. "Go to sleep, honey. Rest. I'll be here when you wake up."

She settled against him, wrapping her arm around his chest, her leg over his. She nuzzled his hair, catching the jasmine fragrance of her bath water. He drew the blanket over her shoulder and kissed her forehead. "I'll be here," he repeated.

"Good old Harrison," she whispered as sleep slid over her and she gave herself to it.

During the night, she reached out and sensed he came awake instantly. He took her hand, placing it over the steady slow beat of his heart. "What is it?"

"I believe that Cleopatra wanted me to find Maria. To try to find the coins and unite them with the Langtry family. I always felt that Cutter Canyon—it called to me, you know? Do you believe me?"

His hesitation was slight, but to her that meant that

Harrison mulled her thought. "Yes. You're a strong woman with definite instincts. You have her blood."

"You're not like your father at all, Harrison," she whispered, because she knew he thought of another dark inheritance. She drifted sleepily beside him, a peaceful harbor after a horrible nightmare. "Don't think for a moment that you are . . . it's going to start raining soon."

"How do you know?" he asked against her forehead, his fingers laced with hers. His nightmares were no less than hers; the scarring on his hand reminded her of his anguished expression as he dug at the rocks.

"Clouds are one thing, and they're building up on the mountains. But my senses—the feel on my skin— are another. Listen to the frogs. They've quieted a little. I've missed frogs . . . and home." The pale sheer curtain at the open window fluttered, soft with fragrances that the gentle breeze swept into the room. Michaela smiled against Harrison's shoulder. Cleopatra had been right—men were difficult, arrogant, bullying, hardheaded beasts at times, but one that could be trusted was one to capture and keep.

His smile curved against her cheek, the stubble familiar and reassuring. "Frogs. After all you've been through, you've missed frogs."

"Cleopatra wants those coins returned to the Langtrys. I can feel her pressing need in me. It's like an ache." Then because she was too tired to deal with more, Michaela gripped the hair on his chest, tugging lightly. "Don't forget what I said about running you down like a dog, Harrison."

The rumbling sound was Harrison's chuckle, his chest vibrating gently. "I might like it."

He came to her in the night as she wanted, his gentle seeking kiss telling of his need for her, for what ran strong between them. Michaela opened herself to him, restlessly arching to his caress as the heat grew, the rising wind churning in the curtains. He was too careful, she thought, and knew that this lovemaking was a reassurance, a gentle time to give comfort and to take it, to cherish what had grown between them . . . placing the past and tomorrow apart from the tenderness between them. She sought his body, sliding her hands lower, finding him, releasing him from his clothing. His mouth was open upon her skin, easing away the nightshirt she wore, his breath warm upon her throat, her face. Harrison took a steady path to her breasts, cupping one, molding the softness to his lips, suckling gently. His hands ran over her hips, molding them, caressing. . . . They were rough with scars and calluses, and somehow true and warm and safe. She sighed and touched him, possessed him, and then he came heavily and so warm over her, to her bidding, locking them deep and true. Then she let the world spin away and gave herself to him.

In San Francisco, Aaron Gallagher slammed down the telephone and began pacing his private gym. His man in Shiloh had said that Michaela's home was protected tonight by "A big guy. Tough looking. Looks like he's staying the night. Ran by the Langtry ranch. The lights are off in the house—looks empty. No one answering their telephone, but the machine. Checked with the nearest airport and both Mr. and Mrs. had boarded earlier in the day."

There was no chance for Aaron's man to slip into her house tonight, to steal her Langtry coin. The coin on Aaron's chest seemed to burn, reminding him of his failure to obtain the rest—the break-in to the Langtrys was timed for their absence. Aaron's best man had failed to find the rest of the coins. "Idiot. It looks like I have to do everything myself."

Aaron stopped to preen in the full length mirror, flexing his gym-sculpted muscles. Through his attorneys, Harrison Kane had flatly turned down Aaron's first probe to buy KANE. Harrison hadn't waited for business hours, or a discussion, or a formal letter.

The coins had to be his and Aaron brooded his next move. The Langtrys knew all about Kane and would despite any gossip. Therefore, the trusting tie between the Langtrys and Kane needed to be cut. But how?

Aaron frowned, noting the harsh light overhead. It had just shot through the hair on top of his head, catching a gleam from his scalp. He probed his thinning hair and whipped a tube of hair replenisher from his pocket, quickly applying it. Not trusting the damage a comb would do, he patted his hair gently. For a moment, he thought he heard a woman laugh softly near the huge windows overlooking San Francisco's dazzling night lights. Perhaps he was just remembering how the Kane woman had— He shook his head. The Kane woman had cackled eerily, almost like a bone raked up an old-fashioned washboard.

He gave himself to thinking about the coins . . . how all six would look and feel in his hands, making him powerful.

Harrison sniffed at his bare shoulder. The delicate feminine scent matched that of his recent shampoo. Taking a bath and shampooing in an old-fashioned tub with claw feet was a first—fitting his body into it, his knees doubled. The small colorful array of bottles beneath the small oval mirror fascinated him. A variety of brushes stood in a pottery mug, obviously crafted by Faith. He wondered briefly about the use of the tiny cotton squares. He hurried to rise from the bath, slashing away the clinging bubbles. Methodically, he prowled through the calls he'd made upon waking. Josy Daniels had expected to take over the morning and noon show. She was prepared to cover Michaela's segments and her own, but surprisingly Dwight wanted to do his share, too.

Culley's terse description of the break-in confirmed that professionals had been at work. Harrison frowned—there was something about the way Culley always watched him, as if searching for something in Harrison . . .

Harrison stared at his reflection in the steamy mirror. The tiny disposable feminine razor was useless on his two-day-old beard. Had it been that long since he'd shaved? He'd been very careful to avoid chafing her skin while they made love on the mountain, and that seemed an eternity ago. The towel he had used last night lay on the cream cotton rug, spotted with his blood. He tugged up the clean boxer shorts from Michaela's overflowing laundry basket. From the filled baskets and clothing on the floor, it looked like she decided to wash everything at once. Harrison bent to retrieve the towel, studying it. To remove blood required soaking, and he'd had plenty of experience with that. The image of his father's death ripped through Harrison, and he pushed it firmly away.

Thunder rolled nearby and a moment later, lightning zigzagged across the cloudy morning sky as he closed Michaela's bedroom window. She still continued to sleep soundly. He watched her, and tried to understand what had happened last night—*she was angry with him for not being with her.* He'd expected her fury for another reason, because of his family, because he'd known all along that the baby was dead. He bent to cover Michaela's bare shoulder with the hand-stitched quilt. She moved restlessly, frowning slightly and he hesitated, unused to giving comfort, before placing his hand on her hair, smoothing it, the silky strands snagging softly upon his rough hands. She settled again, snuggling down into the bed they had shared.

The tiny closet was crammed to overflowing with her clothing, business suits hanging from a holder on the door, shoes spilling out onto the hardwood floor of the bedroom. The bed's frame wasn't ultra modern as he expected; rather it was old, a bit scarred and needing refinishing. The posts cornering it weren't tall and elegant, but short and square and sturdy, matching the night stand stacked with files and books. But the dresser was polished and old and obviously treasured, the oval mirror held between two curving posts. Michaela's costume jewelry filled a basket, necklaces and earrings hung from stands, easy to reach and select.

But there on the doily, gleaming in the dim light, was the coin she treasured. It seemed to warm to his fingertips, as if calling out to him to help Michaela return the rest of the coins to Langtry keeping. But how? He'd done his best. He touched the turquoise ring in the center of the chain, placed so meticulously that he knew Michaela's thoughts were of Maria, mourning her. Maybe he'd missed something crucial in the file—

On his way to the kitchen, he stopped and saw the living room for the first time; he'd been too startled with Michaela's reaction to him to notice. A vacuum cleaner stood in one corner, attachments scattered across the rug as if the user had used them all. The couch cushions stood at odd angles, as if freshly vacuumed. Window cleaner and rags sat on a small table; the lemony scent said they'd had recent use. "From the looks of it, she tried to clean everything away at once, including the past—and me."

The male Langtrys would probably clean up with something a bit harder than lemon oil and laundry detergent . . . and Harrison wouldn't blame them. Faith was certain to hate him now.

Last night, Michaela was alone and needing. It was logical—or not—that she turn to the man with whom she had recently made love. It wasn't logical that she turn to a man who had deceived her for years, who was the child of a family who had ruined her own.

Perhaps she had turned to him because they were together in this nightmare. Trauma made for strange decisions; she could regret last night in the clarity of day.

Harrison prowled into the kitchen, thrust the blood-spotted towel into the washing machine and set it on cold. He'd promised Michaela to stay, and he would. His methodical mind dissected her running down the walkway toward him, her bare legs flashing in the moonlight, her breasts shimmering beneath his T-shirt. There was no misreading the fury in her expression.

And she'd needed him. No one had ever needed him in his lifetime. Harrison turned the unique thought as he considered the huge stove dominating her tiny kitchen. Obviously harvested from the recesses of a storeroom, the stove was the most fascinating one he'd seen, filled with large gas burners, enameled ovens, a shelf running across the top. He experimented with the sturdy levers and knobs as he made coffee. He'd expected a sleek modern version, where controls ran smoothly without buttons. This stove was definitely meant for a man. He wondered distantly if he could cook Michaela a proper meal, given a stove like this.

Women's logic had always escaped him, especially Michaela's, so wide open with him. He glanced out at another lightning bolt and wondered how she would feel about him this morning, after she had rested— after they'd come together, gently needing each other in the night. It was best, perhaps, Harrison thought, his mind dissecting the possibilities, to wait and see. Once her reaction to him was clear, he could determine how to— He smiled tightly, reminding himself that he was a contemporary man with little experience in the feminine arenas. Intimacy wasn't in his experience. With Michaela, he felt more like a frontiersman determined to capture a bride.

He studied the small kitchen, splashed with yellows, an aged blue glass fruit jar filled with daisies. Cozy, he thought, and settled in to explore the new feeling. He liked "cozy" with Michaela, the scent of laundry and lemon, and brownies enveloping him. He wanted to return to the woman sleeping in bed, to love her again, but he wouldn't. Michaela was too exhausted, fragile, vulnerable.

Vulnerable? Hell, he was vulnerable. After rest, when she was thinking clearly, Michaela could detest him.

He lifted the foil wrapper covering a pan on the stove's massive warming shelf. The fragrant, mouthwatering aroma of chocolate rose to tempt him. He meticulously counted the eight various pans of brownies, obviously freshly baked and knew that

Michaela must have had all the ovens on at once. He considered the nut-filled brownies and the emotional woman of last night. She'd remembered his preferences and he took that as encouragement that he ranked favorably high as a prospective lifetime mate. Or did he?

How could Michaela possibly overlook the fact that he was the son of Julia and Harrison Kane, the half-brother to her missing sister?

thirteen

The third coin came from her mother's people. They seemed most eager to be free of it after my wife's visit to their camp. In return, I placed aside a section of our land where they could hunt and fish and live as they wish. I will protect them with my life, despite the wars of red and white. I often wonder what Cleopatra said to bring fear to those stalwart warrior's eyes. She will not tell me, and we argued most heatedly about a wife's good obedience. 'Twas the pleasure of mending that fiery rift that almost made my stalwart heart swoon. . . .

Zachariah Langtry's Journal

Fearing Harrison had left, Michaela leaped from her bed and hurried into the kitchen. She had to tell him that she could manage now—without him—that she was rested and able to—she found Harrison, dressed only in his boxer shorts, his bare, slightly hairy legs sprawled from his chair onto another. She remembered the gentle rhythmic scrape of those legs against her, the powerful muscles sliding against hers, bunching and— Unable to move, Michaela couldn't breathe, her body tensing as his hand swept across his chest, rubbing the wedge of hair thoughtfully.

Outside a thunderstorm raged, furious rains slashing at the windows, the day dark and broody beyond the brightly lit kitchen. The rain, snaking down the windows, made shadows on his face as he concentrated. He picked up a pen, scrawled a note on a pad, and scowled at it. *Who was he?* She'd known him all her life and suddenly Harrison was new and fascinating, her heart racing just to look at him.

She'd seen those black thick brows draw together before, the steel gray of his eyes, that hard lock of muscle crossing his jaw when he saw something he didn't like. The dim light slid across his lashes, and drew fringed shadows on those hard, blunt cheekbones. The jut of his brow over his deep-set eyes tightened. Harrison was too rugged and fierce to be called handsome. His finger jabbed at the paper, traced the printed line, and his hand closed into a big, hard fist.

Yet beauty roamed in him, in the flow of his tanned skin gleaming in the half-light, in the way his shoulders moved, the lift of his chest muscles, that flat rippling stomach. He'd bathed, and her finger craved to smooth the damp curls at his nape, to rub that taut muscled neck. Her body tensed, remembering the way he held her, as if nothing could tear him away from her. His big hands had moved under her hips, lifting her. . . .

Harrison closed the file he'd been studying, the deep frown easing away as he saw her. The snaking patterns of the rain shifted on his face as he smiled.

"Good morning, dear heart. Sleep well?" he asked cheerfully, as if he had been comfortably sitting in her kitchen every other morning she awoke. He'd worked his way through half of a pan of brownies. His gaze traveled slowly over her rumpled hair, the faded flannel robe over her nightshirt and down her bare legs. He inhaled roughly as he studied her feet and slapped closed the thick file on her table. "I thought you couldn't cook."

"I was just trying out the recipe from the Monday cooking show—Mrs. Little's favorite brownie recipe. I did the interview, remember? And make sure you leave some for Roark and Culley." She'd been thinking of Harrison, needing his arms around her, furiously whipping the batter and chopping the nuts and keeping herself from tearing after him. She'd fought her pride; she wouldn't let everyone in Shiloh know that she needed him more desperately than he needed her.

He carefully replaced the brownie that he had just picked up. "These are for Culley and Roark?"

"I wanted to wrap my hands around someone's thick neck last night, and squeeze. That neck wasn't Culley's or Roark's." He wasn't certain of her yet, even after the beautiful lovemaking of the night. But then, she wasn't certain of herself at the moment. Harrison was too big and overpowering, her body pounding with the need to feast upon him. Another part of her mind was with her mother and the closing of a long, painful search. She glanced at the clock on the wall and blinked. "I've missed the morning show and I'm about to miss the noon one. I've got to hurry—you let me oversleep, Harrison!"

He slowly placed the coffee cup he'd been holding on the small table she'd salvaged from her mother's storage—it was the table her parents used when they were first married. "You're staying home today and you're resting. Josy and Dwight are stepping in, sharing duties to cover your spots."

"You know why I want to be there. I want to know anything that is breaking about Maria's death."

"The sheriff has called already. He'll call here with any more news. You are going to rest today," he said firmly. "You are going to take one of those long, relaxing bubble baths, eat something healthy, and get some more sleep."

"It's been a long time since anyone tried to tell me I needed a bath and a nap." Michaela uncurled her fists; only Harrison would dare try to order her to stay out of the unfolding story. She wanted any information possible, to gather it to her, to hoard and dissect it, even though she knew nothing would change the past.

Harrison's left eyebrow lifted, challenging her. "Don't even think about fighting me on this, dear heart. I'm seeing that you do just that."

Michaela poured herself a cup of coffee, dumping sugar and milk into it. On the Oregon coast, her parents would be standing beside that tiny grave. Maria's remains were being evaluated by a forensics team, and nothing in the world was right—except Harrison, dressed in his shorts, sitting and eating brownies at her kitchen table. Outside, the fierce summer wind raged, and rain had bowed Mrs. Atkins' herb beds. Inside, Michaela felt as battered, fighting to keep from crying. Her hand shook as she stirred the coffee with a spoon. She hit the counter with the spoon and it clattered to the floor between them. "I'm trying to establish myself as an anchor. This is *my* story."

"You're too close to it. You're running on nerves, Michaela. You're not thinking clearly. You want to help, to do something for Maria and for your mother; there's nothing anyone can do now. Last night—"

"Yes, what about last night?" She turned to him, anger simmering. "Where were you? The station's call letters—KANE. It wasn't your ego that named Kane Corporation or Kane Bank, or the television station, was it? You thought you'd draw your mother back somehow, get the information from her."

From Harrison's dark, guarded expression, Michaela knew she had hit the truth. "Julia Kane is a highly intelligent woman, a genius, if you will. My father used that, before she turned on him. Under an assumed name, she's likely to have subscribed to Shiloh's newspaper, and probably kept tabs on everything for years—if she's alive. I check every name that subscribes to the paper. I thought it was worth a chance to stir her up. She's unpredictable, brilliant and devious. I wanted her confirmation about what happened to Sable. . . . You can't go out in that storm, dressed like that—"

When she turned to Harrison, leveling a cool look at him, he placed the brownies aside. "Fine. I'm coming with you."

"Wait a minute," she ordered, placing her free hand upon his chest, staying him. "You've never skipped work a day in your life. Why now?"

"I've got more important considerations," he said slowly, in the thoughtful way that meant he'd reasoned and weighed and had come to a conclusion he wasn't likely to change.

"Such as?" she asked, her heart thumping wildly, but no more unsteadily than his, beating heavily beneath her palm.

He inhaled slowly. "I think it is important for me to understand the female mind better—namely yours. What the hell is a feminine side? I'm not certain if I like that remark or not."

"Stop bristling." Michaela pushed open the door and the storm welcomed her with a slash of lightning. She'd needed the fresh wash of rain, the wind lifting her hair, the scents of earth, cattle, and freshly baled hay.

"Women," Harrison grumbled darkly behind her as he jammed on his western boots.

When the burros and Harrison's gelding had had their treats, Harrison took the metal bowl from Michaela. He placed it over her head for protection from the rain. He knocked lightly on it. "I don't suppose we could go in now?"

The rain hammered at the bowl and Michaela met his wary look. "You realize that it's almost one o'clock in the afternoon, and you're standing in full sight of the highway—wearing nothing but your shorts and your boots, don't you? And darn, those well-combed waves are just curling everywhere."

He glanced at the highway and slashed away the raindrops running down his face. "See what you've done? My executive image will never been the same," he said wryly, unbothered as the mail woman honked her horn and gave a "Woo! Woo!"

Harrison tilted Michaela's mixing bowl-hat, peering down at her. For a moment, the slashing cold rain seemed to heat, pouring warmly over her.

His hair was waving damply down his forehead, curls nipped low on his nape, making him seem sleek and foreign and new. Rain beaded on his eyebrows, his cheeks and on his shoulders, forming into tiny rivulets that slid into that curling wedge of hair on his chest and lower. The wind whipped through his hair, lifting it away now and he seemed like a dark warlord intent upon one thing—her. He took her breath away with the realization of how much he wanted her, how dark and glowing those smoky eyes could be, watching her, waiting—

Yet she'd known him all her life—she'd made love with him. Michaela tensed as she realized that the slow warmth moving up her cheeks was a blush. She closed her eyes and moved into the novelty of being new and clean and touched only by Harrison. She realized that nothing else had passed before, nothing that mattered.

His finger smoothed her wet cheek, testing the warmth and time seemed to stand still, the rain almost musical on the metal bowl. Then he slowly bent to kiss her experimentally, as if testing her reaction to him. The kiss lingered and brushed and warmed and searched. His deep voice was dark and rough, curling intimately around her—just for her, despite the rain and the nearby highway traffic. "I've never been needed before. It's a new experience, okay? I'm in an adjustment period."

"So am I," she admitted softly, placing her hands on his chest, on that solid warm beat. She skimmed his nipples gently with her thumbs and a ripple passed quickly through his tall, hard body. Harrison was very susceptible to her touch. That knowledge hurled through her and centered in a warm glow deep within her. She dug her fingertips in slightly, then smoothed his wet, gleaming shoulders with her palms. He inhaled sharply, his stomach tightening and one glance lower on his body told her that he was already aroused, his rain-soaked shorts leaving no doubt.

"I feel like I'm getting sized— You're upset and exhausted. You don't know what you want. I won't have your father accusing me of taking advantage of you. I've done enough—"

He stopped as she kissed the corner of his mouth,

taking the taste into her, savoring it. "Oh, Harrison. Can't you take a hint?"

He blinked at her and blew away the raindrop clinging to his nose. "What? What hint?" he asked urgently.

She stood on tiptoe to kiss him, to lock her arms around the safety that never changed, no matter how the world tumbled around her. Then his arms were circling her waist, lifting her off her feet. The mixing bowl tumbled to the mud and her firemen's boots slid away as he continued to hungrily kiss her, carrying her into the house.

Inside, she laughed up at him—this new Harrison—and then her breath caught at the stormy dark hunger of his eyes, consuming, burning her. His mouth was a hot brand on hers, and she met him fiercely, hands tugging at damp clothing and until he pulled her against him.

The bold surge of his desire nudged her stomach as his hands, rough and trembling, coursed over her, heating, sensitizing. She slid her fingers through that damp curling hair, holding his mouth slanted to hers, the fit too tight and deep to be severed, even for a moment. When her palms slid to frame those hard bones of his jaw, the stubble rough against her skin, Harrison trembled. "You're—you're burning, already damp against me—"

She moved then and the blunt pressure slid, resting intimately within her thighs. Harrison closed his eyes, shaking fiercely as his tongue surged deeply within her keeping. She trusted his strength as he lowered her to the kitchen's cotton rug, in front of the huge stove.

Heart racing, her hunger surging out of control, feverish, Michaela opened herself to him and caught him tightly against her. She sighed with the filling, the locking of her body to his. The pounding rhythm of his body was no sweet thing, rather a claiming just as she wanted, her own needs as demanding as she hurled herself into the steaming torrent, flying quickly to that ultimate release, holding Harrison tight and deep and safe. His mouth tugged at her breasts, suckling, nibbling, churning the river of heat staking her on that ultimate plane where only he existed. With a long, shuddering sigh, Harrison gave himself to her, his features honed fiercely above her, skin taut across his face, his powerful shoulders. While his body rhythm ran on deep inside her, Michaela withdrew into herself, focused on that intimate pleasure, giving herself to it.

When she could open her eyes, Harrison's body still locked with hers, she found him staring at her, frowning. She couldn't stop the bubble of laughter sliding warm within her. "Shocked, Harrison?"

His big hand had locked to the stove as if it were his safety. "You'll have bruises on your backside. I—"

"I can't move now, but if I could, I'd snuggle in bed and sleep forever," she heard herself murmur. "Good old Harrison. You're so dependable."

His cocky, boyish grin curved against her hand as she patted his cheek. "Yes, I am, aren't I?"

"No doubt about it."

Then Harrison was easing from her, lifting her and carrying her back to bed. This time, she poured herself over him, taking him gently within, rocking slowly as Harrison covered her back with the blanket. She smiled as another release shook them, and slid gently off to sleep in his arms.

"You're right. Your mother is a very intelligent woman. She's covered her trail well. She knew how to change identities like another woman would change clothes. And she knows how to make money—and to ruin people, like she did your father," Michaela said as she studied Harrison's files. He'd done everything he could to find Sable and his mother, but the trail was too cold by the time he had started hunting. Harrison had meticulously followed every clue to its bitter end. With little knowledge of the mind's quirks, anyone could see that Julia was brilliant at deception. But only a sick and battered mind would play games as Julia had done, the cruelty of the faked death certificates, the extravagantly crafted, step-by-step falsehoods. Harrison had starred one interview from a sympathetic woman who had tended Julia during an illness—"Her mind twisted through passages I cannot understand, and then suddenly the next moment, she was as normal as you and I. At first I thought it was the flu working at her, and then I knew she needed more help for her mind than for her body. She reworked my retirement portfolio and I've never seen anything like the way she could manage paperwork or make money grow. She was gone as quickly as she came, leaving no trace of where to find her. There was nothing on her bed but the sad wig she always wore."

Michaela watched Harrison test the stove's flames; he was like a boy with a new train set, prowling through the ovens, trying each of the large burners. "Go ahead, cook something," Michaela said and picked up the files, carrying them into her living room. She settled down to Harrison's notes once more, ignoring the clattering of pans in the kitchen.

"No baby," he'd written on every entry after the time Sable would have been two years old.

The pictures of newborns Harrison and Sable were an exact, startling match. She traced Sable's picture and wondered how anyone could steal away a six-week-old baby. Michaela thought of two-year-old Sable's grave, nestled amid lush Northwest ferns and towering pines. Faith would be there now, mourning the child she'd lost. Michaela wiped away the tears trailing down her cheeks and found Harrison standing in the doorway, his arms folded across his chest. "I'm sorry, Michaela. I'd change it all, if I could."

She slashed away the tears. "You did everything you could. This research must have cost a fortune and the time—"

"I should have turned to Jacob, told him what I knew. But I wasn't certain what Faith had told him. Even if I voiced my suspicions about my mother without mentioning the rape, I knew it would have to come out eventually. Even after my father's death—it was all so mixed-up."

"You wanted to protect my mother. They'll understand that."

"I'd give my life to protect her," Harrison stated solemnly.

"From the looks of these files, it looks as if you have already done that. Come here and hold me," she whispered, her throat tight with tears that would not stop flowing.

Three days later, Faith looked up from her pottery wheel. It was spinning and empty, just as she had been. Harrison stood in the shadows of the shelves lined with her students' work.

Pain sliced through her once more. There would be no more wondering about how Sable would look now, if she had Harrison's dark brown waving hair, if her blue eyes had turned to gray. She leaned back in her chair, not quite ready to let go of the child she would never see toddle or play. Then, because life moved on and she must help the boy who had carried a huge dirty secret into manhood, she stood. "Harrison, come sit by me outside."

He followed her to the patio, where she folded away a student's easel. In the distance, the mountains surged into the clear blue sky. Mark Jeffries' tractor hummed, the sound blending with the birdcalls and the scent of herbs bordering the patio. Faith eased into a wooden chair, feeling very old, as if she had passed through centuries in only a few days. Harrison, dressed in a blue cotton shirt, worn jeans and his boots, sat slowly beside her, She smiled briefly at the crease in his jeans, that military edge ground into him too young. There was nothing to remind her of his father now. Harrison looked so horribly worn, and her mind went skipping back to images of him on the mountain. His hands had been torn, blood wiped on his pants.

She took his hand in hers and listened to the mockingbird's trill, the hum of that tractor as it passed, cutting hay for bailing. She'd managed her daily routines, the image of that tiny grave set amid the Cascade ferns and soaring pines held tight within her. Jacob—wonderful Jacob—did not know now how to hold her, his body stiff in bed beside her. The past slashed at him, too, and she would have to wait for him to accept all that had passed those twenty-eight years ago. And here was the man who had bled for her, who had known everything.

"Julia was once my friend. She was brilliant, you know. Just as you are, a fine mind for numbers. She loved you very much."

His hand, big and rough, tightened on hers, the tremble telling her that his emotions were tightly tethered. But he'd come to make his peace, and she would give him what she could. His head was down, one hand hanging limply between his knees. Faith reached to touch his hair, then drew back her hand. Harrison was a man apart, not like his father, or like the child she'd held close for years. His voice came deep and rough as though scraping on his throat, the words pulled from his soul, "I'm sorry, Faith."

"You didn't need to come back, Harrison. But you did. And you're trying to right something you didn't do, had no part of. Don't. Don't do it for me, or for anyone. I know how hard you're struggling with this, and how you've worked to make my dreams come true. But it's time for your own dreams now."

Harrison turned to look at her. "Michaela should have never been on that mountain, never seen Maria's . . . Maria like that. I wanted time alone with her and that's what happened."

Faith smiled and squeezed his hand. "My daughter would be a hard woman to catch. She runs fast."

Harrison nodded in grim agreement. "She does that."

"Her heart is strong and she trusts her instincts. Sometimes, I think she has more of Cleopatra in her, than of me." Faith's instincts told her to believe in the beating heart beneath her fist, to believe her baby was still alive. After twenty-seven years, it would take time to adjust, she told herself.

She inhaled the morning air, the scent of the newly mown field. Whatever else she felt inside her, she had to give her family and Harrison peace. "If Maria's body had never been found, I'd still be—trapped. Now I know. Sable should stay there, my little girl, where the ferns drip dew on her tiny grave and the ocean winds sway through the tall trees. I didn't feel it was right to bring her back here, to disturb her again. It's time for it all to end. But you're still a member of this family, only now there's nothing to fear. Someday you'll have a child, and you bring her to me to hold, will you?"

She touched the waving dark brown hair, the red lights shimmering in it. Her daughter would have had hair like that—Faith inhaled quickly and knew she had to move on, for the sake of those who loved her.

Harrison's expression was haunted. "I don't know that I know how to love, Faith. I don't know that I have anything to offer."

"You have yourself and that is enough, and love is how you clasp it close and hold it dear. You know how to do that already, Harrison." She stroked that hair, then tore herself away from that tiny grave. She'd known a young cowboy, rawhide rough, and with a charm that could knock any woman's sensibilities away. It had been a long, good life with Jacob Langtry and she intended to have more—

"Michaela is very much like you. She's like Jacob, too, but she's unshakable when she believes."

"She's a Langtry. She isn't easy. You're alike in so many ways."

"She says I've got a feminine side," Harrison grumbled darkly.

"You do, and you're insulted just like Roark would be. And all hell would break loose if I ever told Jacob that, but he is a good listener . . . he tries to understand, like you do. You're strong and brave and true and honest and that's what is important. Michaela may not trust herself now, but on one level she does trust you, because you never change—you've always been solid and good." Faith closed her eyes and gave herself to the pleasant morning and the young man trying to understand, trying to do his best in a situation created long ago.

That night, Harrison stepped into the mountain clearing, his hands raised. The rifle bore pointed at him didn't waver and Jacob Langtry's hard expression didn't soften. "So you knew all along," Jacob said at first thrust.

In the fire between them, a pine knot laden with pitch, ignited. A shower of sparks shot high into the smoke spiraling into the mountain night.

Harrison nodded. "Since I was fifteen."

Jacob's rifle barrel slowly lowered and he crouched down by the fire, sitting on his heels western-style. "I'd have killed him," he stated. "Beat him to a pulp. Even now, the thought of him touching her, hurting her, makes my gut turn sour. My wife wanted to protect me. She didn't tell, but I knew something was wrong when I came back. There was fear in her eyes those first days, and my Faith isn't a weak woman. I thought I'd done something wrong every time she cringed away from me."

His black eyes were hard on Harrison, pinning him. "You rode up here at midnight? Well, then, it would be inhospitable of me not to offer you coffee, wouldn't it?"

He nodded at the blackened camp pot by the fire, and Harrison bent to pour a cup into a pottery mug.

He noted the mug and knew that camp gear usually included cups that wouldn't break, but Jacob wanted to brood, holding something his wife had made. "I'm sorry, Jacob. I wanted to tell you."

Jacob's expression was fierce, his words a shot. "Why the hell didn't you, then? I raised hell all over this country and back to find that baby."

"I thought it was Faith's choice."

"Damn right it was, and she didn't tell me. That hurt. I went over that file Michaela gave me. You think I don't know you did everything you could and ten years after the trail was cold? A boy, pitting himself against a man's job. Now, how do you think that seems—you not trusting me? My daughter is afraid I'll hurt you, boy. She came to me, laid out the rules. Now what do you think of that?"

Harrison slowly nodded, jarred by the thought that Michaela would protect him. In his lifetime, no one had. "This is between you and me."

"And Faith. Every time she looks at you, she's seeing her baby. She's wondering what Sable would look like as a woman. There was nothing in the paperwork at the cemetery about the woman who paid cash for the burial. The caretaker had long ago died and there was just this little stone marker with an angel on it— Sable Kane Lantry . . . dammit! It didn't make any difference to me, she was my baby, too!"

Harrison took a deep steadying breath, and for a moment listened to the sounds, the cool August night signaling September when the trembling aspens would flame across the mountains. Jacob was snarling and hurt, Faith was quietly bleeding, and Harrison had never played matchmaker. Surprisingly, the task came easily to him. Perhaps it was because he cared deeply for both of them and they were so right for each other. It was only logical. "I think your wife needs you now. And you're up here acting like an old bear."

"Damn right I am." Jacob spit into the fire, hatred burning inside him that couldn't be satisfied. It left a bitter taste. "There are just some animals you kill, because you know they are going to kill again, tear the life from something wonderful and special. That's what I would have done to him. She's down there, not talking to me, sitting at her wheel, and making pots. Oh, she told me everything—twenty-eight years too late to kill him. . . . It tore me apart to watch her at that baby's grave . . . she'd picked a little bouquet of Wyoming wildflowers. She held them all the way on the plane and then put them on her baby's grave—I always wondered what it was between her and you and now I know. . . . That's a hard wound to heal."

Harrison tossed the coffee into the fire, watching it sizzle on the burning wood. "You must have known—somehow."

"Didn't matter. I've plowed all through this years ago. You think I didn't know—feel—that that baby wasn't mine with that cap of red curls when no Langtry baby had anything but hair black and glossy and straight? Sure, I felt it deep down inside, but I loved Faith then, and I do now. Faith says the baby is sleeping now and— She sang that old lullaby by the grave, knelt down and rocked herself as if holding that baby. I didn't know what to do. Are Roark and Culley keeping close watch? Dammit, if Faith knew that someone had broken into the house, knocked Culley in the head and—you just turned pale, boy. You didn't know there was rough stuff, did you? Culley walked in on them—two big men, faces covered. May had time off and wasn't around, thank God."

Harrison closed his eyes. He didn't often play hunches, but this time, his bet was on Aaron Gallagher. Gallagher wasn't the kind to be run off easily and now he'd come back—for what? "Faith needs you, Jacob. Let's ride down."

"You're doing all this for her, aren't you? Trying to get Julia Kane to come calling, so Faith can have the rest of the answers? You've driven yourself for years, boy. Don't you think I know that? You think I don't honor a man who has tried his honest best and more?" Jacob eyed the younger man, wearing a white dress shirt tucked into his jeans, his boots worn with use. He'd come from work, stripped away his business trappings to do what he felt was right. Harrison always did what he thought was right and good and Jacob could find no fault with that.

He traced Harrison's weary shadows. Now Harrison was after his daughter, for sure. Michaela had a sleek look to her, like a woman well loved and one who hadn't yet set the terms for their changing relationship. Jacob took in Harrison's big build, the muscles straining at his shirt. The boy wasn't pushing paper alone; he'd be a hard one to take down. "So you came to bring me back, did you? Think you can?"

"I think you'd better see to the woman who loves and needs you, instead of hiding out up here." His expression brooding, Harrison looked at Jacob. "Michaela thinks I've got a feminine side. What do you think of that?"

Jacob laughed for the first time in days. "She's like her mother and you're in for what is now called a 'learning experience.' If Faith holes up with her potting wheel too long, I just may have to go down to Donovan's Bar and Grill. . . . She sure was a pretty sight when she'd come haul me back home in the old days. Made me feel real good. I just went to get her to come after me like that. I'd sweet talk her and we'd dance a bit and make up . . ."

Harrison wondered if Michaela would do the same and found himself grinning, imagining the sight of her coming for him. "I'm a little behind on . . . courting, but I hear country dancing is popular. I've had some ballroom lessons. What do you know about the Texas two-step?"

"You didn't have much time for that, did you?" Jacob picked up a stick and drew a pattern in the dirt. Then he grinned at Harrison. "Oh, hell. Stand up. I'll show you, but if you tell anyone about this, you're dead meat. And stay your distance."

Harrison stood and in an awkward moment Jacob showed him the dance positions of man and woman. As Jacob concentrated on the rhythm he was humming, Harrison couldn't resist asking, "Honey? You're coming home tonight, aren't you?"

Jacob sputtered, then smiled wryly. "You won't be so sassy when Michaela gets to you."

"She already has."

"Not enough to stop you from matchmaking, though, right?"

"Jacob, I came up here to dance," Harrison said, smothering a grin.

Jacob pushed him away, and reached out to playfully riffle his hair as though he were a son. "Well, do it, then. It's too cold and damp up here after the rain— could come another thunderstorm and I'm past my rain slicker days. I'm going to Donovan's to see if that key he gave me still works. Then I'm going to sit there and wait until my Faith comes after me. Probably not what some upscale psychologist would say to do, but it's always worked. We'll have a real war this time, no doubt, then the air will clear—maybe. Mount up if you're coming with me."

fourteen

I tracked the old hide-hunter into the mountains, fearing for my family when he'd peered inside our cabin. There in Cutter Canyon, I drew my revolver as he turned, a big bear of a man. He placed a Langtry coin on a black rock near the river and called, "Yer wife be wantin' that. She's a strong woman. I hear yer a good man, and fierce when yer loved ones is bothered. You should have what belongs to your blood." I never saw him again. Four coins now lay within my keeping and my bride was none surprised. . . .

Zachariah Langtry's Journal

Harrison glanced in his rear-view mirror. Michaela's red S.U.V. was so close he could see her frown through the windshield. He pulled his pickup into her driveway and got out, watching her slam her vehicle door and sail toward him, full steam. He'd prefer that wide open fury any day, and the passion that went with it, to that of his cold upbringing. When Michaela was angry, there was a really enticing flounce to her hair, making it gleam blue-black in the late August sunshine. Her red business suit and television makeup said she hadn't taken time off and those long legs, exposed by her short skirt, quickly closed the distance between them. There in the bright Wyoming afternoon, the Langtry medallion on her chest bumped gently as she walked, and Harrison prayed that the legend was true, that it would keep her safe. The burn of those fabulous blue eyes went right to his heart, warming it after a chilling encounter with Aaron Gallagher.

Two days ago Gallagher hadn't liked Harrison's surprise visit, announced by sending Ricco sprawling on the floor between them. Gallagher wasn't a man who would take no, and he wanted the station, Michaela and something else. He had the look of a man who couldn't stand to leave anything alone, not until he tore it apart. To his bad luck, Harrison was already experienced with a man like that, his father.

Harrison inhaled slowly, his chest tight with the ache to hold Michaela, to reassure himself that she was safe. Gallagher would be coming for what he wanted—to take, or to destroy. Harrison's visit was to inform him that the takings weren't going to be easy. The cold cutting words with deadly meanings weren't new to Harrison. He knew how to give them back and Gallagher wanted to take him apart. Some men had to be "bull of the woods," had to prove themselves viciously, and Gallagher was one of them, his gaze taking in Harrison's build, the back alley fighting unexpected when Ricco tried to hold him.

Gallagher had already started his campaign to ruin Harrison by carefully feeding information and suspicions to Kane board members. At an impromptu conference call in his hotel room, Harrison had doubted the international backers would support him. Anonymous files concerning very personal information about his father's suicide, the embezzlement, the bankruptcy, and his mother's borderline insanity had been methodically sent to the backers. "Entertaining material, n'est-ce pas?" Jacques L'Tour had murmured with humor in his tone. "But I am certain that we have more pressing business than this, like our next Christmas party—Cannes or the ski slopes?"

Harrison breathed slowly; he'd come from nowhere, started with nothing. He'd wanted to give the Langtrys back their baby, his half-sister, and he'd failed. His need to hold Michaela terrified him, to fuse his mouth to hers and forget everything that had happened in the last three days, the discovery that Gallagher would be closing in. He tensed, strapping in his emotions, because *he wasn't certain he could restrain himself if she opened herself to him, as he knew she could. Locked deep in his passion for her, he could hurt her, bruise that smooth, soft skin. He'd seen enough with his father to know what a man's strength could do to a woman.*

He swallowed heavily and braced himself for the woman bearing down on him. Her sky blue gaze cut at him, ripping down his dress shirt and suit slacks, creased from traveling, his opened collar and dangling tie. "Okay, four days ago, you and my father were down at Donovan's getting pie-eyed all night. I can understand that. I've seen enough of male bonding rituals and I know that he's down and wanting comfort, reassurance . . . and Mom to come after him. Which she did. Seeing the two of you men, well over six feet, two-stepping together at five o'clock in the morning, would be enough to terrify anyone. I know it did me. And that silly grin when you picked me up and twirled me around—well, that part was okay. You were lucky the sheriff didn't throw you in jail with Donovan signing the complaint. Of course, he was there and so was Roark. Culley knew better and stayed to watch the ranch. You've been gone three days—What's this?" she asked, as Harrison retrieved the big bouquet of French tulips from his front seat and held them out to her.

"You're not a rose. You're one of these," he said, hoping that he wasn't offending her. The flowers were long stemmed, and gracefully bent, the blooms elegant. "I appreciate you taking me to the lake to let me recover from Jacob's reassurance party. There's nothing like a dip in an icy mountain lake to clear the brain. Not that I appreciated being pushed in like that."

He'd felt so free and happy then, treading water and splashing her. Michaela had laughed at him, the morning sunlight glittering gold on the water. Then, to warm him, she'd moved over him in the rear of her S.U.V., his first experience at making out in a car. He hadn't done too badly, taking her again, loving her.

Michaela took the elegant bouquet, nuzzling it. "I . . . uh . . . you left that afternoon, just packed up and drove out of town. I don't know where you've been, or . . . ." Over the bouquet, she intently searched his face. "Thank you."

Harrison felt encouraged—giving gifts, other than business necessities, was new to him. He'd reveled in shopping for the flowers, the high-end camera and attachments. If that sudden look of awareness in Michaela's eyes was any gauge, the traditional gift-giving, male to female, still held as a point-maker. He reached inside the car for a large parcel, holding it out to her. "They go with this. It's your new camera, complete with every lens, filter, and accessory possible."

Her gaze remained steady on his face. "What happened to your lip? It's cut."

Ricco's ring had done small damage. Gallagher was the real danger, a man sizing an opponent he wanted to fight. Harrison wasn't giving him that pleasure, but he would defend what he loved; he was beginning to realize how deeply he'd loved Michaela for years. "Move in with me," he said quietly, and with lowered lids studied her reaction.

He wanted to protect her. He wanted to listen to her breathing beside him in the night and know that she was unharmed. Usually picking his words, he was stunned by his voiced need to have her close. He held the box containing the camera beneath this arm, the tulips washing fragrance into the hot still air between Michaela and himself.

Michaela leaned her forehead against his chest, so that he couldn't see her expression. The florist's green tissue paper crinkled as she shook her head "no."

Harrison closed his eyes, his body alive with exposed nerves, his gut hollow and aching— He'd hoped for just that instant . . . and yet he'd known she wouldn't want that commitment to him. "It's because of withholding what I knew, isn't it? You don't trust me now?"

That glossy, silky hair shifted as she shook her head again. "I've waded all through that. The trail was ten years cold when you took it up and you were only a boy, already torn apart. It's me . . . I've lived with a man—"

Harrison's hand moved before he knew it, wrapping in those silky strands, pulling gently until her face lifted to his. The setting sun hit that dynamic face, those beautiful eyes caught the brilliant blue sky and met his steadily.

"I'm not him," he said, realizing that his voice held a harsh, growling frustration. Had she loved Dolph so much that there was no place for him? Harrison swallowed, realizing that he hadn't exactly courted her, hadn't said the right things to win her. He should have waited for a candlelight dinner and soft music and an engagement ring on her hand.

He sucked in the late afternoon air, scented of an alfalfa field newly cut, and coming rain, and

Michaela's unique, seductive scent. His chest ached as if something had been torn from him. In business he knew the right protocol; in romance—something he'd never taken time to dissect—he needed smoothing.

"I'm sorting out my life now, Harrison. I won't be pushed. Everything is happening too fast."

Too fast, he thought dully. *He'd waited a lifetime for her and Gallagher wouldn't wait*— Harrison forced his fingers to release her hair. The gesture was too primitive, but that was how he felt with Michaela—as if they had mated and she was the other half of his heart and soul. He knew there would be no other woman for him, his life empty without her. The seductive summer breeze webbed her hair along his dark skin in a gleaming caress. A soft shadow slid over her face, despite the clear sky, and he shook his head. "You're afraid you'll fail again. You're not certain that you won't leave town to find a better job and you don't want ties. You're not going to fail at anything you do—you never have—but it's your decision."

"Yes, it is, and I'm not ready to make that one yet. Harrison?" she asked as he handed her the box and walked to the bed of his pickup.

He hefted a big box up onto his shoulder before turning to look down at her. His "What?" was impatient, the lick of temper behind it.

Michaela considered that edgy control. He'd been gone for three days, and now *he* was angry with her?

She turned the idea. Harrison was a logical man; he'd understand that she'd want explanations and good ones . . . especially if he wanted to deepen their relationship by living together. And he wasn't delivering— Why?

"Aaron Gallagher has contributed a hefty sum to the Shiloh Historical Society. He's offered to buy Kane House and help build a new modern facility for them. Mrs. D'Renaud is in favor of selling the house you donated to them. Aaron wants to live in Kane House, refurnish it as it was. He likes Shiloh. He wants to settle down here. He's a very friendly man."

"Uh-huh." Harrison knew what Gallagher wanted and it wasn't a feeling of coming home. Gallagher was quickly taking moves to box Harrison in, to force a confrontation. Michaela was one prize and Gallagher was hunting something else that just didn't fit. If he touched Michaela— Harrison felt the live rage ripple through his body and he forced himself to look away from those searching sky-blue eyes.

"I'm afraid Mrs. D'Renaud has withdrawn her support of the television station. It has to do with—"

"I know—with my background and bad publicity." He'd expected Gallagher to make suggestions, to remind the community of the Kane heritage.

In the safety of her Seattle sanatorium room, Julia Kane's mind slid from the murky shadows that prowled around her, sometimes devouring her. In her lucid moments, she knew she was losing against the darkness threatening to consume her forever. The sanatorium's drugs only delayed her encounters with the past and her guilt, and dulled the remnants of her brilliant mind. Her attorney called her Julia Kane, though on the records she was Julia Monroe. He knew he had to please her whims, or she wouldn't do the trick he wanted most—to make money for him. In his way, he feared her, just as she had feared—who had she feared? Who was the man who had hurt her so horribly?

She took the stack of newspapers from her attorney. She wouldn't let him know that one special paper interested her more and skimmed the rest, hoarding the financial facts into her mind to use later. In the Cheyenne, Wyoming, paper was a news lead about the discovery of Maria Alvarez's body.

Her hand shaking, Julia signaled the man away. He'd let her search through the papers, recognizing "money-makers," and then he'd come back—meanwhile . . . When he was gone. Julia tore open the paper and read quickly. Hikers had found the body where Julia had placed it, starting the avalanche to conceal it. An anonymous source had revealed new facts in the disappearance case of the Langtry baby. The Langtrys would not disclose the source . . . Faith and Jacob had gone to see the grave . . .

She crushed the paper in her bony hands. They'd never find her; she'd been too thorough. They'd gotten the postcard she'd had one of the released patients send from New York. Years ago, she'd had to leave town sooner than she'd wanted because a man was asking about her. She'd escaped with his business card. He was an investigator and she'd had the postcard sent to him; she'd wanted to destroy any hope that the Langtrys retained for the baby. It was her baby, after all, not Faith's. Sable Kane Langtry on the tiny stone was brilliant as usual. She'd made so many perfect arrangements for that tiny grave, concealing her identity well, falsifying records easily. She smiled, pleased that she could remember so much, then the darkness clawed at her. She began to rock in her bed, the newspaper against her . . . *Soft-ly, slow-ly . . . the mornin' will creep. . . .*

Her mind slid back into the shadows, where she forgot and she remembered. *Why did that song taunt her? Who sang it? Why did the big gold coin keep haunting her, torturing her, burning her mind? Why did that Indian woman stalk her nightmares? Who was that little boy playing in her mind?*

Michaela knew she had hurt him and it was more than refusing his offer to move in with him. Harrison was too logical not to expect her to want a sorting-out time. Still he'd drawn inside himself, into that icy shell of automatic, dispatched answers. The breeze riffled through his usually neat hair, playing in the curls at his nape. He stood immobile, the cardboard box braced easily on his shoulder, as if he were taking the sight into him, hoarding it. He looked at the late August dancing across the sunflowers in her tiny field, the burro herd grazing peacefully, the soaring mountains jutting up into the late evening sun. Harrison moved his hand across his chest, rubbing it, and she ached to touch him there, where his heart lay wounded and shielded.

Then her gaze snagged on his big hand, on the raw scrapes across his knuckles and her throat tightened painfully. Harrison wasn't a man to brawl, he was a thinking man, he—

He looked as if he'd come back from a war, shadows beneath his eyes, the lines deeper on his face, and those smoky eyes were guarded. The cut on his lip reminded her of another time, when his nose had been broken. He hadn't explained his absence and yet she— He couldn't be brawling in a tavern, not Harrison. She shook that thought aside as another one hit her. *He wouldn't touch another woman, not after making love with her so beautifully.*

Harrison had been raised without gifts and kindness and he'd said he'd never given a woman flowers. The French tulips swayed gently in her arms. They were seductive, unique, a dainty blend of yellows and reds. Harrison would have chosen them specifically to suit her, not a casual purchase, because he cared.

He'd held his personal life tightly in his fist, giving it to no one. And yet he had wanted her to move in with him. For Harrison, that was no easy offer.

"Would Aaron Gallagher's purchase of Kane House bother you?" she asked quietly, as a humming-bird came hovering near her tulips. It zipped away in a blue-green neon bolt to feed upon the liquid hung from her front porch. Life moved on just as quickly, from daylight to shadows.

"Yes, it will bother me. Immensely." The clipped, harsh answer startled her. Harrison had separated himself from Kane House and everything in it, and now the violence within him shook the air.

He looked down at her as she stood holding his

bouquet and the boxed camera and his expression gentled. "I'm going to learn how to grow those tulips and apples, and maybe those herbs you love, too. I thought I'd turn that old garden over—it's been needing care—and maybe get one of those tillers. It's come to me that I've never done much with my life—like growing and making things. For a time when I was so determined to get my start, I was a hachet man, tearing companies apart and selling them off. I destroyed other men's dreams—"

Harrison scanned the old garden. "Your mother makes homemade jam. She always makes certain I get a jar and at first I couldn't open them—they seemed so special and from the heart. It seems to me that homegrown is better, more caring. People need to care more, which brings me to Faith and Jacob. How are they?"

Michaela reeled from Harrison's plans to garden, a contrast to the dedicated businessman who never took time for anything but money-building. "They're okay, I think . . . working on it. Maria's family came yesterday to retrieve her body . . . the forensics report showed a blow crushed her skull."

Harrison stiffened, his body humming with tension. "My mother was amazingly strong when she was—when she wasn't calm."

Michaela ached to tear him away from those clinging shadows. She'd moved past her fiery anger that he'd been gone, offering no explanation, into wanting to hold him tight. "You're supposed to call Mother when you get back. She's gotten a few new patrons for her cultural center though Dad wanted her to turn down a donation from Aaron and she agreed."

She didn't understand Faith's reaction, the intensity with which she spoke of turning down Gallagher's offer . . . as if she didn't want any part of him. Michaela realized that Harrison had been holding his breath, his fingers digging into the cardboard. "Good. By the way, I told you to take some time off. I expected you to do just that. I'm calling Roark and we're installing this security system tonight," he said finally and walked into her house, leaving her in the dry Wyoming evening.

"That's it?" Riveted by her emotions, Michaela stared at the open door. Her body trembled in the wash of sunset into the valley, the mountain shadows fingering over the lush fields. He hadn't held her close against him. "Hello, honey, I'm home. Where's my kiss?" she whispered to the summer breeze as it mocked her.

She knew that if she followed Harrison, he'd be too cool, too logical, his shields closed. She wanted the unguarded man, who'd kissed her in laughter and in passion. She knew herself well enough to know that she too could withdraw and the standoff could hurt them both. Inhaling the fragrance of Mrs. Atkins' climbing scarlet roses, Michaela listened to her instincts. Then she carefully placed the camera box inside her S.U.V. She scribbled a thank-you note on an envelope and placed it on his windshield. Then, still holding the tulips tight against her, because she knew that Harrison had chosen them carefully, she drove away.

Two hours later, Harrison's sleek black pickup squalled to a stop beside her four-by-four, dust hurled around it. From his living room, Michaela watched him stalk up the walkway of his house. She'd scrubbed off her make-up, taken a shower, carefully unpacked the camera and the accessories he'd given her. Every minute of that time, she'd dissected how Harrison had looked, the way he'd closed himself away again, a man with too many scars. Now, dressed only in his shirt, she was good and ready for any mood he could throw at her. A big powerful man, his dress shirt open and his feet in black socks, he placed one hand on the gate she had locked and vaulted over it. She recognized that fierce scowl, the slice of those steel gray eyes, that lock of his jaw and he wasn't behind those cool, logical shields now.

She waited until he slammed into the house. He placed his hands on his hips, and as his eyes adjusted to shadows, he searched for her. He found her just as she hurled a pair of balled socks at him. He caught the missile, threw the crushed envelope to the floor, and frowned at her. "Next time you can thank me to my face, not some prim little bloodless note you'd give to someone you barely know. What do you mean, dear heart, to call and say 'it's only fair that if you're in my house, then I'm in yours'? And what are you doing to my things? I usually *fold* my socks," he said thoughtfully as he opened the ball, paired the socks neatly and folded them. He placed them on the back of the couch.

"True. That's why I unfolded every one of them and balled them the right way. Just wait until you see your underwear box—there's nothing folded there. I mixed your T-shirts and your undershorts. Think of that, Harrison—your T-shirts are in your undershorts box and your shorts are in the T-shirt box. And every pair of your shoes, lined up against that wall, does not match." She began pelting him with the balled socks, his cat leaping upon the ones rolling on the floor.

"Women!" Harrison scrubbed his hands over his face as if trying to step into the correct universe. As if he were trying to make sense of her actions, and plan his next move, Harrison scooped up the balled socks and folded them. He placed them in a precise row across the back of the couch. "You're not being logical, you know. It's difficult when you're so volatile."

He smoothed that broken nose, studying her. "I did something wrong, didn't I? I'm new to this relationship business—intimacy and trying to please you—but that's no excuse—"

" 'Volatile?' How should I be? You were gone for three days, Harrison, not one. And without a word."

"Business," he explained slowly. "I should have kissed you hello, shouldn't I have? The welcome home kiss you weren't going to give me?"

" 'Business.' That's no explanation. You just shut another door, Harrison."

He nodded thoughtfully. "So I did. *Should* I have kissed you?"

"It was important . . . yes, you should have. One of those mind-blowing kisses that told me you missed me."

"That I did." The admission was solemn, as if Harrison was absorbing and correcting any future mistakes. He sniffed lightly and frowned. "More brownies?"

"Don't think they're for you, not someone who acts as if he can just walk off when he wants to. You listened to me when I told you about how I thought Cleopatra was calling me, trying to tell me something, and you understood. You held me when I cried—you were there for me. Don't you think you take a part of that with you every place you go? Men with good feminine sides are hard to find, you know." Was she reasonable? Was she hurt? Yes, but only Harrison mattered now, and the darkness stalking him.

"What the hell is this feminine side business?" He raked his hand through his hair, and then as if to test her reaction threw back a ball of socks, hitting her lightly.

For a moment the air stilled between them and then he smiled. It was just a curve of his hard mouth, just that lick of pleasure.

"Miss me, did you, dear heart?" he asked, picking up another ball and pelting her as she ran behind a chair, carrying his socks in one arm and hurling them back at him with the other.

Then, as she was laughing, the air stilled again, the cat swiping at the sockballs, rolling them. The shadows seemed to shift and tighten and warm as Harrison stood very still watching her. Her breath locked tight inside her, waiting. . . . Those gray eyes flickered down her body, heating her skin, stirring that liquid heat within her. And then, because she knew that she couldn't lose him back to the shadows, she eased his shirt from her body, letting it pool to the floor.

For a moment, Harrison didn't move, as if locked in place, then he quickly crossed the distance between them. He tugged her into his arms and held her close, his big body trembling in her arms. "I'll always come back," he whispered roughly against her forehead, his kisses short and fierce. "I'll always be faithful . . . and I'm never going to hurt you. . . ."

She knew then that he'd wanted her too badly when he'd arrived, and he feared— His trembling hands caressed lightly, skimming her breasts, her back, as if reassuring himself that nothing had happened to her. Then his mouth came down hungrily upon hers, just as she wanted, with all the heat and storms and passion that lived within Harrison. She gave him back everything, pouring into him, wrapping her arms around his shoulders, digging her hands into that thick, shaggy mass of waves. Held hard against her, shaking and very, very warm, Harrison breathed roughly against her cheek. He found her ears, his teeth tugging gently on her lobes, then there was just that flick of his tongue that staked the chords within her body. "Harrison—" she sighed, wanting him safe within her, locked so close that nothing could come between them.

He swept her up, high against him, his mouth devouring hers, meeting her passion, just as she wanted, and hurried into the hallway shadows with her.

Harrison's hunger was exactly as she craved, genuine, trembling, too powerful to be denied. His mouth locked on hers, hot and seeking. His arms caught her hard and safe to his chest, the pounding of his heart enveloping her as though it were her own, his fingers splayed open on her thigh, digging in slightly, possessively, claiming her.

In the new bedroom, he came down upon her, and eager for each other, they quickly dealt with his clothing. There would be gentler times, she knew, but in the deep heat of the night, she needed all of him, all pretense, all leashes stripped away.

The pounding fever shot quickly through them, until they moved as one in their passion. Each touch, the skimming of hands and lips and flesh seared, reassured. Riveted by the intense stake of passion, Michaela could not move, holding him tight as they tumbled over the edge.

Harrison lay heavy upon her, and his weight pleasured her, letting her know that he'd given everything a man could give during passion. Their lovemaking was no methodical, practiced event, but a searing truth. She smoothed his back, loving the relaxed flow of muscles, tensed in his passion only heartbeats ago.

Lazy and sweet and intimate, Harrison's trembling hand smoothed her shoulder, her arm, until he held her hand, his thumb caressing the back.

"Did I hurt you?" he whispered raggedly against her throat.

"No. I wanted you just as desperately. Call me shameful." She sensed his withdrawal, his fears. Harrison was always very careful of her, and this time, rising over her, his body clenched with passion, he'd held her hands beside her head.

His smile curved along her throat. "Okay, you're shameful and you've wasted me. I'll never be the same."

He raised above her, his expression serious now in the shadows. She smoothed his tousled hair away from his face. With her thumbs, she smoothed his brows, and then his jutting cheekbones, framing his face with her hands. "You're not like him, Harrison. You're not capable of rape, and you would love your children. You'd be an ideal family man, a perfect father."

"How can you be so certain?" he asked raggedly.

"Because I've known you all my life, and I'm shameful and I'm never wrong," she whispered back, searching those hard features and watching them soften into the roughish smile she wanted.

"Such confidence. You want me, don't you?" he teased, grinning widely now as her hand lowered over the hair on his chest. He looked down their joined bodies and those gray eyes flickered and darkened as he met her eyes. "I'll be coming for you and you know it, don't you?"

Then his fingers began to move lightly, thoroughly, and she forgot about everything else—

fifteen

Only one Langtry coin remained to be found, five already in my keeping. This day, that last coin gleamed in my fist, for I had traded my first Langtry stud. Pride glowed in my sweetheart's black eyes, and she chided me that I was too bold, too arrogant and swaggering. When I chased her, laughing into the wood, I wondered at how she could love me, a man who had little to give but my heart and soul. That night, I dreamed of Obediah, his skin gleaming with sweat. My honor had not fled, yet clung sturdily to me, for I had survived and had become respected in my new life. I came to see that I had honored my father's dreams and I had tried against circumstances to meet another honor, in another time. Now I am respected in this new land. Can it be that his curse

*had held true? Or was it my wife's love that had
united all six coins? What is this power women have
to make men strong, when they would give up hope?*

Zachariah Lantry's Journal

Harrison carefully placed his briefcase on his desk.
Before the events of the last week, it had been his custom to come in early and work before the bank's staff
arrived. Behind in his workload, Harrison would
have liked to stay in bed, holding Michaela close this
morning, but she had driven home before dawn to
prepare for her morning wake-up show.

On his way to work, Michaela's red four-by-four
appeared beside him. She'd signaled for him to catch
and then a large tinfoil-wrapped square sailed
through his open window before she turned toward
KANE. The missile had smelled like freshly baked
brownies and Harrison had carefully placed it on the
seat beside him.

His secretary came in, placing a cup of coffee on his
desk, and Harrison smiled at her. "Good morning,
Kay."

"Good morning. I'll be back in with the letters for
you to sign—" Kay stood very still, peering at him.
"Are you feeling all right, Mr. Kane?"

"I'm feeling *excellent*, thank you. And you?" Harrison smiled warmly at her again. Kay had always been
a wonderful person, trying her best to please him, to
be efficient. She needed a bigger Christmas bonus.

Clearly flustered, she blinked rapidly at his smile,

"I . . . um . . . I'll just do those letters now," she said, before hurrying out the door and closing it.

Harrison clicked on the television, recently installed so that he could watch Michaela's wake-up show. He frowned at the segment taped earlier in the season, featuring Michaela's visit to Lobo Mike's Rattlesnake Farm. The "milking" process of extracting venom from live snakes to be used in anti-venom was not an interview that he wanted Michaela to do again. Dwight and Michaela were at the anchor desk, chatting warmly, and everything seemed "cozy," Harrison decided. Dwight seemed a little on edge, his smile too cheerful. Harrison tossed away the notion that Dwight was disturbed and carefully opened his briefcase.

He stared at the tinfoil square he saw there, enjoying the sight of it and the warm, fuzzy feeling it had created. He carefully removed it from his briefcase. A man unused to gifts, he carefully opened the foil. Harrison ran his finger across the brownies, treasuring them and the woman who had thought of him. He settled down to enjoy his morning coffee, a brownie baked just for him, and Michaela's morning news segment.

The huge floral arrangement on the anchor desk caused him to frown. They weren't his tulips. He punched the line to the news room, and Jerry, an intern, picked up the line. "Who sent the bouquet on the anchor desk?" Harrison asked. "You don't know? Find out and call me back."

Two minutes later, he wasn't pleased to discover that Aaron Gallagher had brought the solid orchid bouquet . . . and he was sitting nearby. He was drinking coffee and chatting with the crew—and waiting for Michaela to finish her segment.

Harrison's finger traced his broken nose. A fast game player, Gallagher would want Michaela alone, avoiding Harrison and a confrontation for now. Gallagher had dismissed Harrison's warning to stay away from the Langtrys and Shiloh. That meant he was ready to play rough, and Michaela was right in the middle. There was nothing to do now but to wait for Gallagher to make his move.

On second thought, Harrison picked up the telephone and rang the intern again. "I spoke too sharply to you a moment ago. I apologize. What's going on at the station this morning? Did that segment at Faith's cultural center go well?"

He smiled briefly as Jerry nervously updated him, then Harrison asked, "I suppose Dwight is wearing his pajama bottoms. I hope he is in a good mood this morning."

Jerry's words were slow and well chosen. Dwight was courteous this morning, cheerful and fully dressed in a suit, shocking everyone. And Harrison knew then who Gallagher had picked as an inside informant.

She'd made him angry. Michaela Langtry had refused to have lunch or dinner with him . . . there was a red mark— a small scrape on her throat—that she hadn't concealed, and that meant that Kane was grooving with a woman Gallagher had to have. She'd gone to lunch with

Mooney, that fawning buffalo, and she had plans for dinner—Kane, no doubt.

On the other hand, Kane may have been her bedtime entertainment, but she wasn't exactly in his pocket. Michaela Langtry was her own woman . . . until she was Gallagher property.

Aaron Gallagher paced the caretaker's living quarters in Kane House. Victoria and her cronies hadn't objected when he wanted to sample a few nights in the house. Ricco, too noticeable with his knife-scarred face and dangerous appearance, waited in a motel a safe distance away from Shiloh. Gallagher had learned a long time ago to make some of his players invisible, until they were needed.

Gallagher ran his hand across the Langtry coin fastened to the thick gold chain on his neck. Michaela wasn't as easily managed as the D'Renaud woman and Dwight Brown. Brown had gotten in too deep with gambling debts, and he'd said the wrong things. He was vulnerable and ready to cooperate, providing inside information Gallagher needed—like Kane's working hours away from the station, like Michaela's love for orchids.

Ricco, a professional, hadn't been able to locate the coins in the Langtry house. That meant each Langtry still wore them. Michaela's had gleamed on her gray suit that morning. A classy woman, she used no jewelry, except the coin. *She should have paid more attention to him. . . .*

Gallagher looked in the bathroom mirror, peering at the scalp revealed more each day. He feared to comb his hair now. He turned his bare shoulders to view the hair on them. It was new and thick in an unbecoming gray. "A good wax job will take care of that."

He considered the deep lines between his brows. "Cosmetic surgery is easy now. No problem."

But the Langtrys had refused a second anonymous bid from Gallagher for the coins and Michaela had refused to date him. That wouldn't do at all. Kane had to be removed from the picture.

Kane House was opulent, though the old woman had said it was much more elegant when the Kanes resided in it. Gallagher snarled at the man who had had all the advantages in growing up. And now Kane had Michaela in his bed.

Gallagher had expected the Langtrys to shun Kane and they hadn't.

Gallagher had to have those coins, and the woman. Then everything would fall into place and he'd be even more powerful. He needed to move quickly.

The old house settled into the night, creaking around him. Outside, the wind howled around the house's corners. There was almost a fluid lilt to the sound, like the lullaby the old woman sang in the sanatorium. The room was suddenly cold, but then Gallagher knew that drafts were common. A door creaked and slammed shut, and he held very still, listening, as the house creaked and settled once more.

Now, after going over Kane's financial resources, Gallagher could easily see his inheritance from the madwoman. She'd given him her astounding ability to pick financial winners. Kane had been handed everything, while Gallagher had had to haul his butt up from the Oklahoma slums.

He sorted through his options. Culley Blackwolf looked like hard times and rawhide, a man who kept to himself. He wouldn't break easy. Roark Langtry was just as tough as Jacob. They were men who would fight to the death for what they held dear. Their only weaknesses were the women they loved, Faith and Michaela.

Anger slapped Gallagher. *Michaela really shouldn't have refused him.*

Michaela ran her hand over the French tulips that Harrison had given her. Their tall, elegant stems were beautiful and simple in the clear glass vase.

The bouquet contrasted her primitive emotions concerning Harrison. He'd come to the station and the quiet, deadly swords between him and Aaron were clearly drawn. Harrison had closed his shields, his expression grim as he stood off set, watching her give the noon news. After the evening news, Harrison and Dwight had been locked away in his office. She had the impression that he was protecting her from Gallagher—or else he didn't trust her.

She wasn't certain that she trusted herself. Or Harrison. She wasn't ready for the relationship that seemed to be exploding beyond her control. Their intimacy on the mountain, their shared experience in discovering Maria and the past was a deep link. But was it enough?

The day had been filled with odd little edges, swaggering males squaring off, and Gallagher's sly insinuations still clung to her. Over morning coffee, he'd insinuated that Harrison owed "big money," and that he was like his father, embezzling from those who trusted him. In his turn, Harrison stared coldly, impassively at Gallagher over her head and the testosterone hovering in the air had added to the headache brought on by the heavy scent added to the orchid bouquet. For his part, Dwight was too polite and eager to please, and none of it made sense.

Dolph had just called. He'd apologized smoothly, congratulating her on the success of her interviews and her mother's art cultural center segments. Michaela instantly recognized his shielded feelers about Maria's death, the kidnaped baby. It was a good story, and it was hers to be handled exclusively, with taste and conscience. Dolph's sensationalism would hurt too many people. She recognized the desperation in his voice, a career in the balance, if he didn't produce a headlining story soon. She'd helped him before, and now he needed her again.

Had it really been like that? So cold, so icily perfect, as they plowed through their growing careers? So unreal and heartless? Could she really have wanted those perfect children with Dolph?

She shook her head and looked out at the Atkins' climbing roses, blooming blood-red on the trellis. As brilliant as the blood on Harrison's hands as he'd tried to dig Maria from her tomb.

Michaela shivered, fighting the talons of that nightmare. Everything was happening too fast, tearing at her.

She answered the telephone and Harrison's deep voice skittered along her skin, lifted the hair on her nape. The background sound, shifting of paper and a scribbling pen, did not hide his tired frustration. "I'm working late tonight. I'd like to see you, but I'm sorry—researching the details of this merger won't wait."

He sounded so grim, she could practically see him working at his desk. His shirt would be open at the throat, his tie dangling open. He'd have that hard eagle-like look, pouncing on facts and digesting them, just the Harrison she loved to tease. "There is no need for you to apologize. I've got plans of my own."

Paper crackled at the other end of the line and the static silence was telling. Harrison inhaled slowly. "I see. May I ask what they are?"

So proper, she thought, taking a tulip and sliding its smooth petals against her face. Harrison's tension practically simmered across the lines as he waited. He always responded so nicely, and at just the perfect moment. She moved into her living room and lay down on the couch, stroking the tulip across her lips. "I'm going to take a nice long bubble bath, sliding deep down in the water and letting it wave gently around my body. I'm going to slowly soap my legs, one at a time, and then my arms and my—"

At the other end of the line, paper crunched again, and Michaela smiled. "And then I'm going to dress in something nice and lacy and lie on my bed and try those relaxing exercises—you know the ones where you stretch every muscle. Or I might do yoga stretches with my new video."

"You enjoy that, don't you—tormenting me?" Harrison asked raggedly, after a long, meaningful groan. "Why don't you come to the studio office? I'll order carry-in for dinner."

"Can't. I'm standing here without my clothes. Gosh, these tulips feel great against my skin, so soft—"

A half hour later, Michaela heard a door slam and looked out of her window. "Good old Harrison," she murmured, as his long strides took him quickly up her herb-lined pathway. His hair was uncombed as though he'd been running his hands through it, the shaggy lengths curling at his nape. His dress shirt was opened slightly. He hadn't taken time to shave, a dark stubble running around his jaw. He had that fierce warlord look, a man on the hunt, and pleasure riveted her bare feet to the floor. It seemed like seconds passed before they were both undressed.

This was what she wanted, no schedules for intimacy, no methodical adjustments and rituals, just the sheer need running hot and wild between them—the reassurance of passion and heat that she hadn't thought possible, her heart pounding before. Their bodies were damp, blending, sliding, all the textures and colors she'd wanted in her life raised so vividly nothing else existed. "Harrison—"

"Say my name again. Say it," he demanded roughly against her breast, tugging at it until the fierce cords tightened deep within her. He held her

there, hands joined with hers, hard body meeting
hers. Her senses filled with the taste and the solid feel
of Harrison. Had he always been there? Had he
always been the one?

"Harrison . . ." she whispered as her passion came
running too swiftly to catch and hold and control. . . .

Later she held him close, smoothing his broad
shoulders. His weight rested comfortably against her,
all those textures and edges resting for a time, and she
studied the coin she'd hung from a necklace rack. Was
this what Cleopatra found, this peace in simply holding a man close? Was this what made a woman want
to give him a child?

Long after she slept, curled against him, Harrison
would study the coin. It shimmered in the night, a soft
glow, almost peacefully as if it were keeping all harm
away from Michaela. He nuzzled her forehead, inhaling her fragrance, and wondered at the tenderness
within him. The Langtry legend was true, that the
women had *hearts as soft and sweet as the summer mist
over a mountain meadow.* Only a heart like that could
forgive as Michaela had seemed to do. But could he
capture her heart, hold it close and safe without harm-
ing her again?

Harrison closed his eyes and inhaled the fragrance
of her hair. Dwight was also vulnerable, and he'd
been too eager to talk. He'd known Gallagher from
the coast, and Gallagher had discovered that Dwight
owed gambling debts to the wrong people. Gallagher
had threatened to "leak" information. Harrison had

other plans for Dwight, who would soon be traveling as a low-profile tourist in Italy.

Then she stirred against him, and the whimpering began, the sound of the old lullaby, *Soft-ly, slow-ly....*

He gathered her closer, rocking her against him. That night had torn her away from safety. Could she ever forget that it was his parents who began the turmoil? Could she ever truly forgive?

The coin glimmered softly in the moonlight and an autumn leaf tumbled down the window outside. Michaela shivered in her sleep and Harrison drew the quilt over her bare shoulder, holding her close.

He had to protect her. Gallagher was out there somewhere, waiting for his chance.

The next morning, Michaela breezed into Harrison's television office. "Harrison, we can't wait. We need a local weather segment up and running before the snow sets in. And what is this about Dwight leaving the station? Spending time with his mother dying? I'd have thought—"

She stopped midstride. A four-year-old girl was sitting on Harrison's lap, her miniature tea set placed on his desk. Harrison's big hand was wrapped around a tiny cup and he was in the middle of sipping an imaginary drink. A well-loved doll was flopped over the shoulder of his suit jacket. "Sarah has new socks with lace. Her mother is Ann, our technician, and brought her to work today. Her grandmother usually keeps her, but today she isn't feeling well," he said very formally to Michaela.

Rocked by the image of Harrison holding the little girl, Michaela closed the door. "I see."

"Sit down and have some tea with us. Sarah, this is Michaela Langtry, the pretty woman you saw on my television." Despite his busy schedule, Harrison acted as if he had nothing else to do but to play tea party with the little girl.

For the next fifteen minutes until Sarah's mother came to collect her, Michaela was fascinated by this new Harrison. He stood at one point, pointing to the burros out in the field, the child straddling his hip.

"Well, that was interesting," Michaela said, after he solemnly returned Sarah's good-bye kiss.

"Yes, it was. I really enjoyed learning about her doll. You used to be like that—really sweet—when you weren't terrorizing everyone, including me. Playing tea party and dolls wasn't exactly Roark's or my idea of a manly time. You used to have some real temper fits, though, that I'll bet Sarah never has."

Michaela laughed, the memories floating between them. "You're right. I always meant to have my way. Harrison, she's got you wrapped around her little finger."

"Uh-huh. You did, too. It was either do as you said or get myself lassoed and made to do it anyway." He smiled at that and leaned back in his chair, placing his arms behind his head. She felt that tug of awareness, that warming, tender emotion circling her. "Hey!" he exclaimed in a delighted tone, as she came to sit on his lap. "What's this?"

"I'll just bet no woman has ever sat on your lap.

They would have wrinkled your creases and that wouldn't be permitted. It's virgin, so to speak," Michaela teased and watched that slow, roguish smile spread across his face. She traced her fingertip over the corner of his mouth and his teeth caught it, then kissed it.

His hand drew her face close, his nose rubbing hers playfully. "I've been saving myself for you, doll," he murmured in a Humphrey Bogart imitation.

She lay in his arms, looking up at him. He seemed so relaxed, his hair waving through her fingers, his eyes had that dark drowsy look that said he wanted her. But there was tenderness flowing between them, too, like warm golden threads. "Who are you?"

He framed her face with his big calloused hands and leaned close. The answer came slow and true, in the tone that said Harrison was taking a vow. "Didn't you know? I'm the man you're going to marry."

sixteen

Years ago, I had bought her life from the hangman, and she'd had to marry me. So much had passed between, binding us together, including the new babe strapped to her back and my fine son riding her hip. She came to me in the meadow that day, as our horses raced in the glorious morning sun. She placed all six coins in my hand and her soft dark eyes filled with me and nothing else. Then she placed her hand over mine and the coins. She spoke often with gestures, rather than words as was her way. I knew she believed her debt paid and that her honor had been met. If she stayed with me now, it was because I held her heart and that was no small treasure to hold dear.

Zachariah Langtry's Journal

Harrison swung up into the mare's saddle and she didn't like it. In the Langtry corral, the newly purchased animal hadn't been ridden lately, her elderly owner selling her. "She's been broken once, but I haven't been able to ride her. Pretty is a good horse and strong of heart, but she's got her own mind," Tom Wheeler had said. That statement reminded Harrison of Michaela, who had been on edge for three days and keeping distance between them.

The first of autumn chill hovered in the shining September morning. After battling Michaela about the local weather spots she wanted, working at the bank, and a late night call from an investor that demanded research, Harrison needed sunshine and physical work. He needed a day away from paper and the sly threats from Gallagher. He hovered near Michaela, calling her at the station. There was nothing to do until Gallagher made his move—and he would.

The headstrong mare was perfect to take Harrison's mind off Michaela's distraction, whatever it was. He'd whipped through the paperwork at the bank, worked on the station's budget, and tried to let her work out her mood. One fierce glare of those blue eyes wasn't exactly encouraging, but three days without holding her close was enough. Whatever burned her needed clearing.

Of course, by trying to ride the unbroken mare, he was showing off like some head-over-heels in love schoolboy. Michaela's car was parked at the Langtry house and more than likely she was watching now, waiting for him to be tossed on his butt. But maybe he'd get a chance to— Real dumb to play rodeo and show off, Harrison thought when Roark shouted, "Let her rip!" and the mare started to buck.

Pretty stomped, stiff-legged, and spun and headed into the corral fence, trying to dislodge him. Harrison held tight, pitting himself against the horse, wearing her down. She tossed him once, three times, and he hauled himself back up on her, aching and cursing and determined to tame her.

Finally, an hour later, sweating, dusty, smelling of horse and leather, Harrison rode the mare around the corral. Experienced horsemen, Jacob, Culley, and Roark stood on the corral boards. "Good job, boy," Jacob called.

"You wasted it, old son," Roark noted with a wide grin. "She's not here."

Harrison rode the mare to the men. "What do you mean?"

Roark's grin widened as did Jacob's and Culley's. "Took off early this morning . . . rode into the mountains. Mom packed her lunch after their powwow this morning. Seems my sister is not happy with you, or any man, and needs a day of peace."

"She's not in the house?" Harrison repeated, and damned his aching muscles and the bruises that would be appearing soon.

"Well, I'm sure glad you showed up, so eager to help us with this mare, boy. None of us wanted to ride her down like you did." Jacob's chuckle grew into guffaws as he took his hat off and swiped it against his jeans. He wiped away tears of laughter as Roark stood grinning, his hat tilted back on his head, hands tucked in his back pockets. Culley's grin was shielded by his hand as he patted the mare.

"Which way did she go?" Harrison's body chilled. Gallagher could— When Roark pointed and opened the gate, Harrison rode the mare through it. Then because she wanted to run, and because he needed to know that Michaela was safe, he leaned forward and the mare responded, racing through the fields, sailing over a fence. "Come on, Pretty."

Old Tom had been right, the mare was strong. She quickly picked her way over the mountain path, as though she sensed Harrison's desperate fears for Michaela's safety. The Langtrys couldn't know how dangerous Gallagher could be—

Gallagher paced in Kane House caretaker's apartment. On a Saturday morning, he should be waking up in his San Francisco bed and all six of the coins should be stored in his vault.

He was losing his hair too quickly, the bald sheen defined now. He thought of the old woman, her mind almost gone, and a trickle of fear chilled his body. Could it be that the legendary curse was true?

He stripped free his belt and looked down at the burned red patches on his upper thighs. He grabbed the tube of ointment, smearing it on the tender flesh. Michaela's little payback for holding her arm, for showing him that she would not be detained or controlled, would cost her. The spilled coffee had stopped him then, only delaying his ownership of her.

He jerked up his pants and winced painfully when the tug on his zipper took flesh. He cursed and shook his head. With years of practice, he sliced away what he didn't want to believe. Only part of the curse was true, that whoever held all the Langtry coins would be powerful. Gallagher preened in the mirror. He was virile, his muscles toned. He turned slightly to the mirror and found a softening at his middle. Sucking in air, he grabbed the telephone and dialed Ricco. "I want them hit with everything tonight. Get the girl and take her up to that old cabin, where she can't be heard. I don't want any interruptions, and make certain that nothing happens to Mr. Kane. I've got special plans for him."

Gallagher slammed down the receiver. "Michaela really shouldn't have turned me down. She didn't make me happy."

At eleven o'clock in the morning, Michaela stretched on her blanket. She awakened to the beautiful meadow, birds singing in the trees, the aspen leaves shimmering like fire in the sunlight. Lying face down, she yawned and welcomed the first relaxation in three days.

She flipped to her back, her body alert, her senses telling her that she wasn't alone. She brushed away the strand of hair from her eyes and looked up to see Harrison. His expression wasn't friendly as he sat on his heels, western-fashion, beside her. Michaela blinked; Harrison was always meticulously neat, and now a fine film of dust covered his hair, his western clothing sweaty and dirty. He had a dangerous gun-slinger look that she'd never seen, as if he had found the exact choice for a shootout. "Having a good day?" he asked without warmth.

"How did you know I was here?" She sat up and smoothed her clothes, crossing her arms around her knees to stop them from shaking. She hadn't been pre-pared for Harrison or anyone else to find her.

"Broken branches, overturned rocks—all new. The usual things. Your dad taught me how to track, remember? The fresh banana peel made it easier . . . the question is, why are you up here alone?"

"That isn't a question, that's a demand."

"You're damn right it is. I want to understand."

She started to rise to her feet and his hand on her shoulder pushed her down flat on her back. "You're not going anywhere until we talk. You've been run-ning from me for three days—"

"Maybe I've had my fill of testosterone."

"Gallagher, you mean. Couldn't be me, because I've 'got a feminine side.' " His taunt underlined his bad mood.

Harrison usually controlled his darker side and she could feel it simmering in the golden autumn air, waiting to catch fire. He was set to push now, and she'd never liked being pushed or controlled. From his look, he was ready for a battle. Her own temper wasn't that stable and she wanted time to think—when Harrison was near, solid thinking became instinctive and too emotional. "I came up here for peace and quiet. To shoot a few pictures with my new camera— I mean you. He doesn't matter."

"Well, that's something at least. And I matter? Me and my 'feminine' side?"

She frowned at him, refusing to admit that his dark looks at her, his withdrawn silence had both hurt and angered her. "Let me up, Harrison."

His gaze ran slowly down her body, dressed in a long-sleeve, pink plaid cotton blouse tucked into her jeans. That unique spark ignited in the sweet autumn air as though he had passed his hand over her, touching her with his wide safe palm, those strong fingers. She stood shakily and didn't look at him as he came to his feet, towering over her. In a suit, he was devastating, but looking like this, all rugged male, she could have— She pushed back the impulse to grab his face, lock one hand in his hair and draw that hard mouth down to hers. Gallagher's presence had shoved certain facts at her, and she wasn't certain about Harrison now. "They got you to ride that mare, didn't they? They took bets on it this morning."

His indrawn breath hissed raggedly. From the dirt and the sweat on him, she knew he'd ridden the mare—the mare standing tethered to the white bark of an aspen tree beside her horse. That would be Harrison, working on a project until he'd gotten his way. Michaela stopped to collect her camera bag, and walked a distance from the horses, chestnut coats gleaming in the sun. The dappled sunlight hitting the gold straw of the meadow, the bluish-white contrast of the aspen trunks framed the horses beautifully, heads bent to graze. "Hold this," she said, handing him the camera bag.

She took out the camera and made the light adjustments. "I've decided to shoot all the pictures I want, practicing with it. When I'm old and can't hike—to find peace like today—" she underlined, "then I'll paint from the pictures."

Michaela leveled a look at Harrison. "It is a Saturday, you know. I'm on my own time. I'm not responsible to you. Not anymore."

Harrison's narrowed eyes and dangerous look said he didn't agree. But typical of Harrison, he was staying on track, getting to the bottom of the problem. "What's going on with Gallagher and you? He's calling the station for you and he turns up at the station waiting for you," he asked, standing still as she moved to the left, going down on one knee for the camera shots.

"It seems he doesn't like you. He wants to date me. And he's offered me a top spot as an anchor in San Francisco."

She took more shots, aware of Harrison's tension in the sunlit meadow. "Are you taking it?"

"I've got a contract, remember? And I just bought my house." A chipmunk chattered, leaping from fallen log to the trunk of a lodgepole pine, and Michaela quickly framed the shot, clicking the shutter.

Harrison slowly placed the camera bag on a rock and stood, looking down at her. "Let's have it, then. Come on, you're always right there, holding nothing back and these last three days—"

"These last three days you've been glaring at me every time I talk to Gallagher. I know what he is. Don't you think I have better judgment than to get mixed up with him? You've been snarling, Harrison, and I don't like it. I've done nothing to—" She looked down to the wrist he'd just snagged, his fingers firm and possessive.

He brought her hand slowly to his lips, looking over it to her. "I don't want you hurt. He can be . . . violent when refused. You don't know what violence is, Michaela. You haven't experienced—"

She tugged her hand away. Harrison could be too persuasive, and when he looked at her like that— close and dark and intimate—she'd started melting and forgiving. She didn't want to forgive him just yet. "What do you think happened that night in New York, when James decided to make his move?"

The ugliness of that night, the lust written on James Charis's face slashed at her. She fought tears, the camera shaking in her hand as she clicked a series of shots up at the fiery aspens, the daylight skimming through the leaves.

"I know what violence is," she heard herself say unevenly, as an image of her torn clothing and James's rage hit her. Her own violence came on the second betrayal, when Dolph wanted her to "play along with James. He can help both our careers."

Michaela moved around the clearing taking shots, taking in the birds and the beauty and pushing away her terror and horror and violent anger at Dolph's reaction. She turned suddenly, framing Harrison, and his savage expression startled her. His fists clenched at his side, he looked as if he could kill— She didn't take the last shot, but carefully returned the camera to the bag, zipping it closed. "I handled it, Harrison. My kick boxing lessons paid off. James wasn't expecting that, or for me to be aggressive . . . or for me to file a company complaint against him. It was handled all very discreetly, of course, because the network wouldn't want bad publicity. But that isn't the issue now, is it? The problem is you lied to me. We're lovers and *you lied to me.*"

She wiped away the burning tears and turned from him. "Silky was having an affair with Dwight. You didn't know that, did you? He came to her the night he left. She said he was scared stiff and running and that you had helped him get to safety."

She turned to him, crossing her arms protectively in front of herself. "I found the file you had on me— you were very thorough. I'd expected that and I could live with the fact that you kept tabs on me. I know what you were trying to do for my mother. Your very exact file was created *prior* to when we made love. I considered that event a commitment, Harrison— when we made love, a reassurance of trust. Neither one of us give ourselves easily, so making love— You told me that Dwight's mother was dying and he wanted to spend time with her. You didn't trust me enough to tell me the truth. You made me feel safe and I trusted you. Do you know what that is for me— to feel safe? And *you lied to me.*"

Harrison stood with his legs braced wide upon the

meadow, as if taking a physical blow. His rugged features tightened, a pulse hammering in his temple, his jaw taut, a muscle moving beneath the tanned skin. "I didn't know Charis had hurt you."

"A few bruises on my arm, and nothing more." Her dress had been torn, fighting him, and her lips were swollen from his unwanted kiss. But he had limped away from the encounter, cursing her.

The deadly silence that followed almost frightened her. Then Harrison ran his hand through his hair. "I should have told you everything, but I didn't think you needed to be involved—"

She threw up her hands. " 'Involved?' I'm supposed to be your right hand at the station. I'm working at KANE every day and we've— 'Involved?' Yes, I'd say so."

"Okay, I was trying to protect you and evidently, you prefer hard facts. Dwight had gotten himself into trouble and Gallagher was using him to spy on the station and us. I thought it best to get Dwight to safety." Harrison studied her and ran his finger down his nose. "How long is it going to take you to get over this?"

"Oh, you're going to pay, Mr. Harrison Kane II."

He tilted his head to one side, considering her mood. "I don't suppose you'd let me hold you, would you? Just to know that you're safe?"

"Why?" She shivered with the need to have him do just that, but pride kept her apart.

"Because Ms. Langtry, anything could happen to you up here—including that—" He nodded toward the bear lumbering on the other side of the meadow. It paused, caught the scent of the humans, and stopped to watch them. The horses started nickering and prancing, but the bear, its mouth stained red, sniffed, coughed and grunted. Harrison and Michaela stood very still as the bear moved off into the brush and disappeared. The light "grizzled" tips of the bear's hide marked him as a fierce grizzly, once common in the Rockies. At seven hundred pounds, it could crush a man in a deathly hug, and one swipe could tear away flesh. Zachariah's claw necklace was fashioned from such a bear long ago.

When the brush was very silent, Michaela slashed her hand between them, setting up an emotional fence. "You've got to trust me, Harrison, and that's how it has to be. Those are the terms. He's on his way across the stream and up the next hill. I think it's safe now. . . ." Harrison glanced at her, then walked to the trail the bear had taken, moving cautiously into the brush. Michaela shook her head and was just about to go after him, when he returned. "Are you taking that job in San Francisco?"

"Huh. And leave the chance to make you pay? I don't think so," she stated firmly.

"The paycheck is better, the career opportunities better." He was pushing now, shoving choices at her when he already knew the answers. He knew she'd chosen heart and home. Harrison was baiting her, until she admitted everything out in the clear autumn air, dismissing any doubts between them. He moved slowly toward her and Michaela backed up a step. When Harrison looked like that, he meant business. And he had focused on her, watching her in that way that made her heart dance. Her mind went spinning like the golden leaves falling around them. He reached out his finger and stroked away the clinging web of hair on her cheek. "I was worried about you, up here and defenseless. You believed in me, gave me sunshine when I had none. You—"

His mouth curved gently at the thought. "You needed me. I've never been needed for myself, for the comfort I could give. I was terrified that I wouldn't know how. You terrify me. If anything happened to you, what would happen to my heart? It would still beat, but my life, my hopes and dreams, would be gone with you."

With that, he touched her hair again, his thumb cruising over the sleek strands. Then he left her, a tall, broad-shouldered man walking toward the frothing creek nearby. Michaela tried to find her heart, her breath, her body— *What would happen to my heart?*

Harrison wasn't a man to talk about his emotions, and yet—*what would happen to my heart . . . ?*

When Michaela could move, the falling golden leaves spiraled around her. She walked slowly to the creek. Harrison had removed his long-sleeved shirt, dropping it to a flat rock. In a gesture that said he wasn't immune to the unsteady emotions between them, he tore off his white undershirt. She leaned back against a trembling aspen, studying him and he glanced at her. That awareness sprung between them, alive, tangible, simmering, erotic, sweet, exciting.

He touched the softness she'd hidden for so long, the deep feminine feeling brought on by male appreciation, of what she was, of what she could be—

"There's something else you should know. In those three days I was away, I met with Dwight's creditors. His debts were extensive. I paid them. I've always known how to make money, but the station called for a personal investment and Dwight's debts—my finances are pretty well stripped now."

Michaela threw a rock and it splashed in the water in front of him. Harrison didn't move as she asked, "Is that important? Do you think it matters to me? Is that what you think of me, that I want a man who can take care of me? I'll have you know that I—"

Harrison's expression was grim. "A man likes to know he can take care of a woman. Yes, it's important to me."

She shook her head. "Not really. Not to me. The truth is worth far more."

Harrison shook his head. "It's more than sex. You're a part of me. I'm hoping that someday you'll see that we could be a part of each other. The problem is that there's been no time. Everything jumped into fast motion that first time we made love. I knew there was no going back then, living without you," he said quietly over the calling of the birds, the wind rustling the leaves that would soon fall.

She'd known then, too, that there was no going back, the urgency to claim him too strong.

Then he crouched beside the bubbling stream, the golden leaves floating down it, as he bent to rinse his hair, to scrub his face, arms, and chest. The wind toyed with her hair, lifting it, as she considered his male beauty, the shift of muscles beneath his dark skin, that intense profile. Using his T-shirt as a towel, he ran it across his hair, scrubbing at his face and hands. A man who meticulously prepared for any event, he'd rushed to find her, forgetting everything else. He'd been sweaty and dirty, corral dust clinging to him. He rubbed his T-shirt over his chest. Then those smoky gray eyes locked on her, his deep voice uneven and fierce. "Don't ever do this again, Michaela. Nothing can happen to you."

She walked slowly to him, taking the damp T-shirt. She wet it again, wringing it, then circled to his back, smoothing the taut muscles. He stood very still under her touch and she stroked his hair, longer now than his usual cut, the ends curling around her fingers. "I have feelings for you," she whispered, realizing that she'd never really given herself to any relationship, except this one. "They hurt."

Harrison's expression tightened, the past haunting him. "Because it's always going to stand between us, isn't it? My parents and my silence?"

"It's me, Harrison, and nothing more. I've guarded myself for too long. Roark tells me I've chosen men I could control. He's wrong. You are definitely not in that basket." She stroked the T-shirt down his arms, and just for a time, rested her cheek against his back.

She moved on instinct now, trusting herself and Harrison. "You challenge me. It's both exciting and infuriating and you know it. Then there are the softer feelings that I never thought myself able to give. I never believed I'd need anyone so much. It's terrifying."

He breathed suddenly as if he'd been holding his breath for too long. "I'm not experienced at this. I make mistakes."

"Shh." She'd never tended a man before, never knew how much quiet pleasure there was in the simple task. She wondered briefly if that was how Cleopatra felt, tending Zachariah's wounds and later when his dark moods came upon him, his honor challenging his pride.

Michaela stood in front of him, lifting the cloth to dab away the droplets clinging to his forehead, those fierce eyebrows, his cheekbones cut broadly in a harsh face. He watched her intently now as if he couldn't move. His heart leaped to her touch as she dabbed the cloth across that intriguing wedge of hair, beaded with water. She looked up at him and dropped the garment. "Your hair needs cutting," she whispered, smoothing the rumpled waves with her fingers, delighting in the warmth, the texture that carried to her heart. "But I like it this way."

"You cut it once. I was the laughingstock of the town that summer."

"You wore that ball cap all summer, even when it was over a hundred degrees."

"That was my macho stage. I was trying to impress you, but you were too busy with Billie What-His-Name."

"Don't touch me, Harrison. Just let me—" She leaned against him, placed her cheek over his heart and listened to the wild, strong beat. "I'm still fighting myself, you know. I'm not certain that I trust my judgment with men. I've had to fight so long and so hard for myself that adjusting to someone else in my life isn't easy. I'm just getting back my confidence and believing that I didn't fail, that it wasn't me. I'm building a new, fresh life here, getting back so much."

He breathed raggedly, his body taut. A shudder ripped through him, and yet he did not move. "I know. Everything came all at once and you were vulnerable."

"So were you. I'll never forget how you looked on the mountain and how much I needed you to hold me . . . how much I needed to hold you."

Michaela stood back, looking up at his fierce expression, his emotions visible, unlike Harrison's usual shield. She placed her hand along his cheek and he gripped her wrist suddenly, pressing his mouth into her palm. Against it, he whispered unevenly, "Just don't leave me, not now. I don't know about love, or if I can."

He'd given her another deep truth, hoarded too long away in the dark. Michaela placed her other hand on his hair, stroking it. The pleasure in touching him, reassuring him came quietly, unbidden, and safe. "You can."

He trembled and looked away, and Michaela urged his face back to hers. She lifted her lips to his, just a brush of a kiss, a taste. She enjoyed the flavor of his surprise, the new softness within herself. She'd never acted as a woman, tending her man before and yet, the task was not unpleasant. She stepped back, and following her instincts, she bent to take his shirts. She crouched and washed them in the stream. Aware of Harrison trying to control the urge to sweep her into his arms, she spread his clothing onto the bushes to dry and walked slowly back to the blanket.

A big man moving in the meadow's dappled autumn shadows, Harrison's gray eyes locked with hers. "Why did you do that—wash my shirts?" he asked huskily.

"It seemed the natural thing to do. I've lived for years without feeling natural as if a part of me hadn't unfolded yet. I like being natural with you. Doing what feels so right. Do you mind?" she asked as she began unbuttoning her blouse.

Harrison watched her closely as his finger prowled across her breasts, sliding just under her bra. "Natural is always appreciated," he said formally.

He ran his thumb over the crest of her breast, hardening it and Michaela closed her eyes, taking that slow perfect touch into her, letting it simmer and heat. "Make love to me, Harrison, and never keep anything from me again."

"So all is forgiven, hmm? I have no little wars to worry about, no payback for not telling you about

Dwight?" He nuzzled her cheek with his and the scent of him filled her, warmed her.

"I wouldn't say that, but you're safe enough for now," she said. She smiled against his lips as his arms came around her, lifting her feet off the ground. Michaela gave herself to his hunger, fed upon it and him. Nothing else mattered, but Harrison in her arms.

seventeen

She knew that wherever she went, I would follow, for she had my heart. Against all others, I would keep her and our children safe, no matter the cost. There came times when I would do just that, and she never failed to trust me.

Zachariah Langtry's Journal

"One thing is for certain, life with Michaela around is never dull," Harrison grumbled as he placed one hand on a fence post. He ached in every muscle, the mare's bucking taking its toll hours later. The walk down the mountain path had lessened his anger. He'd left Michaela sleeping on the blanket and had gone to bathe buck-naked in the creek. He'd heard a noise, terror running through him, the rocks cutting at his feet as he ran into the clearing. No Michaela, no horse, no—the note stuck on a branch where the horses had been tethered simply said "Payback." He hadn't appreciated the smiley face leering at him.

Before they'd made love, she'd leaned against him, smoothed his arms, and nuzzled his chest, the caresses almost ritualistic, as though she were fitting herself to him. The beauty of that moment, that simple feminine gesture with the tending of his clothing had shaken and stunned him. In the meadow, they'd made love slowly, beautifully, completely, and she'd left him to walk home.

At five o'clock the mountains' evening shadows were creeping upon the Langtry fields. The three-hour walk was easy enough, but Harrison had other plans when he awoke, like asking Michaela again to move in with him. He wasn't going to push her into marriage, rather let her get used to the idea. Gallagher was an added reason to keep Michaela close. With a lazy swish of his tail, the Langtry stud eyed Harrison. Then, as if wanting no part of Harrison's mood, the horse lifted his tail and raced away.

Roark came to ride beside Harrison. His grin flashed beneath the shadows of his western hat.

"Don't say it," Harrison ordered tightly.

"Okay, I won't." In the easy manner of a horseman used to hours in the saddle, Roark held the reins loosely, threaded through his gloves. "I found Cleopatra's ring and her journal. They were in that old hunter's cabin. When I was in that meadow by Cutter

Canyon, the glint of metal shot from that old broken down cabin. He'd placed Cleopatra's metal box inside another, and there was the ring. He'd hacked off the branch that had grown around it, embedding it in the wood. Something inside me always said that I'd find them. It gave me a purpose in those first months when I lost my wife and baby."

Harrison stopped walking. He turned to look up at Roark. A charmer when he wanted, Roark could easily attract any woman. But there would be no peace for Roark, with his heart lingering over what he could not have.

Harrison patted Roark's horse. If anything happened to Michaela, he would be just as empty. "I'm glad."

"I couldn't read it. It seemed too personal, a woman writing about her life, setting it down for the children that would follow. Mom and Michaela spent time with it, carefully opening those old pages. Then Michaela said something about cooking dinner, baking brownies and getting a shower curtain installed for her bathtub. She borrowed Dad's tool box and said she wanted to do it herself. She seemed pretty happy. Happier than I've seen her in a long time."

"I see." Harrison didn't really understand, but he was trying. If he understood the Michaela-situation correctly, she'd evened the score for his mistake, and now she was settling into domesticity. Harrison didn't trust that image at all. "She's not a plumber."

"When did anything stop her? There's probably water running everywhere now. You'll just have to finish the job. I don't want to be near either one of you tonight." Roark's grin flashed again. "You must have really stepped into a cow pile, Harrison. Can't remember when you ever walked home from a date. Of course, I can't remember you having dates."

"That's going to change." Harrison jerked open the door to his pickup and slid inside. "We both know she's just keeping things even. I made a mistake, a bad one. I won't make it again."

"She's a fast game when she wants to play, and she hasn't wanted to do that in a good long while. Maybe you'd better rest up before trying to find her."

"Not likely." Harrison revved his pickup to bury Roark's laughter.

Julia Kane pressed her fingers to her throbbing temples. Who was he, the little boy who played in her mind? He was so solemn, watching her. She'd loved him, but hated him, too . . . because he looked like someone else who had hurt her.

She gathered the blanket around her, huddling in the shadows. There was another man with cold blue eyes who had come to her, asking questions she could not answer.

The faces went around in her mind, taunting her. Who was the baby? She wore pink—a girl maybe. But she looked like the little boy.

What did the man with blue eyes want? He was a hurting man and she'd been afraid of him.

Big shining gold coins spilled into her mind, pounding the pain there. The nurse came, and Julia greedily devoured the pills that would take away the faces tormenting her.

Saturday nights were usually quiet in Shiloh, except at Donovan's Bar and Grill, and at seven o'clock, Michaela was not with her friends, in her home, or Donovan's. Her parents and Roark were not answering their telephones.

Harrison sat outside Donovan's, the neon sign spilling through his windshield. In that filtered light, his knuckles were blood-red, his hands locked on the steering wheel. *Where was she?*

The tool box was open on the bathroom floor, the oblong piping upon which the curtain would hang was in the tub. The directions were spread across the sink. She'd had a bath, the tiny feminine room scented of her. The casserole was in the stove's warming oven, baking chocolate and eggs waited beside a mixing bowl. The recipe book was opened. The mixing spoon lay on the floor and Harrison picked it up, his fear growing. He had replaced the eggs in the refrigerator and checked the alarm system, which Michaela had deactivated. Her message machine had been empty.

Her camera bag was gone, her car in the driveway. Harrison went to the back porch, and saw the burros circling, waiting for their treat. He methodically took apples from their bucket, halved them into the mixing bowl and fought his fear. The burros weren't friendly, but they took the apples. They were missing her, too.

Then the fire siren cut through the night and peo-

ple poured from Donovan's. Harrison saw the trucks
heading toward KANE and knew the war had begun.

He arrived moments after the fire trucks to find
Josy Daniels and Mooney frantic with worry as smoke
filled the news room.

The fire was small, occurring in the hallway near
the news room. A highly flammable rag had been
placed in Mooney's not-so-secret ashtray—an old
milk can he'd partially filled with sand. Hidden
behind a file cabinet, the can's tight lid had kept tell-
tale cigarette smoke contained and choked the possi-
bility of fire. But someone had drilled holes in the lid
and strategically placed a small button so that the lid
could not fully close. Another hole had been drilled,
and a stealthily concealed rag, saturated with fluid,
had led into the wall. The fire had burned for hours
undetected by alarms before bursting through the
wall. Water and debris and smoke now filled the
room.

Mooney's apologies mixed with his tears, and Harrison tried to calm him. "It's arson, Mooney. Not your
fault."

"I said I'd stopped smoking, but I hadn't," Mooney
sobbed.

"It's not your fault," Harrison repeated as the sheriff stood nearby, asking questions and the fire depart-
ment hacked into the wall, seeking potential
smoldering wood.

"No wonder Michaela loves you. You're such a
swell guy. She says your bark is worse than your bite
and that you're really soft as a marshmallow inside

and sweet . . . I love you, too," Mooney sobbed and flung his arms around Harrison.

"Mooney, this is a small fire, little damage and—" Harrison tried to push gently free of Mooney's three-hundred-plus-pound bulk. Mooney continued to sob and Harrison noted the grins around the news room. "I love you, too, Mooney," Harrison said finally, in an effort to appease the grieving camera man.

Harrison firmly freed himself and turned to the sheriff and firemen. They stared at him and suddenly stopped laughing. "I'm not having a good day," Harrison warned. "Let's do what we have to do here and get this mess cleaned up. Has anyone seen Michaela Langtry?"

"She's off this weekend, Harrison," Josy said. "I heard her say something yesterday about a day spa."

Harrison's mind tripped back to the wooden spoon lying on Michaela's kitchen floor, to the unfinished shower project, her tool box and waiting directions. "Any other ideas?"

"Call for you, Mr. Kane," one of the technicians called.

Harrison held his breath, praying it was Michaela. "If playing hide and seek is a joke, Michaela, it's not—"

"I take my wife, my son, and my top man to dinner at the Corral Roadhouse on the highway, and what the hell happens? Someone breaks into Faith's studio and damn well breaks the place to pieces. They broke my cup," Jacob yelled indignantly. "My wife made that cup for me, one of her first, and I'd had coffee with her this morning, leaving it at the studio. Damn. They broke my cup. Now, where in my daughter? She didn't get hurt in the fire, did she?"

"Jacob, I think we may have a problem," Harrison stated very carefully. He glanced at Sheriff Marlon Amadeo. If Gallagher had taken Michaela, one wrong move from the sheriff and his officers could mean her life. For now, it was better to wait. Perhaps Michaela had ridden to town with a friend, maybe— "I'm going to go to a private line. Hold on."

An hour later, Harrison returned to Michaela's darkened home. She hadn't returned and after waiting a little longer, he finished the task of installing the shower rod. In the bathroom mirror, his face was covered with stubble, and he hadn't changed clothing since he'd ridden the mare. Shadows darkened his eyes and lines cut through his face. He wasn't tired, rather riding on nerves, and he needed to be more in charge if Michaela was in danger. Sensing it was going to be a long night, he prowled through Michaela's closet, found his laundered clothing from their trip at Cutter Canyon, and brought the telephone into the bathroom. He stepped into the shower, alert to the telephone's ring.

Dressed now, Harrison brewed coffee for the long night ahead. He bent to pull Michaela's ironing board into position, and damned whatever macho show-off reasons he had for breaking the mare. As the iron heated, he ate without tasting. With an unsteady sigh, he picked up a blouse from Michaela's laundry basket and began ironing methodically. *If only he could hold her, to know that—*

Harrison pushed away his needs and began matching and folding her socks. After that, he cleaned and lubricated her vacuum cleaner and tensed each time a car drove by on the highway. He double checked the silent telephone. The Langtrys wouldn't call, keeping the line free. He'd agreed to call them at any word of Michaela.

At midnight, the call came from Michaela. "He wants all of the coins, Harrison. And the bear claw necklace. He wants you to come alone. He'll let you know where. Please don't—"

"Are you all right? Did he hurt you?" Harrison asked, but the line was cut dead.

Soft-ly, slow-ly . . . the mornin' will creep. . . . Michaela dragged herself awake, her muscles aching. Ropes bit into her wrists. She was cold, shivering, and the small battery heater a distance away did not help her. She'd refused Gallagher's invitation to sleep with him—in his sleeping bag—or with Ricco. She lay on a shack's cot, dirty rags serving as the mattress. The bruise on her cheek came from Gallagher. He hadn't liked her wooden spoon applied to the area between his legs.

For that, she'd been forced to trudge up the mountain tied behind his horse—Gallagher hadn't liked her opinion of his poor horse riding skills, or the blunders he and his men made night riding in the mountains.

When she couldn't get up the last time, she'd been roughly slung over a horse. At their destination, she'd been tossed onto a cot.

Dream your sweet dreams and do not weep.... How many hours had it been since she'd opened her front door to Gallagher, expecting to see Harrison?

Cornbread in the mornin' it will keep... The birds were beginning to chirp outside the rough cabin and Michaela caught the tang of pine and spruce in the morning air.

Drift soft-ly, slow-ly 'tis time to sleep... Harrison? Where are you? Michaela closed her eyes and prayed that Harrison was safe.

Gallagher came to stand over her and sipped his coffee. He wore her coin now and another. "Your boyfriend should be coming soon. He's going to bring the rest of the coins to me . . . and the bear claws. You didn't like being packed up here across a saddle, did you?"

She stared at him and tried not to wince as his hand came down to her throat. He suddenly jerked her denim coat, bringing her to sit upright. "How did you get that other coin?" she asked.

"Harrison's mother. Isn't that a kick? The old woman told my brother about it, both of them nutsos. I've got another one taped to my holster—bought it from a con man. So that makes three for me, and three coming with your boyfriend. I'll have all six. And you. Won't that be fun?"

"You know where Harrison's mother is?"

"In a private Seattle sanatorium. Uses her real

name, but the records are private. Who would have thought it? It doesn't matter where her body is. Her brain is shot. She's still got it when it comes to investments though. Kane got his smarts from her. He won't need them, though, honey. Not after today."

A cool damp finger of mist curled through the broken window and layered the single room. Gallagher's cold blue eyes ran down her body and Michaela didn't try to shield her disgust. He smiled and patted his thinning hair. "There are ways to make you willing, you know. But they're not as much fun as what I have planned. You're thinking Kane will come to the rescue, right? I've got men stationed on the trail. If he isn't alone, everyone pays."

Ricco moved, peering out the window. He nodded and Gallagher said, "Show time. Bring her outside, Ricco."

Through the morning's layers of mist, Michaela saw the man and knew it wasn't Harrison. Roark's build was leaner, his western hat pulled low on his head. Michaela closed her eyes, Ricco hauling her up beside him. She knew without doubt that Gallagher's men weren't there anymore. Her father and Culley would have removed them silently during the night.

She shivered, if they saw that it was Roark and not Harrison— Where was Harrison?

Roark tossed the bag through the mist and it fell at Gallagher's feet. He bent to tear it open and held the coins to the dim morning light, examining them. He slid the bear claw necklace over his head and stood, holding the bag Roark had thrown.

Michaela noted a shadow and her heart raced. "Good old Harrison," she murmured.

Gallagher swung to her. "What?"

"I said I'd like to know more about Harrison's mother."

"Just what I told you. And you're not in a position to ask favors, lady."

Harrison moved then, a big man appearing suddenly from the mist to tear Ricco away from her. Ricco went down easily with the hard punch. Gallagher took his gun from his shoulder holster and pointed it at Harrison. "You—"

Michaela's kick hit Gallagher's hand and the automatic discharged, flying into the wet grass.

"Let's see what you've got now," Harrison said coolly as he whipped away the rope from Michaela's wrists.

Gallagher scanned the field, the tall western men moving into it. "My men—"

"Left. They didn't like the choices and they weren't trained for mountains at night. I think the Langtry dogs scared them a little." Harrison's punch to his jaw took him reeling backward. "All you have to do is to get through me and run up that trail. There's a highway on the other side, and you just might have a chance—if they don't catch you. But you have to go through me, first," Harrison repeated too softly.

Gallagher's blow was packed with fear, determination and rage. It sent Harrison staggering backward. Then Michaela followed her instincts and leaped upon Gallagher's back and all four men in the meadow yelled angrily at her. In the free-for-all, someone tried to pull her free of Gallagher as he was swatting back at her, yelling because his ear was twisted painfully. Taking that distraction, Harrison reached across Gallagher's shoulder and placed his large hand on Michaela's face. Harrison shoved gently. "Would you let me handle this?" he demanded.

"Mmmft! I'm helping here, Harrison," she returned hotly, as Roark finally pried her free.

But Gallagher and Harrison were trading blows now, back alley fighting mixed with trained punches. Locked in a fierce battle, the men were equally matched, Harrison skillfully dodging and blocking blows, dancing in place while Gallagher seemed to tire.

Michaela placed her hands on her hips. Harrison had crouched, slamming blows into Gallagher's head and body. He had that lowered neck, tight stance of a boxer, and he seemed to dance over the ground as though he were in a professional ring, wearing down his opponent. "Apparently, you don't need my help," she said.

Culley studied the movements with appreciation. "It seems our boy has had some training in bare-knuckle fights."

Michaela turned to him. "Harrison?"

"I thought he needed to know a thing or two before he left for the big wide world," Jacob murmured with undisguised pride. "Looks like he's practiced a bit since then."

Gallagher reeled, staggered and went down, and

Harrison dived upon him. With one hand on the other man's throat, Harrison lifted the two coins free and tossed them away. He hauled Gallagher to his feet.

His expression was too savage and Michaela shivered. She hadn't seen him so fierce— "Harrison! Were you in brawls like this before?" Michaela called.

"I suppose I should have told you that, too," Harrison said, pushing Gallagher away. Obviously defeated, Gallagher sagged against the old cabin.

Unable to wait longer, Michaela ran into Harrison's arms, holding him tightly. "If anything happens to you . . . *what would happen to my heart?*" she asked, repeating his words to her, feeling them tight inside her.

Harrison's arms tightened around her, his face buried in her hair. He shook, his fear for her, rather than for himself. "If he hurt you—"

Gallagher had pushed away from the cabin, running toward the trail leading to freedom.

"I'll get them all," he cursed as he powered into the fast dash, counting on the strength from his laps at the gym. One hand held down the bear claw necklace; he'd have that at least until he could kill them all. His running shoes quickly ate up the rocky trail. The Langtrys and Kane were not far behind, but then he was smarter— Then he looked up at the bear, who had just risen to his back feet. The tree behind it was marked with its claws, the bark torn away. Terror staked Gallagher immobile, his scream frozen as the silent grizzly moved in with a deadly embrace. Gallagher's last thought was that the bear had seen the claw necklace and had come for revenge. One swipe tore it from his throat.

Michaela's body froze instantly when she saw Harrison stand in front of the bear mauling Gallagher. Guns drawn, Jacob, Culley and Roark stood beside her. "Don't move," Roark said quietly. "Those claw marks on that tree say the bear marked his territory for mating. Gallagher couldn't have picked a worse place. Stand still, Michaela."

Instead, she inched toward Harrison. She placed her hand on his back. "Don't you dare—"

"Get back." The harsh order hit her like a fist.

"What would happen to my heart?" she whispered to him again. He stiffened at that, but did not move. "Please don't try to help him, Harrison. He's already dead."

"Drop him," Harrison was saying too quietly, his head was down, eyes averted so as not to challenge the beast. For the first time, Michaela noted the large empty sheath at his back, the large, evil knife held in his hand. "Drop him," Harrison repeated quietly, firmly, as his long legs locked in a fighter's stance.

Michaela's hand went to her pounding heart. *Harrison sounded as if he would*—Terror sucked the warmth from her body. One glance at his jaw and she knew he meant to have his way. "Harrison . . ."

"Hush."

With a loud grunt that sounded of disgust, the bear took one last swipe at Gallagher's lifeless body, rolling it, before ambling away.

The others moved slowly toward the body, making

certain that the bear was out of range. Roark bent to test the pulse in Gallagher's throat and looked at her, shaking his head "no."

In one efficient movement, Harrison threw the big hunting knife. A silver streak in the autumn day, the blade lodged into a tree with a solid whack. He tugged Michaela close against him. "Listen, let's get this straight, okay?" he whispered unevenly into her hair. "It's a role-playing thing. I'm bigger. I'm stronger. That's the deal. I'm supposed to protect you. You're supposed to kiss me and make me feel better. You're supposed to spoil me and wait on my every wish—but you are not supposed to kick a loaded gun from a man's hand. You are not supposed to follow me to ask a grizzly to release a man. That's the job description."

She held him tighter, and wasn't certain who was shaking the most. Harrison's heart pounded wildly beneath her cheek. "So I'm supposed to watch you get mauled, too? I don't think so."

Harrison's smile moved slowly against her cheek. "I don't think even that bear would take you on, once he got a taste of your temper."

She shivered against him. "Where did you get that knife?"

"It's just standard camping equipment. The handle has fishing line, a compass, and other essentials in it. Nothing special."

He turned her face up to him, and frowned, kissing the bruise Gallagher had given her. "Oh, my,"

Michaela exclaimed, examining his swelling bruises, his cut lip. "They said you knew how to brawl—Harrison, you didn't, did you?"

He smiled tightly, then touched his swelling lip. "Not often. I don't suppose you've got an ice pack handy."

Michaela shivered and stepped back. She wrapped her arms around herself, staring at the hard-looking big man in front of her, his mouth too swollen to kiss. She leaned forward anyway and lightly brushed her lips over his. "All these secrets have got to stop, Harrison. *Who are you?*"

"I am one very tired, aching man. Part of that is due to a very long walk down the mountain, thanks to you. What did he tell you about my mother?"

Michaela tried to see his face, but everything was sliding away. "She's alive . . . Harrison, I've never done this before, but . . . I think I'm going to faint."

Good old Harrison, she would remember thinking as her legs gave way and he swung her up into his arms.

"Just look at that—look at my hands shaking," Michaela said furiously that evening as Harrison sat in her parents' hot tub. She picked up a soft cloth and began scrubbing his ears. "I'll just go get another ice pack for your face. And oh, those hands. Don't get them in water."

"This is more like it. Me man, you woman. Me master, you slave."

She tugged his hair with just enough pressure to let

him know what she thought of his premise. "Fat chance. I'll be right back. Do not put those hands in water."

Alone in the sunset, Harrison placed his glass of wine on the rim, and leaned back, closing his eyes. He wasn't used to her fussing over him, but after today, the feeling did soothe the raw edges.

His mother had been easily located by a friend in the health care industry. She'd been in the sanatorium all the while. Harrison felt so old and worn, his journey almost at an end.

Would she remember him? Would it finally be over? He closed his eyes, dreading whatever new truths were yet to be unfolded.

As the water bubbled soothingly and the steam rose around Harrison, the old lullaby came circling him, the one she used to sing to him. *Soft-ly, slow-ly . . . the mornin' will creep. . . .*

Michaela's hands moved through his hair. Her thumbs smoothed the lines between his brows. "You're going to use those aching muscles for full advantage, aren't you? Having me wait on you?"

"Trying to impress you isn't easy. I'm not in shape for breaking horses."

"Well, let's go to my house and see if you're in shape for other things," she whispered lightly against his torn lip.

He opened his eyes, staring into her soft blue ones. "You'll be gentle, won't you?"

Her impish smile delighted him and he reached to tug her into the hot tub with him, holding her on his lap. "One question. Why did you take your camera, of all things?"

Michaela smoothed his jaw and kissed the bruise there. "I thought I might have to protect you. Blinding him with the flash would give me the advantage. And it was a gift you gave to me."

His expression darkened as the frightening day slid by on the hot tub's steam. Harrison held her tighter. "You could have been killed."

"You know what I thought when I saw you? I thought 'good old Harrison.' He always comes through. I never doubted that for a moment."

The long lounging gown she wore did not constrict his roving caresses, which had to stop too soon. She was just snuggling against him, those featherlight kisses making him woozy when Roark, Jacob, Faith, and Culley came to sit on the benches around the tub. Harrison held very still. It all seemed so natural, a family sitting together in the setting sun, Michaela nestling against him. He hadn't thought of her as a cuddling woman, but then he hadn't thought of himself as a man with a heart. He drew the pleasure into him, savoring it with a sigh.

"Michaela and I read Cleopatra's journal," Faith said as she smoothed the coins on the black velvet cloth. "All six are returned to us and that is what she wanted—for Zachariah's heirs to have his legacy. They both fought so hard for their lives, and she believed in Obediah's curse. Cleopatra tells a beautiful story, blending so well with Zachariah's. Now we have her ring, her journal and the coins."

Faith looked at Harrison. "Julia was once my friend. I would like to know that she's being treated well. If she ... if she can remember any details about Sable, I'd so like to hear them. Can you do that, Harrison?"

She hesitated and looked at her husband. "And if you can, if she understands, please tell her that I forgive her."

Jacob's arm circled his wife. She would never have the child she'd missed and that unspoken thought cruised through the evening hour. Because Jacob wasn't certain how to tell her of his heart just then, he chose another familiar method. He lifted his new mug, studying it. "Don't know that I like this one as well."

Soft-ly, slow-ly. ... the mornin' will creep ... Michaela awoke, fear racing through her, her body damp with sweat. Harrison had turned, bending over her in the night, his hand smoothing her tumbled hair. She closed her eyes and trembled, trying to pull herself from the nightmare.

They hadn't talked about Gallagher and now Harrison whispered roughly, "Did he—? Did he hurt you?"

"No. You would have known hours ago," she said too harshly. The old lullaby still echoed in her bedroom.

"No, I might not have. You keep secrets, too, dear heart. You've got to forgive yourself. You were a four-year-old child when Sable was stolen. What could you have done?"

"I don't want logic now, Harrison," she stated shakily. "I'm still seeing you fighting him, that savage look on your face. I didn't know you then. And that knife . . . you could have been killed. Just hold me."

He drew her head down to his shoulder, smoothing her hair with one hand and holding her against him with his other arm. "It's all over, Michaela. We'll sort the rest of this through. It's just going to take time."

"How can you be so certain?"

"Because I know you. You were there when I was fifteen and when I was eighteen, and today—" He paused and tilted her face up for a kiss. "Today, when your hand was on my back as I faced that bear, I knew you were unshakable and—"

He held her as she cried, his expression grim in the feminine room. Would the past ever stop tearing at them? *Soft-ly, slow-ly . . . the mornin' will creep. . . .*

eighteen

I wish I could give my true love the journal she had lost. She'd wanted to share her heart with our children and grandchildren. But the ring and her journal seem eternally lost, never to be shared with the women who will either marry or carry her blood. It is enough for us, I think, that we have each other. I have made my peace with pride and honor, and my wife had no little part in the doing. We've come so far, and though Cleopatra believes Obediah's curse and the legend of the coins has made us strong through the years, I believe it is our love. Truly, she is my heart.

Zachariah Langtry's Journal

Seated outside the door that led to his mother's room, Michaela glanced at Harrison. He was dressed impeccably in a gray suit. Nothing remained of the fierce man who had battled Gallagher the week before. Harrison was too quiet, and Michaela mourned his reckoning with his mother. At night, he held her close, but shadows circled them both. Michaela had lived with a stranger once, and now, even with Harrison close against her, she feared losing him to the past. September's beautiful foliage had gone unnoticed by him, and he'd plunged into work, forging time for his trip to the oceanside sanatorium.

He hadn't wanted his bruises to frighten Julia; the reports of her condition said she was very unstable and easily upset. Despite Harrison's grumbling, Michaela's skill with cosmetics concealed his fading bruises.

He held her hand, studying the slender, pale contrast to his wide callused palms, his strong fingers. "Fine thing when a man wears makeup," he grumbled, but leaned back against her free hand as it stroked his hair, the waved length brushing his collar.

She brought his hand to her lips, kissing it, and held it safe, tucked beneath her chin. Harrison glanced at her, shaking his head. He eased his hand away from her care. "Don't feel sorry for me, Michaela. I won't have that."

"I wouldn't think of it," she returned, determined to keep his mood from darkening. She was terrified now, fighting for courage, because Harrison seemed so far away from the man who wanted her desperately in the night. "We're just traveling buddies."

"There was no need to bring your camera. It's not like a happy reunion." He glanced down at her dark blue jacket and white blouse, the practical matching slacks. "You're not wearing your coin."

"I thought it might upset her."

"I want you to wear it. You shouldn't be here. You don't need to go through this. There's no telling what she'll say." Harrison spoke harshly and Michaela nodded. His edges were all out there and she wanted to hold him safe against the pain. He rubbed his hand roughly across his face, as if he were too weary to deal with his encounter.

"I want earrings from you, Harrison," she said to distract him. He'd faced a dangerous bear with nothing in his hand but a knife; he'd survived the past and struggled to make it right, and now he dreaded the moment of reckoning. She could help him now, if only for a moment.

He turned to her. "Huh?"

"Gifts. I want gifts," she said, pushing him back from the darkness. "And you need to help me weed the herb garden, and when are you going to till that old garden for fall?"

For the first time, humor lurked around his hard mouth. "Nag."

"Well, then, there are the salsa dancing lessons. I need a partner. I saw you dance around Gallagher like you were Mohammed Ali—light as a . . ."

Harrison bent to brush his lips against hers. "Okay, okay."

"And photography is an art form, you know. You gave me a camera and I need a nude to—"

Harrison blinked and straightened. "Hell, no. It's bad enough I'm wearing makeup."

"And you're so pretty, too," she cooed and settled back to watch Harrison blush.

"If you tell Jacob or Roark, I'll never live it down."

"So you'll take those salsa dancing lessons with me?" she pushed with a grin, then at the sound of movements within Julia's room, Harrison tensed, expression going flat.

The door opened and a nurse wheeled a small, frail woman out into the hallway. The nurse nodded to Harrison, indicating he should follow. The small woman with white hair, terrified blue eyes and a too pale, thin face clutched a stack of newspapers as though it were her Bible. The nurse spoke soothingly, "No, you can't have your medicine just now. There now, Julia. Don't be frightened. It's so beautiful today. We've got you all dressed in pink, with a pretty shawl, for your visitors. They'll see you out on the patio where you can view the waves you love so much."

"Will they want to talk about finances?" Fear threaded Julia's high-pitched voice. "Is it my executor?"

As the wheelchair moved out onto the sunlit patio, Harrison stood. As usual, he'd been thorough in his research. "Executor, my foot. The guy has his hands in her money so bad that—"

Michaela slid her hand through his. "You'll take care of it. Let's go meet your mother."

The ocean surf pounded at the rocks below and the nurse sat quietly to one side, lifting her knitting bag onto her lap. Julia's terror locked in her eyes when she saw— "Him, that's him. That's the man who hurt me."

She crushed the papers to her thin chest and the nurse shook her head, speaking in that same monotone. "Julia, this is your son. He may look like someone else, but he is your son. His name is Harrison."

Beside Michaela, Harrison's big body tensed. "Hello, Mother," he said in that same monotone.

Tears squeezed from Julia's eyes as she stared at him. "You look different. Maybe you're not him."

Michaela put her hand to her throat. Harrison had his father's features, but there was kindness and vulnerability there, and great strength.

Harrison sat slowly and Julia's fear-filled gaze swung to Michaela. "I saw you. You're that Indian woman, Cleopatra. Why are your eyes so blue? Faith Langtry's eyes, that's what they are!"

Harrison breathed in sharply and took Michaela's hand, pulling her down to sit beside him. "This is Michaela Langtry. She's come to see you."

Julia shrunk back in her wheelchair, pulling her papers up to her face. "I don't want to see her. Make her go away."

Michaela nodded and eased a distance away, as Harrison leaned forward, speaking quietly to Julia. She could only guess the immense control he'd exerted to keep his voice low, when his emotions were tangled and hurting. Eventually, Julia showed him her newspapers, and for the next half hour, Harrison and she discussed financial reports.

Then suddenly, Julia screamed shrilly, "Yes, I took that Langtry baby. Harrison gave it to Faith Langtry, but it was really my baby. I couldn't bear looking at her anymore, because she looked like the little boy."

Harrison's hard face had paled and he glanced wearily at Michaela as Julia began to sing *Soft-ly, slow-ly. . . . the mornin' will creep. . . .*

Julia leaned into the salt air, with the sound of the waves smashing into the rocks below the cliff. The strong wind pressed her long white gown against her thin body, and the black waves spread out endlessly before her.

She couldn't bear more pain, and seeing her son today had opened up the past . . . she remembered everything too vividly. . . . She'd managed to leave him a note, some small thing to give him after all the pain she'd caused—*I love you. Mother*, she'd written simply, forcing herself to remember the letters.

The exact business letter she had written earlier, addressed to her son, was already in the mailbox. It listed her accounts and ones her executor didn't know about. She wanted Harrison to have what remained, and the executor who had taken so much, needed a sturdy auditing. Her son would know what to do— she'd tested him with the financial reports and asked him about the bank.

Now she wanted to be with her husband. Her love

for him had never stopped, but it had twisted into something dark and evil within her. Faith Langtry had said she forgave Julia, but how could any woman—?

Faith Langtry's daughter was strong, too, and love flew between her and Harrison. The Langtrys were bred to give love, to fight for it.

Julia wiped at the tears flowing down her cheeks. She should have protected her son, but she hadn't. She'd had a child she'd abandoned, and now he was an adult, a good man.

"Mrs. Kane!" the nurse called to her.

Julia smiled serenely before she hurled herself into the night. "I'm coming, dear husband," she whispered to the wind rushing through her hair, the waves and rocks below.

Harrison sat at his desk, Julia's effects in front of him. She had a keen financial mind, leaving exact figures and where they could be found. She had been right; her executor had been skimming from her accounts. He opened the small envelope and read the note within: *I love you. Mother.*

Michaela was on tape, her voice carrying from the television set. The program centered on area pioneers, laced with interviews from their descendants.

Harrison rubbed the ache in his chest. It was mid-September now, the leaves falling, and snow due on the mountains any day. Michaela hadn't pushed him in the month that had passed, but she deserved more than a man who brooded and couldn't sleep at the midnight hour.

She was a woman meant to have children, and he feared what ran through his blood, the darkness and the ability to hurt. The Langtry coin gleamed on her purple suit, and Harrison shook his head, rubbing his face with his hands. He had so little to give—

He frowned and caught the balled socks that had just hit him on the head.

"You're just needing time, Harrison," Michaela said fiercely. "You're healing, and that's all that matters."

"Well, then, I'm going to take time to deal with it," he returned. "And you're wrong. You matter. It's important to me that I give you everything in me, not just portions here and there. I'm going to work this out."

"I see," she answered stiffly, pain ricocheting through her. "And you're going to do that without me?"

"You're a . . . a lovely distraction. Look at you—standing there in my T-shirt and nothing else. How am I supposed to concentrate on making myself romantic? Think of it this way—I'm old-fashioned, it seems. I want a traditional relationship. I want to learn how to treat the woman I want to marry. How to make myself appealing. I want you to have everything possible in this relationship, including dating and gifts and whatever the hell comes with it."

"You're not being logical. We've been through too much to—" *Was she losing him?*

"That's exactly right. We've skipped from A to C and missed B. I want B—for you. Do you think I want to give you less than Jacob gave your mother? Than Roark gave his wife?"

Harrison rose to his feet and walked slowly toward her. "I've got to go through the steps. It's important to me. I'm asking you to understand."

He lifted her chin with his fingertip. "You've been too quiet, backing away from every argument, when once you would have flown at me, everything right out there in the open. I can't have less than the truth from you, either. I won't have you guarded around me, afraid to speak that vivid, creative mind. Not once have you pushed the weather segment you want, argued about the necessity of local reporting. You've been holding your punches, dear heart, and that isn't the relationship I want."

"You're making this very complicated, Harrison. You always do," she whispered.

"The point is, sweetheart, that you're not ramrodding this relationship. We both are. You haven't forgiven yourself for that night, and it's time you did. I can't bear to wake up at night, to hear you crying in your sleep. Do what you have to do. It's important," he repeated and then drew her into his arms for one of those mind-blasting tender kisses.

She didn't understand, Michaela decided that night in her tiny house—without Harrison. He had that grim, pulled-inside himself look, and he was set upon resolving the past.

Michaela swallowed the tightness in her throat and dashed away the tears. Everything had come so fast—

her love for him, startling her. Yet there it was, raw and bold and unchangeable.

She held the Langtry coin, meant to bring good luck to the wearer and damned Harrison for being right. She had to come to terms with herself over that night.

Cleopatra's journal lay waiting, and with trembling hands, Michaela picked it up to read. . . .

Such a strange beast, I thought, laying my hands on the man's wounds. He watched me closely, his eyes the color of sun in honey. His name came hard to my lips. Zachariah Langtry he is called.

Later when I defended myself against the man who would have me, this Zachariah came, giving five of his family coins for me. I must marry him, they said, for a woman such as myself must have a master to tame her.

So we were married, me standing with the hangman's noose around my neck, did have little choice. When we were wed, his lips touched mine. The strange new touch tasted of something I had not known, but that warmed me. So we were wed, and the learning of him, how strong and brave my husband is, was to come much later. We fought, the would-be master and I, with my soul and heart telling me that this was right. Like the tiny milkweed seeds blowing in the wind, we discovered what was true between us. Nothing else mattered. He is in my heart always.

Cleopatra Langtry

Harrison tossed aside the wood he had just split in two for the cabin's fire. Michaela was riding up the mountain to him, steam shooting from Diamond's nostrils. Harrison smiled briefly, and ran his hand across his three-day-old beard. He'd expected her sooner than three days, but then, Michaela was never really predictable. His sweetheart had that dark hunter's look to her, her eyes—above the thick woolen scarf—finding him on the mountain.

He piled the wood into his arms and walked into the old cabin. Busy with cleaning it, chinking the old logs against the winter's cold, had helped him sort through the darkness of the past. Now the cabin was clean and starkly unfurnished, smelling of the wood stacked by the stove. The large window overlooking Cutter Canyon was new and no easy task to pack up the mountain. His bridal gift to Michaela would give her an unsurpassed view, and he thought of her in the morning mist overlooking the mountains that meant so much to her.

The three days they had been apart had not been easy, and Harrison had warred with old wounds. There was only one logical conclusion. If he wanted a new life with Michaela, the old would have to die. He'd come to terms now with the past, grappling with it through the long, empty nights.

Harrison took off his coat and hung it on a peg, then sat down to wait. When Michaela came calling, anything was possible.

Her footsteps sounded a march up the wooden

steps. She flung open the door and searched the shadows, finding him. "You've got it all wrong, dear heart," she stated as she slammed the door behind her.

"How so?" he asked, his heart pounding at the sight of her, all steamed up and ready to fight.

His love went to the stove, ripped off her mittens and glared at him. She warmed her hands near the stove.

"I watched children playing for hours. Small four-year-old children. I knew that after playing hard all day, they couldn't possible awake during the night. There was nothing I could have done as a child. I know that now—I feel it inside."

He nodded, and settled back to enjoy the storm.

She tore off the blood-red scarf and her blue eyes burned warmth into the empty place in his heart, the place that had missed her. "Secondly, I'm not exactly traditional. Thirdly, I couldn't ramrod you into anything if I wanted to."

"That party at my house?" he asked gently, pushing her, for he would have his due from her.

"Well, *that* was a necessity. Sometimes you have to be dragged into what's best for you."

"Like you?" He fought a smile, because Michaela looked as if she was just getting warmed up, plowing right through every instinct she had, emotions wide-open and real.

She stood, tall and dressed in a warm dark red sweater and long, tight-fitting jeans. "My feet are cold and it's your fault."

"Okay." He accepted that responsibility as she sat to tear off her boots.

She sat in a chair near him, put her feet in his lap and ordered, "Rub."

He chafed her feet as ordered and then gently eased the socks away. "Balled or folded?"

"Balled. Does that make a difference?" She sucked in her breath as he lifted her foot to kiss the insole. "What do you want from me?"

"Honesty. Just everything you're doing right now." He wrapped his hands around her ankles. He slowly drew her chair close to his, then lifted her into his lap. "You have to know that you're not a failure. You couldn't have pulled the station together as you have if you were."

"I know. I've thought about that and how I've always trusted you, feeling safe with you. I trust myself now. I'm more confident. I know that I have a woman's feelings . . . you've given me that." Michaela watched him carefully. "Harrison, there's really no point in us being apart. You could move in with me."

"Or you could move in with me and change your name in front of a minister, but that's not really the point now, is it?"

"What are your terms?" she asked smoothing his hair, playing with it as he loved.

"There's that little 'I love you' thing. That would be nice."

"You first." She looked down to see his hand slowly, possessively close over her breast.

"You first," he returned, kissing the side of her throat and easing his hand up under her sweater. He slid the sweater from her, then the thermal undershirt, until Michaela's lacy bra was free to his roaming hand.

"You first," she whispered as he bent to kiss her there, to arch her body against his mouth.

"Love," he whispered against her curved body when they were both lying on the small old metal bed, their clothing upon the floor.

"Come to me—" she whispered desperately, and with a sigh took his body into hers.

It was no gentle lovemaking, rather the burning away of the past, the forging of the new, the tempest raging between them, hunger and future mixed into a heady blend. Deep within they met, hurled against each other, blinded by the heat that came churning suddenly, pounding at them. They lay quietly in the aftermath, hearts pounding, bodies still trembling. Michaela raised slightly, and Harrison eased back the silky hair from her damp cheek. Her blue eyes were drowsy and warm with what had just passed between them. "I do love you, Harrison."

"I know." He drifted in the pleasure and the future, his love snuggled next to him.

She tugged the hair on his chest lightly. "Don't you have something to say?"

"Only 'ouch!'" He captured her hand, lacing his fingers with hers. "I thought I'd wait for the right romantic moment."

When she gasped, her flashfire mood shifting, Harrison held her tighter as she struggled against him. "Let me up."

"No. I'm having too much fun." Then, off-balance, Harrison began to slide off the narrow bed, taking Michaela with him.

Lying on the floor, she grinned up at him and he began to laugh, feeling as if he had everything he never thought possible. "Okay, I love you," he said finally, and watched those fabulous blue eyes soften upon him.

"You know what they say about us Langtrys, don't you?" she asked against his lips.

"That I do. *It was said that when the wild heart of a Langtry is captured, it will remain true forever.*"

"Yes, never doubt it, my love," she whispered. As she rested her head upon his shoulder she saw her coin. It gleamed upon the chair where Harrison had placed it. *Go to sleep, Cleopatra. Your work is done.*

The Langtry coins were united now, and outside the old cabin, the eerie mountain winds seem to ease as if Cleopatra was ready to finally rest quietly with her husband, Zachariah. *Soft-ly, slow-ly . . .*

Every now and then a love story comes along
that's so unforgettable, you know
it will stay with you forever . . .

YOU MADE ME LOVE YOU
An Avon Contemporary Romance
by
Neesa Hart

YOU MADE ME LOVE YOU is a story that explores
the depths of the human heart and the true power of
love. A heartbroken widower is convinced he has
everything he needs—his work and his daughter. But
then a generous, pretty woman comes into his life,
making him ache with long-forgotten desires . . .

YOU MADE ME LOVE YOU will make you experience the power of falling in love—again and again.
Don't miss it!

ACA 1100